Praise for Chris Simms

'Chris Simms combines psychological insight with gritty realism to give the reader a genuinely exciting story' *Crime Time*

'Simms keeps you guessing' *Daily Telegraph*

'An exciting new psychological thriller' *Daily Mail*

'This highly polished study of madness and murder shows how well Simms' talent is maturing after his previous fine work . . . filled with insight and not lacking in some dark humour . . . a must-read for those who like their crime fiction psychological. If you've not read Simms before, this is a great starting point' *Shots* magazine

'*Outside the White Lines* was one of my favourite thrillers of last year. Definitely a talent to watch' Sarah Broadhurst, *Bookseller*

'A promising debut . . . the characterisation is merciless, convincing and very gripping' *Morning Star*

'Simms' fresh approach, and the way the story weaves between three vewpoints, makes this one of the most promising debuts in crime for some time. From the prologue's brutal first pages to the satisfying crunch of the final chapter, the prose is spare, lean and mean' *City Life* (Manchester)

'A thriller should, ideally, star characters one can care about, move briskly without any signs of sagging, and leave an indelible impression long after the last page is closed. On all counts, Simms succeeds marvellously . . . a wonderful display of talent from a soon-to-be star of the crime fiction world' *January* magazine

'A very robust and creepy tale that had me riveted for an evening with dark characters that still reverberate in my head . . . a rapidly developing talent in the world of crime fiction' *Deadly Pleasures*

'An ingeniously plotted psychological thriller . . . reading Chris Simms is like watching a Danny Boyle film – strong characters in a present-day setting, enlarged with splashes of violence'
Ottakar's Bookshop

Chris Simms is married with four children and works as a freelance copywriter. This is his second novel in a compelling new series starring DI Jon Spicer, following the acclaimed novel *Killing the Beasts*, which was selected as a Best Crime Book for 2005 by *Shots* magazine. *Pecking Order*, Simms' second novel, was selected as a Best British Crime Novel by *Deadly Pleasures* magazine, and Chris has been named one of Waterstone's 25 'authors of the future'. He lives in Manchester. Visit his website at www.chrissimms.info.

By Chris Simms

Outside the White Line
Pecking Order
Killing the Beasts
Shifting Skin

SHIFTING SKIN

Chris Simms

An Orion paperback

First published in Great Britain in 2006
by Orion
This paperback edition published in 2007
by Orion Books Ltd,
Orion House, 5 Upper Saint Martin's Lane,
London, WC2H 9EA
An Hachette Livre UK company

1 3 5 7 9 10 8 6 4 2

A CIP catalogue record for this book is available
from the British Library

ISBN 978-0-7528-8168-3

Typeset by Deltatype Ltd, Birkenhead, Merseyside
Printed and bound in Great Britain by
Clays Ltd, St Ives plc

The Orion Publishing Group's policy is to use papers that
are natural, renewable and recyclable products and
made from wood grown in sustainable forests. The logging
and manufacturing processes are expected to conform to
the environment regulations of the country of origin.

www.orionbooks.co.uk

To the boglins, big and small.

I'm a different person, yeah
Turned my world around

'Lola's Theme', Shapeshifters

Chapter 1

Jon Spicer looked around what used to be his weight training room and sighed. Bare plaster walls faced him, exposed surfaces still raw from where he'd scrubbed them with sandpaper. The carpet was hidden by dust sheets that stretched from skirting board to skirting board. In the corner the steam machine looked like the victim of a clumsy shave, scraps of dry wallpaper stuck all over it.

He started peeling apart last week's local paper, separating the pages and laying them across the small table in the middle of the room. Immediately, and even as he tried to look away, his eyes were snagged by the front-page headline: BUTCHER OF BELLE VUE STRIKES AGAIN.

Quickly he flipped the page over, but it was too late. The horrific details of his latest case came streaming into the last place on earth he wanted them: the nursery.

The latest victim, Carol Miller, had been a midwife at Stepping Hill hospital. She was good-looking, her strong facial features complemented by a curvy, full figure. The sort of woman his dad would refer to in his strong Lancashire accent as 'proper breeding material'. In his own way, he would have been right. She'd given birth to a thickset baby the year before. Jon had watched as the infant drained an entire bottle of milk without pausing for breath, blissfully unaware of the tears streaming down the face of his grandmother above him. Jon had sat with his tongue frozen in his mouth, thanking God the bereavement counsellor had come with him to inform the woman that her only child was dead. The counsellor had kept up a soothing murmur, the actual words of secondary importance to the comforting tone of her voice.

'What will become of our Davey?' the woman had gasped.

'His father's not around and I'm not well. What will become of him when I'm gone?'

The wrinkles round her eyes deepened and she started sobbing again. Jon could feel her looking at him and he kept his eyes fixed on the counsellor, willing her to break the silence with an answer. Say something, he pleaded in his head, because if you don't I'm going to fucking cry.

Pushing the memory away, he picked up the paint tray and decorating implements. He banged them down on the table, then placed the tin of paint next to the tray. Getting his blunt nails under the lid, he began to pull, increasing the force until the pain in his fingers got too much. 'Bastard,' he cursed, glaring at the tin like it was trying to insult him. He glanced around for a suitable tool, and spotted the scraper lying next to the steam machine. Only able to fit the corner of its blade under the lid's rim, he cautiously increased the downward pressure. The seal broke with a pop and the blade jerked upwards, gouging into his thumb. Pain shot through his hand and he drew the scraper back, ready to slash the side of the tin in retaliation.

Get a grip, he told himself, placing it on the table and examining his thumb. The red line ran across his knuckle, merging with an old scar from where an opposition player had stamped on his hand while wearing illegal rugby studs. Jon sucked the back of his thumb, then blew a thin stream of air on to the wet skin, the coolness detracting from the pain. He peered into the open tin, frowning at the purplish red paint inside. Then he picked up the plastic spoon and scooped a dollop of viscous liquid into the tray.

Immediately an image of the pathologist dropping Carol Miller's liver into a stainless steel tray appeared in his head. As the pathologist had stepped across to the mortuary's scales, Jon couldn't help staring at the corpse on the autopsy table before him.

She had been found early in the morning, naked except for her knickers, stretched out in the middle of a small park in Belle Vue. The skin from her upper thighs, stomach, chest and neck lay in a neat pile beside her, muscles, tendons, ligaments and subcutaneous fat exposed to the world. The Home Office pathologist who attended the crime scene quickly concluded that she had been moved there from another location. Lifting one of Carol's arms, he pointed to the long grass beneath it. 'No blood. If she'd been flayed here, this whole area would be soaked.'

Jon had stepped out of the white tent shrouding the body and looked around. He was standing in the centre circle of a badly neglected football pitch. It had rained during the night, washing valuable forensic evidence off the body and blurring the many footprints in the patches of mud around it. The area was overlooked by residential properties. Dotted in the unkempt turf was lump after lump of dogshit – apart from late at night, the animals' owners must be using the area as a toilet for their pets almost continually. Even now a woman with a brindle Staffy was hovering beyond the perimeter tape, surreptitiously watching. The ghoul. Jon walked round the white tent, putting it between him and the woman's inquisitive glances. He looked at the modern, cheap council stock, ground-floor windows elongated and narrow to deter burglars. They had a defensive appearance, like machine-gun slits in pillboxes.

Beyond them a large church spire thrust upwards, the flat grey sky making the green copper stand out. Jon shook his head: there was little evidence of the forces of good in this grim place. He dropped his eyes back to earth, looking at the scattering of seagulls waiting at the far end of the pitch. Their hunched postures made them appear resentful of his presence on their feeding ground.

Behind him came the low rumble of traffic, a steady stream of it passing along the A57. He moved away from it, stepping between the team preparing to go over the immediate area on their hands and knees, and walked over to the park's perimeter fence. Rubbish was piled against its base, deposited there by the unrelenting wind that blew across the bleak expanse of grass. At the top of the park was a basketball court, the cracked concrete furred with patches of moss. Fragments of glass crunched under his foot as he paced across it. On his left he counted another gate into the park. That was the fifth. By the time he'd circled the perimeter he'd counted seven more. Twelve possible entry points for the killer. The whole place would need sealing off. He halted under a wiry tree, noticed the beginnings of leaf buds on the bare twigs above him. He took a little comfort in the thought that spring would soon be here to transform the desolate place.

Why take the risk of leaving the body here, in a park overlooked by so many houses? Perhaps the victim was being made an example of. Some sort of warning?

Jon had to agree with the pathologist. There was no way this was where the killer had carried out his ... what? Surgical procedure? He walked back to the tent and stepped inside. 'There was a bit of disagreement about the first victim – whether her killer had any surgical knowledge. Assuming the same person is responsible for this one, what's your opinion?'

The pathologist was about to take a glove off. He stopped, allowing the rubber to snap back over his wrist. 'As I understand it, the first victim only had the skin from her chest and upper arms removed?'

Jon nodded.

'And here we see he's removed the skin from her throat, chest, stomach and upper thighs. In both cases it's not a particularly difficult procedure to perform. Anyone with the most basic knowledge of surgery, probably even a butcher, could manage it.'

'Really?' Jon was surprised.

The pathologist smiled. 'Ever peeled the skin off a raw chicken breast? Not much more to it than that. You just use the tip of a very fine scalpel to help divide it from the layer beneath – something to think about next time you're making a casserole.'

Jon felt a wave of revulsion at the pathologist's reply. He'd sat in on a lot of post mortems over the years. But he never could get used to the macabre comments that bounced between the mortuary staff with the same ease as the pre-match banter in his rugby club's changing room.

'So he may not have medical training?' he asked, suddenly aware of the muscles moving beneath his flesh.

The pathologist stood up and removed his gloves. 'He's got some skill, but it could have been gained from practising on dead pigs, for all I know.'

★

'Jon! Have you seen the local paper from last week?' Alice's voice, calling up from the bottom of the stairs.

He blinked once or twice, waiting for the images to fade. Then he looked at the sheets of newspaper covering the table in front of him. 'Yeah, it's up here.'

'You're not using it to cover that table are you?'

'Well, it's last week's, babe. This week's is by the sofa, I think.'

She began puffing up the stairs, slow footsteps eventually reaching the top. 'There was something in the classified section I wanted,' she announced, slightly out of breath.

Jon turned to the doorway. His girlfriend stood there, strands of blond hair haphazard on her shoulders, football-shaped stomach forcing its way between her T-shirt and tracksuit bottoms.

Jon's eyes moved from the strange blue line that had appeared beneath the tightly stretched skin. 'What was it?'

'One of those abdominal crunchers.'

'I thought you were buying Chloe's off her?'

'Someone else beat me to it. She forgot to mention she'd also put an ad up on the noticeboard at her hospital.'

'That was good of her.' Jon lifted the tray off the table and put it on the floor. He peeled the paint-covered spoon off a sheet of newspaper, leaving a thick daub of red behind. 'Are you sure this shade isn't too bright?' Carol Miller's blood was still in his mind.

'Jon, it's going to be a nursery. We want it bright and cheerful.'

'Yeah, but red? Isn't it meant to close a room in? That's why they paint the ceilings of boozers with it.'

'Ah,' she countered, 'but we're only using it for the skirting boards and doorframe. The rest of the room will be in that bumblebee yellow.'

Jon started shuffling through the pages, scanning the columns of advertisements.

'There you go.' She stepped over and slid a page towards her. 'Health and Beauty section.' She traced a finger down the 'A' column. 'I thought so: ab cruncher, ten pounds. Bargain.' She tore the corner of the page off.

Jon looked at her enormous bump. 'Are you sure that's a good idea at this time?'

Alice giggled. 'It's for afterwards, stupid. God, if I can hardly do my own shoelaces up, how will I use one of these? But once the little one's arrived, I can start working my abdominals and pelvic floor, get my stomach back in shape.'

Jon stepped behind her and spread his fingers across her swollen belly. 'I quite like you with a bit of a pot.'

She laid her hands over his, leaned back against his chest and turned her head to look up at him. 'Will you still like it when it's just a saggy fold of flesh?'

Jon made an effort to smile. 'Of course. It will be a part of you.'

She squeezed his hands. 'And what about the pelvic floor stuff? Pissing in my knickers every time I run up the stairs?'

She had plunged him into something he had no knowledge of and he tried to drop his hands away. She clutched them tight, laughter rippling through her. 'It's all part of the process. You'd better get used to this sort of stuff. Just be thankful it won't be you in a few week's time, legs up in stirrups, squeezing out a great big bundle of joy.'

Jon grinned. 'You know I'd share the pain with you if I could.'

'Yeah, right.' She released his hands and headed out of the room, trailing the scrap of newspaper behind her.

Jon put the paint tray back on the table, eyes drawn once again to the clot of congealing paint. A conversation with Carol Miller's mum began playing in his head. He'd asked what her daughter's state of mind had been like. How happy she was. The old lady had replied that her daughter had been unhappy with her weight ever since giving birth to Davey. She'd tried all sorts of diets but never succeeded in removing the two stone her pregnancy had left her with. At the time Jon had begun to screen out the answer, letting the mother ramble to a conclusion, his next question already lined up. But now he scrutinised her words more carefully.

The old lady had said Carol had tried Weight Watchers and a soup diet, but recently she'd returned from work having spotted something that had given her fresh hope.

'Ali?' he called. 'Your mate Chloe's ab cruncher. You said she'd sold it on the noticeboard at her hospital.'

'Yeah.' Her voice floated up from the front room.

Jon stared down at the classified section of the newspaper. Buffered up against the last column of the 'Health and Beauty' entries was the start of the 'Personal Services' section: ad after ad of massage parlours, adult saunas and escort services. He looked back at 'Health and Beauty', seeing the unwanted mountain bikes, exercise bikes, mini-steppers, rowing machines, power sliders and flexi steps. He smiled cynically at the two sections' proximity: if attempts at making yourself look good failed, you only had to travel across the page and buy yourself a shag.

In the front room he crouched down to stroke his boxer dog's ears. 'This noticeboard, is it in the hospital reception or something?'

Alice put the torn-off corner of newspaper on the table. 'No, it's in the staff room of A and E, I think. I know all sorts of stuff gets pinned up there. It's how she found her flat. One of the consultants was advertising.'

'Do you reckon every hospital department has one?'

'I'd have thought most would. Why, what's on your mind?'

He made his voice sound casual, 'Nothing much. It just started off a train of thought.'

'About this case you're on?' Her voice had dropped a notch. The previous year, Jon's hunt for the Chewing Gum Killer had placed his family in extreme danger. The nature of his work was an area they both still skirted round nervously.

Jon nodded and stood up. 'I just need to pop out. I won't be long.'

Alice's eyes slid to the clock on the video. 'Half past eight at night? Can't it wait until tomorrow?'

But the thought was an itch he couldn't ignore. 'I'll be back in no time.'

She let out a long sigh and Punch glanced up, sensing her frustration as it billowed across the room. 'Well, at least wash the paint off your hands.'

He stood at the kitchen sink, one hand under the stream of

water, watching the curls of red snaking down the plug hole. So far his delving into Carol Miller's life had revealed very little. She hadn't been seeing anyone since her husband had disappeared two months after the baby was born. The grandmother had found herself looking after Davey a lot more than she had planned – Carol's income had plummeted and she'd been forced back into midwifery as a locum, filling in last-minute staff shortages at Stepping Hill hospital's maternity ward. Usually that meant weekends and evenings.

Although she still had the terraced house in Bredbury, the rent was getting harder and harder to meet. The grandmother had been expecting Carol to ask about moving back in very soon. Until, that is, she turned up in a Belle Vue park with large portions of her skin cut off.

He dried his hands on the tea towel, pulled a jacket on over his old rugby shirt, then tucked his warrant card into the breast pocket. On his way to the front door he paused at the door into the front room. Punch's big brown eyes watched him dolefully. Alice kept staring at the magazine on her lap.

'Want anything from the shop at the garage?' he asked.

'No thanks.'

'OK, I won't be long.' He bent over the arm of the sofa and dropped an awkward kiss on the top of her head.

He pulled up in the car park of Stepping Hill hospital twenty minutes later, then followed the signs directing him to the maternity suite.

The front doors were locked; a notice instructed him to buzz the intercom if the time was outside normal office hours. A camera stared down at him from its wire cage above the door. Jon got his warrant card out, held it towards the lens and pressed the button.

His arm was beginning to ache by the time a crackly voice said, 'Hello?'

'DI Spicer, Greater Manchester Police.' He pushed the door but it remained locked.

'Yes?' the voice said.

'For fuck's sake,' Jon muttered under his breath before looking up and saying, 'I'm investigating the murder of Carol Miller.'

'Oh.' The lock buzzed open.

The foyer smelled fresh, the painted walls almost pristine. He wondered if the maternity ward they would be going to for their baby's birth at Withington hospital would be so recently decorated.

A sign by the lifts told him that reception was on the third floor. As he waited for the lift to arrive blue light began to flicker across the walls around him. He turned to see an ambulance pulling up in the emergency bay outside. The driver jumped out and jogged round to the rear of the vehicle. Seconds later the back doors were thrown open and a gurney was wheeled out. The mouth of the woman lying on it was drawn tight and Jon could hear her moans, low and guttural, through the glass. Two male paramedics started pushing her towards the doors, the woman's partner flapping along behind, a large bag hanging from his arm.

As they wheeled her into the foyer the lift arrived. 'Hold the doors!' one of the paramedics called. Then he looked down, 'Nearly there. Keep breathing and don't, whatever you do, start to push.'

Jon had stepped into the lift and he kept his finger on the button with two arrows pointing away from each other.

'Cheers, mate,' one of the paramedics said with a smile. 'This pair of charlies' – he nodded jovially at the couple – 'didn't want to bother anyone by coming in early. Waited until her contractions were nice and close. A bit too close, though!'

Damp hair plastering her forehead, the woman was deaf to his attempt at humour, eyes tightly shut, focus directed entirely inwards. The moaning began again and Jon saw a glance of concern flit between the two paramedics. He wondered if he could jump back out of the lift, but the doors were sliding shut.

Jon looked at her partner, searching for clues as to how he should handle himself when it was his turn. The man began to brush strands of hair from her forehead and Jon thought what a futile gesture of comfort it was. But what else could he do? He was no more part of the process, no more able to share in what she was going through, than the rest of them. Jesus, thought Jon, everything about parenthood scares me shitless.

'God,' she growled. Her tone was masculine, like someone straining to lift a barbell in a gym. She began a shallow and desperate panting and her eyes snapped open, the look in them giving Jon the impression of a wild animal in pain. Her eyes settled on him for a second before shutting again, and somehow he felt guilty for being a man.

At last the lift came to a halt and the doors opened. A mid-wife was waiting for them and the group sped off to the nearest delivery room. Jon found himself alone in a corridor plastered with thank you cards and badly taken snaps of women lying on beds, tiny babies clutched in their arms. He leaned closer for a better look, alarmed at the lines of exhaustion on so many of the new mums' pale faces. Except for the pride shining out from their sunken eyes, they looked ideally suited to a hospital ward. And the babies. So small, so fragile. Dough-like features as if their faces had not yet formed, and some with plastic nasal tubes taped to their tiny cheeks. Not for the first time he looked at his thick fingers with their network of nicks and cuts from rugby matches and thought he was the last person on earth suited to this sort of thing.

'Can I help you?'

Guiltily he dropped his hands to his sides and looked at the bird-like woman who had appeared silently at his side. 'DI Jon Spicer.' He started fumbling for his ID, uncomfortably aware that he was wearing trainers, paint-flecked tracksuit bottoms and an old rugby shirt beneath his jacket.

'I just spoke to someone on the intercom about—'

'Yes, I heard. I'm Sister Cooper.' In order to meet his eyes she had to bend her head back. 'They certainly breed them big in the police nowadays.' Her eyes snagged on the bump in the bridge of his nose before dropping to the club badge on his chest, where they found an explanation for his injury. 'Rugby player?'

Jon nodded, never sure whether the admission would bring a knowing smile or a wary look.

Sister Cooper smiled. 'So was my husband. He's confined to criticising it from his armchair nowadays.'

'Oh well,' said Jon. 'I suppose you get to spend more time with him at the weekends now.'

'More's the shame,' she rolled her eyes theatrically. 'Always under my feet, he is. Like a lost puppy, now he doesn't play.'

Jon laughed.

'Please.' She waved him on down the corridor and into a staff room. A couple of other midwives were sitting on the padded blue seats that lined two sides of the room. 'Do you need to speak in private?'

The midwives had obviously been tipped off he was coming and were already beginning to stand. 'No, that's fine,' said Jon, gesturing. 'Please don't get up. I just need to check something.' He moved a copy of the local newspaper out of the way and took a seat, aware of the fact that his towering form didn't exactly encourage a relaxed atmosphere. 'I was talking to Carol Miller's mother and she mentioned Carol was trying to lose a bit of weight. She said Carol had come back from work excited about discovering a new way to regain her shape. I'm interested to know if you have a staff noticeboard where people advertise things for sale.'

'It's right behind you.' Sister Cooper pointed above his head.

Jon craned round and saw a noticeboard plastered with pieces of paper. He stood up and started to scan them.

Salsa lessons. Spanish teacher. Thursday evenings.

Panasonic video camera.

Income tax and preparation of accounts.

Garden maintenance and lawn-mowing services.

Britax Excel 3 in 1 travel system.

'Did she mention anything to any of you?' he asked over his shoulder.

One of the midwives said, 'Yes. Is there an ad for a rowing machine up there? One time she was talking about how effective rowing machines are for burning off calories.'

All three of them joined him and they began searching through the notices together. Within two minutes they'd checked the entire board, but without success.

Jon was about to give up when Sister Cooper announced, 'Here you are.' She was lifting up a large sheet with a photo of a Nissan Micra for sale. Beneath it was a plain postcard.

York Sprinter Rower. Computer screen showing strokes, time, distance, calories. Cost £139, will accept £80. Never used. Call ext. 241 and ask for Pete.

Jon removed it, hoping none of the women had seen the extension number. 'I just need to borrow this. Thanks very much for your help. I won't take up any more of your time.' Hoping his exit wasn't too abrupt, he started for the door.

'DI Spicer?' It was Sister Cooper's voice. He turned round. 'How are Davey and the grandmother? Are they coping?'

'Social services are helping out. Apparently there's a cousin as well...' His voice fell away.

Sister Cooper gave a tight smile and Jon retreated from the room, a woman's shrieks following him all the way to the end of the corridor.

Outside he walked round to the hospital's main reception and approached a woman behind the desk. Discreetly he placed his warrant card on the formica surface and asked if there was a list of internal phone numbers he could look at. She opened a drawer and removed a clipboard with several sheets of A4 pinned to the front. He traced a finger down the columns, searching for extension 241. Eventually he found it within the section headed 'Porter's lodge.'

Chapter 2

She found herself lying on the kitchen floor, blood clogging the vision in her right eye, cheek pressed against the fake marble tile. There was a piece of pasta beneath the cooker and she wondered whether the small brush in the cupboard under the sink would be able to reach it. He hated mess. Her face was one big blot of pain. Bottles clinked in the front room.

What's happened to our marriage? she thought. It was good once. It was normal. If only we still had Emily, things wouldn't have ended up like this.

Slowly she got to her knees, feeling as if the weight of her skull had trebled. Drips of blood fell onto the floor with a steady ticking sound. Reaching up, she curled her fingers over the edge of the sink and got stiffly to her feet. The J-cloth smelled faintly of sour milk as she dabbed the blood from her eye.

'Taped over Man United. Stupid bitch.'

It wouldn't be long before he came for her again, rage re-stoked by the alcohol. She opened the cupboard door, leaned forward and tried to reach the floor cleaner, spotting her gin hidden behind the bleach just before her vision darkened. She heard a bottle bang down on the coffee table in the front room, followed by a sharp intake of breath.

He was really going for it. She changed her mind about cleaning up, knowing how the whisky set his demons free. Following a routine that was getting more and more frequent, she grabbed her handbag off the top of the fridge and unbolted the back door.

As she walked unsteadily to her car she thought about how their life had gone wrong. He'd always got a bit lively after a drink or two. Things would get knocked over in the front room if his football team let in a stupid goal. She'd seen the occasional flash of aggression in the pub. Not enough to attract other people's attention. Just sneers at young and boisterous groups. People he felt were lacking in respect.

But he hadn't drunk enough for her to perceive it as a problem. That only happened when his career started to stall. As he was passed over for promotion again and again, the resentment began to build, a dark anger at the world. Trying to get him to talk about it only led to accusations of being a nag.

As she reversed out of the drive he appeared on the front doorstep. The surprise on his face turned to a snarl and he staggered across the lawn. 'Where are you going?'

Her hands were shaking as she got into first gear and accelerated away, the whisky bottle bursting against the back windscreen.

As usual she drove aimlessly, the occasional heaving sob doubling her over the steering wheel. The bleeding above her right eye had started again and the tissue box in the glove compartment was empty. Looking around, she realised she was driving through Belle Vue. The bright lights of a bingo hall were on her left and she turned into the car park, pulled up next to an empty coach and walked towards the entrance. A ripple of nudges went through a group of elderly women in the foyer and they stared at her through the plate-glass windows.

'Can I use your toilets, please?' she asked the red-coated man at the door.

He looked her up and down. A woman in her late thirties with messed-up hair and a bloodied face. 'Are you a member?'

'I'm sorry?' she replied, taken aback by his callousness.

'Have you got your membership card with you?'

She shut her eyes. 'I just want to use your toilets.'

'It's members only.'

She opened her eyes, saw his look of undisguised distaste. Shame suddenly filled her and she turned away from him. There was a motel on the other side of the car park, its neon-lit sign advertising rooms for £39.95 a night. She set off across the tarmac, trying to keep some dignity in her step.

A low hedge separated the two properties and she squeezed through a gap into a dark and empty car park. Directly behind the building she was just able to make out the greyhound racing stadium, unlit floodlights looming in the dark. She pushed open the motel's front door, immediately noticing an ashtray on the counter overflowing with butts. To her side was a rack for holding pamphlets. '*Manchester's Attractions*', said the card at the top, but the shelves below were empty.

She pinged the bell, then immediately placed her hand on the metal dome to stop its sharp echo. The office door opened slightly and a thin woman with lank brown hair slid through the gap. Her pale, narrow face emphasised her large brown eyes, which moved around like those of a frightened deer.

The woman who had just walked in off the car park was immediately reminded of a girl from her school. She'd come from a poor home and always wore second-hand uniforms and jumble-sale shoes. Her stick legs were never clad in tights, and during cold weather the skin almost went blue. The girl constantly suffered from a runny nose – colds in winter, hay fever in summer. As a result, a hanky was always pressed to her face and the playground joke was that her thinness resulted from her losing so much fluid through her nose.

She gestured towards the inner doors. 'I just need to clean up. Can I use your toilets? Please?'

The receptionist's eyes went to the doors behind her as if she was expecting more than just a lone woman. 'Jesus, you need more than a sink.' She stepped back into the office and almost immediately re-emerged with a green first-aid case. 'Here. I don't think this has ever been used before. I'm pretty sure it's full.'

She put it down on the counter and unclipped the lid. Inside were bandages, plasters, safety pins, antiseptic cream and a pair of blunt scissors. 'The toilets are just through those doors. Wash the blood off and we'll get you patched up.'

'Thank you.'

The hinge on the door into the toilets was stiff and the place smelled awful. She stood in front of the mirror and looked fearfully at her face. God. Her right eye was swollen half shut, dried blood caked her cheek and clotted her eyebrow. A fresh drip emerged from the split in her skin and caught in her eyelash.

She looked around for paper towels but the dispenser was empty. So were the toilet-roll holders in the first two cubicles. The last had a small stack of tissues piled on the cistern.

Five minutes later she stepped back into the reception, a tissue pressed to her eyebrow. 'Seems it doesn't want to stop.'

The receptionist frowned in sympathy. 'Was it a john?'

'Sorry?'

'Your face? Was it … ?'

Her mobile phone started to ring. Picking it out of her handbag, she saw her husband's name on the screen. She turned it off and dropped it back. 'Jeff. My husband.' The admission brought tears to her eyes.

The receptionist's face softened further. 'Let me see your face, you poor love.'

'Really, you don't need to. I can do it myself.'

The receptionist peered at the cut. 'These butterfly plasters might do it.' She smeared antiseptic cream over the cut, then applied two of the plasters. 'I've got some ice in the back. It will help with the swelling. You look like you could do with a cup of coffee as well. I'm Dawn, by the way.'

'Fiona. Thank you so much for this,' she replied.

The back office looked as dilapidated as the rest of the motel, but the chairs were soft and the coffee hot. She sat down, and her resolve to return to her car instantly crumbled. Reaching for her handbag, she took out a packet of cigarettes and held it out to Dawn.

'Cheers,' she said, sliding one out.

Fiona held a flame to it and then to her own, took a deep drag and sat back in the seat. Bustling around the room, Dawn wrapped some ice cubes in a bandage and passed it across. Fiona regarded her, thinking that her concern seemed to extend beyond mere sympathy. 'This has happened to you as well, hasn't it?'

Those eyes again. They moved with a look of perpetual alarm. 'How could you tell?' she asked.

Fiona was surprised at how quickly her crestfallen look had appeared. She guessed Dawn was used to people seeing through her fragile front to the vulnerable person beneath. 'Your kindness. It's the sort of thing one shows to a fellow … you know.'

'Survivor. The word you're looking for is "survivor".' But it didn't ring true, coming from her lips. Dawn sat down. 'I've suffered, yes. But in the past, not now. I'm with a good person now.' The comment was more than emphatic: it was defiant.

'I'm glad for you.'

'And you? How long has he been doing this to you?'

Breaking eye contact, Fiona lowered the ice pack and read-justed the cubes inside. 'On and off over the last few years.'

'On and off? But more and more often?'

Fiona pressed the ice pack against her forehead and shut her eyes. More and more often? In truth, she couldn't tell; her recent past had merged into one long nightmare. 'He's under a lot of pressure at work. He's always so sorry afterwards.'

'You mean, once he's sober?'

Fiona opened her eyes, surprised at the accuracy of the guess.

Dawn leaned forward, anger in her voice. 'They're always sorry the next morning. But that doesn't last for long. In fact, it lasts for less and less time. It's a cycle, don't you see? It's a cycle that just gets faster and faster. You have to get out of it.'

Fiona closed her eyes again, but the tears had escaped down her cheeks. 'You know that's not so easy. We've been married almost twenty years. I haven't anywhere else to go.' She started getting ready to stand. 'In fact, I should get home. He'll be asleep now. It'll be safe.'

'He's not coming back,' Dawn said quietly.

'Sorry?' Fiona replied, half out of her seat.

'The man you married. You're hoping he'll come back one day, aren't you?'

Fiona pictured her husband of all those years ago. Slim, a full head of hair, the quantity surveyor eager to work his way up the construction company. She thought of him now. Overweight, balding, face ravaged by drink, the strength she'd once found so reassuring now used against her.

'He's gone,' Dawn continued, laying a hand on her shoulder. 'Don't go back there tonight. Stay here – there are plenty of empty rooms.'

Fiona gave a hollow laugh. 'I don't have any money.'

'Sod the money.'

'I can't have you risking your job because of me. What if your manager found out?'

Dawn smiled. 'I'm the night manager. As long as you're out before the day manager arrives at seven, there's no problem.'

Fiona looked around the room uncertainly. 'Who actually owns this place?'

'Some business conglomerate down in London. I've never seen them. It was built for the Commonwealth Games last summer and it's been dying on its arse ever since. Please don't go back to him. You'd only be setting the whole process in motion again.'

Fiona sighed. 'Staying the night here won't achieve anything, other than to aggravate him further. I'll have to face him at some point.'

'Why? Have you left any children back there?'

Fiona gave an aggressive shake of her head. She couldn't face that one, not now.

'Then put a stop to it for ever. Leave him.'

Fiona stared at the floor. 'Don't think it hasn't occurred to me. But leave him for where?'

'Get a good night's rest, and tomorrow I'll put you in touch with some people. There are houses you can go to, places where you'll be safe.'

'You mean women's refuges?' Fiona said. 'But they're for ...'

'Battered women.' Dawn completed the sentence for her. 'Women from all walks of life, of all ages.' Her voice dropped to a whisper. 'Women just like you.'

Dawn got to her feet and removed a bottle of brandy from a cupboard. The sight of it made Fiona's stomach clench with longing. 'You could do with a splash of this,' said Dawn.

Trying not to appear too eager, Fiona extended her cup, watching the rich chestnut liquid as it glugged from the bottle. As she took a thankful sip, more tears spilled silently down her cheeks. 'Is that how you escaped? By going to a women's refuge?'

'More than once,' Dawn replied, taking a generous sip herself.

'I'd begun to believe that I was one of those women who always fall for the bastards of this world.'

'And now?'

'Now I'm happy. You know what I reckon is most important? Companionship. A partner in life who treats you as equal. To be honest, sex isn't really that important.'

Fiona almost shuddered at the thought of what her drunken husband would do to her in the bedroom.

The outer doors of the motel opened, and low voices sounded in the foyer.

'Dawn!' A woman calling. 'You back there?'

'Two seconds,' Dawn whispered, getting up. 'Yeah, hang on.' She hurried into the reception area.

'Got a spare room?' The woman's voice again.

'Yup. For the night or ...?'

'An hour.'

Fiona leaned forwards to see out the door. The woman was standing on the other side of the counter, hair tied in a ponytail, long red nails tapping impatiently on the fake wooden surface. Next to her was a man in a suit, looking awkward.

'That's twenty pounds,' Dawn said to him.

'Ah. Right.' He fumbled for his wallet. The money was handed over, but Dawn didn't open the till. Instead the notes went straight into her back pocket. She passed the woman a key. 'Number four's free.'

The couple went out through the doors and Dawn came back into the office. Fiona looked at her inquisitively and she shrugged. 'That conglomerate? I couldn't live on what they pay me. It's the only way to make ends meet.'

Fiona's mind was working, 'Earlier on, when you asked if it was a john, you meant a ... You thought I was a ...'

Dawn looked embarrassed. 'I wasn't sure. Your clothes weren't right, but most women who book in here are working girls. I'm sorry. As soon as you started speaking, I could tell you weren't.'

Fiona took a gulp of her drink, suddenly realising why the man in the bingo hall had been so callous earlier. She laughed at how her life had shifted.

'What?' asked Dawn, smiling nervously.

'Nothing,' said Fiona. 'It's just that if anyone had told me this morning that I'd be sipping brandy in a brothel in Belle Vue tonight, I'd have thought them mad.'

Dawn's face relaxed and she held the bottle out again.

Fiona extended her cup but, before tipping the bottle, Dawn said, 'So you'll stay here tonight?'

Fiona felt like she was teetering on the edge of a cliff. 'What are these refuge places like?'

'Heaven compared to what you're suffering at home.'

Fiona took a deep breath. 'OK. I'll give it a go.'

Dawn's face broke into a smile and she topped up Fiona's cup with brandy.

Fiona wrapped a towel round herself and tried to step out of the shower. The brandy was coursing through her veins and she had to grab at the shower curtain. A couple of hoops were ripped off before she regained her balance. Wiping steam from the bathroom mirror, she looked at her face. Aside from the injuries, a good-looking woman with wavy brown collar-length hair looked back.

'You can do it,' she said slowly, words slightly slurred. 'You can leave him.'

The ice had reduced the swelling a bit and she hoped the bruising wouldn't be too obvious. She wished she had her make-up bag with her. Instead, all she had was a miniature tooth-brush and tiny tube of toothpaste Dawn had found in a desk drawer.

Not surprisingly, acting as night manager of a run-down brothel wasn't Dawn's life ambition. As they had worked their way through far too much brandy, she had outlined her plan to emigrate with her partner to Holland, as soon as they'd put enough money aside. Renting rooms out by the hour was going a long way towards letting them realise their plan.

Fiona hung the towel on the rail, then, not trusting her balance, sat on the toilet to put her knickers back on. Carefully she walked across to the bed, peeled back the bedclothes and climbed in. The sheets had worn thin from washing, but they were cool and clean. She flicked the light off and let her head fall to the side.

She woke with a start some time later, certain that someone had opened the door. Her head was spinning and she had to feel at her sides to make sure she was still lying in bed. Keeping absolutely still, she heard a set of room keys fall to the carpet. But the sound was from the next room, not hers. Jesus, the walls were thin.

Groggily, she got up on one elbow and pressed a button on her watch. Its face lit up: 3:36 a.m.

A feminine giggle, the door shut and then she heard a man's voice, words indistinct. The bed creaked as someone sat on it. The woman said something, words impossible to make out. Shoes hit the floor and a belt jangled loudly as it was clumsily unbuckled. Fiona's eyes widened. Surely it wasn't a prostitute and her client?

She could hear the murmur of voices, and the bed creaked as they moved about on it. Fiona lay back and started breathing slowly, unable to resist trying to listen. Silence for a few minutes, then the bed began to creak rhythmically. The man started to grunt lightly. Oh God, they were having sex and she could hear everything. Fiona raised her hands to her ears, squirming.

He began grunting more loudly, then said something and the creaking stopped. Her voice now. More creaking and Fiona guessed they were changing positions. The belt buckle jangled once more. Fiona shut her eyes, embarrassed yet fascinated by the noises. Now the creaking started again, accompanied by gasping. Their movements got wilder and she wondered what the man had requested. Jesus, it was starting to sound like a wrestling match. The headboard started banging against the wall and the gasping was replaced by a stifled moan. Fiona opened her eyes. It wasn't the sound of pleasure. The moan changed to a choking noise. Fiona sat up, all attention. In the darkness it felt like the bed was lurching away from under her. The girl was fighting for breath. Was he strangling her? She listened as the movements and noises became weaker. Finally they stopped.

Fiona kept absolutely still, nausea building in her stomach. The belt buckle again, then the bed creaking. A single pair of footsteps crossed the room. The bathroom taps came on for a while. Fiona willed someone to say something. If they started speaking again, she would know the girl was all right. The footsteps came back across the room.

Still no talking. The bed creaked, there was a grunt of effort and then something heavy thudded to the floor. Fiona slipped out of bed, heart racing. The footsteps moved around for a while before they crossed the room, slower, more laborious. Concentrating on keeping her balance, she tiptoed over to her door and peered through the spyhole. Like a nightmare sequence in a horror film, the fish-eye lens gave a distorted view of the corridor. She heard the door to the next room open and her view was suddenly filled by brown material. She glimpsed wavy chestnut hair, then he was gone. Moments later the door at the other end of the corridor from reception banged shut.

She went into the bathroom and splashed cold water on her face. Had she really just heard a prostitute being murdered? Two glasses were by the sink and she filled one, gulped the water down. Her eyes were bloodshot and her head felt full of cotton wool. She drank another glass, then went back to bed. A chill went through her and she drew the covers up. The person had been carrying something over his shoulder, obscuring Fiona's view of his face. But whatever he was carrying, it was heavy.

She should go and tell Dawn. She'd started to fold the covers back when the doors from reception burst open. Drunken laughter. Someone running down the corridor, turning and running back. A key turned and a door slammed shut. Fiona sank back down in the bed. Everything seemed worse at night, she told herself. At home innocent rattles became the sounds of burglars testing the patio doors, the creak of wood the sound of a rapist's foot on the stairs. She decided to wait until morning, see if daylight could put things in perspective. Uneasily, she lay back and closed her eyes.

As soon as her watch reached six thirty, Fiona climbed out of bed, wincing as the action set off a pounding in her head. She drew the curtains. Weak daylight filtered into the room, the streetlights lining the A57 still on. Mist filled the bingo hall's car park. Thank God, her car was still there, the only vehicle left. She examined her face in the bathroom mirror. The cut above her eyebrow still looked nasty: some swelling remained and the beginnings of a bruise was gathering below the skin, screaming that she was married to a wife beater. While she dressed, nose wrinkling at the stale smell trapped in her clothes, she thought over what had happened in the night. She decided to tell Dawn, see what she reckoned.

Out in the corridor Fiona looked uneasily at the next room. The door hadn't shut properly. She pushed with her fingertips and it swung open. The room was identical to the one she'd slept in. She walked nervously past the bathroom doorway into the main part of the room. The top blanket was stretched tautly across the bed, the pillows plumped up.

Nothing looked as if it had been touched. Fiona glanced into the bathroom. The sink was bone dry, every surface wiped clean. The possibility that she had imagined the entire thing occurred and, fearful of seeing an abused woman with the beginnings of madness staring back at her, Fiona avoided her reflection in the mirror.

No. She couldn't deny the glimpsed figure passing across the view from her spyhole. Staring at the bed once again, she thought of the object on his shoulder. It had been wrapped in something brown – the same shade as the blanket covering the bed. Fiona turned and checked the top shelf of the flimsy wardrobe. One spare pillow, but no spare blanket. The discovery gave her suspicions some foundation and she got down on her hands and knees, scanned under the bed. A small white object lay against the skirting board. The tips of her fingers just reached it and she slid it out from the shadows.

Looping curled script gave the business card an exclusive air: *Cheshire Consorts. Evening companions for the discerning gentleman.*

Fiona flicked the card over. Scrawled in biro on the back was the name Alexia, followed by a mobile phone number.

She went to the window, eager for a glimpse of normal life going on outside the horrible scenario unfurling before her. The daylight was getting stronger, more cars flowing past on the A57 towards the city centre. Back out in the corridor, she saw Dawn emerge from the room nearest reception and dump a pile of sheets into a linen cart.

'I was just coming to give you a knock. The day manager's due any minute. I need you out of here.'

Fiona hurried down the corridor, gulping back the emotion that threatened to erupt as tears. 'Dawn, I know this sounds mad but, I think I heard someone being strangled last night.'

'Where? Outside your window?'

'No. In the next room.'

'What do you mean?'

'I could hear everything through the walls.' She breathed deeply, forcing herself to slow down. 'A couple came in just after three thirty this morning. At first the sounds were them, you know, having sex. But then they changed to choking. It was horrible. I'm certain he killed her. Not a word was said after the struggling stopped. I heard him moving around the room, there was a loud bump and then he walked across the view from my spyhole, carrying something wrapped in a blanket over his shoulder.'

'I'd have seen him come through reception,' Dawn stated flatly.

'He went out the other way, through the fire-escape door at the other end of the corridor.'

Dawn's eyes skittered nervously towards the door to room number nine. 'No, I don't think anyone was in that room last night. Listen, Fiona, you've got to leave. I could lose my job here.' She opened the doors to reception and beckoned. 'Come on.'

Fiona hesitated, looking back down the corridor, wondering if the sounds could have come from another room. She pressed her fingers against her temples, trying to suppress the ache pulsating through her skull. 'But Dawn, that door wasn't properly shut. I looked inside and the spare blanket is missing.'

Dawn's voice was agitated. 'Half the spare blankets are missing in this place. Please, you've got to go.' Her hand flapped more desperately.

Fiona walked reluctantly through the double doors and across the reception area to the exit. Dawn produced a sheet of paper.

'Here. This place is run by decent people. I rang last night after you went to bed. They're expecting you to call.'

She looked at the number, knowing she had nowhere else to go. 'Thank you, Dawn. You've been so kind.' As she folded the paper into her pocket she felt the business card in there already. 'Look! There was this as well. Under the bed.'

But Dawn's eyes were on the main road. 'That's him.'

Fiona looked, saw a silver Volvo turning into the car park.

'Take care, Fiona.' The outer doors swung shut.

Chapter 3

'Come on, boy.' The man waited as his elderly labrador climbed slowly down the front steps and on to the garden path.

Once on the pavement the man glanced towards the A57 and the park on the other side. Ever since the lady's body had been found there he'd been put off walking his dog around its litter-strewn confines.

Instead he turned in the other direction, walking along Mount Road, the greyhound racing stadium on his right. This early in the morning the neighbourhood was unusually quiet. Mist filled the street and, as he paused to light a cigarette, the only sound was the scrape of the match and the drip of water hitting the damp pavement as it fell from the glistening tree to his side.

The man continued past a shop. Tip-Top Electricals, all appliances bought and sold. Fridges. Freezers. Washing Machines.

After a couple of boarded-up houses he came to the offices that stood on the corner of the grassy area around which he now walked his dog. *Belle Vue Housing Offices* said the graffiti-covered sign, a few crocuses flowering in the bare earth beneath it. The building's windows were clad in metal grilles, and a spiked rail ran below all the gutters.

The sun had seemed about to come out, but now its promising glow faded once again. The morning felt heavy and subdued, as if waiting for something to give it a kick-start. He breathed out smoke and it soon churned to a stop in the motionless air above his head, hanging there like a phantom.

His dog began to pull excitedly at the lead. 'Bit eager today, Prince,' he said, not sharing that enthusiasm. He undid the clip and watched the animal disappear into the thick haze.

He stepped over the tyre tracks joy-riders had gouged in the grass, and walked for a short while. 'Prince!'

No response.

He waited half a minute, then tried again. Tutting, he cut across the verge in the direction the dog had vanished, soon spotting paw-prints in the dew-covered grass. As he moved forwards the mist seemed to recede at the same pace, never allowing him to see more than about fifteen metres ahead. Eventually he discerned a dark form in front of him. 'Prince,' he said impatiently, 'what are you doing?'

Prince's head was down, nuzzling a discarded white sack.

'Come on, will you.'

The dog looked up, a bluish loop in its teeth.

The man squinted, then walked closer. It wasn't a sack. It was a corpse, white skin ending at an expanse of red where the abdomen began. The swathe of raw flesh continued upwards to where the person's face should have been.

The dog began to slink guiltily away, the section of intestine dangling from its jaws.

Jon Spicer walked into the incident room expecting to be one of the first people in. But there was a man sitting at the desk opposite his. Late twenties, dark brown hair that had been freshly cut, crisp pale-blue shirt. So this is my new partner, Jon thought.

The day before, his boss, Detective Chief Inspector McCloughlin, had mentioned with a meaningful wink that he was being paired up with someone. New resources had been released to the murder investigation and Rick Saville, promoted to detective sergeant only a few months before, was one of seven new officers assigned to it. McCloughlin had described him as 'slick'. Scrutinising him from across the room, Jon wasn't sure if the word applied to his ability as an officer or to his appearance.

He thought about the meaning of McCloughlin's wink. Last summer he'd fallen out with the DCI over the Chewing Gum Killer investigation. Jon suspected Rick Saville had been paired with him to report everything they did back to McCloughlin.

Easy, he told himself. Reserve judgement. As he crossed the room Saville glanced up, spotted him and immediately began to rise.

'In early,' said Jon, taking his suit jacket off and hanging it on the back of his chair. 'Rick Saville, isn't it?'

'Yeah. Good to meet you.' Not overdoing his smile.

Jon shook the sergeant's hand, feeling slightly less pressure returned. Jon kept his grip, waiting for the subtle press of fingers that would indicate membership of the Masons. Nothing happened. Maybe he was a DS this early in his career because he actually merited the rank.

'Where are you joining us from?'

Rick sat down. 'I've just completed a stint at Chester House – a project for reducing bureaucracy.'

'And did it amount to anything, apart from producing more paperwork?'

Rick smiled briefly, though his eyes remained guarded. 'Not really.'

'I take it you're on the accelerated promotion scheme, then?'

He nodded. 'I did my two years' probationary down in Chester, but all the action's up here, so I applied for the fast track with Greater Manchester Police as soon as I could.'

'Graduate?'

'Yes, Exeter University. History and Law. You?'

Jon shook his head. 'Joined as a bobby over twelve years ago.'

'You've done bloody well to make DI by now, then.'

'Cheers. How do you find the accelerated promotion scheme?'

Rick kept his hands on the table, interview-style. 'Very challenging, to be honest. It's all the tests – they never seem to end.'

Jon leaned back and looked at the paperwork spread out on Rick's desk. Statements from friends, relatives and associates of the Butcher's second victim.

Rick saw the direction of Jon's gaze. 'A bit of homework. All these tests I do, it's a hard habit to break.'

Jon sat down. 'Any first impressions?' he asked, turning his computer on.

Rick tipped his head to one side. 'Not really. I just wanted to familiarise myself. But this second victim, Carol Miller, she seems to have been called in on a lot of evenings and weekends to cover the maternity ward.'

Jon shrugged. 'That's the nature of locum work, isn't it? You're on call for when the full-time staff cry off. Which is usually evenings and weekends.'

Rick tapped a biro on the pile of documents, neither agreeing nor disagreeing. 'Her last twenty-four hours ... She left the baby with her mum just after five in the afternoon, but she wasn't on duty in Stepping Hill until seven. You don't leave your baby two hours earlier than you need to, surely? Yet Carol Miller's mum was under the impression her daughter had left to go directly to work. So what was she up to?'

Grudgingly, Jon admitted to himself that he was impressed. Of course, the discrepancy hadn't escaped the investigating team. Many suspected Carol was hiding something. Attention had turned to her phone records. 'That's what a few of us are wondering. Maybe she just needed a break from the little one, but didn't want to admit it.' He opened his briefcase and took out a perspex folder. Inside was the card from the maternity ward's noticeboard.

His first thought was to keep everything back from his new partner, at least until he could be certain if he was McCloughlin's stooge or not. He glanced across the desk. Rick's eyes were roving back and forth across a witness statement. Skim-reading – something Jon couldn't master, hard as he'd tried. Watching the younger officer absorbing information like a sponge, he suddenly felt threatened.

He looked at the card again, knowing that teamwork was far more effective.

'I had a thought yesterday, sparked by something my missus said. Carol Miller was always trying to lose weight, but never very successfully. Then she got excited about something she'd spotted at work. Last night I checked the staff noticeboard on the maternity ward at Stepping Hill hospital. One of the midwives mentioned Carol had been talking about getting a rowing machine. I found this.' He spun the postcard across the desk.

Rick trapped it under one hand and picked it up. 'A rowing machine. Did you try the extension number?'

Jon shook his head, 'I thought it might be more interesting to catch him face to face. His shift starts later this morning.'

By now the room was filling up with members of the investigating team. Behind their desks was McCloughlin's private office, separated from the rest of the room by a flimsy partition wall. The phone on his desk began to ring.

'Where's the boss?' asked Rick, the word sounding odd coming out of his mouth.

Jon shrugged as Rick got up. He skirted eagerly round his desk, stepped into the office and picked up the receiver. Far too keen, Jon thought, knowing he would now have to take a message. Turning his head slightly to the side, he listened to his new partner.

'Hello. DCI McCloughlin's phone ... No, he's in a meeting I think ... Well, I don't know. I mean, I don't know where the meeting is. Can I take ... Right, I see. Hang on.' He now sounded totally flustered. 'Jon? This guy's insisting on talking to the SIO.'

Jon swivelled in his seat. 'Who is it?'

'The radio operator downstairs. Can you ... ?' He held the phone out as if it was a piece of equipment he no longer knew how to operate.

'DI Spicer here.'

'Jon, it's Sergeant Innes,' voice sounding strained. 'Who's the tool that picked up the phone?'

'My new partner.'

He heard an exasperated sigh. 'Where's McCloughlin?'

'I don't know. Have you tried his mobile?'

'It's switched off. A call's come just come in from near a patch of waste ground by the Belle Vue Housing Offices. Are you near a box?'

'Hang on.' He transferred the call to the phone on his desk and turned to his computer screen. 'I am now. Go ahead.'

'Have a look at this FWIN.'

Jon typed the Force-Wide Incident Number in and the operations room report filled the screen. 'Oh, shit, another body.'

'Yes. Minus her outer layer – and I don't mean clothes. I've told the nearest uniformed units to get over there and secure the scene. The major-incident wagon's also on its way.'

Jon scanned through for the exact location of the incident. 'Off Mount Road? I don't believe it.'

Anger surged through him. The bodies were being dumped right on their doorstep, and Jon felt as if the killer was deliberately goading him. He felt his grip tightening on the telephone receiver. 'OK, we'll get over there. Leave a message on McCloughlin's voicemail will you?'

Before he'd hung up, Rick was in his face. 'Mount Road? Where's that?'

'Put it this way. With the traffic at the moment, it would probably be faster to walk there.'

Despite that, they drove, Jon anxiously listening to the police radio for any sign of McCloughlin's whereabouts as they fought through the commuters clogging the A6, siren only slightly speeding their progress.

Finally they turned off the main road on to Kirkmanshulme Lane, only to join the end of a stationary queue of cars. The oncoming lane was just as choked, and Jon realised there was no way of cutting through. 'Bollocks,' he said, his fingers drumming angrily on the steering wheel.

Rick looked out of the side window. 'Belle Vue. Strange name for such a grim-looking area.'

Jon glanced at his passenger, then at the surroundings beyond their windscreen. 'Belle Vue? In its day this was the biggest leisure park in Britain. There was a zoo, complete with mangy lions and miserable bears, a huge roller coaster, boating lakes, dodgems, miniature steam railway. Even a speed-racing track.'

'Where?' asked Rick, twisting in his seat, trying to find evidence of what Jon had just described.

'This whole area. The speedway track was over there, where that car auction site is. One of my earliest memories is of coming out here with my dad, getting sprayed with the red grit that the bikes used to kick up as they roared past. I used to wear a pair of old flying goggles to protect my eyes. They still race, but at the greyhound track nowadays. Of course, you're not allowed to perch on the barriers at the bends any more.'

'I bet there was hardly any trouble, either.'

Hearing the wistful note in his voice, Jon let out a short cough. 'Don't you believe it. There's no harking back to a lost golden era with Manchester. The housing around this area was shocking – still is, in fact.' He nodded at the road in front. 'There are houses just up the road in Gorton on the market for five grand. Negative equity is alive and well around here. When the leisure park was first built it was surrounded by back-to-back terraces crammed in around the cotton factories and chemical works. Smoking chimneys, open drains, the stench from the knacker's yards.'

'You make it sound like a Lowry painting,' Rick laughed, a note of disbelief in his voice.

Jon's eyes narrowed slightly. 'That's because it was, man. Lowry painted life as he saw it, no gloss. When my family first moved over here from Galway they lived in an area called Little Ireland in Ancoats. You've never heard of it?'

Looking a little bored, Rick shook his head.

'Engels described it in his *Condition of the Working Classes in England*,' Jon replied, resisting the temptation to make a comment about his partner's university education. 'It was the worst slum he'd ever seen. Hundreds of Irish families shared cellars as their homes, slept on straw. You're from Chester. Did you never learn about the region's history at school?'

Rick reddened. 'I went to boarding school down in Surrey.'

Jon clenched his teeth. Should have bloody guessed.

Rick broke the awkward silence. 'So it wasn't all polite promenading, then?'

Jon sighed. 'People needed an escape. Working in a factory all week was tough back then. That's what led to the music halls and drinking dens. I've read about what used to go on and it was pretty much the same as today, including the drunks, the prostitutes, the gangs.'

'Gangs?'

Enjoying the fact he was giving a history lesson to a graduate in the subject, Jon nodded. 'Scuttlers, they were called. Peaked caps, bell-bottom trousers. They'd form a group and steam into people – knock them down and rob them. Manchester's always had gangs. Three lads from one were arrested for breaking into the zoo. They got into the bird enclosure and kicked a load of penguins and pelicans to death.'

'Recently?'

'No, late fifties. My granddad told me about it. They all got packed off to borstal.' He paused, then couldn't resist adding, 'Their grandkids are probably the ones mugging clueless southerners who come to study at Manchester University today.'

Rick started to pick nervously at a thumbnail. The last comment had definitely hit home.

Eventually they started inching past the huge expanse of a multiplex cinema's car park. It was empty except for a group of lads racing radio-controlled cars across the smooth asphalt.

A pang of guilt played in Jon's head. Trying to make up for his cutting remark, he said, 'The lake was right there, massive thing with an island in the middle. The roller coaster was called The Bobs, one of those old, creaking wooden things. The cars rattled round it, looking like they were about to fall off at any moment. There's not much my old man admits to being scared of, but he happily let me know that The Bobs terrified him half to death. I was too small to be allowed on – probably saved me from a lifetime of nightmares.'

'So it was all here when you were growing up?' Rick asked, sounding chastened.

'Yeah, just, though it was well past its heyday by the time I was old enough to visit.'

'What happened to it?'

'It closed down during the seventies, bit by bit. Bigger and better attractions elsewhere: Chester Zoo, Alton Towers, Blackpool. Plus tastes change – there used to be a huge ballroom where they held the national brass band contest. Not much demand for stuff like that any more.'

Rick was staring at the cinema. 'How long's that been here?'

'The Showcase? Early nineties, maybe. After the last parts of the park were demolished this place was waste ground for over a decade. The facelift started with that. Burger King and Pizza

Hut sprang up on the back of it, and so did the bingo hall. But I hear they're all struggling again. The Printworks in the city centre is dragging huge numbers of cinema customers away. If the Showcase folds, it'll revert to wasteland again, I suppose.' Jon thought about the processes of decay and regeneration that seemed to wash regularly across the city like a tide lapping at a beach.

At last they turned on to Mount Road and a couple of minutes later they pulled up by the Belle Vue Housing Office. Council workers were crowded in the car park, staring through the metal struts of the fence. The mist had burned away, and across the grass several uniformed officers were attempting to keep a small gathering of locals at bay. Jon and Rick started across the grass, warrant cards ready.

'Has someone been killed?' A council worker in a shiny grey suit called through the fence. The eager note in his voice riled Jon. 'It looks like a corpse.'

Jon paused and stared at the man, took in his pallid skin and fish-like eyes. 'So do you.' He carried on, leaving gasps of shock behind him.

Without turning his head, Rick murmured, 'Please, don't mince your words.'

He smiled to indicate sarcasm but Jon's face remained stormy. 'One thing I hate is members of the public getting a thrill from this sort of thing.'

As they reached the rendezvous point in the outer ring of tape Jon noticed a young man nearby lining up the crime scene in the viewfinder of his camera phone. 'If I hear that click, I'll impound your phone as evidence.'

The man lowered the phone, an uncertain expression on his face. A uniform stepped over and, as he noted down their names, Jon nodded towards the man with the phone. 'Take his name and address.' Then, louder, 'The perpetrator of a crime often returns to where he committed it.' The man looked as if he wished he'd stayed at home.

Jon and Rick proceeded to the inner cordon. The pathologist and crime-scene manager had yet to arrive, so no one was entering the circle of tape. Beyond it was the body. Like the first two victims, she was naked except for a pair of knickers. Unlike the first two victims, her face had been removed.

Jon felt his throat contract. Shit, we've got an evil bastard on our hands.

Rick looked away first. 'That's grotesque. It's like something from that exhibition.'

Jon turned his head. 'What exhibition?'

Rick looked up at the sky. 'What's his name? Von Hagen, that's it. He removes the skin from corpses, preserves them, then puts them in various poses. The exhibition was down in London not long ago.'

They turned back to the dead woman and regarded her for a little longer before Rick added, 'She seems too young to have lost that many teeth.'

Jon nodded. The smooth and supple skin that remained on the corpse's limbs was that of a young woman, yet half of her teeth were missing. Keeping his eyes on the body, Jon began walking round the perimeter. With each step the sense that he was viewing some sort of display increased. 'You should investigate that.'

Rick looked at him enquiringly.

'That Von Hagen thing. It occurred to me when looking at Carol Miller's body – why risk dumping it in the middle of a public park? He must be trying to make some sort of a point. I thought it was a warning, but maybe it's a display.'

He looked around. Once again houses bordered the grass: a council terrace down one side, more-expensive-looking properties with large rear gardens on the other. Several worried owners stood behind their fences, exchanging comments. Above the roofs he could just make out the tops of the floodlights that ringed the greyhound track. A solitary phone mast towered over the scene, topped by ugly panels of grey metal. 'If only there was a camera on that.'

About five minutes later the Home Office pathologist arrived.

'Fast mover,' observed Jon as the pathologist folded his long limbs into a white suit.

'The call came through when I was on my way to work. It

35

was easier to come straight here.' He slipped on white overshoes and, laying down footplates before him, approached the body.

While Jon waited for him to complete his initial examination, the major-incident wagon pulled up in the Housing Offices car park. Several officers approached the crime scene, carrying poles and a white plastic canopy. As soon as the pathologist had properly surveyed the body Jon said, 'What do you reckon?'

'Well' – the pathologist stood up, one knee popping loudly – 'she's been here most of the night. There was a heavy dew and some mist this morning. I don't know when the dew point occurred – I noticed my car had a light covering when I took the dog out for a walk at about eleven o'clock last night.' He looked at the sun, still low in the sky. 'The side of the body still hidden from the sun is soaking, as is her hair.'

'Any idea on time of death?'

'Rigor mortis is pretty well established. The facial muscles are stiff, though whether the fact that they've lost their layer of skin is relevant I'd have to find out. Despite that, the limbs are also going. Her being out here all night would have delayed its onset, but I'd say she was killed a good twelve hours ago, maybe more.'

'And the lack of blood around the body. She was moved here?'

'Just like last time. One thing I'm not sure about is the damage to her abdomen. The wounds are very rough.'

'Dog bites,' said Jon.

The pathologist looked dismayed and Jon was pleased to have broken through his professional detachment.

'What's your opinion now on this guy's medical skills?' Jon asked, hands in his pockets.

The doctor looked at him, regret tugging at the corners of his eyes. 'To remove a face in its entirety like this takes a lot of time and skill.' He crouched, extending a finger to the victim's hairline. 'He's created a coronal flap by cutting from one ear, across the top of the forehead to the other ear. Then he's peeled the skin away – not particularly hard where the forehead is concerned, since the peri-cranial flesh is quite loose and you only have the frontalis muscle to worry about.' He pointed to his own forehead and raised his eyebrows. 'That's the one that lets you do that. Next, I imagine he made incisions down the sides of the face and right along the jawline. This is where it would have got complicated. The muscles in your body are attached to your bones by tendons. Your facial muscles differ from all your other muscles in that they attach directly to other muscles or to the skin, which is why the human face is capable of such an amazing array of expressions. The movement of one muscle has an effect on its neighbour – a kind of ripple effect, if you like.

'Whoever did this has divided the skin from the ocular muscles – which surround the eye – almost perfectly.' He pointed to an exposed eyeball. 'Just a tiny nick here, then he's carried on down the face, leaving all the muscles around the nose perfectly intact – I forget their names, *levator* and *Compressor naris* or something. Next, he reached the mouth. He's removed her lips, with the result she now looks like she's grinning for kingdom come. Perhaps that's what he wanted.'

'So he's had formal training of some description?' Jon asked, relieved to look away from the mutilated corpse.

'He's got surgical knowledge, without a doubt. The key to surgery is all about finding a plane – the layer between the dermis, or outer layer of skin, and the sub-dermal tissue. Once you've found your plane, you make your incision along it and the skin lifts away quite easily. But to find your plane and keep it while navigating all the contours of the face and its delicate arrangement of muscles? That's quite a feat.'

Jon nodded his thanks and turned away. When he got his hands on whoever was doing this, the bastard had better admit to everything straight away. Otherwise it would take more than the duty officer to stop him visiting the sick fuck in his cell and beating a confession out of him with his bare hands.

By the time McCloughlin showed up, the body was shrouded by a white tent. The pathologist and photographer were inside and flashes kept going off, making it appear like they were in there enjoying a particularly morbid party.

'DI Spicer,' McCloughlin announced, rubbing his hands together. 'First to the scene again?'

The comment wasn't accompanied by a smile. On the

Chewing Gum Killer case, Jon had arrived at a crime scene ahead of McCloughlin and the observations he'd made had eventually led him to the killer. It still bristled with McCloughlin.

'Sir, I picked up the call to your desk phone,' Rick intervened.

McCloughlin didn't seem bothered and Jon glanced at Rick. So, the arrangement you have with McCloughlin extends to taking his phonecalls?

'And Jon took the opportunity of teaching you how to crack a case all by yourself?' McCloughlin walked off without waiting for an answer.

Rick spoke from the corner of his mouth. 'Someone got out of bed the wrong side.'

Jon's hands were clenched tight in his pockets. 'I guess that's our cue to bugger off.'

As they set off back to the car Jon spotted a petite figure with tousled black hair hurrying across the grass towards him. She was struggling slightly with what looked like a large plastic toolbox: Nikki Kingston, the crime-scene manager. He'd used just to fancy her, but with what they'd gone through during the Chewing Gum Killer investigation, the bond between them had deepened to a level he'd never dare let Alice know about. 'Nikki, you've got this one?'

She smiled up at him. 'Jon Spicer. My lucky day.' Her eyes lingered on his for another heartbeat before she turned to Rick.

Jon coughed. 'Nikki Kingston, crime-scene manager. DS Rick Saville, my new partner.'

Rick's businesslike exterior underwent a fractional softening, and Jon noticed a lightness in his touch as he clasped her hand.

Nikki turned back to Jon. Something was sparking in her eyes and jealousy jabbed him in the chest. 'So, am I reporting to you?' she asked.

He shook his head, 'I'm on another part of the investigation. Carol Miller, mainly.'

Her eyes widened. 'You mean this one's connected to the Butcher? I was just told it was a naked body in a field.'

'It is. Except her face is about two feet away from the rest of her.'

'Oh, Jesus,' Nikki winced.

Jon gave her a grim smile. 'See you in the incident room.'

She turned and started towards the crime scene again.

The walk back to their car took Jon and Rick past a makeshift ramp made from an old door and a few breezeblocks. Bicycle tyres had scoured the grass in front of it and left muddy tracks across the door's surface. As they stepped round it Jon spotted something.

'Nikki!' he called.

She turned, saw the urgency of his wave and came back.

'Is that a latex glove?' Jon said, pointing. It lay in the long grass beneath the door, fingers slightly curled as if caught in the act of trying to crawl from their sight.

She squatted down to get a closer look. 'Yes, and that looks like blood covering it.' She examined the ramp. It had been knocked out of alignment with the breezeblocks. Treading carefully, she scrutinised the area around the door. Pointing to a heel mark in the muddy patch by the foot of the ramp, she said, 'Looks like someone could have bumped into it.'

Jon looked back at the tent covering the body. With a finger he drew a line in the air back towards the road. The ramp was right in the way.

'What are you thinking?' asked Rick.

'Our man dumps the body and sets off back to his vehicle. Only it's dark. He walks full into this ramp, stumbles and drops the glove.'

Nikki was nodding with excitement, 'Don't go any nearer. There's another footprint there, too. We need to get this area taped off.' She turned towards the main crime scene.

'Nikki!' He caught her hand. 'When McCloughlin asks, it was Rick who found the glove.'

'No way,' Rick protested. 'It was your find.'

Jon didn't take his eyes off Nikki. 'You heard me?'

'Whatever,' Nikki replied with a frown, twisting her fingers from his grip and running away.

In the car Jon began indicating to do a U-turn, then changed his mind. 'Let's go for a coffee. If we get back to the incident room now, everyone's going to be pumping us for information, and there's no way I'm taking the wind out of McCloughlin's sails.'

'Why's he got it in for you?' Rick asked.

Jon ran a hand over his knee, wondering how much Rick knew. 'It's old history. I had a stroke of luck.'

'The Chewing Gum Killer?'

Jon looked out the side window and nodded.

'That was the favourite topic of conversation last summer in Chester House.'

'Well, there you go. You know already.'

'Yeah, but it was McCloughlin's case. He was SIO, he gave the interviews on the TV and to the press when it was all over.'

'His case, but my collar. You know how it is,' Jon said guardedly.

'So why did you tell the CSM to say it was me who found the glove?'

'We shouldn't have even been there before him. The last thing I needed was to find what may turn out to be a crucial piece of evidence.'

'So you got her to tell McCloughlin it was my find?'

'Yeah,' Jon answered, hating the fact that Saville now had something on him.

In the coffee shop, Jon tipped a sachet of white sugar into his black coffee. Rick carefully tapped half a sachet of brown sugar into his latte, then reached for the pot of chocolate powder to dust the foam on top. When he spotted Jon watching him, he suddenly changed his mind.

'Anyway, back to the present,' said Rick, sitting down. 'First victim.'

Jon took a seat opposite him. 'Angela Rowlands.'

Rick sat forwards. 'Forty-two years old. Divorced for just under two years. Got the three-bedroom semi in Droylesden as part of the settlement. Worked part-time as a legal secretary in a solicitor's just off Deansgate.'

Jon nodded. 'You've done your homework.'

'That's just surface stuff. I'm hoping you know something more interesting.'

Jon took a sip of coffee and grimaced slightly with pleasure at its sharp taste. 'Her daughter, Lucy, lives down near Castlefield, doing very well in web site design. Lucy told us her mum had been very lonely since the divorce. Hurt too. The husband dumped her for a "younger model", to use Lucy's words. Rowland's stage in life: mid-forties, married for twenty years. She was in a routine. It was safe and comfy, but totally devoid of single men. Lucy had encouraged her to get out and start trying to meet someone, but apparently the idea terrified her.'

'Don't blame her,' Rick leaned back. 'Playing the field after being out of it for that long?' He shook his head.

'Exactly. Apparently, Lucy took her to a singles' night at a bar in town. Lucy did very well, but her mum didn't get a second glance. After that Lucy suggested she try dating agencies – but only the upmarket ones.'

Rick toyed with his drink. 'Ones that advertise in the broadsheets?'

'Yup. And at several hundred quid just to join, they're not cheap.'

'So we've got her coming into contact with various men, none of whom had a previous social connection with her. Have we got the list of people she had dates with?'

'Only just. They were reluctant at first, because their members' records are strictly confidential. Then someone pointed out to them that having the Butcher of Belle Vue on their books was probably more of a risk to their profits than a few disgruntled members. Rowland received dozens of member profiles, but only had around fifteen actual dates, we think. Each one's being looked into now.'

Jon downed his coffee in one gulp. 'According to Lucy, she hadn't had much luck with any of them. Her confidence was low. Before the divorce she'd only ever dressed up for a few gin and tonics at their local every Friday. Now her wardrobe was hopelessly out of date.' He tapped a forefinger on the table to emphasise his next point. 'Then she mentioned to her daughter over the phone that she'd decided to do something. She sounded nervous and excited. She wouldn't say what, just that it was something she should have done a long time ago.'

'Did Lucy find out what she was up to?'

Jon shook his head. 'Next time she saw her mum, it was in the mortuary. We've gone over her phone records and bank statements, but nothing of much help there.'

Both men were silent as they turned possibilities over. Jon looked up. 'What about the porter selling this rowing machine? That was a surgical glove back there. They must be two a penny in hospitals. How about nipping over to Stepping Hill hospital?'

Rick looked uncomfortable. 'Shouldn't we run it by McCloughlin first?'

'Strictly speaking, yes.'

Rick hesitated before pulling out his mobile. 'I'll give him a quick ring, then. May as well play things by the book.'

Jon gave a noncommittal shrug as Rick made the call.

Chapter 4

Rick snapped his phone shut. 'Yeah, he says to get over there, but stressed just for a chat. What did he think we were going to do, batter him?'

Jon knew the comment was directed at him. In McCloughlin's view, Jon's temper was his Achilles' heel, a constant threat to his career.

Half an hour later Jon laid his warrant card on the counter in the main reception at Stepping Hill hospital. A different woman looked up at him.

'Could I use the phone please?' he asked. 'Internal call.'

'Here you are.' She turned it round and put it on the counter.

Jon dialled 241. He was about to give up when the phone was answered. 'Is Pete around?'

'Pete Gray?'

'I don't know his surname.'

'Well, there's only one Pete works in here. He's on his way with some supplies to the surgical wards. Left two minutes ago.'

'Cheers.' Jon handed the phone back and looked at the site map. A very cheerful volunteer with the name 'Sue' on her badge pointed out the way they needed to go. Thanking her, they set off down a long corridor, passing a procession of hospital staff, patients and visitors. Soon they reached a T-junction and followed the overhead sign. At the next crossroads, they could see the surgical ward immediately in front. Jon glanced to his left; a man with a large paunch was swaggering towards them, pushing a trolley piled with boxes. As he got nearer Jon said to Rick, 'Check out the box on top of his pile.'

The label said: *Mediquip Inc. Powder-free surgical gloves. Sterile. 24 boxes of 200.*

'Pete Gray?' Jon asked. Taking in the porter's jet-black laquered quiff, Jon guessed he was in his late forties and clinging to the same haircut of twenty years ago. When baldness hit, it was going to hit hard. The heavy gold neck chain seemed incongruous with the simple white overalls he was wearing.

'Yes?' he said, slowing down.

Jon held his warrant card up. 'DI Spicer and DS Saville, Greater Manchester Police. Once you've dropped that lot off, can we have a quick word?'

The porter seemed to think about this for a second, eyes fixed on Jon's badge. Nervously he raised a hand to his chin. No wedding ring. 'Here? What's it about?'

'Perhaps a café area would be more comfortable,' Jon replied, ignoring the second question.

Pete's eyes flicked from Jon to Rick and back again. 'OK.'

He pushed the trolley through the double doors, Jon and Rick watching him through the windows.

'Him selling a rowing machine? No wonder. He obviously didn't get much use out of it,' Rick said quietly.

Pete re-emerged and, confidently now, led them to a quiet café area round the corner. After they'd all got a drink, Pete walked over to a table with a discarded copy of the *Sun* on it, peeling back the front page to stare at the page three girl beneath. 'I wouldn't kick her out of bed. Tits are fake, though.'

Jon studied his face. With the build-up of flab on his cheeks and below his jaw, there was a faint resemblance to a Las Vegas-era Elvis. In his younger days he'd probably been quite the ladies' man. The way he passed judgement on a topless model some thirty years younger than him suggested that he thought he still was.

'How long have you worked here, Pete?' Jon placed a white plastic stirrer in his upturned cup lid.

Pete finished pouring a third sachet of sugar into his coffee. 'About eight years.'

'Ever have to work nights? I could never get used to them when I was in uniform.'

Pete's shoulders relaxed a little. 'I don't mind them, actually.'

Jon stretched his legs out to the side of the table, took a sip

44

of coffee. Allowing a note of boredom into his voice, he said, 'This is just routine stuff because your name was thrown up as part of an ongoing investigation – it shouldn't take long. Were you working yesterday?'

'Yeah, I finish at eight in the evening.'

He wasn't quite sure why, but Jon was getting a feeling about the man. Keeping it casual, he looked away, appearing to be more interested in the Give Blood poster on the wall. He was about to ask his next question when Rick jumped in, 'What did you do for the rest of the night?'

A wary expression slid across Pete's face. 'Watched a couple of videos.'

Jon tried to steer the conversation back to just a chat. 'A couple? You a film buff?'

'Just Elvis ones.'

'I think I've only ever seen *Viva Las Vegas*. What else was he in?'

'Loads.'

The man had clammed up and Jon could tell he was only going to get more tense. Cursing Rick for having jumped in so clumsily, he decided to go for it. 'Did anyone watch them with you?'

'No, I live alone.' Guarded now.

'Pete, are you into exercise?'

'Not really.'

'What about rowing?'

He shook his head.

'You've never tried a rowing machine?'

Pete blinked. 'Oh, yeah. I've tried it a couple of times.'

'At a gym?'

'No, I bought one. The thing's still in my house.'

'Must clutter the place up. Ever considered selling it?'

The stream of questions was irritating Pete and he tried to reverse the flow. 'Why? You want to buy it?'

Jon laid his forearms on the table. 'Did Carol Miller want to buy it?'

He watched as connections came together in the other man's head. 'I've never laid eyes on her.'

'Was she looking to buy your rowing machine? The one you're trying to sell on the noticeboard of the maternity ward?'

Pete ran a hand back and forth across his chin, eyes shifting to the side. 'We spoke. She was interested, but she never followed it up.'

'You spoke? You mean over the telephone?'

'That's right. She rang me – internal call.'

No record of calls made on an internal phone system, Jon thought. He was considering his next question when Pete spoke first. 'I don't like where this is going. I'm not prepared to continue.' He finished his coffee and got up.

Jon shrugged. 'One last thing before you go. I've been meaning to see *Viva Las Vegas* again for a long time. Where do you hire your Elvis videos from?' He could check on Pete Gray's story with the shop.

'I have my own collection.' He walked quickly away.

Jon waited until he'd disappeared round the corner. 'Well, that got him all shook up.' Rick's face was blank, completely missing the joke.

Jon pulled an evidence bag from his pocket, then, using the end of a pen, picked up the cup Pete had been drinking from and dropped it inside.

'What are you taking that for?' asked Rick.

'It'll have his prints and DNA on it.'

His partner laughed incredulously. 'You're not seriously thinking of trying to use that as evidence in court?'

Jon gritted his teeth and waited for the flash of annoyance to pass. 'No. But it could come in useful if any DNA's recovered from the third victim's body.'

With a little shake of his head, Rick stood up.

As they crossed the canteen Jon stared at the back of Rick's neck, thinking that his new partner had a lot to learn and deciding that he wasn't the one who'd do the teaching.

Chapter 5

The woman shook her head. 'Don't worry, love. We've had women turn up here in just their nighties before. Barefoot and everything.'

Fiona saw the woman's eyes shift to the cut above her eyebrow yet again. She turned away to look around the bedroom. It was more like a nun's cell: narrow single bed, tiny table next to it, simple wardrobe in the corner. The only splash of colour was three dahlias in the vase on the bedside table.

'Talking of nighties, we've got spare ones, or pyjamas if you prefer. Clothes and basic toiletries, too. A lot of people donate items.'

Fiona smiled. 'Thank you, Hazel, you're so kind. I don't know what to say.'

'You can say that we can take some photographs of your face.'

Her voice had hardened and Fiona looked at her with surprise.

'Photographic evidence makes it more difficult for him to get away with it.' She was staring intently into Fiona's eyes.

'I ... I don't know. What do you mean, "get away with it"?'

Hazel backed off. 'I'm sorry. I shouldn't let it anger me like this. What I mean is, if there comes a time when you want to press charges or divorce him, it helps to have some kind of record. A written diary is good, but photos are far, far preferable. There's no pressure for you to do anything now, except get better. But it helps if we can get some record while the injuries are still fresh.'

They stepped out of the room, Hazel gesturing to the many doors in the short corridor. 'With the exception of the two

47

family rooms and the old servant's quarters up in the attic, all the bedrooms have been divided. It's a bit like a mini-hotel, complete with my office just inside the front door. Shall we go down?'

'Actually, do you mind if I make a quick call in private?' Fiona said, glancing back into the empty room.

'Certainly,' Hazel replied. 'But I must stress that this address has to remain a secret.'

Fiona nodded and then went into her room and closed the door. She lifted her mobile out of her handbag and switched it on. Before she'd even found the business card from Cheshire Consorts, her phone was beeping with answerphone messages.

She listened to the first, heard Jeff's drunken threats, and deleted it. The next three were him again, angrier and more drunk, remorseful and pleading, then snarling and vicious. She deleted them, too. The last was from that morning, a colleague from the salon ringing to see if she was OK.

Noticing her battery charge was getting low, she reached into her handbag and took the card from Cheshire Consorts out.

What the hell am I doing? she thought. Isn't my life messed up enough without getting involved in this?

She was about to screw the card up when a memory from the day her daughter died bobbed up. She'd been lying there, listening to Emily's light footsteps as she ran out of the house. Just lying there, not doing a thing. At some point every single day of her life since, she'd paused and thought: If only I'd got up ...

She ran a hand across her forehead, trying to wipe the thought away. Opening her eyes she stared at the card again. Damn it, she'd let down one vulnerable person in her life. She wasn't about to do it again with this Alexia. She took a breath in and called the mobile number written on the back of the card.

When it was eventually answered, all Fiona could hear was what sounded like traffic going past. After a few seconds she tentatively said, 'Hello? Is that Alexia?'

'You what?' A male voice, pitched high with the question.

'I'm trying to get hold of Alexia. Is she there?'

'Who's this?'

'A friend.'

'From where?'

'From...' Fiona searched for an answer, but failed to find one. 'Put Alexia on, please.'

Silence. 'Who are you?' Fiona demanded. 'Why have you got Alexia's phone?'

Still no reply.

'It was you in that motel room last night, wasn't it? What have you done to her?'

The phone went dead.

Fiona stabbed at the redial button, but got the 'number unobtainable' signal. She hugged herself, waiting for her heart to slow down.

The office door was open. Hazel waved her in and said, 'OK. If you could sit in the corner.' She opened a drawer and took out a Polaroid camera. 'Now, if you'll lift your hair away from your face. Lovely.' The flash went off. 'I'll just get a close up of that cut on your eyebrow. Has a doctor seen it yet?'

Fiona shook her head. 'I was planning to go to A and E later on.'

'I think you should,' Hazel replied. 'You don't want to end up with a scar.'

She photographed Fiona head on and from the other side. 'Great. How about a cup of tea while I get your file sorted out?'

Two other women were sitting at the kitchen table, one hunched over the late morning edition of the local paper, a cigarette in her hand.

'Sarah, Cathy, this is Fiona. She'll be with us for a few days.' Hazel retreated from the room and Sarah got up and reached for the kettle. Fiona sensed a well-established routine.

'Brew?' Sarah asked.

'Thanks,' Fiona replied. She fought the urge to brush an imaginary hair from her forehead, knowing the gesture was just an attempt to hide her injury. Nervously she reached for her cigarettes, realising she only had a few left. She held the pack out anyway. 'Cigarette anyone?'

Cathy looked up and Fiona saw livid burns running down the side of her face. A large chunk of her self-consciousness evaporated.

'No, thanks,' Cathy smiled, holding up her own by way of an explanation.

The headline on the paper's front page caught Fiona's eye: HAS THE BUTCHER CLAIMED ANOTHER?

'Milk? Sugar?' Sarah asked, but her voice seemed to be coming from far away.

Fiona's voice came out as a croak, 'Can I?'

'Be my guest.' Cathy slid the paper across and the front page filled Fiona's vision.

A grainy photo, which, judging from the elevation, had been taken from an upstairs window. There was a garden in the foreground. On the grassy area beyond stood a cluster of uniformed policemen and a few onlookers in plain clothes. A tent was being hastily erected.

Fiona's hand went to her mouth as she read the opening paragraph.

> A dog walker made a gruesome discovery early this morning on waste ground almost in the shadow of Belle Vue's famous greyhound racing stadium. As yet police have refused to confirm whether the Butcher has claimed another victim but, as our reporter at the scene can confirm, substantial swathes of the victim's skin had been removed.

Fiona looked up and turned desperately from one woman to the other.

Cathy's chair scraped slightly as she shied away, 'Do you know something about this?'

'I heard ... I heard something last night. I was in a motel. Oh God.'

'What did you hear?' Sarah's hand was frozen on a carton of milk.

'Something horrible.' Fiona stood up and hurried back to the office.

Hazel was writing Fiona's name at the top of some sort of form. She looked up. 'What's wrong?'

'I need to use your phone. Please.'

'Of course. Here.' Quickly she evacuated her seat. 'Are you OK?'

'I just have to... ' The sentence was left unfinished as she began dialling a number. 'Janine, it's Fiona. Is Alice there?'

'Fiona! We tried your home number and mobile when you didn't come in this morning. Everything OK?'

'I'll tell you later. Just put Alice on, will you?'

'OK. She's just finishing with a customer. Wait a second.'

Fiona kept her head down, discouraging any questions from Hazel who was hovering at the door.

'Hi, Fiona. How are you?'

'Alice, your other half. Jon. He's in the police, right? Quite high up?'

'Yes, he works on major incidents. What's wrong?'

'Listen, I need to speak to him. It's about this Butcher of Belle Vue thing.'

Chapter 6

They had just pulled up in the car park of Longsight police station when Jon's mobile began a stifled warble in his pocket.

He glanced at the caller's identity and was surprised to see Alice's name. She always tried to avoid calling him at work. Afraid it was because the baby was coming early, he signalled to Rick that he'd catch him up. 'Ali. Are you OK?'

'Fine. Can you talk?'

Relieved, Jon leaned an elbow on the car roof. 'Yeah. What's up?'

'I work with a woman called Fiona. She does make-up and facials.'

'The one with the violent husband?'

Alice's voice dropped to a whisper. 'Yeah.'

There was a moment's silence as each waited for the other to go on.

Alice spoke first. 'She called me just now. She wants to meet you.'

'About the husband? Ali, I'd love to sort him out, but there are trained officers she can speak to in the Domestic Violence—'

'She thinks she heard someone being killed last night.'

'What?'

'She thinks she heard someone being killed last night.'

'Where?'

'In the room next to hers. She was staying in some run-down motel in Belle Vue.'

Jon cupped a hand over his ear to hear more clearly. 'You said Belle Vue?'

Forty minutes later he found himself sitting with another coffee. He thought back to Rick reaching for the chocolate powder, then changing his mind. Strangely self-conscious behaviour.

As his eyes scanned the people passing the window, he searched his memory for the one time he'd met Fiona. It was a few years ago when the salon staff were out celebrating Melvyn's birthday. Jon was coming off a late shift and had agreed to pick Alice up at the end of the night.

When he'd arrived at the wine-bar he could see the evening had been a good one. Empty bottles littered the table and they were all sitting around with pissed looks on their faces. Jon had taken a seat next to Melvyn and Alice. On spotting him, Melvyn introduced everyone, then instantly reached for a bottle of wine and began filling a glass.

'Just a small one,' Jon had smiled, his outstretched hand palm down.

'Bollocks. Get a taxi,' Melvyn replied, filling it right up.

Jon shook his head, the grin still on his face. 'It'll take hours to catch you lot up and this place shuts in ten minutes.'

Alice had slumped against his shoulder and was fumbling with a packet of cigarettes as she resumed an earnest discussion with Melvyn about who was the sexiest, Ewan McGregor, Johnny Depp or Keanu Reeves.

God, she's going to be hung over in the morning, Jon thought, lighting one for himself and looking around. Fiona was at the other end of the table, clutching a glass of wine, deep in a serious-looking conversation with the woman at her side.

Jon had found himself studying her. She should have been quite a glamorous woman but something was marring the impression. Her face was pleasantly proportioned, no single feature standing out as wrong. Her light brown hair had been professionally cut and styled, probably by Melvyn, Jon had guessed. She was wearing a pale blue cashmere top, the neckline cut just low enough to show off a glittery necklace.

But everything was being undermined by something. Ready to look away the moment her eyes turned towards his, he scrutinised her more closely. Was it her eyebrows? Had she plucked them a little too vigorously? Applied liner at a slightly harsh angle?

Finally it came to him. The negative impression wasn't as a result of any single feature, it was more the expression on her face. The lines at the corners of her eyes and at the edges of her mouth all emphasised it. They slanted downwards and the skin along her jawline seemed loose and somehow tired.

Her face hinted at the slow and cumulative effects of pain. He'd seen a similar drawn look appear on his granddad's face as the cancer really began to take hold. Jon was just wondering what was eating her when something caused alarm to flicker in her eyes.

He looked to his right and saw a heavy man standing just inside the door. His arms were crossed and a large belly pressed out over his belt. He nodded towards the door and Jon spotted a set of car keys hanging from one hand.

Fiona started scrabbling around for her handbag, hurriedly saying goodbye to the colleague she'd been talking to. Her movement was picked up by Melvyn and he glanced round for an explanation. Seeing the man by the door, he called out sarcastically, 'Jeff! Good to see you. Joining us for a quick one?'

The man stayed exactly where he was and shook his head.

'Yeah, and fuck you, too,' Melvyn muttered.

Fiona was now standing, agitation and embarrassment on her face. 'See you all on Monday,' she said, struggling slightly with her words.

Melvyn got up and hugged her, then watched with a pained expression as she lurched across the bar and out the door. Jon looked around and saw similar emotions on everyone else's face.

Melvyn sat back down with a sigh. 'Fucking arsehole.'

'That's Fiona's other half?' Jon asked.

His question had gone unanswered as they all broke into conversations about why she stayed with him.

A woman walked through the coffee shop doors. She was wearing a strange mish-mash of clothes, her hair was down over her forehead and she tried to keep her head bowed as she glanced quickly round the room. Their eyes met. Simultaneously recognising her and seeing the damage to her face, Jon held up a hand.

She moved towards him. 'How did you know it was me?'

'We were introduced once. I was picking Alice up from the

pub. You were there with the other staff from the salon.' She was looking blankly at him. 'Jesus, you really were pissed.' He touched the scar above his own eyebrow and smiled. 'Besides, Alice said we had something in common.'

Her eyes dropped in embarrassment and Jon cursed his clumsy attempt at breaking the ice.

'What else did she say about me?' she asked.

He chose his words more carefully. 'Not a lot. Just that your husband gives you a hard time.'

She sat down, lit a cigarette and looked him in the eyes. 'My soon to be ex-husband.'

Jon hoped so, but he'd heard that line plenty of times before. Abusive relationships fought hard to keep their participants in place. 'I can put you in touch with specially trained officers. Start the ball rolling to make sure he can't come near you again.'

She shook her head. 'Thanks, but it's OK.'

'Where are you staying?' said Jon, eyes straying hungrily to the smoke curling from the tip of her cigarette.

'Sorry, would you like one?' She held the pack out.

Jon pursed his lips. He'd agreed with Alice to give up last year. Apart from one lapse, he hadn't smoked in almost six months. Most of the time it was becoming less and less of a problem, but certain occasions brought on an urge like the need for a cool drink on a summer's day. A little voice told him it would be OK. She was a fellow smoker. She'd understand. Word would never get back to Alice. He wrestled the temptation down with a shake of his head. 'Trying to give up, thanks. So, where are you staying?'

'I've got a room just round the corner.' She gestured vaguely towards the street.

'In the refuge on Stanhope Street?' Jon kept his voice low.

Fiona's face went from shock to realisation. 'Sorry. They told me to keep the address secret. I should have known the police would know about it.'

'How long are you there for?'

She sighed, and a tremor passed across her lower lip. 'I don't know. I really don't know.'

'Are you OK, Fiona? We don't have to do this if you're not.'

She smiled bleakly. 'Am I OK? I've just walked out on my husband. And then what I heard last night …' She ground the cigarette out, drilling the filter hard into the ashtray. 'Be strong, Fiona. Be strong,' she said under her breath. Then she looked up. 'I want to tell you about last night.' Despite her determined tone, a shiver went through her.

'Can I get you a coffee first?'

She smiled. 'Thanks. A latte, please.'

Jon returned a couple of minutes later. He placed a froth-filled cup before her just as she lit another cigarette. 'Take your time,' he said, sitting down.

Fiona told her story, starting from when she'd staggered into the foyer of the Platinum Inn and had sat with Dawn in the back office, sharing a few drinks. She began to falter when she had to describe the sound of the couple undressing.

'OK, Fiona,' Jon helped her along. 'They were on the bed by now.'

She nodded.

'And I'm guessing you could hear them getting down to business? Pardon the pun.'

'Yes. But then I heard them speak again and they moved. Changed – you know – positions I suppose. And that's when the struggling began. And this awful choking sound. She was fighting to breathe.'

Jon knew the autopsies on Angela Rowlands and Carol Miller had shown evidence of strangulation. In the background the milk steamer's splutters ground to a halt.

'Eventually they stopped moving. Then one person got up, went to the bathroom and the taps came on. He wandered about the room for a bit, went back to the bed.' She broke to spoon foam into her mouth, fingers trembling. 'Then there was a thump, like something heavy being dragged off the bed and onto the floor.'

Jon tried to keep his thoughts objective, but he couldn't stop the waves of excitement running through him. He dragged his eyes from the tip of her cigarette again.

'I crept across to my door and looked through the spyhole. One person left that room, moving slowly, something big and heavy wrapped in a blanket over his shoulder.'

'Did you see his face?'

'No, just a flash of reddish-brown hair, but I reckon that was the girl's, poking out from the top of the blanket. He headed away from reception to the door at the other end of the corridor. He must have left through the fire exit.'

'Did any sort of an alarm go off?'

Fiona shook her head. 'You should see the place. It's falling apart. I doubt the alarms even work.'

Jon ran the information through his head. The motel was a few minutes' walk from where the third body had been found. But where had the victim's skin been removed? Did the killer have a van in the car park or had he even left the building at all? Could he have taken her to a storage room or perhaps the basement?

'Fiona, do you know what time of night this was?'

She nodded emphatically. 'Three thirty in the morning they woke me coming into their room. He left at about four I'd imagine.'

Jon's excitement vanished. 'You're absolutely sure on that?'

'Yes, I looked at my watch.'

'And it was three thirty in the morning?'

'Yes. Three thirty-six, to be exact.'

An image of the killer had just started to materialise in his head. Blurred and indistinct maybe, but just enough to create a tingle in his veins. It was a sensation he found completely addictive. Now the hazy silhouette evaporated like a mirage. His lips tensed in regret. 'Fiona, I'm telling you this in confidence. The body found at just after six this morning. It had been there all night, not placed there just before dawn.'

Fiona frowned. 'But I heard ... What I heard, it wasn't just sex.' Her jaw set tight. 'I really think I heard someone being killed.'

Jon took a deep breath and looked up at the ceiling, wondering how much brandy she'd shared with the receptionist. Halogen bulbs glared down at him.

'And I found this.' Fiona patted her pockets and pulled out a slightly crumpled business card. 'It was under the bed.'

'Under which bed?'

'The one in the next room. Number nine. The door hadn't shut properly. I looked around it this morning.'

'And?'

'And it was spotless. The bed looked like no one had slept in it. The bathroom was immaculate. Everything had been wiped clean – to destroy evidence, I suppose. This was the only thing there. Oh, and the spare blanket was missing, too.'

The card was still in her outstretched hand, shaking slightly.

Jon looked at it. It could have been lying there for days. 'Fiona, you were attacked by your husband last night. You mentioned you had quite a bit of brandy with the night receptionist—'

'Don't say I imagined it!' she hissed.

'I'm not. I'm certain you heard something. But this motel – it's used on an hourly basis by prostitutes and their clients. All sorts are going on. Doors banging, people coming and going right through the night.'

'I heard what I heard.' The card was thrust defiantly towards him.

Reluctantly Jon took it, read the printed writing then flipped it over.

Fiona jabbed a finger at the scrawled biro. 'I tried her number. A man answered. He hung up on me and when I tried again the number had gone dead.'

Jon raised an eyebrow.

'Go on. Try it yourself.'

As he took his mobile out he got a surreptitious look at his watch. This was taking up too much time. He rang the number. It went through to a number unavailable announcement.

'See?' Fiona insisted. Her voice was beginning to grate. 'He's stolen her stuff. The phone's probably been shoved down some drain by now.'

'OK.' Jon got ready to stand up. 'This Platinum Inn. I'll stop by and ask some questions, I'll speak to Cheshire Consorts and I'll check who this mobile number is registered to.'

Fiona relaxed a little. 'Thank you.'

'I've really got to go. I'll call you. Have you got a mobile?'

She gave him her number.

★

When he walked into the incident room on the top floor of Longsight station, a new buzz was in the air.

Rick was at his desk, a couple of other officers complimenting him on spotting the glove. Jon saw the look of pleasure on his face, the easy way he was taking credit for the find. You'll go far in this job, he thought.

As he got to their desks Rick finally saw him. 'It was blood on that glove.'

Jon sat down. 'That's great news. Anything on who the girl is?'

'No. She's been fingerprinted and a DNA sample's been taken. All missing reports for young female adults are being checked now, and word's gone out to the neighbouring forces to do the same.'

'Door-to-door around Belle Vue?'

'As we speak.'

The other two officers moved off and Rick quietly said, 'McCloughlin announced that I'd found the glove to the whole room. It's been a good way of meeting everyone.'

That surprised Jon, and he thought that maybe there was no link between Rick and McCloughlin. But then he realised Rick could easily have told McCloughlin the true story and the announcement to the incident room could be just McCloughlin keeping up the pretence. 'What about that footprint?'

'The CSM – what was her name?'

'Nikki Kingston,' Jon replied, slightly irritated at the defensive note in his voice.

'Apparently, she shoved a bucket over it and sent for a casting kit.'

Jon grinned in admiration of her efficiency.

'But the best is yet to come,' Rick carried on.

'Go on.'

'The glove. She's testing it for fingerprints, something about amino acid deposits in sweat showing up on latex. If whoever dropped that glove is on NAFIS, we could have his name and address in a few hours.'

Jon looked around. 'No wonder everyone's looking so happy.'

Rick stood up. 'I'm desperate for a leak.'

Jon waited until Rick had gone out, then picked up the phone and dialled Nikki's number. 'Nikki, it's Jon. This glove.'

'Bloody hell, Jon. Anyone else and I'd tell them to call back later. It's right in front of me. We've already lifted a partial from the wrist where he gripped it to pull it on.'

'Enough for a match?'

'No. But there should be others – on the inside at the finger-tips, for instance. If he wasn't wearing them long enough to get them all smudged, they could prove useful.'

'Great. Listen, can you tell me who made the glove? Can you see the word "Mediquip" on it?'

'Hang on. There's something on the back.' Her words were drawn out and Jon could tell she was squinting, face inches from the glove. 'Yes. It says "Size 8" and "Mediquip Inc". Good news?'

'Could well be,' Jon replied, trying to suppress the excitement in his voice. He placed the bag with Pete Gray's cup in on the desk. 'Last thing, Nikki,' he said, lowering his voice. 'Can you run a couple of tests on a cup for me? Fingerprints and, hope-fully, saliva for DNA.'

'Are you taking the piss?'

'I don't mean straight away,' he protested. 'Just when you get the chance.'

She sighed. 'You owe me. Big time. Where's it come from, anyway?'

'A suspect left it behind at an interview.'

'So this is an unofficial test?'

'Yeah.' Jon smiled. 'If it links him to what I'm hoping, we'll pull him in on something else and then run a DNA mouth swab in line with the Police and Criminal Evidence Act.' Seeing Rick coming back in, he quickly hid the cup in his drawer. 'Right, I'll leave you to it.'

'Sure there's nothing else?' she said sarcastically.

'No, that'll do for the moment. Cheers.' He hung up as Rick sat down. 'I've just spoken to the CSM. The glove you found at the crime scene was made by a company called Mediquip.'

Rick raised a finger. 'Same as the ones Pete Gray was wheel-ing to the surgical ward.'

Jon winked. 'Have a check on the PNC, see if he's got any priors. I'll see what the internet has on Mediquip.'

Less than a minute later, Jon was reading out the company's home page in an American accent. 'Mediquip is one of the world's leading manufacturers of latex and vinyl gloves for surgical and medical use. Our factory employs the very latest quality control standards in order to produce a range of gloves recognised across the globe for their reliability.' A row of thumbnail-sized photos popped up across the the screen. 'Powder-free vinyl. PE gloves for industrial use. Powder-free in natural colour. Latex surgical sterilised by EO gas. Copolymer sterile latex. Pre-powdered nitrile examination.' He scanned the column on the left of the screen. 'Here we go: suppliers.' He keyed 'United Kingdom' into the search field. Four names came up, one based in Manchester: Protex Ltd, Unit 15, Europa Business Park, Denton.

Rick's eyes were on his own screen. 'Pete Gray. Cautioned for sexual harassment back in eighty-nine. Was going to court, but charges were dropped by his then wife, Helen Gray. There's an addendum to contact the Domestic Violence Unit for more information.'

He called the unit and got them to pull their intelligence file on Pete Gray. There were two other incidents involving violence towards females, one in 1993 and another in 1999. Neither had resulted in a caution or conviction.

'So he's not had his DNA added to the national database,' Rick announced, hanging up the phone.

'Looks like he has an attitude problem with the ladies, though,' Jon replied, printing off the contact details for Protex. 'OK. I think it's time for a word with McCloughlin.'

As he got up, he saw the business card for Cheshire Consorts lying on his desk. Flipping it over, he looked at the mobile phone number scrawled there and groaned. He'd assured Fiona that he'd look into it, and now he'd have to waste valuable time keeping his promise.

'Two seconds, I just need to do a favour for a colleague of my girlfriend. She thinks she heard someone being strangled in the room next to her in a motel last night.'

Rick smirked at Jon's tone. 'Whereabouts?'

'Belle Vue,' Jon replied, picking up the phone.

'Really? Near where the body was this morning?'

Jon nodded. 'Yeah, but don't get excited. Whatever she thinks she heard, it was at three thirty in the morning. The third victim's time of death was hours before that.'

He called the communications liaison office. 'DI Spicer here. Could you run a check on a mobile phone number for me, please?'

Next he flipped the card over and rang Cheshire Consorts itself. 'Hello, this is DI Spicer from Greater Manchester Police. Who am I speaking to, please?'

'Joanne Perkins. Are you on duty, Detective Inspector, or is this call for leisure purposes?'

But for a calculating note, the voice was very seductive. Jon imagined long, shimmering blond hair, arched eyebrows and full red lips. 'I'm on duty, yes. Could I speak to the manager or owner, please?'

'You are. I'm manager and owner.'

'Ms Perkins—'

'Please, call me "Miss". You'll find we're feminine, not feminist, at Cheshire Consorts.'

Jon smiled; the lady was good. 'Miss Perkins. Do you have a girl on your books called Alexia?'

'Why?'

'A possible missing person. We have reason to believe she worked as an escort for your company.'

A cigarette lighter flicked and breath was exhaled against the mouthpiece. He could almost feel the smoke washing over his face. 'No surname?'

Jon shook his head. 'Afraid not.'

'No, I don't.' The answer was too abrupt.

'Have any girls failed to check back with you since their last job?'

'DI Spicer, I'm not their nanny. The customer gives his credit card number to me, I send the girl to him. Apart from passing a percentage of his payment to the girl, I'm out of the equation.'

That was more like it, Jon thought. Cold and selfish. He guessed her experience of customers wasn't limited to just the management side of things. 'And you're sure no one of that name works for you? It sounds like an alias to me.'

'All my girls use aliases. Go to Cheshire Consorts dot com. They're all listed there. Now this is a business line. I really must go.'

Jon made sure he got the phone down first. Small recompense for being brushed off. A few seconds later he knocked on McCloughlin's door, opened it and let Rick step in first. McCloughlin's face lit up. 'DS Saville.' His eyes moved to Jon. 'And DI Spicer.' Less enthusiasm in his voice. 'Sit down.'

'Sir,' Jon began, 'we spoke to Pete Gray, the porter at Stepping Hill hospital.'

'And?'

'As soon as Carol Miller was mentioned, his mouth clammed shut. In fact, he got up and walked away, not prepared to talk any further.'

'Interesting.'

Rick spoke up. 'He was arrested for sexual harassment in 1989. His ex-wife.'

McCloughlin inclined his head. 'And I can tell you have more.'

Jon nodded. 'When we saw him at the hospital, Rick noticed he was wheeling a box of surgical gloves. They're manufactured by a US company called Mediquip, but distributed in this region by a British firm called Protex Ltd.'

McCloughlin's eyes lingered suspiciously on Jon before turning to Rick. 'Have you called Protex yet? We could do with knowing who the area rep is, at least.'

'Not yet,' said Rick. 'We—I've only just got the information.'

McCloughlin obviously sensed Rick wasn't being straight. He pushed his phone across the desk. 'Make the call.'

Rick looked down. The only thing on his lap was Pete Gray's record. Sheepishly he looked at Jon. 'I think you have the company's details?'

Jon whipped the sheet out from his notebook. From the corner of his eye he saw McCloughlin's lip beginning to curl.

Rick called the number, introduced himself and asked to speak to the sales rep for the north-west. He started jotting information down. 'Since when? ... I see ... And his name's Gordon Dean? ... Where was he staying? ... OK ... No, if we hear anything we'll call back.' He hung up, looking baffled. 'It appears he's vanished. He was staying in Manchester, seeing clients around town yesterday. Since then they've been trying to contact him. He missed a big sales meeting this morning.'

Without lifting his forearm from his desk, McCloughlin pointed a finger at the door. 'A blood-spattered glove is dropped at a murder scene and the area rep for that company goes missing the very next morning? I don't need to tell you which lead to pursue, gentlemen.'

As they made for the door, McCloughlin called Jon back. Without looking up, he said, 'Next time, don't use your partner to front up information that you've sourced. Understood?'

'Sir.' Jon closed the door quietly behind him.

Chapter 7

The body in the bed didn't move.

Sunlight slanted in through the open window, spilling across the crumpled white sheets and creating a lunar landscape of miniature ravines. Silence dominated the room, pierced at regular intervals by a thin whistle. It came from the bandages encasing the patient's face.

Eventually a hand slid upwards. A forefinger and thumb picked delicately at the nostril holes and shoulders flinched as pain lanced outwards. After a few moments the patient tried again, this time successfully getting the tip of a varnished nail into a nostril that still throbbed from where the blows had landed. A large flake of dried blood was prised away and a sob of self-pity was released.

The hand fell back on to the sheet as a soft whirring came from the window. A robin had alighted on the metal arm holding the window open. Head cocked to one side, it surveyed the room with a keen eye.

From the bed, a pair of swollen and bloodshot eyes looked back, hungry for company of any kind. The patient tried to encourage the bird forward with a kissing sound, tears spilling over the layers of gauze.

Chapter 8

Immaculate grass borders flanked the entrance to the Europa Business Park. The spotless white gates were open and, as soon as they turned in, the car tyres seemed to start gliding over the smooth tarmac. A large sign stood at a fork in the road. Rick's eyes moved over it. 'Units ten to twenty. Right turn.'

Jon spun the wheel and they followed the gently curving avenue. Side roads branched off to low buildings made from a type of corrugated material that appeared to come in only three colours: blue, green and white. Protex Ltd had chosen white.

They parked in one of the spaces reserved for visitors directly in front of reception. Grey glass doors slid silently open as they approached them and they stepped into a foyer which was tidy to the point of being unwelcoming. A photo of a proudly beaming man was on their right. Directly below it a brass plaque: *Keith Bradley founded this company in 1973.*

And doesn't his tie just show it, thought Jon, making an effort not to wince at the ugly splashes of colour jumping off the man's chest.

Photos of various gloves lined the wall, each one bathed in coloured lighting to add interest to a totally lifeless product.

A young woman with a headset cutting into her wavy brown hair nodded to them from behind the reception desk. 'Can I help you?'

They held up their warrant cards and her smile slipped.

'Could we speak to your head of human resources, please?' Jon asked.

'One moment.' She pressed a button on the switchboard. 'Martin, I have two policemen wishing to speak with you.' She listened for a second, then looked up. 'Could I ask what it's in relation to?'

Jon leaned closer and, for the benefit of the person on the other end of the line, said loudly, 'Gordon Dean.'

The receptionist listened again. 'He'll be right down. Please take a seat.'

Jon glanced at the chairs. Like everything else, they were stiff and unused. He remained standing. A minute later footsteps could be heard on the stairs. A middle-aged man in shirt and tie walked over to them. 'Martin Appleforth, head of HR.' He hesitated, not knowing who to shake hands with first.

Jon stepped forward. 'DI Spicer and DS Saville.'

Appleforth's office was slightly too warm. The blinds on the end window were lowered, but sunlight cut through the gaps, one sliver dissecting the photo of a plain-looking woman trying to smile in some crowded beauty spot.

'I hope Gordon's all right? Has something happened?' He positioned his pen in the exact midpoint of a Protex notepad.

'We're not sure at present,' answered Jon, unbuttoning his jacket. 'What sort of employee is he?'

Appleforth turned one palm upwards, as if the necessary information would drop into it. 'Hard-working, reliable. He's been with us for around eight years.'

'And his sales patch is the whole of the north-west?'

'The Manchester area and south into Cheshire. Another rep takes care of the Liverpool area and up into the Lake District as far as the Scottish border.'

'So Mr Dean has a company car?' asked Rick.

'Yes, a silver Passat – same as me, in fact.'

'Do you have his registration?'

Appleforth swivelled in his seat, consulted a sheet of paper pinned to his noticeboard and read out the registration.

Jon noted it down. 'What sort of companies do you deal with?'

'Hospitals and GP practices mainly, as you can imagine, but any sort of business in the health sector. Private surgeries, NHS clinics, even a few tattoo parlours and beauty salons, though I class them in the cosmetics sector.'

'Tell me, do you have a contract with Stepping Hill hospital in Stockport?' Jon asked, thinking of Pete Gray.

'I'd have to phone the sales department.'

'And it would be useful if we could have the list of clients Mr Dean saw in the last three days. Is that possible?'

'Again, I'd have to ask the sales department.'

'How old is Mr Dean?'

'Late thirties, I'd have thought.'

'Married?'

'Yes.' Appleforth looked down at his desk and rubbed a forefinger against his temple. 'Angela, if I remember.' Jon guessed he'd just been looking at Gordon Dean's file.

'Have you spoken to his wife today?' Rick asked.

'Yes.' Appleforth admitted. 'She rang earlier, very worried. When I said he hadn't shown up for the meeting here, she said she was going to report him as missing.' He looked at them as if they should already know this.

Rick nodded ambiguously. 'Which station did she go to?'

'Her local one in Stoke.'

'I see. Mr Appleforth, we could do with speaking to her ourselves. Could you give us her phone number?'

He reached for the mouse, but his hand stayed hovering above it. 'I'm not sure if I should give his personal details out...' His eyes were calculating. 'She said the police told her that, although he's missing, they couldn't treat it as anything but low priority for a few more days. How come you're here now?'

'Mr Appleforth.' Jon hunched forward in his seat, shoulders suddenly tight against his jacket. The desire to move the investigation forward was nagging away at him and there was no way an officious little prick like this was going to slow things down. 'We're investigating a serious crime here, one the press are also very interested in. There's reason to believe that Mr Dean, in his capacity as a sales rep for Protex, could help us. Now, I don't want this turning into a matter for your PR department.'

Appleforth hesitated a moment longer before clicking his mouse. Sure enough, Gordon Dean's details, including his address in Stoke, were already up on his desktop. 'We'd appreciate being kept up to date with Mr Dean's whereabouts.'

Jon sat back. 'Of course.'

They were heading back out of Appleforth's office when Jon

paused in the doorway. 'Does Mr Dean have a workstation in the building?'

'Yes, office number five at the end of the corridor.'

'May we take a quick look inside?'

Appleforth hesitated but, unable to think of a decent reason why not, nodded and got up. He led Jon and Rick along the silent corridor, past smoked-glass windows and shiny wooden doors. They stood back at number five, allowing him to open the door for them.

To Jon's annoyance Appleforth used the opportunity to step in ahead of them and position himself in the corner by the window. 'What are you looking for?' he asked.

Jon shrugged. 'Nothing specifically.'

The room was small, too small for three men. Jon tried to look around, but his view was obscured by Rick and Appleforth. Picking up on his look of annoyance, Rick stepped back and watched from the doorway. Immediately in front of Jon was a small desk with a computer monitor and keyboard taking up one half. A phone with a notepad occupied the opposite corner and between them sat a desk tidy. Jon looked at the three cylindrical tubes, noting each one held a different colour of biro, blue, red and black. The shallower tray at the front was filled with paperclips. Jon looked again; they were actually stacked in neat little piles of decreasing size.

He examined the rest of the room. A filing cabinet was next to Appleforth, each drawer clearly marked: A – F, G – L, M – R, S – Z. Next to the cabinet was a bin. Jon craned forwards, it was spotlessly clean inside. His eyes wandered over the bare walls. No pictures, prints or photographs. He reached round the desk and tried the uppermost drawer. Locked. 'Does he ever actually work here?'

Appleforth looked confused. 'Yes. He's on the road most of the time, but here about three times a week I'd say.'

'And is he as neat in his personal appearance as his office suggests?'

Appleforth frowned briefly. 'I suppose so. And we'd expect him to be, too. Protex is a medical supplies company. We need to be neat, organised, efficient.'

'Clinical,' Rick added from the doorway.

'I'm sorry?' Appleforth asked.

'Nothing,' Jon replied, glaring at Rick.

At that time of day the drive down to Stoke took just over an hour. Rush hour, and you could double that, Jon thought. Gordon Dean's house was in a private development bordering agricultural land, cows dotting the fields alongside. The cluster of houses was large, all of them detached and with separate garages. They pulled to a halt outside Ravenscroft. Fake wooden timbers criss-crossed the front of the house, lattice windows adding another feeble period touch.

They'd phoned en route and Mrs Dean opened the door as they walked up the front path. She ushered them into a spacious living room dominated by pastel shades and the scent of polish. The pale pink carpet was covered in hoover marks and a yellow duster lay on the coffee table. 'I'm sorry,' she said, removing it. 'I need to be doing something.' Her eyes searched theirs, seeking information from their expressions.

'I'm afraid we haven't anything to tell you as to your husband's whereabouts as yet,' Jon said, turning and gesturing to the large sofa and its plumped-up cushions.

'Oh, sorry, please.' She perched nervously on the edge of a matching armchair and her fingers started teasing the corners of the duster. As Jon sat down he realised the room had the same feeling of sterility as her husband's office at Protex.

Jon took out his notebook. 'When did you last speak to your husband, Mrs Dean?'

'Yesterday morning, when he set off for Manchester. But he should have rung this morning. He always rings me between eight and nine if he's staying in a hotel.'

'And how often is that?'

'Three or four times a month. Usually he stays in Manchester. Most of his big clients are around there, so he saves hours of driving by booking into a hotel.'

'Does he stay in a particular one?'

'Yes. They built a Novotel for the Commonwealth Games last summer. That's his usual one nowadays.'

'I see. Mrs Dean, this may sound silly, but have you looked in your husband's wardrobe?'

'Why?' Voice defensive.

'To see if any of his clothes are missing.'

'Yes, I have,' she replied with a stiff nod. 'The hangers aren't jangling.'

Jon wondered what she was holding back. 'And you've been trying his mobile?'

'Yes. It just rings through to answerphone.'

Thinking of the precise incisions that had been employed to remove the third victim's face, Jon leaned forwards. 'Mrs Dean, how did your husband come to work for a medical company? Does he have an interest in that area himself?'

'Sorry, I don't quite understand you.'

'Did he read medicine or have ambitions to practise it?'

'Oh no. He worked for a paper merchant's before this job, a manufacturer of franking machines before that. According to Gordon, it's all just sales at the end of the day.'

Jon glanced around. 'Does your husband have an office here?'

She pointed through the archway into the adjoining dining room. 'He plugs his laptop in there.'

Jon looked. On the table in the far corner of the room was a small printer. Two box files stood on a shelf unit beside it. 'May we?'

Mrs Dean nodded.

As Jon crossed into the other room, he was aware of her trailing along behind. He said, 'Could I be cheeky and ask for a cup of tea?'

'Of course. I do apologise, I should have offered.'

Once she was out of the room Jon and Rick each took a file. They put them on the dining table, sat down, opened the lids and started flicking through. Jon's contained plastic folders with information on Gordon Dean's clients. Rick's was used for receipts and literature about Protex products. Both men were so absorbed in their task, they didn't hear Mrs Dean come back into the living room.

'Are you looking for anything in particular?' She was standing by the coffee table, carrying a tray with a teapot, milk jug and three cups.

Jon shook his head. 'Not really. We're just trying to get an idea of his typical movements.'

She put the tray down and approached them. Rick was flicking through the receipts for that month. Mrs Dean watched him, fingers of one hand massaging the thumb of the other. Jon waited for her to come out with whatever it was she wanted to say.

Eventually she spoke. 'I had a look through his suits earlier on. I found some statements there.'

Jon raised his chin. 'What sort of statements?'

'Credit card ones. The bills go direct to his office, but it's not a company credit card. They're old statements from the last two months.'

'Do you still have them?'

She dropped her hands to her sides. 'I'd never go through his pockets normally ...'

Jon stood up. 'I understand, Mrs Dean, but these are special circumstances.'

She nodded in agreement. 'They're here.' She opened the drawer beneath the dining table but, rather than get them out, walked back into the living room. 'Do you take milk and sugar?'

'One, please.' Jon's eyes were on the sheets of paper as Rick shook his head politely at Mrs Dean. Jon put the statements on the table and sat down. The card had taken quite a hammering. 'Piccolino's. That's the new Italian near the town hall,' he murmured.

'Twenty-six quid. Probably a meal for one,' Rick whispered back.

'Via Venice, Stock, Don Antonio's. He likes his Italian food.' Jon pointed at an item on the list. 'Is that a restaurant?'

'You've never heard of Crimson?' Rick's voice was barely audible.

Jon checked that Mrs Dean was still out of earshot and whispered, 'No. But he was there three times last month. What is it?'

72

'It's in the Gay Village, on a side road behind Canal Street. A wine-bar upstairs, cabaret and dance floor downstairs. Very trendy.'

'With who?'

'It started as a gay venue. There's a drag queen called Miss Tonguelash. All sorts go nowadays to hear her bitching.'

Jon glanced at Rick, ready to ask how he knew so much about a place in Manchester's Gay Village. But his partner's eyes were frozen on the statement, a red flush creeping up his neck. The words died in Jon's throat.

Mrs Dean walked back through the archway. As she held the china cups out, they began to rattle in their saucers. Tea started to spill. 'He's not coming back. The bastard.'

The word seemed so foreign coming from her lips. She started to cry. Jon quickly stood up and took the drinks from her quivering hands. Rick pulled a chair out and she collapsed into it, raising a hand to her face.

Awkwardly, Jon stood to the side. Rick fetched her cup of tea and sat down next to her. Taking her hand in his, he said quietly, 'Why do you say that, Mrs Dean?'

She looked up, tears brimming. 'Those.' She pointed accusingly at the credit card statements. 'He's been hiding something for a long time now. There's always been something distant about him, but recently there's been a change. He's found someone else, I know it.'

'How has he changed recently?' Rick asked.

She extracted her hand from his and pulled a hanky out of her cardigan cuff. 'His behaviour. Like he's having a midlife crisis. He was talking about getting a motorbike, for God's sake. And he got a tattoo. Of all things.'

Jon sat down. 'What sort of tattoo?'

'A ladybird, on his shoulder. What came over him? He's thirty-nine.'

Jon looked at the framed photo on the wall: Mrs Dean standing stiffly next to a thin man with a sweeping side parting and feeble moustache, the Eiffel Tower rising into the sky behind them. They were in the city of romance but a good ten inches separated them.

Jon searched the walls for photos of children. There were none. 'Mrs Dean, is there anyone Gordon may have gone to? A close friend, a son, a daughter?'

'We don't have children,' she replied, the corner of her left eye beginning to tick. 'I've already called all the people I could think of. No one's heard from him.'

Jon's eyes went back to the snap of them in Paris. 'Mrs Dean, it would be a great help if we could have a recent photo of your husband.'

They drove back up the M6 in the last light of day. Jon's mind switching between Gordon Dean's disappearance and Rick's intimate knowledge of a bar in the Gay Village. Was the bloke a homosexual? Something odd was definitely going on.

As they approached the Knutsford services the sky darkened and, minutes later, drops of rain started hitting their windscreen.

'Welcome to Manchester,' Jon commented with ironic cheer.

The manager at the Novotel was a woman of around forty, with wiry ginger hair fighting to break free from a cluster of hairclips. 'How may I help you?' An Eastern European accent added a brusqueness to her greeting.

Jon checked her name tag. 'Hello, Kristina. I'm DI Spicer, this is DS Saville.' The enthusiastic way she responded to the sight of their warrant cards surprised him. Perhaps it was something to do with attitudes to authority in her native country. She listened to their request, then looked at the computer before confirming that Gordon Dean had booked in the day before. 'The room is now occupied by another guest.'

'So Mr Dean checked out. Can you tell me at what time?' asked Jon.

'It is not possible to say. Many guests leave the key in the door, others drop it in the box at the end of the counter. The room is paid for at check-in and should be vacated by eleven the next morning.'

'Can you tell us if anything was left in his room? Bags, a laptop, that sort of thing?' Rick asked.

'I will check Lost Property.' She disappeared into the back room, returning a minute later. 'No, nothing from his room.'

Jon pondered the information. Gordon must have returned at some stage, packed his things and moved on. He pointed to the CCTV camera above the entrance. 'Do you keep the tapes from previous days?'

She nodded. 'For the last two weeks only. But I would need permission from head office before you can take one. They are shut now, I'm sorry.'

Jon tapped a finger on the counter. More and more, he suspected that Gordon Dean had simply eloped. However, he knew McCloughlin would be tracking him closely on this one. 'Actually, Kristina, we could seize the tape as evidence here and now. But don't worry, I'm happy if you could just put in a request for us to borrow yesterday's.'

Chapter 9

Jon clicked his biro shut and dropped it on the pile of paper and messages on his desk. Among them was a note saying the check he'd requested on the mobile phone number Fiona Wilson had given him had shown it to be a pay-as-you-go: untraceable. It was almost ten o'clock at night and the incident room was nearly empty.

'I'm calling it a day,' he announced.

Rick stretched his arms above his head. 'Yeah, good idea.' He pushed a batch of forms aside. 'This can wait until tomorrow. I'd never have believed getting someone's credit-card records would take so long.'

'That's data protection,' Jon replied. 'Lots more paperwork for us.' As he got up he saw the card from Cheshire Consorts on his desk. Shit, he'd promised Fiona he'd have a word at the motel. 'One more job to do,' he said, sitting down again.

Rick was hesitating, jacket draped over an arm.

'That favour for my other half's friend? I said I'd check the motel she stayed in. You get on.' Jon nodded towards the door.

'Oh. OK, see you tomorrow.'

Jon tried to look up the number for the motel but couldn't find it in the Yellow Pages. However, a quick visit wouldn't take him too far out of his way.

In the deserted car park he was surprised to see Rick standing by his vehicle. Jon was parked almost next to it. 'Car not starting?'

Rick flicked a distracted glance at his Golf. 'No, it's fine. I just wanted to get something sorted out.'

This'll be interesting, thought Jon, crossing his arms.

Rick's chest filled out slightly as he nervously breathed in.

'Back at Gordon Dean's house, you looked at me when I was describing that place called Crimson.'

Jon nodded, surprised that this wasn't about McCloughlin.

Rick swallowed. 'I hope the fact that I'm gay won't affect how we work together.'

Jon was suddenly relieved that it was dark: Rick couldn't see his blush. 'No. Of course not.'

Rick continued facing him a moment longer. 'Good. It's best that we dealt with it straight away.'

'Absolutely. And it's really not an issue for me,' Jon replied, hearing his language slipping into the politically correct. 'I'll see you tomorrow.'

'See you tomorrow.'

Simultaneously they unlocked their cars, opened the doors and got in. As Jon turned the ignition key, he heard Rick's engine start, too. Both sets of lights came on together. Jon leaned forward and gestured to Rick. The other car drove quickly away. Jon sat back in his seat. Jesus, his partner had just admitted he was gay. He wondered if it was common knowledge around the incident room.

Despite all the anti-discrimination regulations, homosexuality was still something plenty of his colleagues regarded as a laughable affliction. They were usually the same officers who believed most blacks were thieving, lazy niggers.

He hadn't received any piss-take comments about working with a poof, so he concluded that no one could know. Then he remembered McCloughlin's wink on telling Jon that he was getting a partner. Could it have been a hint?

Five minutes later he pulled into the Platinum Inn's car park and looked across to the greyhound stadium behind. The floodlights were on and a crackly voice was announcing the runners for the final race.

Jon glanced around the car park. Two other cars, a Ford Mondeo and a Citroën Xara. Salesman choices. He pushed open the doors to reception. The place had obviously seen better days. The glut of cheap chain hotels in the town centre was slowly strangling it to death. Another few months and it would be boarded up, and shortly after that probably burned down by local kids.

Behind the counter was an alarmingly thin woman. You've had a tough paper round, thought Jon. He held up his warrant card. 'DI Jon Spicer. And you are?'

'Dawn Poole, night manager.'

'Just the person I need to speak to. Were you on duty last night?'

'I'm on duty every night.'

Jon looked around, not envying her lonely job in an area where women's corpses were turning up, stripped of their skin. 'Seems quiet. How's business?'

She shrugged. 'It's been busier.'

'Who do you get staying here? Company reps, mainly?'

'Mainly. Some younger sorts having a night out in Manchester. Three to a room can work out cheaper for them than a taxi home, specially if they manage to sneak in an extra mate.'

'Who else?'

'That's about it.'

'So if I take a seat here, there's no chance of any couples coming in to book rooms by the hour?'

Her mouth tensed up and she pointed to the tariff sheet on the wall. 'The rates are for the night only.'

'Come on, Dawn.' Jon leaned on the counter, sensing it wouldn't take much to make her crumble. It never did with the mouse-like types. Usually they'd do whatever it took to keep attention off them. 'This place is used as a knocking shop. I don't work Vice. Help me out here and I won't need to get them involved.'

She crossed her arms, the bones in her elbows jutting out painfully. 'What do you want to know?'

That's more like it, he thought. 'The girls you get coming in here, do you know their names?'

'Some of them.'

'Ever heard of an Alexia?'

The skin below her eyes flinched. 'I don't think so.'

Jon didn't break his stare. 'You don't think so? How about a yes or a no?'

She dropped her head. 'No, I haven't.'

He took a breath in. 'Last night, someone heard something.

It could have been the sound of an assault. Did you have any trouble? A girl coming out of her room looking injured?'

'No.' She was still looking down.

'Look at me, please. It was around three thirty in the morning.'

'No. That Fiona what's-her-name made a report, right? Listen, she staggered in pouring with blood. I helped patch her up, gave her some booze.'

'How much?'

'A lot. There wasn't much left in the bottle by the time she went to bed. Probably shouldn't have given her any, the state she was in. Totally stressed out, she was. Then she thinks she heard something in the middle of the night.' Bony fingers fiddled with her necklace. She sighed. 'Look, it can get pretty busy here, but I'd have noticed. Honestly.'

'What about side doors? Emergency exits? Is there one at the other end of this corridor?' He pointed through the double doors at the corridor beyond.

'Yes.'

'If someone left by that route would it set off an alarm?'

'No, it doesn't work on that door. But why would they? It leads straight out to the bin area. They'd have to walk right round the building to get back to the car park.'

'My informant believes the commotion was coming from room nine. How about I take a look in it?'

Dawn handed him a key. 'Be my guest.'

Jon could tell searching the room was going to be a waste of time. His eyes shifted to the clock in the back office. Quarter past ten and he was dog tired. He knew she was holding something back. Probably just afraid of him finding out that she was putting the night's takings straight into her pocket.

He weighed up the two women's stories. Given the third victim's time of death, Fiona's emotional state and the hefty amount of booze it appeared she'd got through, he decided her claim was a waste of time. He gave the key back. 'OK, Dawn, take care.'

Her mouth opened with surprise. 'That's it?'

Out in the car park he glanced towards the rear of the building.

It was plunged in shadow and he'd have to get a torch if he was to look around properly. Bollocks to that, he thought.

In his car, he called Fiona's mobile. 'It's Jon Spicer.'

'Have you been to the motel?'

'I'm in the car park right now. I've spoken to the night manager, Dawn Poole.'

'That's her. What did she say?' The words were slurred and Jon wondered how much she'd been drinking.

'She didn't notice anything suspicious last night.'

'Well, did you check the room?'

'It was spotless, like you said. And there was nothing round the back of the building, either.'

'What about Cheshire Consorts? Did you call them?'

'Yes. The owner told me there's no Alexia on her books.'

'She could be lying.'

'There's a web site. Have a look yourself. All the girls are listed there.'

'So what now? I really think I heard someone being killed.' Her voice was rising.

'Fiona, there's nothing more I can do. I'll keep an eye on the police computer. If an unidentified female body shows up, I'll look into it.'

'That's it? You're not doing anything else?'

A wave of irritation washed across him and he ran a hand through his cropped brown hair. 'What do you suggest I do?'

'I don't know. You're the policeman. If this was an angelic little girl or a copper's wife, things would be different, wouldn't they?'

Jon felt his jaw clench. 'You think you heard something. You were traumatised and pissed.' He paused to let the comment sink in. 'You could contact the Missing Persons Bureau, I suppose, but without a surname I doubt they can help. I can't think of anything else.'

'So you're washing your hands of it?'

'For fuck's sake, Fiona, I'm working on a big murder case. You can probably guess which one. I don't have time for this.'

Her voice was twisted with sarcasm. 'No, I suppose not. After all, it's only another whore who's disappeared.'

Jon hung up.

Ten minutes later he pushed his front door open. Claws scrabbled in the kitchen and Punch peered eagerly through the doorway. The dog gave a delighted *hrrmph!* through its squashed nose and bounded down the hall.

Jon scooped the animal up and began rocking it in his arms like a baby. Punch craned forwards, trying to lick Jon's face. 'Who's my stupid boy?' Jon said, lifting his chin and allowing a wet tongue to lap at his throat.

'I don't know how you can stand that.' Alice had come out of the TV room. She was wearing a dressing gown and clutching a mug in both hands.

Jon put Punch down. 'What a day. How are you, babe?'

'Good,' she smiled. 'Have you eaten?'

'Only some crap pizza, unfortunately.' He hung his jacket on the banister post and walked over to her. Careful not to put any pressure on her swollen stomach, he hugged her lightly. 'How's the bump?'

'Fine. I could feel some kicking earlier. Here.' She took his hand and placed it on her stomach, inside her dressing gown. 'On the right there, that's where the legs are.'

They stood motionless, Punch staring up at them with a bemused look on his face. Jon was careful to maintain an inquisitive smile, although privately he felt freaked out every time something began moving independently inside Alice's body. He kept his hand there for a few seconds longer. 'No. The little thing must be asleep.' With a twinge of guilty relief, he slid his hand out of her dressing gown, went into the kitchen and cracked open a beer.

As soon as he took a seat, Punch lay down on the lino floor and rested his head on Jon's foot.

'Did you ring Fiona?'

Jon sighed. 'Rang her, met her and went to that motel. She's got quite a temper, hasn't she?'

Alice grinned. 'Fiona? Yes, she's got a strong sense of right and wrong.'

'So why has she stuck by a husband who knocks her around for so long?'

Alice gave a sad frown. 'We've tried to work that out in the salon many times. You should hear her with customers who don't keep their appointments. She's straight on the phone asking where they are, demanding to know why they haven't shown up. But then she goes home and seems to adopt this submissive personality with her husband.'

'What the hell does she see in him?'

Alice ran her hands through her long hair. 'I don't think it was that bad to begin with. She's always reluctant to talk about it – pride I suppose – but I think they were happy for a while. God knows, something happened to turn it sour.'

He ran a finger down his beer can. 'Has she got a problem with the booze?'

'Why do you say that?'

'The night manager at the motel she stayed in said she'd downed a load of brandy, and she was slurring her words on the phone tonight as well.'

Alice nodded. 'She turns up for work late sometimes. There's always a legitimate excuse, but you can smell it on her some mornings. If it was a big chain salon she'd have probably lost her job by now. Lucky for her Melvyn's happy to turn a blind eye.'

'Well, she certainly believes she heard something the other night. And she certainly wasn't happy when I said I couldn't do much.'

'Can't you?'

He took a long gulp, almost shuddering as the ice-cold beer went down his throat and hit his stomach. 'I'm not convinced she heard anything more than a bit of energetic shagging.'

'Why not?'

He hooked a nail under the tab of the can, lifted it up and then let it snap back with a ping. 'She only heard something. There's no evidence of anything else. The night manager says she didn't see anything, and I believe her. Didn't believe everything she told me, but I believed her on that count. All Fiona has is this.' He flicked the card from Cheshire Consorts on to the table. 'It could have been lying in the room for weeks, if not months, judging by the state of the place. A name that's probably made up, and a disconnected mobile phone number that isn't registered to anyone.'

Alice bit her lip. 'Oh, well. She's got her own life to sort out. She'll let it drop soon, I expect.'

Jon took another gulp of beer. 'The other big news is that I can't decide whether my new partner's reporting everything I do straight back to McCloughlin.'

Alice rolled her eyes. 'You mean he's still sulking about ...' She stopped, unwilling to refer directly to the case that had almost cost them so much last summer.

'Just a hunch, but yeah.'

Alice blew a strand of blond hair out of her eyes. 'The arsehole.'

He gave a rueful smile. 'Oh, and another thing about my new partner. He's gay.'

'So?'

Jon examined his knuckles.

'Oh, please. Don't tell me you're scared he'll threaten your masculinity by trying it on with you?'

Jon picked at the can's tab again. 'Well, I don't know. It makes things awkward, you have to admit.'

'Why? It only makes things awkward in your head. Don't flatter yourself. A big grunt like you with scars all over your face? He might prefer smooth-skinned, gentle types.'

'Let's hope so.'

Alice sighed. 'Surely you've worked with other gay officers?'

Jon shook his head. 'It's not like your job, Ali. We don't have people flouncing around like Melvyn.'

'Not every gay man's as camp as Melvyn. Besides, he puts a lot of that on for the blue-rinse brigade.' She smiled. 'The old dears reckon it's like getting their hair done by Graham Norton.'

'Yeah, well, this is the police.'

Alice put a hand on her hip and extended one foot slightly in front of the other. Jon called it her barrister stance, because it was a posture she adopted whenever they got into one of their verbal tussles.

They'd started seeing each other almost twelve years ago after a chance meeting in a city centre pub. Jon and several team mates were sitting at the centre table to watch the final of the 1991 Rugby World Cup on the pub's giant screen. As the match ground its way to England's eventual defeat at the hands of Australia, a few of his friends had got increasingly annoyed at the referee's decisions.

When the drinks on Alice's table were all knocked over she had no hesitation in standing up to have a go at their entire group. Before offering to replace them, Jon had watched her feistiness with admiration. It was the first thing he'd noticed about her and whenever it reappeared he was reminded why he'd fallen in love with her.

'What about all the equal opportunities stuff we're always hearing about?' she demanded. 'Those posters around town … What was the headline? Something about "All walks of life walk the beat"?'

Jon rolled his eyes, relishing every second of the exchange. The recruitment campaign posters, with their Home Office allocation of ethnic minorities in the photo, had generated plenty of jokes around the station, but not many non-white job applicants. Besides, bobbies walking the beat? They were too busy stuck at their desks completing paperwork for that.

'There's a culture in the police, Alice. You know it, I know it. It doesn't matter how much lip-service they pay to the drive for ethnic minority officers and all that.'

'And all that,' Alice tutted. 'Watch out, Jon, you might find yourself left behind in the last millennium.'

'I don't agree with it, Ali, but it's life. Besides, you say society's changing, but what you actually mean is that your experience of society's changing. I'd say that, on the whole, the age-old prejudices are just as alive and healthy as ever.' He thought about the poster's headline. 'It's just that your walk of life doesn't take you into contact with them.' He gave her a glib smile and waited for her response.

She scowled. 'You're bound to get racists and anti-gays in the deprived areas you get called out to. You always will until people are educated differently.'

Jon laughed. 'I'm not talking about housing estates. I'm talking about country estates. Those living at the top of the pile, not the bottom: the aristocracy, the establishment, the elite, whatever you want to call it.' He pictured the huddles of senior officers, the judges, the politicians. Old, white, married and male. 'I'm talking about people who've had the best educations money can buy. It's that lot who are most against change. The system suits them just fine. After all, it was created by them, their fathers and their fathers' fathers.'

Alice was silent for a moment. 'That's depressing.'

Jon realised he'd come out of this one on top, but the victory gave him precious little satisfaction. 'That's life,' he shrugged. 'Anyway, don't worry. I'm not going to creep around the canteen whispering to everyone that Rick's gay.'

'I know that.' She tipped her head back to yawn and saw the clock on the wall. 'You coming to bed?'

Jon finished his beer and nodded.

Chapter 10

Dawn Poole could almost see the waves of pain radiating out from the back of the patient's throat with every swallow. Breathing was obviously still difficult because, after a few more sips, the straw was released.

'Enough?' Dawn asked, her concern showing in her face.

The patient leaned back against the pillows and gave a single slow nod.

Dawn put the carton down. 'You're being so brave.' She ran her fingers gently through the short spikes of hair on the patient's head. The haircut reminded her of a singer's, someone who sang of bruised feelings and life's injustices. Annie Lennox? Sinead O'Connor? She couldn't remember.

Bloodshot eyes turned towards the window. A finger was held up, red nail varnish contrasting with the white sheets. 'Can you crumble a biscuit on the window sill?'

The words were little more than a rasping whisper. Unsure if she'd heard correctly, Dawn stood. 'Crumble biscuit on the window sill?'

The patient nodded. 'For a robin. It lands there.'

She smiled uncertainly. 'Of course, my darling.' She took a digestive biscuit from the untouched packet and broke off a small piece. 'Outside? Here?' she asked.

'And on the inside, too.'

Dawn began crumbling the biscuit between her forefinger and thumb.

Chapter 11

Take a few moments to browse through our selection of handpicked ladies. Prices start at £150 per hour.

Fiona stared at the computer screen. Jon was right: all the girls were listed there. She read a few of their details.

Becky, age 19. Holly, age 20. NEW! Kim, age 20. Mel, age 22. The list went right down to women in their forties. By each name was a tab saying, *More info.*

Fiona clicked on Mel's.

A new screen popped up giving the girl's height, bust, dress size, hair, ethnic origin and occupation (5'6", 34C, 10, brunette, shoulder-length straight, white British, customer service adviser).

At the base of the screen was a subheading, *Reviews.* Fiona clicked on it and was taken to a different page called 'Punter Opinion'. The report was enthusiastic but matter-of-fact, like a review of a well-designed electrical item. The punter would definitely be seeing Mel again, it concluded.

Appalled at the commercial sophistication of the process, Fiona went back to the main listings page. She scanned down the column of names; the word '*NEW!*' was by about a quarter of them. The girls obviously came and went fairly frequently. Alexia could easily be an ex-employee.

Trepidation made her hesitate as she reached for her mobile. But all-too-familiar feelings of guilt flared up in response, and with them a determination to find out if Alexia was OK. Knowing she couldn't live with herself if she did nothing, she slowly dialled the number at the top of the screen. A woman answered almost immediately, her voice warm and attractive.

Fiona wasn't sure what to say. Suddenly, the words were coming out of her mouth. 'Hello. I'd like to speak to someone about working for Cheshire Consorts.'

'What's your background, love?' The voice had lost some of its pleasantness and become more matter-of-fact.

'Well, my name's Fiona. I work as a beauty therapist, specialising in manicures. I've also done a course in Swedish massage, but that was some time ago. What else? Um, I enjoy going out to the theatre when I—'

The woman cut her off. 'You're new to this, aren't you?'

'Yes.'

'How old are you, Fiona?'

'Late thirties. Thirty-eight.'

'That's OK. Some of my busiest escorts are your age.' A small crumb of encouragement; Fiona's spirits lifted. 'Why don't you come and see me?'

'I'd like that.'

The address was a house in Mellor. Fiona had heard of the area. Big houses at top prices. More expensive than where she used to live. She closed Hazel's computer down, then went to the kitchen. 'Cathy,' she said, nerves making her stomach feel light and empty. 'Could I borrow some make-up, please?'

A short while later she was driving along the M60 ring road. She turned off on to the A626, following it all the way to Marple Bridge and the turning for Mellor. The road was narrow, leading through a pretty little village, antiques shops dotting the high street.

The road went up a hill and Fiona spotted a pub called the Royal Oak. She parked outside it as instructed and looked across the road to number 133. It was a large semi-detached house with a wooden front door. Nothing remotely seedy or dangerous about it. Crossing the road, she knocked a couple of times and waited on the steep stone steps. The door opened to reveal a woman about her age with an immaculately cut brown bob. She wore hardly any make-up and the skin was stretched tight over her cheekbones. Slightly sunken eyes looked down and her thin lips parted. 'Fiona?'

Conscious of the generous layer of concealer masking the worst of her injury, Fiona smiled. 'Yes.'

'Come in. First room on the right.'

She stepped past the woman, sensing that she was being assessed. She sat down in a pleasantly decorated front room. Although it was homely, something was missing. Fiona looked around. No family photos.

The woman sat down in a leather chair by a corner table which held a computer, printer, boxes of disks and other business gear. She surveyed her visitor. 'My name's Joanne Perkins. What happened to your face?'

Fiona lifted her fingers to her eyebrow. 'Some trouble with my ex.'

'Fiona, I don't send girls out with damaged faces. The men pay a lot of money, so they expect some class.' Her eyes shifted to Fiona's borrowed shirt and too-large skirt.

Fiona coughed self-consciously. 'To be honest, I've just left my husband. I didn't have time to pack much. These aren't my clothes.'

The phone rang. Joanne held up a finger at Fiona, then picked it up. 'Cheshire Consorts ... Yes, that's right, sir ... Whereabouts are you? ... The one at the airport? ... What sort of time? ... And who did you have in mind? ... Victoria? Oh, she's lovely, she really is.' She turned to the computer, clicked the mouse a couple of times and consulted the screen. 'I think she's available. If I can I take your telephone number, I'll get Victoria to give you a call.' She jotted a number down. 'And your name is? ... OK, Gerald, you two have a chat, and if you like the sound of each other I'll call you back to confirm the booking. Is that all right? ... Lovely. Do you have a credit card? ... No, don't give me the details now. Wait till I call you back, OK? Victoria will ring you shortly.'

She hung up, consulted the screen again and dialled a number. 'Victoria? It's Jo. Can you do a booking at the Radisson, Manchester Airport, for ten o'clock tonight? ... He sounds fine – salesman I imagine ... OK, he's called Gerald. Here's his number.' She read it out and hung up. Turning back to Fiona, she said, 'Now, you've just moved out?'

'Yes.' Fiona blinked, shocked at how prosaic Jo made selling sex seem.

'Your life's just been turned upside down. You need cash.'

'No,' Fiona protested. 'Well, yes. Things are all different. But—'

'I don't take on people who are going through stuff like that.'

'I'm sorting myself out.'

'Could you stand up?'

Slowly, Fiona did so. Her hands fluttered nervously and she had to make a conscious effort not to fold her arms. They hung at her sides, feeling awkward. She looked at a point on the wall well above Joanne's head.

'You aren't at all comfortable about this, are you? Somehow I don't think you really want to work in this business.'

Fiona's shoulders relaxed. 'No.' Gratefully, she sat down again. 'I'm looking for a girl. She's gone missing.'

'You're not the only one.' Joanne's lips tightened to a thinner line, and she lit a cigarette.

Fiona nodded awkwardly. 'I'm sorry. It was me who asked the police to ring you.'

Joanne took a sharp drag on her cigarette, shadows deepening beneath her cheekbones. 'Is this girl your daughter?'

The question caught Fiona off guard and a sudden image of Emily caused her eyes to sting. 'No. She was in the next room of a motel I was staying at. I heard something terrible happening to her. Like she was being strangled. I checked her room the next morning, but all I found was one of your cards with her name and a mobile phone number written on the back.' Joanne's face darkened at the news. 'I really want to know what happened to her,' Fiona concluded.

The phone went, and Joanne picked up. 'Cheshire Consorts ... Hi, Victoria. You're happy with it, then? ... Yeah, I thought he sounded quite nice, too, and he offered his credit-card number straight off ... OK, I'll ring him to confirm it.' She called the man back. 'Gerald? Hello, it's Cheshire Consorts. Victoria would be delighted to meet you at ten o'clock. If I could take your credit card details, we can confirm the booking. I gather that you agreed an hour with Victoria, so the charge is £150. OK, the name on the credit card is?' She took the rest of the details down. 'Thank you for using Cheshire Consorts,

Mr Richmond, and I hope you enjoy your night.'

She replaced the phone, looked at Fiona and took another drag. 'No one of her name has ever worked for Cheshire Consorts. I checked after that pushy detective called. I turn away a lot of girls who'd like to work for me. Usually ones with drug habits – they're unreliable and they'll try and give their own phone numbers to clients to cut me out of future deals. I've been in the business long enough to spot them and I've worked harder than you can imagine to be where I am today.' She waved a hand towards the window and the pleasant surroundings beyond. 'I've got here because I only employ real ladies. Now, I don't know how one of my cards came to be in that motel room, God knows, there are enough men around town who use my escort agency. But I did have someone in here calling herself Alicia a while back.'

Fiona frowned. 'Sorry, you mean Alexia?'

Now Joanne looked confused. 'No, she said she was called Alicia, and that copper said Alicia, too, unless I misheard him.'

'You must have done. It was definitely Alexia written on the back of the card,' Fiona replied, wishing she hadn't given it to Jon.

Joanne sighed. 'I don't know. Maybe it was Alexia, then. No one of that name has worked for me, either.'

'How can you be sure without checking?'

Joanne said impatiently, 'Because I help them choose their working names.' She pointed to a Perspex container of business cards. 'After the interview I noticed half my cards had gone.'

'Why would she take your cards?'

'Trying to gain a bit of credibility, I'd imagine – at the expense of my business's reputation. The best place you can start searching for that little bitch is back where she crawled from.'

Fiona raised her eyebrows questioningly.

Joanne stood up. 'She claimed she was working the massage parlours. I'm fairly sure she said the Hurlington Health Club. You know where that is?'

Fiona shook her head.

'Just past the Apollo on the A57. You can't miss it. All the windows are blacked out, for a start.'

Fiona ignored Joanne's movement towards the door. 'What did she look like?'

Joanne sighed. 'Skinny little thing – a good sign she was using. About your height, late teens, early twenties. Hair darkish brown. Down to about here.' She held a hand to her collarbone. 'She was still pretty, not for much longer. The bruises round her eye certainly didn't help.'

'Bruises? Someone had been hitting her?' Fiona asked with dismay, imagining the wretched life the poor girl must lead.

An indifferent shrug. 'Goes with the territory, that end of the market.'

Fiona almost felt sick, acutely aware that Emily would have been roughly that age now. She held the image of the girl in her mind's eye as she finally stood. 'Thank you. And sorry to have wasted your time.'

Joanne looked her up and down. 'Listen, when your face has cleared up and you've got your own clothes back, call me.'

Fiona stared at her, unsure of what she meant. Realisation struck and she quickly made for the door.

By the time she got back to the outskirts of town, it had gone ten o'clock. The information Joanne had given her burned in her head. The Hurlington Health Club. A skinny girl with dark brown hair, around twenty years old.

The desire to find her dragged Fiona towards the city centre and she found herself driving along the A57 towards the Apollo. A few minutes later purple neon lettering caught her eye. The Hurlington Health Club. It was halfway down a short row of shops, sandwiched between a place selling antique fireplaces and another selling second-hand furniture. The doors and windows of both shops were concealed behind grey metal pull-down shutters.

She eased into a lay-by and looked across the road. The front of the Hurlington Health Club had been returned to something resembling a residential, not business, property. A terracotta pot holding a miniature conifer stood on either side of the front door, and in the front garden a tiny fountain sprinkled water, lit mauve by an underwater light, into a small, square pond.

She peered more closely at the windows. The curtains, of red material which had the heaviness of velvet, were open, but even so it was impossible to see inside. Joanne was right: there was an inner layer of glass and it had been blacked out.

Nervously, she checked in her rear-view mirror. There was no traffic coming. She climbed out and crossed the road. The front gate was open; water tinkled into the square pond. A small sign on the door read: *Open 11 am until late. All major credit cards accepted.*

Fiona took a deep breath and walked quickly towards the door. It opened and a man stepped out, buttoning up his coat. Their eyes met and his immediately moved down to her chest. He stared with no attempt at subtlety.

Fiona shrank back, bumping into the gatepost. He realised she wasn't coming in. The look that came into his eyes reminded Fiona of her husband before he punched her. He moved towards her and she turned and scuttled back across the road to her car.

Once inside she locked the door. He sauntered off towards the small car park by the Apollo. Her eyes turned to the front door again. She couldn't go in now, not at night. Any visit would have to be during the day when, she hoped, the place would be quieter.

Chapter 12

Jon checked his watch. Eight thirty-five, not too early to ring. 'Morning. Martin Appleforth, please. It's Detective Inspector Spicer.'

A few seconds of Handel's *Water Music* before Martin spoke. 'Morning, DI Spicer. I was just going through my emails. The sales department have sent over Gordon's client list as requested. Is there any news of him?'

'I'm afraid not. We're trying to locate his Passat, but nothing yet. And it hasn't shown up on the national database as abandoned or burned-out. Anyway, thanks for getting the information on Mr Dean. Did you find out if your firm has a contract with Stepping Hill hospital?'

'I did and we haven't. Have you an email address I can forward Gordon's client list to?'

Jon gave it to him and the message appeared a few seconds later. There were two attachments, a complete list of Gordon Dean's clients and a shorter one of the people he was due to visit in the last days before he vanished.

Jon dragged his eyes from the screen to see Rick hanging up his jacket. 'All right?'

'Morning.' Rick's voice was reserved, the comment made over his shoulder.

Jon watched him sit down. Rick glanced across, then broke eye contact and reached for the paperwork on his desk.

'I've got the last clients Gordon Dean was due to see,' Jon said.

Rick looked up, the tension around his eyes easing. 'Yeah?'

'On the day before he disappeared he had one client to see in the morning, then another three in the afternoon, two in central Manchester and one in Worsley.'

'Shall we start with his last ones first?'

'I reckon so.' Jon printed the list out. 'Might as well go over to the NHS clinic in Worsley.' He looked at his watch. 'No point in setting off now – the M60 will be a nightmare.'

They spent the next forty or so minutes filling out report sheets until the receiver called across the room to them, 'The preliminary analysis has come in for the footprint recovered at the latest crime scene.'

Heads across the room turned.

'It's a shoe, not a trainer. Size eleven, left foot. Owner likely to weigh in excess of twelve stone. The grip on the sole is quite distinctive and it's completely worn away on the inside edge, suggesting that the wearer pronates quite heavily. As a result, he's highly likely to have an unusual gait.'

The scene in the hospital corridor flashed into Jon's mind. He had thought Pete Gray swaggered as a result of his beer belly. Now he wondered if the swivel in his hips could have been the result of one foot turning inwards with each step.

The clinic in Worsley was tucked away behind the pleasant green. It was part of a cluster of council buildings including a small swimming pool, exercise hall, doctor's surgery and the clinic itself.

The reception area was plastered with a haphazard collection of posters. Professionally produced NHS ones on giving up smoking sat alongside home-printed ones on dieting groups, childcare support and mothers' meetings. Jon looked with interest at a cluster of smaller, handwritten cards advertising everything from breast pumps and second-hand prams to babysitters and exercise bikes.

He heard someone cooing. A young woman in the seating area was bouncing a baby on her knee. The infant's head rocked gently back and forth but its eyes were locked on its mother's, the rest of the world completely irrelevant to them both. She held it up and the sight touched something in Jon. Just as he was about to smile, the baby vomited down its mother's shirt.

'Good morning.' The rosy-cheeked receptionist was studying them through the glass screen.

'Hello, there,' Jon replied as they produced their warrant cards. 'Who could we speak to about the medical supplies the clinic orders?'

'For my sins, that's me,' she replied, sliding a plate with a half-eaten muffin to the side.

'Does that include such things as medical gloves?' asked Rick.

'Yes,' she beamed. 'In fact, I took a new order the other day.'

'From Protex?'

'That's right.' Her voice slowed down. 'From Protex.'

Rick took out Gordon Dean's photo. 'You dealt with this man?'

'Gordon,' she started to smile again, then stopped. 'What is the . . .' Her voice faded away.

'How did he seem to you?' Jon asked.

Her eyes swung between them, settling back on Rick. 'Friendly as ever. He doesn't come in that often. It's a rolling order – once every few months.'

'Do you remember what time he left?'

'I don't know.' She flicked back through her appointments book. 'He came in after the nurse's post-natal clinic started at four. He probably left at about quarter past. Is he in some kind of trouble?'

Rick shook his head. 'No. We just need to trace him. Did he mention anything not related to work?'

'No. I didn't have time to chat that day – the post-natal clinic's always very busy.'

'But you do chat sometimes?' Jon asked.

'Yes, sometimes.'

'What does Gordon like to talk about?'

She thought for a few seconds, then smiled sheepishly. 'Actually, come to think of it, he usually asks about my family and then lets me rabbit on about what my kids have been up to recently.'

'Nothing about himself ?'

'Not really. Just how the job's going, if he's busy. You know, small talk, I suppose.'

They drove back to the city centre, heading for the next client. The business was in a smart modern building just off the prime shopping area of King Street. Eventually they found an empty loading bay on the edge of St Anne's Square. Leaving a police sign on the dashboard, they walked back round and examined the list of companies listed at the entrance. Firms of solicitors seemed to be the dominant force. A uniformed security officer in the lobby directed them towards the lifts. 'Sixth floor. They've got it all to themselves.'

As the lift rose silently, Rick said, 'I've heard of the Paragon Group. Big ads at the back of women's magazines. Must cost a fortune.'

The doors opened on a plush foyer, the green of tropical palms complemented by walls washed with a subtle turquoise paint. The carpet was pale blue, the lighting recessed. The result was very soothing. Trust us, you're in good hands, Jon thought.

The receptionist wore a starched white tunic and her hair was pulled back so tightly it looked like the follicles might bleed. As they approached her desk, she reached for a couple of forms.

Rick stepped up, his warrant card out. 'DS Saville and DI Spicer. May we speak to whoever orders your medical supplies, please.'

She looked confused. 'Oh, I'm sorry. I thought you'd just popped in to enquire about, er . . . We don't have much here.'

'If whoever orders your medical examination gloves could spare us a minute.'

'Oh, that's our head nurse. She's with someone at the moment. Please help yourself to coffee.' She gestured towards an open door. A pot of coffee was in the corner of the room and satellite television played softly on a plasma screen mounted on the wall. A middle-aged woman squirmed with embarrassment as they stepped in. She pulled her magazine tight into her lap, and kept her head bowed over it.

Jesus, you'd have thought it was a sexual diseases clinic, Jon thought as they sat down. He picked up a brochure. It was printed on expensive stock, plenty of white space between the words. Printing costs had obviously not been a problem.

'Here you go,' Rick said, holding a woman's magazine out. The Paragon Group's ad dominated the page. A nude woman was sitting on a polished wooden floor. Her legs and arms were artfully crossed, screening a figure that was faultless. Below it the locations of the group's centres were listed. Every major city seemed to have one.

'Big business,' Rick stated.

Jon turned to the brochure's contents page. Surgery for the face and body, liposuction, hair transplants, tummy tucks, re-shaping and enhancing of genitalia. Curious to see how reveal-ing the images might be, he flicked to an inner page. The photo was harmless: a woman gazed off to the side, a benign smile playing at the edge of her mouth. Ear reshaping, lip reduction and enlargement, chin implants.

'Gentlemen, please come through.'

A statuesque woman in what might have been her mid-thirties stood in the doorway. The same crisp outfit as the receptionist. She led them into an examination room.

'You have a question about our examination gloves?' She picked up a box from the corner of her desk. The label said: *Powder-free surgical gloves. Non-sterile latex.*

'Actually, it's about the person who supplies them,' Rick said.

Her immaculately painted lips contracted to form the word 'Oh?'

'Gordon Dean, he works for Protex,' Rick continued.

'Mr Dean, yes. He was here two days ago.'

'At what time?'

'About quarter past three, I'd guess.'

'And did he stay for long?'

'About three minutes.'

'Did you chat to him? How did he seem?'

'Chat with him?' The suggestion seemed to bemuse her. 'No. I signed for the delivery and he left.'

Jon saw this was going nowhere. He looked around. 'What goes on here, then?'

Her eyes turned to him. 'In terms of what?'

'Treatments. Have you got surgical theatres and doctors hidden away here? It seems very quiet.'

She shook her head. 'The only things performed here are non-surgical procedures requiring, at most, local anaesthetic. Botox injections and laser treatments, for instance. The primary function of this office is for consultations. An initial one with myself or another nurse, then one with a surgeon. Once the paperwork is complete, the patient will see their surgeon for a further pre-operative medical examination and briefing prior to the procedure at a local private hospital nearby. We rent the theatres from them.'

'Who are your surgeons, then?' Jon asked.

'Is this part of the original reason for your visit today or merely curiosity on your part, Detective Inspector?' There was a challenging, almost provocative, look in her eyes.

Jon stared back at her for a moment. 'A bit of both, I suppose.'

'Our surgeons are employed from a variety of backgrounds. But if you're concerned as to their credentials, as some prospective patients are, I can assure you they possess all the necessary qualifications.'

'Fascinating,' Jon replied, irritated by her brittle manner.

The woman seemed to sense this. She leaned forwards to assess him, then turned to Rick. 'You have very good skin. Do you use a moisturising regime?'

'I do.' Rick smiled uncertainly.

She nodded, then turned back to Jon. 'And you, DI Spicer? I suspect that you don't.' She raised a forefinger and touched the skin at the outer edge of her eye sockets. 'Your starbursts show when you speak.'

Wrong-footed by the sudden turn in conversation, Jon was about to ask if that was the new name for laughter lines, but she carried on. 'The scar above your left eyebrow and the bump in your nose – where it has been broken, I presume – are both easily remedied nowadays. We could take years off your face with some very simple procedures.'

Her eyes continued to probe him, and Jon realised she was searching for flaws, imperfections, anything which might trigger an insecurity she could play on. He was thankful that his hair hadn't started to thin.

'Just imagine how delighted your wife would be.'

'I'm not married,' Jon said.

'Many of the men we treat find improvements to their face do their career prospects no harm, either.'

Jon shook his head. 'Are you a nurse or a saleswoman?'

'Just something for you to think about.' She smiled and handed him a business card.

Jon glanced at it, then dropped it back on her desk. 'No, you're all right, thanks,' he said, walking out.

As they headed back towards St Anne's Square an indecipherable phrase was shouted out in front of them. Jon spotted the *Manchester Evening News* seller and the headline on his stand: BUTCHER STILL STALKS BELLE VUE.

The town hall bells started to slowly toll. The chorus came to an end and a single, funereal strike let them know it was one o'clock. Jon's eyes flickered from the gargoyles on its gothic spires to the people around him. Not for the first time, he wondered how close the killer might be at that very moment.

Rick said, 'Shall we get some lunch? I'm starving.'

'Good idea,' Jon agreed.

'The sandwiches are excellent in there,' Rick said, pointing at the Pret a Manger further down the street.

Jon groaned inwardly, thinking of the variety of breads and choices of fancy fillings. He nodded towards a Gregg's bakers on their side of the road. 'They do a decent bacon barm in there.'

Now distaste showed in Rick's face. 'Aren't those places a bit ... you know ... ?'

Jon looked at him. 'If you mean they do no-nonsense stuff without ripping you off, yes.'

Rick glanced in and spotted a couple of construction workers still wearing their hard hats in the queue. 'Shall we just meet back at the car?'

'Your money,' Jon replied. Rick crossed the road, and Jon went into Gregg's.

He ordered two bacon barms with brown sauce and a cup of coffee, then wandered into the square. Rick was already sitting on a bench in front of the ancient church overlooking the square, enjoying the intermittent bursts of sun breaking through the broken cloud above.

Deciding there was no immediate danger of being doused in a sudden spring shower, Jon sat next to him. As he did so he glanced across towards the glass-panelled corner of the Marks & Spencer's built on the site where the IRA bomb had gone off in 1996.

His mind went back to the event and the years leading up to it. He didn't suppose there ever was an ideal time for becoming a copper. He'd joined in 1991 at the age of twenty-one, suddenly finding himself patrolling the streets in a policeman's uniform. He'd kept on expecting members of the public to laughingly point at him in disbelief.

The city's nightclubbing scene was then in its prime and the place was known throughout the world as Madchester. But, as the nineties wore on, venues like the Hacienda were increasingly being taken over by gangs from Cheetham Hill and Salford. Every night was turning into a scrabble for the police station's bullet-proof vests as they were repeatedly called out to shootings. The gangs didn't care who died in their battle to control the lucrative drugs trade, and the press had started to call the city Gunchester.

Many of his colleagues had spent their weekends working undercover in nightclubs and bars, shitting themselves as they tried to gather evidence of drug dealing so the places could be shut down. Even now the thought made Jon almost laugh with relief – thanks to his conspicuous size, and the fact he was playing for the Greater Manchester Police rugby team each Saturday afternoon, it was a role he was spared.

As the Madchester period began to stutter and fizzle the city had seemed to be searching for a new identity. He remembered mentions of somewhere called Canal Street, rumours of it being a safe drinking haven for gays. Sankey's Soap opened in Ancoats. Alice started raving about a local band called Oasis and suddenly Manchester appeared to have rediscovered its spirit.

Then came the coded phone call on the fifteenth of June. A bomb was set to go off in one of the city's busiest shopping areas, just as the Saturday crowds were pouring in.

He remembered running down Market Street in his bobby's uniform, one hand holding his helmet on his head, the other furiously waving members of the public away from the Arndale. Intelligence was shaky and he had no idea when the bomb might go off. The only times he'd sweated so much was on the rugby pitch.

Within an hour they'd cleared an area in the immediate vicinity of a large white van. He was keeping the crowds back from the cordon tape at the far end of Market Street when the thing went off. It was the loudest noise he'd ever heard, a roar that jarred the air so violently it made him stagger. Then came the cascade of glass. Even a good four hundred metres away, shards rained down all around them. Miraculously, no one was killed, but the centre of the city had been devastated.

He looked towards the gleaming building. Another example of how the city had evolved and adapted from its origins as the world's first industrial city.

As he bit into his large flat roll, he spotted Rick sipping from an absurdly small bottle. 'What's in there?'

'Banana and mango smoothie.'

Jon shook his head, thinking of Alice's love of reducing perfectly good fruit and vegetables to mush. 'You should meet my missus.'

It was just a short drive to the next address on the list. The building was on the Rochdale Road, imposing and dark. They parked in the rear yard, next to a brand-new Range Rover. 'Jesus, there's some money to be made in this game,' observed Jon.

They walked back on to the main road, clangs from a construction site clearly audible over the sound of traffic rushing past. Rick gestured to several cranes that towered like sentinels over the nearby roofs. 'Something major's going on over there.'

'That's Ancoats,' Jon replied. 'It's received huge amounts of regeneration money from the EU. The place is finally getting a facelift.'

Rick checked the printout and then the brass plaque by the door. 'This is it. 'The Beauty Centre, Dr O'Connor.'

Jon looked dubiously at the stone surrounding the door. It was stained almost black by exhaust fumes.

Rick had to buzz twice before a voice sounded on the intercom.

'Who is it?' A faint Irish accent, the voice casual and friendly.

Jon was surprised; compared to the glossy organisation they'd just come from, it was hardly a businesslike greeting.

'DS Saville and DI Spicer, Greater Manchester Police.'

Plastic clattered as the handset was dropped. 'Sod it! Sorry, come right up.'

They exchanged a look as the door clicked open, allowing them to enter a softly lit lobby. The air was slightly musty and Jon looked down at the deep-red carpet at his feet. The ground-floor doors were all plastered over and Jon guessed the rooms on the other sides were offices of companies in the adjoining buildings. The only way to go was up the stairs, and the heavy carpeting completely muffled their footsteps as they climbed. At regular intervals were facial portraits of models, a small notice below each photograph. Collagen. Restylane. Hylaform. Laser skin resurfacing. Temporary wrinkle filler. Cool touch laser.

Jon nodded knowingly at Rick, 'Non-surgical procedures only.'

At the top of the stairs was a short corridor with two doors leading off. The one marked 'Treatment Room' was closed, the other open.

'Please come in,' the same voice called from inside.

They entered an office that looked like it should have belonged to a lawyer. A huge wooden desk dominated the end of the room, rows of books weighing down the shelves behind it. The daylight that made it through the windows seemed to be instantly soaked up by the red carpet and wooden wall panels.

A distinguished-looking man was seated behind the desk, wiping the handset of the intercom phone with a cloth for cleaning glasses. 'Slippery bugger. Hope it didn't sound too loud your end. Take a seat, why don't you.'

Jon drank in the Irish lilt. As they walked across the room, he took in the doctor's full head of white hair, guessing he was in his late fifties. Closer, he reassessed the doctor's age. If he was approaching sixty, he wore his years incredibly well. His jawline was firm, the skin around his eyes smooth.

When he smiled, his teeth were perfect. 'How can I be of help?'

Rick took out his sheet of paper. 'Do you run this place all on your own, Dr O'Connor?'

'I have a nurse on the days we carry out procedures. But there's no point in paying her to be here when it's just paperwork that I'm tidying up.'

'Perhaps we should be talking to her. It's about whoever orders your medical supplies.'

'I do a lot of that myself.'

'Including medical gloves?'

'Indeed.'

'We're trying to ascertain the recent movements of a sales rep from Protex.'

'Young Gordon Dean? He was in here only two days ago.' He plucked a tangerine from the pile of fruit in a polished wooden bowl on his desk, then nodded towards it. 'Gentlemen?'

Jon and Rick shook their heads and the doctor held up a finger. 'Five pieces a day.' He leaned forwards conspiratorially. 'If more people kept to that little maxim there'd be a lot less work for me.' He dropped the peel into a bin and popped a segment of tangerine into his mouth.

'How did Gordon Dean seem to you?' Jon asked.

'His usual cheerful self.'

'He normally strikes you as happy?'

'He does. Seems to enjoy his work visits to Manchester, at least.'

'How about non-work issues? His personal life, for instance?'

The doctor paused. 'He's married, I gather. No children, though I don't know why. I'm not sure what answers you're looking for.'

Jon smiled. 'Neither are we. We're just trying to get an idea of him.'

'He's in trouble, I take it?'

'No. We just need to trace him. He seems to have disappeared.

The last time you saw him, was there anything out of the ordinary? Was he agitated or preoccupied, perhaps?'

O'Connor shook his head.

'Was he here for long?'

'No longer than usual. He left at about three o'clock.'

'Did you chat at all?'

'We talked about the current best dining options in Manchester.'

'Those being?'

'Gordon loves his Italian food. He mentioned he was staying over in Manchester, so I recommended a place I visited the other day. Piccolino's. Have you tried it?'

Rick and Jon shook their heads.

'Ah, Gordon had. I think he was eating at one of his regular places. A person's name. Now let me think.' He closed his eyes.

'Don Antonio's?' Jon asked.

The doctor clicked his fingers, opening his eyes and bowing his head fractionally at Jon. 'Don Antonio's. I've not been there myself. Have you?'

'No, but I think we will be.' Jon started to get up, but paused. 'We've just come from the offices of the Paragon Group. What do you think of them?'

The silence was a second too long before he answered. 'A very efficient organisation.'

Jon sank back in his seat. 'And your personal, not professional, opinion?'

Dr O'Connor looked into Jon's eyes. 'My confidential personal opinion?'

'Won't go further than us three,' Jon replied.

'A bunch of mercenary money-grabbers.'

'Go on,' said Jon.

'They'll employ anyone as long as they have one ethic.'

Jon raised his eyebrows in encouragement.

'That they're prepared to treat anyone, regardless of need or suitability.'

'You mean surgery?' asked Rick.

O'Connor nodded. 'Their staff all have medical qualifications and a basic knowledge of cosmetic surgery. But they don't need any sort of track history – actually, they don't need any history or experience at all. Add to that the fact that this is an industry woefully lacking in regulations. New procedures and techniques are appearing all the time, and all too often they're driven by profit rather than patient well-being. Not, in my opinion, a healthy state of affairs.'

'So you've never applied to work for them?'

O'Connor snorted. 'Absolutely not. The reverse, as a matter of fact. They've tried to buy me out once or twice, but I'm not interested. I've also had doctors approach me looking for work. I've turned them away due to their lack of experience, only to hear they're employed by Paragon weeks later.'

'Performing full surgical procedures?' Jon asked.

'Full surgical procedures.'

'As opposed to what you perform here?'

'Correct. I specialise in aesthetic medicine – laser treatments, botox and filler injections, on the whole. Nothing more than skin deep. But the industry's expanding at an incredible rate. Everyone wants a slice of the action, to employ the prevalent terminology. Dentists now offer Botox treatments on the side. Got a medical qualification and a syringe? Then join the party. There are rich pickings for all.'

Jon contemplated the doctor's words. 'Going back to the surgical side of things, how many people would you say are employed in the industry?'

'Nationwide or just Manchester?'

Jon toyed with the idea of letting the doctor know which investigation they were on, suspecting that he'd soon guess. 'Manchester for starters.'

O'Connor frowned. 'Well, Paragon and their three main competitors have a total of around twelve doctors on their books, I'd say. Some of those work as surgeons in local NHS hospitals and do the private stuff on the side to boost their incomes. Of course, if you were going under the knife, that's the type of surgeon you want. In addition, they employ several who do private cosmetic work full time. Those guys may do a couple of days a week in Manchester, one in Leeds and one in Liverpool.

They go where the business is. I'd hesitate to say how many of them are in Manchester altogether. Fifty, maybe?'

'Thanks for your time, Doctor,' Jon said, getting to his feet.

Out on the street Jon wrinkled his nose as a noisy lorry roared past, leaving a light haze of exhaust fumes in its wake. 'We'd better recommend to McCloughlin that all surgeons employed by the likes of the Paragon Group are traced and interviewed.'

'Should be easy to check the alibis of the travelling ones,' Rick said.

'True,' Jon agreed. 'Let's see Gordon Dean's appointments list again.'

Rick got the sheet of paper out, holding it taut against the buffets of air created by passing traffic.

Jon pointed to the final appointment of the morning. 'Jake's, in Affleck's Palace. That's a tattoo artist.' He looked towards Great Ancoats Street. 'It's only over there. Shall we get it done?'

'Why not?' Rick folded the sheet up.

Jon led the way across the main road and into the jumble of narrow streets and derelict cloth shops that made up the Northern Quarter. Soon they rounded the corner of a multi-storey car park, the smell of curry filling the air.

Rick looked at the little café with its never-ending menu painted on the windows. 'That must be the sixth one of those places we've passed.'

Jon nodded. 'This is where Manchester's first curry houses sprang up, serving lunch to all the Indian workers from the mills and warehouses that used to thrive around here. It was only after they'd made enough money from these places that the owners opened up other premises out in Rusholme.'

'You mean the curry mile?' Rick said, referring to the stretch of road just outside the city centre crammed with dozens of glitzy Indian restaurants.

'That's the one,' said Jon. He pointed across another car park to a hulking old warehouse with strange flower-like lamps attached to its walls. 'And that's Affleck's Palace.'

They walked past a row of market stalls selling fruit and vegetables, and stopped by a side entrance to the Palace. Rick looked at a montage of broken tiles mounted on the wall. Blue fragments spelled out, *And on the 6th day, God created MANchester.* He smiled. 'What is this place?'

'Affleck's Palace? Come and take a look.'

They pushed through the doors and found themselves in a room crammed with racks of old denims, corduroy jackets and military-style clothing. Joe Strummer bellowed that they should know their rights, the music unbalanced by the heavier beats of an Eminem track coming from the next room. They went through a doorway into a narrow space lined with T-shirts. Rick pointed out the lettering on one: *Fat people are hard to kidnap.* 'Strange, but true I suppose,' he said.

'Just about sums this place up,' Jon answered. He was about to point out another that read, *Roll me in chocolate and throw me to the lesbians,* but changed his mind.

They crossed into another room, this one piled high with memorabilia. A seventies-style telephone with a blue neon dial glowed from its position on an impossibly chunky Betamax video recorder which sat next to a ZX Spectrum. Finding a flight of stairs, Jon scanned the list of stalls. 'Jake's, third floor.'

When they reached a relatively quieter landing, Rick took the opportunity to speak. 'What a bizarre place.'

'Yeah, it hasn't changed in years. In fact, most of the stuff for sale looks like it hasn't changed in years, either.'

They emerged on to the third floor, the sound of the Fun Lovin' Criminals booming out from a stall selling semi-precious stones and wind chimes. Jon pointed down the narrow aisle. 'It's in the corner I think.'

They passed through four more zones of music before reaching a stall which differed from the rest in that it had a glass front. *Jake's Body Works. 2 for 1 on all piercings.* Close-up photos of tattoos filled the windows, most so fresh they were fringed by angry red skin.

Jon leaned closer, trying to work out the part of the body each image had been drawn on. Nipples, pubic regions and stomach buttons emerged from the patterns. They went inside. There was barely enough room for both of them to stand, but at least the cacophony of music outside dropped a fraction.

A man sat in the corner, shaved head bowed over a manga comic. He looked up, face glinting with clusters of studs. They protruded from his ears, lips, cheeks, nostrils and eyebrows. One ran through the upper part of his nose and Jon wondered how it didn't make him go cross-eyed.

He folded his comic shut. 'A Prince Albert, gentlemen?'

Jon was unsure what he meant, but knew from the man's expression they'd been sussed immediately for police.

He took out his ID card anyway. 'DI Spicer and DS Saville.'

'You don't say,' he interrupted, eyes moving to Rick for a second. 'I'm Jake.' He waved a hand so covered in tattoos, it was almost blue. 'You'll be wanting a seat before we get started.'

The comment was phrased so Jon wasn't sure if the man was referring to them asking questions or getting a Prince Albert, whatever that was. A mischievous light danced in Jake's eyes and Jon wondered just how much pressure would be required to rip the bolt out of the bridge of his nose.

Rick sat down on one of the stools and said, 'We're trying to trace the movements of Gordon Dean. You purchase your medical examination gloves from him.'

Jake's eyes were still on Jon, who remained standing by the door. 'Ease up, man. I'm only fooling around.'

Jon raised and then dropped the corners of his mouth, the smile over in a blink.

Jake turned his attention to Rick. 'Gordon? He was in here two days ago.' He shook his head and laughed.

'Why's that funny?' Rick said, half smiling, too.

Jake clicked a tongue stud against his teeth. 'He was just pass-ing through. He was on a voyage.'

If the man's eyes hadn't been so alert, Jon would have guessed he was on something.

'What sort of voyage?' Rick asked.

Jake leaned back. 'Self-discovery.'

'Meaning?'

'You tell me. After all, you're looking for him. I just spied him off my port bow, heading God knows where. Perhaps you know more about the course he was plotting.'

Jon shook his head. 'Jake, you're making me feel seasick. Just let us know why you thought he was on a voyage.'

Jake burst out laughing. 'OK, man, I like your style. For a start, he came back after his other appointments for another tattoo.' He twisted round, took a large book off the shelf by his head and opened it up. 'This little baby. Right on his left arse cheek.' He tapped a design of a pudgy red imp with red skin, horns and a trident.

'You did his first tattoo?' asked Jon. 'The ladybird?'

'That's right.' Jake looked up and his smile faltered. 'You've seen it? Don't tell me he's in the morgue?'

'Why? Is that where you'd expect him to turn up?' Jon held his eyes.

Jake's shoulders shifted. 'No. The guy was excited, a bit hyper even. But it was more ...' He grasped at the air. 'Positive, you know? He was bursting with energy. He's not dead, is he?'

'As I said, we're trying to trace his movements. We don't know where he is.'

Rick said, 'So he was bursting with energy.'

'Yeah, like he'd just had some good news. Grinning all the time.'

'Didn't say why, though?'

'No. But he was on a mission. Said he was getting a haircut, too. That horrific side parting of his was going.'

'Did he say where was he getting it cut?' Rick said, pen and notebook out.

'Zaney's, downstairs.'

They clattered down the wooden steps, the incessant music and claustrophobic atmosphere beginning to get to Jon.

'Yeah,' said the hairdresser, sweeping a mane of crimson hair off her shoulder, 'he was my last customer. Left just before six. Don't get to lop fringes like his off very often.'

'What sort of cut did you give him?'

'The chopped look. Grade two back and sides, a bit longer on top. All messed up and spiky. He took a pot of extra-strong styling gel to make sure it stayed that way. Oh, and he let me get rid of that moustache, too.'

'Did he say what he was doing, why the sudden drastic change in hairstyle?' Rick asked.

'Nah. Just gave me a good tip and skipped on out the door.'

Rick rubbed his hands as they walked back to their car. 'A voyage of self-discovery. You reckon he was manic? About to go off the rails?'

Jon's hands were in his pockets, eyes on the pavement in front. 'I don't think so. He was still seeing clients, chasing sales targets. Did you notice his house? There was something dead about it. I think the wife's right – Gordon was on the verge of getting out.'

'Yeah, but to do what? I think he was building up to something. Maybe it was his next murder.'

Jon looked away. 'Just a gut reaction, but I can't see it.'

Rick remained silent.

'You don't agree?' Jon asked after a few seconds.

'He was hiding a completely different side of himself from his wife. Maybe he was hiding a lot of rage, too. That tattooist said he was bubbling with excitement. Could have been with the prospect of skinning another woman.'

Jon jangled the change in his pocket, still not convinced. 'By the way, what's a Prince Albert?'

Rick snorted, but kept looking ahead. 'It's a ring. One that goes down your Jap's eye and out under the rim of your fireman's helmet.'

'Oh, sweet Jesus,' Jon groaned.

Chapter 13

Cathy whispered, 'It's ringing.'

Fiona stood on the other side of the desk. She took the tip of a finger out of her mouth and, anxiously chewing a fragment of nail, hissed, 'Don't forget to say it's a personal call if she asks.'

'I know,' Cathy mouthed. 'Hello, could I have the fax number for Jeff Wilson, please?' She jotted a number down. 'And is he in the office at the moment? ... OK, thanks.' She leaned towards the phone in readiness to replace the handset. 'Sorry? ... No, it's a personal call ... No, that's OK, there's no message ... No, really, it's not important.'

She hung up and said, 'Jesus, she was desperate to get my name.'

'It's him,' Fiona said knowingly. 'He goes mad if you fail to take a name and number when someone calls. It was the same for me at home – even though he refused to take messages for me. My friends gave up trying eventually.'

The comment made Cathy look exhausted. 'Fucking men. Anyway, he's in a meeting until lunch.'

Fiona nodded, but didn't move.

'Well, go, then!' Cathy shoved her towards the door.

'Yes, sorry.' She whipped the car keys from her pocket and rushed outside. In her car she immediately began to fret again. What if the meeting was cancelled and his PA said someone had rung asking where he was? Would he guess it was her and rush home?

The mid-morning traffic was light, allowing Fiona to reach the house with reassuring speed. The driveway was empty, but she parked slightly further down the road, ready for a quick getaway if needed. At the mouth of the driveway she paused. If he did reappear and find her, she didn't know what he'd do. But he won't be drunk, she assured herself, using the knowledge to summon up enough resolve to approach the front door.

It opened to reveal that morning's post on the doormat. He's at work, she told herself, stepping inside and bolting the door behind her. She hurried through to the kitchen and unlocked the back door. Her escape route prepared, she went upstairs.

She pulled the big suitcase out from under the bed, opened the wardrobe and hastily started to fold clothes. Then she dragged it across to the dressing table and used her forearm to sweep all her bottles and pots into it. They cascaded onto her clothes, perfume bottles clinking. The noise was brief, but lasted long enough for her to imagine it could have masked the sound of his car pulling up. She looked from the window and saw an empty street. Breathing a sigh of relief, she rushed into the bathroom for all her toiletries.

The suitcase bumped down the stairs and she hauled it into the kitchen. He kept control of all their finances, including her wages from the beauty salon. But she knew some emergency cash was hidden in the biscuit tin. She flipped off the lid only to see a handwritten note: *Rot in hell, you whore.*

She flung the lid against the cooker, a cry of frustration escaping her. Looking around the kitchen, she yanked open the cupboard under the sink. The bottle of gin went into her suitcase, then she grabbed the bleach and squirted it all over the contents of the fridge. After flinging the empty bottle in the sink, she lifted up her suitcase and staggered round the side of the house.

She could hear a vehicle slowly approaching. She crouched down behind the wheelie bin. A driving instructor's car, teenager at the wheel. Breathing out, she dragged the suitcase across the lawn and along the pavement to her car. Only when she was actually pulling away did she dare to believe she'd got away with it.

Her next stop was Melvyn's beauty salon. She parked round the back, then rummaged in the suitcase for her concealing cream. After touching it over her bruises, she walked round to the front of the salon and went in.

Melvyn glanced in the mirror, a segment of wet hair between

two fingers. He met her eyes, and his scissors paused for a moment. 'Where've you been, you bitch?'

Behind him, Janice also paused, halfway through plucking a woman's eyebrow.

Oh Jesus, he's genuinely annoyed. Fiona's knees felt like they were about to buckle as Melvyn looked back down at his customer's head. But then he turned to face her again, a big grin on his face. 'Come here, you gorgeous woman!'

The scissors were discarded and he crossed the floor with small steps, jeans hanging off his hips. Hugging her with unusual force, he whispered in her ear, 'Did that bastard do that to your face?'

He pulled back to get eye contact and Fiona nodded, hand going to her eyebrow as tears welled up.

'Right!' He gestured to a girl sweeping up strands of hair. 'Zoe, get that kettle on and bring out the posh biscuits. You' – he took Fiona's shoulders and directed her towards a chair – 'put your feet up and relax. It's time you had some pampering.'

Fiona fell into the chair, laughter bubbling in her voice. 'Melvyn, really. You don't need—'

'Don't tell me what to do in my bloody salon.' Fingers adjusting his straggles of highlighted hair. 'By the way, Zoe, Fiona. Fiona, Zoe. She's with us on a work placement for a fortnight.'

He went back to his customer, and Zoe smiled uncertainly from under a low-hanging fringe. 'Would you like tea or coffee?'

Alice came out of her side room. Her smile didn't falter when she saw how Fiona looked. 'Hiya, babe, good to have you back.' Slowly, she crossed the room and carefully lowered herself into a seat beside Fiona. 'You OK?'

Fiona nodded too vigorously. 'I've left him. For good, this time.'

'You go, girl,' Melvyn called – his customer looked totally bemused at the goings-on.

'How are you?' Fiona said, looking at Alice's huge stomach.

Alice's face was glowing. 'Great, thanks. Where are you staying?'

'It's not that far away. Some really decent people live there.' She swallowed back her shame. 'It's a refuge, you know.'

Alice nodded. 'Listen, we've got a spare room. It's going to be the nursery, so if you can put up with a few cans of paint while Jon finishes decorating it ...'

Fiona laid a hand on Alice's forearm. 'That's so kind, but I really want to make a go of it on my own.'

'I understand. But if you feel different, the offer's open.' She looked back towards her room. 'Customer's waiting. See you in a bit?' She pushed herself to her feet.

Ten minutes later Melvyn finished with his customer. He slumped down beside Fiona and picked up the carton of biscuits. 'Is that all that's left? Zoe, grab a tenner from the till and get us some nice ones from Marks and Sparks.' He turned to Fiona. 'So you've really moved out?'

'Yeah, I'm getting my own place. I can't stay where I am much longer. Actually ...' She paused awkwardly. 'You know it's pay day next week?'

Melvyn held up a finger. 'Of course, love. You can have your money, and some extra, too. You'll need it for the deposit on your flat.'

He stood up and began to gently knead the back of Fiona's neck. 'Listen, love. About work. We can cover for you. Once you're feeling better and you've settled into your new place, give me a call. We could always come round for a little house-warming do.'

Fiona leaned back and closed her eyes. 'I don't know what to say, Melvyn, except I'll make it up to you.' Suddenly she tensed and her eyes snapped open. 'If he comes looking for me, you mustn't say a thing.'

'Bloody hell, Fiona.' Melvyn lowered his hands. 'I thought I'd trapped a nerve. Don't worry. If that fat bastard comes in, I'll tell him you don't work here any more.'

Fiona smiled.

After they'd finished their cups of tea, Alice caught Fiona on the street outside. 'Jon said you spoke to him,' she said, slightly out of breath with the effort of taking just a few quick steps.

Fiona's face tightened. 'Yes. I'm sorry that I lost my temper.'

'That's all right. He's used to it in his job.'

'Yeah, well, I had good reason. If you'd heard what I heard, Alice … It's right here.' She tapped behind her ear. 'I can't get the noise out of my head. And no one cares. I know your Jon's busy, but no one cares what happened. Well, I do. I'm going to find out what happened to her. The poor thing is little more than a child.' She looked off into the distance.

'Who?' Alice said.

Fiona blinked. 'Oh. I talked to the woman at the escort agency. She does remember someone, though whether she was called Alexia or Alicia I'm not really sure. Whoever she was, the woman wouldn't take her on. Suspected a drug habit and sent her back to the streets, even though she was barely twenty.'

'What are you going to do?'

'I don't know. Try and find out what happened to her.'

'But you don't know if you're even looking for the right girl.'

Fiona shrugged. 'I just need to find out if she's OK.'

Alice was frowning with confusion. 'How?'

'Well, if she was sent back to the streets, I could start asking the girls who work there.'

'Prostitutes?'

Fiona nodded. 'Someone must know her.'

'Fiona, be careful. Until they catch this man …'

'I've shared a house with a monster for long enough. I can watch out for myself, don't you worry,' she replied, not feeling the bravado she was trying to show.

Chapter 14

Tentatively, she inched the door open and looked inside. The curtains had been opened and morning sunlight was streaming in. The air in the room reflected the temperature outside, and she realised the window was open as far as it would go.

The patient was half sitting up in bed, bandaged face directed to the world beyond the window, tips of spiky hair catching the sun's rays.

Seeing him staring off to the side like that reminded Dawn Poole of how they'd first met. It was in the hair care aisle of Boots just over four years ago. She had seen him scrutinising the bottles, a slimly built man not much bigger than her. He looked strangely helpless. He'd sensed her watching and turned awkwardly to face her.

His clumsy request for advice about hair dye had almost made her laugh. She'd assumed he was buying it for his elderly mother or some other female relative. As she explained the different choices that were available, the mixture of vulnerability and embarrassment in his face started to interest her. She wasn't used to a man relying on her for help and then attentively listening to everything she had to say. Normally in her relationships it was the other way round.

She gave him a couple of tips on how best to apply the colouring, and enjoyed the feeling of being needed as he eagerly absorbed her advice. Then he had surprised her by tentatively asking about how to apply false eyelashes.

Realising he was asking for the benefit of himself and not someone else, she had offered to let him know about applying false nails, too. He'd accepted with a smile.

An hour later they were sitting in a coffee shop, him with a large bag of make-up on the seat next to him.

'He came right into the room just now.'

The words were whispered with hardly any movement of the lips and Dawn was reminded of a novice trying to master the art of ventriloquism.

'Who?' she replied, walking into the room and sitting on the end of the bed.

'The robin. I put some crumbs on the bed. He hopped right in and ate them. So beautiful, so delicate.'

She could tell the bandages hid the beginnings of a smile. The feeling of foreboding that had been building since the policeman questioned her dissipated slightly and was replaced by a warm glow of admiration.

She couldn't imagine the pain he was going through. Knowing that she wouldn't have been able to endure it, she took one hand in hers and stroked the smooth skin. 'It's good to see you looking happier.'

The patient was still looking out of the window. 'Speaking, eating, sleeping. Everything still hurts. But now I feel it's worth it again. Worth it for who I'm going to be.'

Dawn nodded. 'That's the attitude. You know, I'm happy just to be out of that miserable motel. The place is falling apart. If it gets inspected, they'll close it straight off.' She hooked a strand of hair over her ear. 'Your dressings are due to be changed later on. I'm sure he'll bring some more painkillers, too.' The room was silent as she judged how to articulate the next sentence. She opted for a casual tone. 'A policeman called at the motel a few nights ago.'

Eyes swivelled towards her, blood still caught in the lower half of their orbits.

'He was asking questions. Someone thought they heard choking coming from one of the rooms. Choking like the person was in serious trouble.'

She waited for a response, but nothing came.

'I told him no one came to me needing help.' She glanced up seeking affirmation, but the patient had turned back to the window.

She reached into the bag and got out some women's magazines and a copy of the local paper. The outside column of the front page was devoted to conjecture about the Butcher's latest victim, who still remained unidentified. 'I brought you some things to read.'

Chapter 15

At 11:17 the next day Jon's computer pinged. Someone had entered the registration of Gordon Dean's car in the Police National Computer's database of stolen or abandoned vehicles. The system had then matched it to the flag he'd left earlier and relayed the alert to his computer.

He raised a hand and clicked his fingers at Rick. 'Bingo! There's a silver Passat at Piccadilly train station that has outstayed its welcome in the short-term car park. Registration matches our man's.'

The car-park attendant looked at their identities with surprise. 'I was just going to get it towed.'

'No need for now,' Jon replied. 'Where is it?'

He led them up to the third floor, Jon's head barely clearing the low concrete ceiling.

'Over in the corner. See it?'

'Cheers.'

They walked over and peered in through the windows. Rick leaned across the bonnet to see on to the dashboard. 'Ticket purchased at five past seven in the morning five days ago. Fits with him checking out of the Novotel and coming straight here.'

Jon checked the back seat. 'Empty. What do you reckon, then?'

'Seems a bit early to be catching a train,' Rick replied.

'Unless you're catching a train to catch a plane. They're practically round the clock to the airport.'

'Why not just drive there?'

'True.' Jon put his hand in his jacket pocket and hooked his fingers under the driver's door handle. To his surprise, it opened.

'That's a result.' He leaned inside; the interior was filled with the chemical smell of a cheap air freshener.

Rick used the same trick to open the passenger door without leaving any prints. He crouched down and popped open the glove compartment with the end of a pen. A tin of mints, a pile of compliments slips and an *A to Z* of Manchester.

Jon pointed at the music system. A tape was poking out of the cassette deck. 'That's a blank tape. Something could have been recorded on it.' He took an evidence bag out of his pocket, pulled it over his hand, removed the tape and placed it in his pocket. Then he pulled up the lever for the boot. Inside were a few crushed boxes of latex gloves, a picnic blanket and a golfing umbrella, the Protex logo just visible among its folds.

'Something heavy squashed those boxes,' Rick observed.

'Yeah,' Jon nodded. 'And my money's on it being some well-packed suitcases.'

Rick put his hands on his knees to push himself upright, then stopped. His head angled to one side and he got down on one knee to lean forwards into the boot. 'Hello, this doesn't look like Mrs Dean's taste in cosmetics.'

'What?' Jon asked, trying to look in.

Rick took out a set of keys and used the tip of one to hook the tiny object up. It stuck to the jagged edge like an exotic insect clinging on for dear life.

'What is that?' Jon frowned.

Rick studied it, rapt as an entomologist discovering a new species. 'A false eyelash. And look at the size of it. That's a real beauty.'

'Yeah,' Jon agreed, now able to see it. 'Normal habitat, stree-tus prostitutus.' He produced another evidence bag from his pocket.

As Rick dropped it in he said, 'The thought of this is making me feel ill, but I wonder if its mate is in the pile of skin that used to be victim number three's face?'

Jon nodded grimly. 'We'd better go over the autopsy report.'

'Maybe he's washing their faces, stripping off all their make-up before stripping off their skin.'

Jon weighed up the comment. Try as he might, the impression he was forming of Gordon Dean didn't fit with that of a killer. Unlike the thought of Pete Gray. Now there was a man he'd like to take somewhere private, a place where he could exert some real pressure. He stopped the thought right there, worried at how easily his mind could switch to the contemplation of violence. 'Let's see what's on this tape.'

Back in their own car, he turned the ignition key until the dashboard lights came on. Then, using an evidence bag as a glove, he carefully slid the cassette into the machine.

It was a recording taken from the radio, the DJ speaking loud and fast, Manchester accent easily apparent. 'OK, people, as I promised before the break, here's the tune that's setting the airwaves on fire at the moment. I heard a whisper from their record company that it's not being released until well into next year, so until then you'll just have to keep tuned to Galaxy FM, because we can't get enough of playing it here.'

A faint chorus of trumpets rapidly grew in strength. Nodding in time as the drumbeat started up, Rick said, 'It's called "Lola's Theme" – can't remember who it's by.'

By now the music was in full flow, female vocals blending with the uplifting tune. The trumpets built higher, reaching a crescendo as the triumphant chorus kicked in.

> *I'm a different person, yeah,*
> *Turned my world around,*
> *I'm a different person, yeah,*
> *Turned my world around.*

When they walked into the incident room, the receiver waved a sheet of paper at them. 'Gordon Dean's most recent credit-card transactions.'

'Cheers, Graham.' Jon made his way to his desk and laid the paper on it. He and Rick both went straight to the transactions on the night when Dean disappeared.

'Jesus Christ!' whistled Rick.

Jon made a quick mental calculation. 'That's over a grand and a half in one night.'

Rick sat down to study the transactions more carefully. 'Don

Antonio's, like Doctor O'Connor said. And Crimson – surprise, surprise. Between those, a few drinks in Taurus and a stop in Natterjacks. He was certainly hitting the pubs and clubs around Canal Street.'

'Are these all places you know?' Jon realised he'd lowered his voice slightly.

Rick nodded. 'Gay ones, on the whole – Natterjacks gets quite a mixed crowd. But look at those last three transactions. £150 from a cashpoint, £9.99 from what looks to be a garage and then another £1,100 from another cashpoint.'

Jon pointed at the date. 'The final one is from the next morning at six forty-three. That one must have maxed his card out, then, twenty minutes later, he's buying a ticket for the car park at Piccadilly station.'

'So he deliberately cleared his bank account,' Rick murmured.

Jon dropped a ten-pound note on the table. 'That says he's holed up in a cottage somewhere, probably in the sack right now.'

Rick matched his money. 'You're on.'

'OK, I'll ring Visa for the exact locations of those two last cashpoints. Shall we drop by Don Antonio's?'

In the dull light of day the Hurlington Health Club looked almost innocent, only the blacked out windows jarring as odd.

Relieved that the place was so much less imposing than the first time she'd tried to visit, Fiona went up the pathway. The door opened into a room dimly lit by a variety of flame-effect lamps. An aquarium bubbled in the left-hand corner, the water glowing with crystalline light that spilled out across darkly coloured sofas.

A young woman wearing a towelling dressing gown was sprinkling fish food in. She turned round, a look of surprise across her face.

'Cindy, someone's here!' Heavy accent, Russian perhaps.

Fiona looked at the counter to her right, empty except for a swipe machine and a pot crammed with cheap biros, cellophane from the stationery shop still clinging to its lower half. A vacuum cleaner came on and an overweight woman with hair coiled on top of her head straightened up behind the counter. The girl by the aquarium slumped on a sofa and perched her bare feet against the rim of the glass coffee table.

'Hello, I'm hoping you can help me.' Fiona stepped off the doormat, almost shouting to make herself heard above the vacuum's aggravating whine.

'You what?' The fat woman's lips remained slightly apart as if the weight of her chins was pulling her lower jaw down.

'I'm trying to find a young woman,' Fiona replied self-consciously as the woman registered the cut to her eyebrow.

She carried on hoovering and Fiona wanted to rip the machine's plug from the wall. 'I think she works here. Or did recently.'

Still the woman said nothing and Fiona felt her words were being absorbed without impression by her bulk. 'Her name is Alexia.'

'She's not working here any more,' the woman snapped without looking up.

'Why? What happened?'

'Who are you?'

'Me? Just someone who knew her once.' The woman's eyes narrowed suspiciously. Clearly, the answer wasn't good enough. Fiona resorted to a lie. 'I'm a friend of her mother's. We're very worried about her.'

'A friend? Who do you work for, social services?'

'No, I'm a beauty therapist.'

Fiona saw the woman look at her hands. She'd given herself a manicure the day before. Since her face was a mess, something needed to look good.

'She did herself no favours by tapping up regulars with her phone number.' She stopped pushing the vacuum in order to jut a thumb towards the door. 'I told her to sling her hook.'

'Where might she have gone?'

The woman swivelled a paw of a hand so her thumb pointed to the floor. 'Only one place she was heading for. Back to the streets.' She shuffled towards Fiona, thrusting the machine back and forth before her.

Fiona retreated a step. 'Which ones?'

'Which ones?' The woman repeated. 'What do you mean?'

'Which streets?' Fiona asked.

'I don't know. Try Minshull, for starters.'

'Minshull Street. Thanks.'

Fiona opened the door and was bathed in dull grey daylight. 'What did this girl look like?'

'I thought you knew her,' the fat woman said.

Fiona retreated on to the front step. 'Shoulder-length hair? Chestnut brown? My height? Thin?'

The woman was looking at the doormat, running the vacuum over it. 'That's her,' she said dismissively, moving the machine back on to the carpet and letting the door swing shut.

Copies of the autopsy report on the Butcher's third victim were doing the rounds of the incident room, several detectives chewing sandwiches as they digested its details.

'Same as the other two,' Jon commented. 'Evidence of being strangled. Blood in the surrounding tissues and fascia suggests he began to remove her skin within minutes of her death.'

Rick was hunched over his photocopied sheets. 'Well, at least she wasn't alive for it. Substantially more flesh taken off, too. And her missing teeth had been removed shortly after her death. Not wrenched out, removed professionally.'

'So along with surgical skills he's got some knowledge of dentistry. Fuck, what are we dealing with here?' Jon asked, an ominous shadow passing over him.

Rick looked up, face slightly pale. 'Why would he take out a selection of her teeth?'

'I reckon he's covering his tracks,' Jon said. 'He's making it as hard as possible to identify her. No face, only a few teeth to compare against dental records – he doesn't want to get caught.'

Rick looked down again. 'Because he wants to carry on. Jesus.' He turned to the photos of the skin itself. The first image was of it piled up next to the corpse on the waste ground. Jon glanced across the table then turned away as memories of having to eat tripe at his grandma's flashed up in his mind. 'No mention of false eyelashes.'

Rick flipped the photo over. The next one was the same pile of skin in the morgue. The pathologist had then taken the pieces of flesh and fitted them together like a grotesque jigsaw.

He turned to the section titled, 'Distinguishing Features'. 'Row of four piercing holes in the upper right ear. Tattoo on the lower left abdomen.'

Jon looked up. 'What of?'

'Betty Boop. Three inches high.'

'Betty Boop? That cartoon character? Oversized head, little kiss-curl, miniskirt and heels?'

'Yeah, I think that's her.'

'Is the cartoon on TV at the moment or something? I've seen that character recently. God, where was it?'

Rick was frowning. 'If he's covering his tracks, why leave her tattoo? Especially when virtually all the skin from the rest of her torso had been removed.'

'He leaves their knickers on. I don't think he saw it. We didn't at the crime scene, remember?'

'You're right,' Rick answered. 'It was under her knickers. He fucked up.'

Jon clicked his fingers. 'It was in the book in Jake's tattoo parlour. That Betty Boop character.'

Rick's eyebrows were raised. 'Gordon Dean and victim three could have got their tattoos done in the same place?'

Jon shrugged. 'Might be worth checking how often that Jake character is asked to do Betty Boop.'

'Back again, gents? I can see you're tempted. You know it's two for one on all body piercings? You could go halves, one nipple each.'

Jon leaned over the desk, his frame filling Jake's vision. He knew his size was intimidating. But when the person was as annoying as this little twat, who gave a shit? Remaining silent, he stared until the provocative smirk began to wilt. Then he raised a hand and swept it towards Jake's head. Jake's shoulders came up, his eyes screwing shut in readiness for the cuff. But Jon's hand carried on over his head and came to rest on the book of tattoos on the shelf by his side. 'Ease up man, I'm only fooling around,' Jon mocked, taking a seat.

Jake's eyes opened again. 'Oh, you're after a tattoo?' But the riposte was delivered weakly.

Jon ignored the comment and flicked through the plastic sheets until he found the right page. 'Betty Boop. How often have you done tattoos of her?'

Jake curled the corners of his mouth downwards. 'Dunno. Not that often. Why?'

'Do you keep a record of tattoos as you do them?'

'Yeah.'

'What about paperwork? Receipts, sales dockets, that kind of stuff?'

He nodded. 'Of course. I keep accounts and pay my tax. Anything to help cover the wages of servants of the state such as yourselves.'

'Good man,' Jon smiled. 'Here's what we need to know. Not counting his latest delivery, when was the last time you bought gloves from Gordon Dean?'

Jake slid a file off the shelf and started working backwards. 'Here, fifteenth of January.'

'Great. Was that also the date you gave him his ladybird tattoo?'

Jake thought. 'Could have been. Yeah, in fact I think it was.'

'Can you tell us which other tattoos you did that day?'

He took a ledger down. Each page covered a month, with names of tattoos and their prices listed. His finger stopped half-way down the entries for January. 'Yeah, there's the ladybird. Twenty-five quid.'

Jon looked at the page. Immediately below it was an entry for Betty Boop, with sixty pounds written in the next column. 'I know it was a few weeks ago, but do you remember who had the Betty Boop tattoo?'

Jake closed his eyes and raised a hand to his face. His fore-finger and thumb twiddled the silver bar in the top of his nose as if it was a dial that turned on memories. 'A young girl. I asked her for ID to check she was eighteen.'

Jon raised his eyebrows. 'And?'

'Yeah, she was. Well, she had one of those proof-of-age cards for pubs.'

'Can you remember the name on the card?'

Jake frowned, silent for a couple of seconds. 'No, sorry.'

'On which part of her body did you do the tattoo?'

He tapped the left-hand pocket of his trousers. 'Here, just below her knicker line.'

'What did she look like?'

'I don't know. About five and a half feet tall. Slim, pretty. Little button nose, brown eyes and short brown hair.'

'How short?'

Jake held a hand to just below his ears.

'Any distinguishing features? Scars, birthmarks, piercings, that sort of thing?'

'Could have had a few piercings at the top of her right ear.'

Jon and Rick exchanged a glance.

'Do you take customers' addresses? Perhaps for a mailing list?' Rick asked.

Jake snorted. 'I'm not that hi-tech. Keeping this thing up to date is about my limit,' he said, hand on the ledger.

Jon glanced at the payment column. 'How did she pay?'

'Cash. That's all I accept.'

'Do you remember if Gordon Dean was in here at the same time as the girl?'

'Yeah, he was. It was busy.' He gestured to the curtain at the back of the tiny room. 'I was doing another one.' He looked at the book. 'There you go, a Maori arm ring, seventy-five quid. They waited out here together while I was doing it.'

'Were they chatting?' Rick asked, leaning forward eagerly.

'I don't know. When the machine's buzzing I can't hear much out here.'

'But they were here for a while, sitting next to each other?'

He nodded. 'Easily for half an hour.'

Jon stood. 'Thanks a lot. You've been a massive help.'

As they trooped back down the stairs, Rick started humming 'I'm in the Money'.

'Don't get cocky,' Jon said, wagging a cautionary finger. 'There's nothing to link him with Angela Rowlands or Carol Miller.'

'True. But Angela Rowlands was in the dating game and Carol Miller disappeared while on some mysterious errand. The sooner more information's entered into HOLMES, the sooner a link to Gordon Dean will emerge. You wait.'

'I am, and I'm not holding my breath.'

Except for a few waiters laying tables, Don Antonio's was deserted. The manager sat down at a table by the door and tilted Gordon Dean's photo to the window. His accent had the necessary elongated vowels for Italian authenticity. 'Ah yes, Mr Dean, he dines here regularly. But this photo is from before his new haircut.'

'And he was most recently in when?' Rick asked.

The manager waved a hand. 'Four or five nights ago?'

'Five,' answered Rick.

The manager looked surprised. 'You know already.'

Rick nodded. 'Where did he sit?'

A finger was pointed across the room. 'The corner table, for two people. But he was alone.'

'And he left at what time?'

'Early – he always eats early. We cleared his table well before eight, I'm sure.'

'Do you remember what he was wearing?'

'Chinos, maybe, a black shirt. Smart casual, as they say.'

'And how did he seem to you? You mentioned he had a new haircut.'

'Yes. Very short and sticking up. His moustache had gone also. He looked like a new man, much younger.'

'Did he seem happy?'

'Of course.' The manager spread his hands. 'Always happy. But yes, he ordered a glass of champagne, even though he had no one to toast it with.'

Back at the station they started typing. A couple of hours later their reports were ready for handing to the receiver, who would read them for any vital information before passing them on to the indexer for entering into HOLMES.

Leaning back in his seat, Rick stretched his arms above his head. 'So, next stop, Gordon's choice of late-night venues?'

Gay Village here I come, Jon thought uneasily. 'Yeah, I suppose so.'

Rick glanced outside at the darkening sky. 'There's no point in going now — far too early. A swift one instead?'

Jon rubbed the back of his hand across his lips, thinking of Pete Gray's duty roster. His shift at Stepping Hill finished at eight o'clock. Under an hour's time. He wondered whether to suggest they follow him, see what he got up to after work.

But then he imagined Rick's response: their orders were to investigate Gordon Dean's disappearance, and that's what they should stick to until instructed otherwise.

Jon clicked his tongue. 'Actually, I'd better show my face at home. My other half will be forgetting who I am.'

'No problem, I've got some stuff to sort out.' Rick's smile was overdone and Jon suddenly wondered if he had someone waiting for him wherever he lived. Rick looked at his watch. 'Shall we meet at around nine?'

Jon was putting his jacket on. 'Sounds fine. Whereabouts?'

'Will you get the train in?'

Jon nodded.

'The Yates's in Piccadilly station, then?'

'OK. See you there.'

Chapter 16

Jon followed the A6 all the way to Stepping Hill hospital. The car park was three-quarters empty and he reversed into a shadowy corner space from where he could watch the porter's lodge unobserved.

I should be at home, he thought guiltily, picturing Alice sitting on her own yet again. Outside, splinters of rain started lacing the air. They hit the windscreen, fragmenting into diagonal lines of minuscule droplets. A swirl of wind pushed a flurry of little needles against the glass from another direction, cutting the lines and creating a crosshatch effect. Seconds later the shower picked up in strength and the delicate effect was lost forever.

Bang on eight o'clock Pete Gray emerged through the doors, a US-style leather flying jacket over his uniform. He made straight for a Staff Only bay and got into a pale blue mini van. Its lights came on and he pulled out, heading for the main road. Keeping his distance, Jon shadowed him back on to the A6, then to a terraced house near Davenport train station.

Jon parked on the opposite side of the road and turned his lights off. The droplets clinging to his windows twinkled under the streetlights as he watched Pete Gray unlock his front door and go into the dark house. The hall lit up, quickly followed by the front room. Gray walked across to the corner, stooped to turn the telly on, then plucked the remote control from a shelf crowded with large books. Standing there, he flicked through a few channels, his other hand wandering round to his buttocks, where it began a lazy scratching.

The flickering light abruptly died and he put the remote back on the shelf, walked over to the front windows and drew the curtains.

Jon's eyes shifted to the blue van parked on the drive. The

rear windows were facing him and he could see a Confederate flag in the corner of one of them. There were another two stickers in the other window, but the writing was too small to be legible.

Jon waited until an upstairs light went on, then climbed out and crossed the road. From the end of the driveway the writing on the stickers was plain to see: *Shaggin' Wagon* and *If it's a-rockin' don't come a-knockin'*. He tried to see into the back, but the windows were heavily tinted. Perfect for ferrying around cargos you didn't want anyone else to see, Jon thought. Back in his car, he jotted down the house number and the van's registration.

'Hi, babe, it's me.'

'In here.' Alice's voice floated back to him from the kitchen.

He shut the front door behind him, eyes fixed on the corridor. Punch's head appeared in the doorway to the living room a second later. Jon dropped to one knee and slapped his thigh. 'Come here, you stupid boy!'

Once their customary wrestling match was over, Jon planted a big kiss on Punch's muzzle, then stood up and walked into the kitchen. Alice's back was to him as she passed the iron over one of his shirts.

'You're late,' she said, looking at him over her shoulder.

'Yeah, I know. Sorry. It's this case.' He stood behind her and slid his hands across her stomach. 'How's you and the bump?'

'We're fine.' Alice smiled, hooking a hand round to stroke his cheek. 'Been snogging your dog again?'

'No,' said Jon guiltily. OK, then, he thought, I'm a liar.

'Well, someone's given you dog-breath.'

Jon glanced down at Punch. 'Haven't you brushed your teeth?'

The dog looked upwards, the skin above its eyes wrinkled into a frown.

Alice resumed her ironing. 'Seriously, Jon, you'll have to be careful about playing around with Punch once the baby arrives. I was reading about these parasites dogs can carry. They can make a baby go blind.'

Jon knew the parasites were only found in dog faeces, but he didn't want to reply in case doing so opened up a wider discussion that led to whether they should keep Punch at all.

'Did you hear me?' Alice said.

'People have kept dogs in family homes for centuries. I've never heard of babies going blind.'

'It's true. I read about it in *Joys of Motherhood*.'

Fucking stupid magazines, Jon thought. Filling their pages with any old shit, nothing more than a vehicle to carry advertisements for extortionate baby equipment. He unwrapped his arms and addressed the back of her head. 'I'll wash my hands each time I've touched Punch.'

'And no kissing him, either. It can't be healthy.'

Still behind her, Jon made a face, then looked down at his dog and gave him a big wink.

'Have you eaten?' Alice asked, folding up the shirt.

'No, but don't worry. I'll just grab a sandwich – I've got to go back out.'

'Again?' Alice's voice had gone up a notch.

Jon sighed and moved into her line of vision. 'We need to trawl some of the bars a suspect was last seen drinking in. See if anyone knows where he is.'

'Which bars?'

'Just some around Canal Street.'

A smirk appeared on Alice's face. 'With your new partner?'

'Yeah, why?' Jon replied, not liking where this was going.

'People will think you're a couple.'

Jon rolled his eyes. 'I hadn't thought about that.'

Alice grinned. 'You'll look lovely together.'

'Yeah, yeah. Actually, what should I wear? I forgot to ask him.'

Alice wasn't able to drop her smile completely. 'For Canal Street? That white ribbed T-shirt I got you from Gap. The fitted one – it shows off your muscles. And your old 501s – they hug your arse beautifully.'

Jon shook his head. 'You're bloody loving this aren't you?'

'Yes,' she giggled. 'It's hilarious watching you squirm. What if any of your rugby mates see you?'

'Well, they're not going to, are they? The last place any of them would drink in is the Gay Village.'

Alice cocked her head to one side. 'You might be surprised.'

'I'm not listening,' Jon said, walking towards the door with a hand held up. If men wanted to shag each other, fine. Just as long as they did it behind closed doors. Problem was, now he was heading behind closed doors himself.

After a quick shower he came back downstairs with his jeans and T-shirt on. Bracing himself, he went into the kitchen.

Alice looked him up and down, eyes lingering at his crutch. 'They'll be like flies around shit,' she lisped in a camp voice.

Jon gripped his temples. 'Just stop it, will you? This is really doing my head in.'

She laughed again. 'Seriously, though, nice touch. Black leather belt and black leather boots.'

Jon studied her face for signs of a piss-take. 'They're my old shoes from when I was in uniform. Doc Martens,' he said uncertainly.

Alice kissed him on the mouth. 'You look fine, honey. And stop worrying, will you? Anyone would think you're about to climb into a cage full of pit-bulls.'

As Jon slapped squares of ham between two slices of granary bread, she started folding the ironing board up.

'Here, I'll do it,' Jon said. Licking margarine from his fingers, he took it from her.

'Cheers,' she answered, one hand on the small of her back. 'Oh, I saw Fiona today. She called into the salon.'

'How was she?' Jon asked, sliding the ironing board into the cupboard under the stairs.

'Can you get the hoover out while you're in there?'

'Alice, forget vacuuming. You should put your feet up.'

'And who'll clean this place?'

'I'll do it. Tomorrow before work, OK?'

Alice shrugged. 'I'll have to get pregnant more often.'

Christ! The prospect of one baby was frightening enough. He looked round, hoping to see an expression on Alice's face that would tell him she was joking. But her back was to him as she sorted through the pile of ironing.

'So how was Fiona?'

Alice's hands paused. 'She worried me, actually. I mean, she's sorting herself out, looking to rent somewhere, so she's finally free of that arsehole she married. But she was going on about what she thinks she heard in that motel room.'

Jon stood in the doorway, arms crossed.

'She's determined to find out what happened to that girl Alexia, or whatever her name was. She went to some escort agency, the one whose business card she found.'

He nodded.

'The owner had interviewed someone, but didn't take her on. So Fiona said she's going to start asking street hookers if they know her.'

Jon pictured what went on in Manchester's red-light areas after dark. It was a sad fact, but even many of his colleagues considered the working girls fair game for a bit of fun. Stories occasionally circulated of prostitutes being invited into the back of police vans, of freebies demanded in return for increased patrols whenever a violent punter was on the prowl. It was a brutal place for Fiona to be wandering around asking questions. 'She needs to be very careful.'

'I know. But she's determined to find out if she's alive. It's like some sort of fixation.'

'Listen, if she tells you anything more about what she's up to, let me know. I don't want her getting into trouble. There's some very nasty operators making their living from those women.'

As Fiona drove through Belle Vue her eyes were drawn to the Platinum Inn. Lights shone behind the curtains in a few of the ground-floor rooms. Several couples were walking along the pavement, and she wondered which were genuine and which were not.

Five minutes later she was driving round the back of Piccadilly station. Spotlights ran along the top of a huge billboard poster. Stretched out in their glare was a bikini-clad woman, leaning towards the camera, lips slightly apart. Fiona just had time to see the ad was for a forthcoming plastic surgery programme on TV before the road turned left, leading her down a dark street bordered by several locked Manchester University buildings. It was a part of town she was unfamiliar with, and she slowed to a crawl. At once she became aware of women she'd been oblivious of a moment before. Now that she was looking properly, she could see more of them, some hanging back in the cobbled side streets that branched off from the road. A sign caught her eye. Minshull Street. One woman stepped to the edge of the kerb and started to beckon. The car passed under a streetlight and, seeing that it was a woman at the wheel, the prostitute's hand fell.

Fiona speeded up a little, shocked by the existence of a world which, until a few seconds ago, she had only been vaguely aware of. She carried on, the bright lights of Canal Street just visible away to her left. The girls here were dressed more gaudily, and had exaggerated perms and overdone lipstick. She glimpsed silver platform shoes and microskirts and couldn't decide if they were just drinkers heading into the Gay Village.

Soon she was approaching the brightly lit area of Whitworth Street. As pubs and restaurants began springing up the girls evaporated away. She did a U-turn and drove back, scanning the dark doorways and shadowy areas under trees. How had they ended up here? she wondered. How many were escaping violent fathers, husbands or partners? She stared at them, feeling sick with the realisation that, in many ways, the only thing separating her from them was the thickness of her car window.

Jon looked around the Yates's pub. A few commuters with coats and briefcases were sipping pints before their trains home. No sign of Rick. He leaned on the bar and decided on a pint of Stella to help settle his nerves.

The change in his hand didn't cover the cost of the drink and, sheepishly, he had dig out another fifty pence while making the decision to never drink there again.

He chose a table in full view of the entrance, put his drink down and started to shrug his leather jacket off. Then he remembered his figure-hugging T-shirt and changed his mind.

The top half of his drink disappeared in two gulps and he began fiddling with a beer mat, pondering the possibility that his new partner was reporting back to McCloughlin. Although he had initially suspected he was, now he wasn't quite so sure. The limited exchange between them at the third victim's crime scene indicated that Rick and McCloughlin had met, but it was a big jump from that to concluding they were in a hidden agreement.

Jon stared at his drink, considering his options like a chess player. Booze. That would be his next move. Get him drinking, then drop in an awkward question or two.

A couple of minutes later Rick walked in, still wearing his suit. Wilting with the realisation he had misjudged his dress, Jon gave a weak wave.

Rick spotted him and crossed the room, taking in Jon's clothes as he did. 'Shit, I didn't think we were going casual.' His eyes caught momentarily on the rip in the knee of Jon's faded jeans.

Jon moved his leg under the table. 'I thought we were trying to mingle a bit.'

There was an awkward pause, broken by Rick's half-chuckle. 'Well, you'll certainly manage that. Drink?'

Jon tipped his glass to the side. 'Go on then. Another Stella please.'

Rick returned with two drinks, Jon eyeing the other glass suspiciously. 'Is that a Coke?'

Rick took a long swallow. 'With a double gin.'

Resisting the temptation to pick up the drink and sniff it, Jon gulped down some more beer.

Rick took out the credit-card company's breakdown of Gordon Dean's last transactions. 'So, his card was swiped in Don Antonio's at seven forty-nine. Next is a bill for thirty-six quid in Taurus. Transaction went through at eight forty-one.'

'What's Taurus?'

'It's a sort of restaurant bar at the very top of Canal Street. Nice cocktails, decent menu. Might as well start there.'

Jon tried to form an impression of Taurus as they walked through the doors – muted lights and clusters of candles were fighting a losing battle with the shadows encroaching from all sides. He almost stumbled on the sloping floor that led up to the tables, half of which were taken by people dining.

The shelves behind the bar at the top of the room glowed with an impressive assortment of spirits. A glass-fronted fridge was stacked full with bottles of champagne.

Jon tried to look relaxed as he perched on a corner stool. A large glass bowl was at his elbow and he casually picked up one of the things in it. Holding it close to his face, he squinted at the writing. *Free safer sex pack for men – two extra-strength condoms and two sachets of water-based lube.*

He dropped it like a hot coal and glanced at Rick, just able to see the smile at the corner of his mouth as he addressed the barman. 'Hi, there. A double gin and coke and …' He looked at Jon. 'Pint of lager?'

'I'll get these,' Jon said, standing up and taking a ten-pound note from his pocket. They watched in silence as the barman poured their drinks. As he placed them on the counter, Rick laid down the photo of Gordon Dean, his warrant card beside it. 'We're trying to trace the movements of this man. He was in here last Thursday night.'

The barman looked barely past the legal age for drinking. He ran a hairless hand across the black top that clung to his perfectly flat stomach. Rings glinted on three of his fingers.

'Black shirt, hair was cut much shorter, and the moustache had gone,' Jon prompted.

The barman snapped his fingers and said to Jon, 'Yeah, he sat where you are now. I remember because he put his credit card behind the bar, even though he was on his own. He was drinking champagne by the glass.'

'Did he remain on his own?' Rick asked, elbows now on the counter.

'Yeah, I think so. He chatted to people a bit as they were waiting for drinks, but no one actually joined him.'

The barman moved off to serve another customer. Jon risked a look at the two women eating at the nearest table. They were engrossed in conversation, a bottle of Pino Grigio between them. He found himself studying them, wondering why they looked slightly odd. Then it clicked: their hair wasn't natural. The styling was overdone and he realised they were wearing wigs. Masculine fingers picked up a wine glass, and Jon looked away.

The barman returned a moment later. 'Why, what's he done?'

Rick put the photo back in his pocket. 'We just need to ask him a few questions. So, do you think he was cruising?'

The barman pouted. 'Not really. He was just getting merrily pissed. He left after a bit – gave me a good tip, as well.'

Rick straightened up. 'Thanks for your help.' Once the barman had moved out of earshot he said to Jon, 'Not much happened for him in here, then.'

Jon had to make an effort not to let his eyes stray back to the couple. 'No, but I guess it was early in the evening. What about all this champagne? He was celebrating something.'

Rick finished his drink. 'Maybe it was a case of him celebrating the anticipation of something. Like his next murder, for instance.'

He's not the killer, Jon thought, knocking back the rest of his pint. 'When did he get to the next place?'

'Natterjacks?' Rick studied the record. 'He paid the entrance fee at eight fifty-six, so he must have gone straight there.'

Music was thumping through the plate-glass windows making up the front of Natterjacks. Two bouncers stood at the entrance, barely acknowledging the flow of customers heading through the doors.

In the small lobby area people were flicking ten-pound notes under the window of the till counter, then heading into the bar. When it was Jon and Rick's turn to pay they flashed their warrant cards at the cashier. 'Mind if we have a quick look around?' asked Rick.

She looked towards the customers behind them and called, 'Next!'

Inside, it was getting towards uncomfortably busy. Throngs of people filled the area in front of the main bar. Jon looked around, relieved that there were at least a few groups of women in the mostly male crowd.

Rick pointed to a flight of stairs. As they headed down them Jon took in the ornately carved wooden balconies. Male faces peered down from all around. He followed Rick into a quieter side bar where the music was lower but the temperature far higher.

'This place is busier than I expected,' Rick said, taking his jacket off and loosening his tie. 'Aren't you hot in that?' he asked, nodding at Jon's battered leather jacket.

'No, I'm all right,' Jon replied, aware of the sheen of sweat on his forehead.

Once again Rick took the initiative with the bar staff. The girl serving them shook her head. 'Wasn't on that night. Hang on, I'll get Steve.' She moved to the till.

A thin man appeared, the low ceiling behind the bar causing him to stoop slightly. After looking at the photo he scratched his head. 'I'm fucked if I know, mate. The capacity of this place is over seven hundred. There are bars and dance floors on three storeys.'

Rick took the photo back and looked at Jon. 'Drink?'

'I'll need a piss first. Where's the men's in this place?'

Rick pointed to the side. 'Nearest ones are down those steps and on the right.'

At the bottom of the steps was a small dance floor. A line of men stood with their backs against the wall, each holding a drink in his hand. As Jon came down the steps he could feel their eyes crawling over him. Suddenly he realised what it must feel like to be a woman. Self-consciously, he wove between the few people dancing, noticing that the song playing was the one on the tape in Gordon Dean's car. Relieved to find that the toilets were empty, he took a corner urinal, hoping no one would come and stand next to him.

Back in the bar upstairs he walked straight over to Rick, 'Listen, there's no point in staying here, is there?'

Rick glanced at him. 'No, you're right. Let's move on.'

Jon made straight for the stairs.

Outside, Rick said, 'That place not really your style?'

'What do you mean?' Jon answered, surprised at how uncomfortable the crude assessment he'd experienced on the stairs had made him.

'Loud music, cramped bars. All that stuff.'

Jon looked up at the sky, relishing the cool air on his face. 'I felt like a right twat. Do you drink in those places out of choice?'

Rick smiled. 'If I'm out to party.'

Jon sighed, not knowing if that was a euphemism for picking up. The basement dance floor hadn't looked like it was being used for much else. 'Nah. Give me a proper boozer any time. Somewhere you can be comfortable and have a conversation.'

As they were talking, Rick had led the way to a darker side street. Halfway up it a red sign seemed to float in the air. Crimson. 'Here we go,' said Rick, examining the printout. He paid to get in here at ten twenty-one, then forked out another thirty-eight quid at two thirty in the morning. Closing time.'

Jon took a deep breath in. 'Is this going to be like the last place?'

Rick couldn't help laughing. 'This isn't like any other place.'

'Oh, Jesus, I don't like the sound of that.'

Dodging the debris scattered across the cobbles, Rick went up to the door. 'Usually there's a queue.' There was a notice stuck to the door. 'Ah. Miss Tonguelash is away. The place is shut for the night.'

Jon looked at him questioningly.

'He owns the place as well as being the resident DJ, cabaret artist and stand-up comedian. Look.' He read out the notice, 'The bitch is back tomorrow.'

'So is it a nightclub or what?'

Rick stared at the doors. 'I'd call it a meeting of many minds. But yeah, basically it's a nightclub.'

'A gay nightclub?'

'Not exclusively, no. We're right on the border here between the Gay Village and the rest of the city. All sorts turn up, gay, straight, lots of cross-dressers. You even get working girls popping in off Minshull Street to grab the free packs of condoms. You know, like the one you were looking at in Taurus.'

Jon felt his face flush. 'But it's ten pounds to get in. That's more than any pack of condoms.'

'No, the entry fee is for the downstairs area where the cabaret and other stuff goes on. It's free to drink upstairs.'

'I can't work out what Gordon Dean was up to, trawling these places. Is he gay? Is he lonely? What?'

'You don't have to be gay to be drinking in the Gay Village.

A lot of people come here because you don't get fights breaking out. A lot of women come here because they know they won't get hit on the whole time.'

Hands in his pockets, Jon looked down at his feet. 'Do you remember ever seeing Gordon Dean? It seems he was a bit of a regular around here.'

Rick shot him a glance. 'No. That occurred to me, too, but I don't think I ever did. Besides, if I had I wouldn't have kept it to myself.'

Jon looked at him quickly. 'I wouldn't blame you if you had. Admitting something like that would certainly get the tongues wagging round the incident room.'

Rick said nothing.

Jon stared off down the street. 'OK. Assuming for a moment Dean killed the Betty Boop girl, do you really think this is where he also picked up Angela Rowlands and Carol Miller? Can you see those two visiting an area like this?'

Rick sniffed. 'Doesn't seem likely.'

'So what's he doing drinking around here on his own?'

'I don't know. But we need to come back when this place is open, that's for sure.'

'Because?'

'I've just realised: the entry fee Dean paid? It was for two people, not one.'

'So maybe he did get lucky that night.'

'Maybe,' Rick replied, looking at his watch. 'Quarter to ten. Time for another drink?'

'On one condition,' Jon replied.

Rick raised an eyebrow.

'I choose the bloody venue.'

Jon marched to the top of the road. They emerged on to the slightly better lit Minshull Street, girls hovering in the shadows beneath the trees bordering an empty parking lot.

'Where are we going?' asked Rick, trying to keep up.

Jon crossed over, heading back towards Piccadilly station. 'A proper pub.'

Standing in the hushed and cosy confines of the Bull's Head a few minutes later, Jon turned an ear towards the low music coming from the speakers and nodded in appreciation. 'Police and Thieves', from the original version of *Black Market Clash*. 'What'll it be?' he asked.

Rick was studying the fireplace and leather-upholstered seats. 'Same again. Cheers.'

They sat at a corner table. Jon leaned back, closed his eyes and stretched his legs out. 'That's a relief.'

Rick looked amused as he took his jacket off and hung it on the back of his chair. 'Do they keep your pipe and slippers behind the bar?'

One of Jon's eyes opened. 'I wish they did.'

Rick chuckled. 'Is that leather jacket welded to your back or what?'

Jon's other eye opened. 'I owe my girlfriend for why I've kept this on all night.'

'How come?'

'When I told her we were going round Canal Street, she recommended I wear this.' He held the jacket open.

Rick couldn't see a single wrinkle in the T-shirt. He laughed and said, 'Is it sleeveless, too?'

'Almost.' He gestured to his upper arm. 'They come to about—' He stopped, realising Rick was taking the piss. 'Yeah, yeah, nice one. You should meet Alice. You'd get along.'

Rick glanced around the pub again. 'It's bizarre to think this place is just a minute away from Canal Street. I didn't know it existed and I must have walked past it dozens of times. I only live round the corner.'

Jon sat forwards and took a long pull on his pint. 'Whereabouts?'

'Off Whitworth Street. In the new development of flats on Venice Street.'

Jon looked blank.

'You know the Japanese restaurant on Whitworth Street?'

'Yeah, Samsi something.'

'The Samsi Yakitori. I live above that.'

Jon was thinking how much a flat in a spot like that would cost. 'That must practically overlook Canal Street.'

Rick nodded.

'What about the noise?'

'Doesn't bother me. Besides, it's what living in the centre of a city's all about. Part of the vibe.'

Jon looked down at the table and noticed Rick's manicured nails. He thought of the hair-removal treatment Alice said Melvyn offered male customers at the salon. 'Back crack and sack', he called it. He wondered if Rick went in for that sort of thing. Still looking down, he said quietly, 'How far back do you and McCloughlin go?'

He raised his eyes and studied Rick's reaction.

His partner didn't blink. 'How do you mean?'

Jon took another sip of beer. 'Have you not worked on an investigation with him before?'

Rick looked bemused. 'Never even met him.'

Jon kept his eyes on Rick, watchful for any body language that suggested otherwise. He spotted nothing. 'I assumed he'd drafted you in because you'd crossed paths somewhere in the past.'

Rick's eyes narrowed for a moment and a smile of realisation flickered across his lips. 'And you thought I might be a plant, sent to keep tabs on the detective who stole his glory over the Chewing Gum Killer?'

Jon held his glass up and tilted it in silent acknowledgement of Rick's powers of deduction.

Rick gave a short, sour laugh. 'Cheers.' His face turned more serious. 'The order appeared in my pigeonhole the day before I met you. Until then I thought I was staying in Chester House for another desk rotation. I've never said a word to McCloughlin before joining this investigation. I think he's a great SIO but I'm not his fucking lackey.'

'I'm sorry. It just seemed a bit dodgy to me, especially given the wink ...' He realised he'd slipped up in his eagerness to appease his partner.

'Wink? What wink?' Rick leaned forwards.

Jon looked away, cursing himself. 'Just something McCloughlin did.'

'I don't follow you. Just something McCloughlin did when?'

Jon sighed, realising he was cornered. 'When McCloughlin

told me I was being paired with you, he gave me this wink.'

Rick frowned and Jon knew he was turning over the implications of what such a signal could have meant. 'As in suggesting something about me?'

Jon sat back, wondering how often Rick had suffered with this kind of thing in the past. 'I suppose so.'

Anger shone in Rick's eyes. 'Word soon gets round, doesn't it? Apart from you, I've told two people in the force that I'm gay. I thought I could trust them both.'

Jon drank from his pint, considering whether to offer some insincere assurance that, career-wise, it didn't make much difference. He decided to stay silent.

After a few seconds Rick took a massive swig of his drink and breathed out. 'Fuck him.'

'Who? McCloughlin?'

Rick nodded.

Jon clinked his glass against Rick's. 'I'll drink to that.'

Both men sat with their own thoughts, but this time the silence between them was relaxed. Jon traced his mind over their encounters with McCloughlin during the investigation so far. In retrospect it seemed obvious there was no agreement between Rick and their SIO. He realised McCloughlin's bitter attitude toward him was, in turn, souring his own perception. He'd have to make an effort not to let it affect him.

Still thinking about his partner, he said, 'So when did you know you were gay?'

'That old chestnut.'

Jon wondered if the question had caused offence. But Rick didn't seem bothered. 'I've always known. It wasn't like a bolt from the blue at eighteen.'

Jon thought about this. 'How do you mean always? You fancied men even as a little kid?'

Rick toyed with his drink. 'Did you fancy women even as a little kid?'

'I don't know. I remember watching *Top of the Pops* and getting pretty excited by Pan's People's dance routines.'

Rick laughed. 'Well, Brian Jackson doing press-ups on *Superstars* made more of an impression on me. But I didn't consciously fancy him – it was just that he was more interesting, somehow.'

'But how did you find it at school? Playgrounds can be pretty brutal places.'

'Never a problem,' Rick stated. 'I'm not a screaming queen. In fact, if it wasn't for this one girl, most people would never have guessed.'

'A girl you turned down?'

'Basically, yes. I confided in her, thinking we were mates. She went off and told her friends, so pretty soon I was rumbled.'

'And?'

'One particular bloke tried to turn things on me. I walked straight up to him and burst his nose. It's the only punch I've ever had to throw. Luckily it was a beauty.'

Jon smiled. 'Sounds it. So no problems after that?'

'None.' Rick finished off his drink 'Again?'

Jon found himself reassessing another preconception about gay men. 'When you started on the gin and Cokes I thought, here we go.'

'Here we go?'

'You know,' Jon faltered. 'Well, I thought, that's a bit of a ladies' drink. Then I thought, two of those and he'll be all over the place. But fair play, you look more sober than me.'

Rick grinned. 'Think about it. Which thing more than any other drains people's money, time and energy, ensuring they have to get up early every single day of the week?'

Jon frowned. 'I don't know. Kids?'

Rick clinked his glass against Jon's. 'Precisely. And what would a segment of the population do if they had no parental responsibility, plenty of cash and lie-ins every weekend? They'd go out and have a good time. Restaurants, bars, clubs, nice holidays. Here's to the power of the pink pound.'

Jon was left to stare into the dregs of his pint, mind wandering to the early-morning feeds now only weeks away.

Chapter 17

The manager of the women's refuge wrapped her arms round Fiona, engulfing her in a fiercely protective hug. 'You take care of yourself,' she whispered, tilting her head back to look Fiona in the eyes. 'And let me know how you're doing.'

Fiona smiled, thinking about the six precious nights she'd spent in the refuge. 'Thank you so much, Hazel. You've been a life-saver. You are a life-saver.' Waving once more to the women on the doorstep, Fiona turned to her car. Her bags were packed safely in the boot and she climbed in.

The drive to her bedsit took less than a quarter of an hour. She had chosen a place with good transport connections to Melvyn's salon. After all, in the absence of anything else, it was now the main part of her life.

She could accept how the majority of her friends had been slowly driven away by her husband's cold and suspicious welcomes every time they tried to visit. Her resolute denials that anything was wrong had hardly helped.

But the rift she'd opened up with her parents was a deep and aching wound. She'd enjoyed a happy childhood, supported and encouraged by a mum and dad she rarely heard argue. That made it all the more painful when she began to realise her marriage to Jeff wasn't destined for the same level of success.

She'd married him in her late teens. At first everything seemed great as he got a graduate job at a firm of surveyors and she completed her final health and beauty qualifications. Then she got pregnant and gave up work. With the birth of their daughter Jeff became more preoccupied with work. He'd been given new responsibilities and they made more demands on his time. Time he seemed only too happy to give.

He started coming home later and later, often smelling of

whisky. It was a way of relaxing, he assured her. The management encouraged a bit of bonding outside work hours.

But his promotion never came and he became more irritable, forever screening the household bills. She was no longer earning and he made her feel guilty about spending money he said wasn't her own. The balance of their relationship had shifted and her role edged more and more to the subservient. It resembled, she realised one day with a mixture of surprise and disappointment, that of her own parents. Dad the breadwinner, mum the housewife. Only her mum had never seemed unhappy with her role. Perhaps she was being selfish in wanting more. So she kept quiet about her doubts, playing the part of happy mum, hoping things would improve.

Then one day he punched her. A simple movement of his arm, but an action that set in motion a chain of events that led to the death of their daughter. After that he retreated into himself, drinking more and more, questioning every penny she spent. Getting his permission to start working again was a huge struggle. He feared the loss of control it would entail and paranoid fear began to consume him: 'You're going to leave me ... You'll meet someone else ... Isn't what I earn good enough?'

He didn't lay another finger on her for many years. But gradually the bullying moved from mental to physical. Pushes and slaps at first, then heavier cuffs. Finally, punches.

She thought about her parents. She'd shut them out after their granddaughter's funeral, too ashamed to admit how the accident had happened. But they'd known something was wrong. She couldn't stand her mother's entreaties, her father's furious stares. Both of them powerless to help her while she refused to admit there was a problem. Now she wanted to make amends but pride prevented her from calling them. Not until she was properly back on her feet.

The bedsit occupied the corner of the ground floor in a large Victorian house in Fallowfield. It was a student area, the bus shelters permanently full of people in faded jeans, baggy tops and battered trainers. How they chose to carry their books vaguely amused her. Some went for simple sports bags, others opted for ethnic-looking canvas pouches. All avoided briefcases, but that was just a matter of time. She smiled wistfully, wondering what Emily would have chosen if she was still alive.

After reversing into the yard at the back of the building so her car was facing towards the road, she removed the spare car key from her purse. Once out of the vehicle, she checked that no one was watching, then slipped it into a crack between two bricks at the base of the wall. That was a quick means of escape, if it was ever needed. After all, if he did somehow track her down and turn up with a few drinks inside him, she knew what he was capable of.

The hallway of the house was littered with unwanted junk mail and a couple of old copies of the Yellow Pages, still wrapped in plastic. A door opened and a man appeared, a box of old cooking utensils in his arms. He looked to be in his late twenties, but he still wore student clothes.

'Morning. You just moving in?' he asked cheerfully.

'Yes,' Fiona nodded, holding her handbag tight against her stomach.

'Me too.'

She smiled, glancing at the box.

'Cooking things. If you ever need any, just help yourself. People have dumped loads of stuff down in the cellar.'

Fiona looked at the door he'd just emerged from. 'Thanks.'

'Are you a mature student?'

Fiona felt herself flush slightly. 'No. I'm, I'm ... just in between places at the moment.'

His smile faded as he assessed her answer, eyes shifting to her damaged eyebrow. 'Sorry, I didn't mean to pry.'

'No, that's fine. So, are you? A student, I mean?'

'Yeah, I'm doing an MA.'

'Which subject?'

Now he looked embarrassed. 'Classical studies. Latin, Greek. Don't ask why. I think it was my mum's idea, really. She wants me to be a journalist.'

Fiona smiled. 'Well, I'd best get sorted out ... ?' She raised her eyebrows enquiringly.

'Oh, it's Raymond. Raymond Waite.'

'Nice to meet you, Raymond. I'm Fiona.' As he carried on up

the stairs, she looked with amusement at his cumbersome trainers, complete with little Perspex windows in the thick soles.

Then she opened the door to her room and looked around, refusing to be dismayed by its dour interior. It was hers, that was the important thing. Another small step towards freedom.

She paused to sniff the air. The fusty smell she'd noticed on her first look-around still remained, despite the window being open. She brought her suitcase in, eyes lingering on it, attracted by the bottle of gin inside. Fighting back the temptation to have just one drink, she picked up her handbag instead. Air freshener, bleach and scouring cream were what she needed. The bare mattress on the single bed was patchy with stains. With some difficulty she lifted it up and saw the underside was only worse. As she headed out of the door, she added a duvet, sheets, towels and a new mattress to her list, aware that the cash Melvyn had given her was rapidly running out.

She returned a while later, ferried the smaller things through to her room, then returned to the car and began trying to pull the new mattress out from where it lay across the boot and folded-down back seats.

A first-floor window opened and she heard hip-hop music before a voice said, 'You need a hand, Fiona?'

She looked up to see Raymond leaning out of the window. 'Would you mind?'

'No problem.'

He shuffled round the corner a few seconds later, crouching to tie the laces of his absurd trainers. The oversized tongues lolling from the tops reminded her of a pair of thirsty spaniels.

They carried the mattress through to her room, and placed it by the side of the bed.

'I don't know what to do with the old one – it's disgusting,' Fiona said.

'Yeah, I see what you mean,' Raymond replied. 'Why not dump it in the cellar? That's what everyone else seems to do with unwanted stuff.'

'Do you think it would be all right?'

'Yeah. Come on, I'll give you a hand.'

They hauled it off the bed and carried it out into the hall.

Raymond kicked the cellar door open, then pushed the mattress down the short flight of stairs. It came to a lopsided halt at the bottom. He flicked the lights on and carried on down, Fiona following uncertainly behind.

'There are all sorts down here,' he said, pointing to the haphazard stacks of boxes. 'Old clothes, crappy portable televisions, records, textbooks, files of work. Do you need any saucepans? There's a whole crate of them in that corner.'

Fiona looked around, shoulders hunching up at the sight of the huge cobwebs nestled in the exposed rafters above her head. Raymond tipped the mattress on its side and slid it across the dusty floor into a side room. In the centre of the room was a table with what looked like a stone top.

'What on earth is that?' Fiona asked.

Raymond leaned the mattress against it. 'This house would have been built for a wealthy merchant. This room was the pantry. In the days before fridges, the servants would have stored meat on it.' He slapped the bare stone with his palm. 'It's always cool down here. See the gutter running round it? They'd cover the meat with muslin and ladle water over it occasionally. It would have kept for days.'

Fiona shivered. 'Well, I never knew that.'

Two hours later, she peeled off her Marigolds and looked around her room. That was more like it. A bunch of flowers on the windowsill; the bed covered by a plump duvet, the creases still showing on its cover.

Once again, she found herself looking at the suitcase. *No*, she thought. A good vacuuming, that's what this place needs. She smiled. It was the perfect excuse to call in at the salon. Melvyn wouldn't mind her borrowing the Dyson.

'Hi there,' she chirped, stepping through the door. She caught a tense look in Melvyn's eyes before his face broke into a smile.

'Fiona!' he said, taking in her designer jeans and crisp white shirt. 'You're looking more shaggable every day. If I didn't swing the other way ...'

'Oh, stop it, Melvyn,' she laughed.

'Cuppa?'

'Thanks, yes.'

Melvyn turned to Zoe, who was replacing curlers on a rack. 'Zoe, will you be Mum?'

Fiona waved a hand. 'Don't you worry. I'll do it.' Without waiting for a reply, she walked across to the kitchen area and started setting out the cups.

'So how are you, darling?' Melvyn asked over his shoulder while wrapping a strand of his customer's hair in tin foil.

'Great, thanks. I'm feeling so much more positive.'

'Brilliant – you look like you do.'

'I've just moved into my own little place. It's not much, but it's a start.'

'Where is it?'

'Ridley Close in Fallowfield.'

'Near City's old ground?'

'That's it.'

Melvyn adjusted the towel round his customer's neck. 'OK, that's you for a half-hour. Are you fine with those magazines? The latest *Heat*'s around here somewhere. It's got a great article about the contestants for that plastic surgery show they're doing on telly soon.'

'I've read it, thanks.' She sat back in her seat and began reading one of the magazines on her lap.

Melvyn scooted over to the kitchen area. 'I bet you've got it all spic and span.'

Fiona nodded. 'Just about. Though I was hoping to borrow the Dyson. Once the place is properly clean, you'll all have to come round for a drink.'

'Just say when.' Melvyn picked up the biscuit tin and gave it a rattle. 'Empty again? God, do we get through them in here. Zoe, be a love and nip down the street for some more biccies.'

As the door shut behind her, Alice appeared from her side room. 'Fiona. I thought I heard you.'

Fiona looked at Alice and her eyes widened. 'You sure your due date is still a few weeks away?'

Alice's shoulders sagged. 'Oh, don't. I feel like a beached whale.'

Laughing, Fiona pointed to the kettle. 'Tea?'

'Thanks.' Alice perched on the edge of a stool and made a cradle for her stomach with her hands.

'Fiona was just saying she's moved into her own place,' Melvyn announced.

'Where is it?' Alice asked.

Fiona grabbed a pen and paper from her handbag. 'Flat 2, 15 Ridley Close. Over in Fallowfield.' She handed the scrap of paper to Alice. 'You're all welcome to come round, but obviously the address has to stay secret. He has no idea where I am.'

Fiona caught that tense look on Melvyn's face again. 'What is it?' she asked.

'Nothing,' he said with a little shrug.

Fiona turned to Alice, but she was watching Melvyn. Fiona looked back at him. 'He's been here hasn't he?'

He didn't answer.

'The bastard,' Fiona hissed, fear and anger flaring up. 'What did he say? What did he do? Did he threaten you? He did, didn't he?'

Melvyn gave her a brief smile. 'Nothing more than a raging poofter like me's used to. Don't worry, he soon ran out of steam. Especially when I blew him a kiss.'

Fiona gasped, one hand over her mouth. 'You didn't!'

'That was a bit much,' Alice added with a grin. 'I thought the veins in his neck were about to burst.'

Fiona felt sick. 'Oh, I'm so sorry.' Her eyes cut to the front of the shop: could she be seen from the street? 'What if he comes back?' Now she felt genuinely scared.

'That's probably why it's best you stay away for a bit,' said Melvyn. 'I told him you don't work here any more. He'll soon give up.'

Alice went over to the reception desk and tucked Fiona's address into the back of the appointments book.

'Thanks, Melvyn, I really appreciate this,' Fiona said more quietly.

Melvyn fidgeted on his stool. 'Only thing is, Fiona, I can pay you your holiday money. But, you know how it works in here. Without you doing any treatments ...'

'You want me to leave? Find a job somewhere else?' Her nausea increased.

'No!' Melvyn protested with a dramatic wave of his hands. 'You're one of the team. I didn't mean that. But what will you do for money? I mean, I could lend you some ...'

Fiona shook her head defiantly. There was no way she was becoming a charity case for her friends. 'I'm fine for now. Listen, I'm just glad you're prepared to give me unpaid leave.'

They all heard the front door open and Fiona shrank backwards. 'Is it him?' she whispered, knowing her face was draining of colour.

Alice looked round the corner. 'Hi, Zoe. Chocolate Hobnobs? Good choice.'

When Fiona eventually set off for her bedsit, the salon's Dyson in the boot of her car, guilt hung heavy over her. She'd caused so much trouble to so many people. Dawn Poole appeared in her head. Another one she owed an apology to. Especially after sending Alice's other half round to question her.

At the end of the street she turned towards the A57, deciding to put things right at the Platinum Inn straight away. When she pulled into the car park a short while later she couldn't decide which slot to take, it was so empty. Inching slowly forwards, she decided on the far side, away from the day manager's silver Volvo and near the gap in the hedge she'd squeezed through several days before.

How hopeless her life had seemed that evening. Not that it was a whole lot better now. She thought about the cramped little bedsit that was her new home. Her money had almost run out and she had no idea how she was going to meet next month's demand for rent.

Her mind turned to her husband and she pictured him during his more pleasant moments. Laughing at something on the radio, delightedly rubbing his hands when his football team scored. She wondered what he was doing, how he was coping without her. He spent so much time at work, he'd never find the opportunity to clean the house. She imagined the state of the kitchen. Maybe she should call and see how he was. If he showed remorse for his violence and agreed to seek counselling, perhaps they could discuss the possibility ...

She shook her head, realising where her train of thought had so insidiously led her. 'What are you doing even considering it?' she asked her reflection in the rear-view mirror, focusing on the first glimmers of a life free of fear. 'You're not going back.'

She turned the radio on. The seven o'clock news on Smooth FM mentioned the Butcher of Belle Vue case. The police still hadn't been able to identify the third victim – once again, anyone who knew of a missing female in her late teens to early twenties with shoulder-length brown hair and a distinctive tattoo on her lower body was asked to call the incident room. A tattoo? she thought. That was a detail they hadn't included before.

A thin figure came hurrying up the path and went into the motel. Dawn. Fiona waited for the day manager to drive off before climbing out.

Dawn's face remained blank as Fiona walked through the doors.

'Hi there,' Fiona announced uncertainly.

'What do you want?' Dawn replied, busying herself with some paperwork.

'I've come to say sorry. I didn't mean to cause you any bother.'

'Didn't you? Well, you fucked up there, then. What did you expect would happen if you went to a copper and told him you heard someone being killed in the next room?'

Fiona sighed. 'What I heard really shook me up. Then, when I read the report in the paper later that morning ... Do you realise her body was found only just down the road?'

'Of course I know that. Jesus, I've got to walk from the bus stop to here every single bloody day.'

'Oh, Dawn,' Fiona frowned in sympathy.

They regarded each other for an instant.

Dawn brushed a stray hair from the counter. 'It's all right, as it happens. He buggered off after a few minutes.'

Fiona kept her voice casual. 'So he didn't go poking around?'

'No, thank God.' Dawn reached for a cigarette, offered one to Fiona. 'I thought he was going to look around the room at least, but he just asked me if I'd ever heard of a girl called Alexia.'

Fiona was seething at Jon's claim to have searched the place. 'And have you?' she asked. 'The woman who owns that escort agency, Cheshire Consorts, reckons someone using that name tried to get a job with her. I think the same girl worked in a massage parlour just down the road near the Apollo. A place called the Hurlington Club.'

Dawn lifted the counter flap. 'You've been busy. Come on, let's have a coffee.'

They went into the back office and sat down on the comfy seats.

'Go on,' Dawn prompted.

'Well, I think it was the same girl. It could have been an Alicia, though – there was a bit of confusion with names.'

Dawn was searching for her cigarettes. 'And what did this girl look like?'

Fiona frowned. 'I don't know. Around my height with shoulder-length brown hair. Pretty, apparently, but quite thin in the face. She may be using drugs.'

Dawn looked up, a pinched expression on her face. 'How old?'

'Young. About twenty at the most.'

Looking relieved for some reason, Dawn opened a desk drawer and drew out a fresh bottle of brandy. 'Doesn't sound like anyone who comes in here. Fancy a splash?'

The glowing liquid shifted in the bottle. Fiona felt the muscles in her throat tighten with the anticipation of its warmth. She knew that having just one drink would be impossible and the thought of ending up in one of the motel's grim rooms again was just enough incentive to turn it down. Swallowing back a rush of saliva, she said, 'No, I'd better not. You know, driving and all that.'

She looked away and listened as Dawn poured a dash into her own cup. There was a clink as the bottle was replaced in the drawer.

'Why are you so determined to find this Alexia? If she even exists.'

Fiona looked fixedly at the tip of her thumb as it probed at the tops of her fingers, like a creature checking its brood. 'I just hate the idea of this poor girl being out there so alone in the world.'

'So do I. But there's only so far you can go. I think you should try and forget it. This search of yours is dangerous, Fiona.'

Fiona's eyes were still locked on her hand and when she finally spoke her voice seemed to have retreated deep inside her chest. 'I had a daughter once. Emily. But she died.' Her thumb foraged about, touching the tip of each finger. Counting them in. 'I lost her because I wasn't there for her.'

'What happened?' Dawn whispered.

'Jeff – my husband – had really gone for me. It was the first time he ever did. He stormed back from work early one afternoon. He'd been drinking and I did something – I don't know what – to aggravate him. He turned round and punched me in the stomach. No warning, nothing. He hit me so hard I knocked the kitchen table over as I fell. Emily saw everything. He'd left the front door open and she ran out into the road shouting for a nee-nar. She was four years old and that was her word for an ambulance.'

Tears broke from Fiona's eyes.

'He'd knocked the wind out of me and I couldn't get up. I could only lie there, gasping like a fish. It was a car. I heard its tyres screeching. I still hear its tyres screeching.' She swallowed a moan, unable to mention the thud of metal on flesh that followed.

Dawn put her drink down and grasped Fiona's hand. 'You can't blame yourself for that, surely?'

'I try not to, but it doesn't help much. After that things were never the same. One moment's loss of control and our lives were ruined. I could see the knowledge of what he'd done eating away inside him. At first I was glad, but I forgave him eventually, trying to salvage something between us. He's never been able to talk about it. I tried so hard to make things work. He was my husband and, despite everything, I still loved him. But the more I reached out to him, the more distant he became. Then, maybe five years ago, he attacked me again. And you know what?' She smiled sorrowfully, shaking her head. 'Afterwards was the only time he'd shown me any affection in years.'

Dawn squeezed her hand. 'Don't waste your time. It's not you who's provoking him. He's the one to blame, not you.'

Fiona nodded. 'I know. But now I've got my head full of the noise of that poor girl choking. Apart from the man who attacked her, I may be the last person to hear her voice.' She looked up at Dawn. 'That room was used, wasn't it? You did let a couple in there.'

Dawn raised her cup to take a sip, using it as a way of breaking eye contact. 'Yes, I think so. It was a pretty busy night, though. People were coming and going and I was a bit worse for wear after all that brandy we drank.'

'But surely you remember handing the key over? Surely you'd remember a couple checking out again?'

'No. The key's missing and the lock doesn't work properly, anyway. And if they went out by the fire escape, I wouldn't have seen a thing. What makes me wonder if it was used at all is the fact it was so immaculate. I certainly didn't clean it.'

'He did. That's what I heard him doing after it all went quiet.'

Dawn shrugged. 'Who knows what happened?' She raised her cup and took a generous sip.

Watching her, Fiona thought, God, I need a drink. She put her coffee cup down. 'I'd better go. Listen, I want you to know how much I appreciate your help that night. Are we still friends?'

Dawn smiled. 'Still friends. I just wish I'd put you in an upstairs room. It's all but untouched up there.'

As Fiona stood she said, 'Oh, I've got a place of my own. It's not much, but I'd love it if you could pop round.'

Dawn looked genuinely pleased. 'I'd love to. So you moved out of Hazel's place. What about your husband?'

Fiona flexed a wrist backwards. 'History. He'll never find me. I've been back and taken all the stuff I need.'

'Good for you. I'm so pleased.' Dawn reached for her handbag and produced an address book.

'I feel so excited.' Fiona said, then dictated her new address and mobile number. 'You'll call me soon?'

Dawn closed the book. 'Will do.'

Fiona ran the Dyson backwards and forwards over the same small, tired square of carpet. After a while she turned it off and looked around the bedsit. There was nothing left to clean. Deep inside her something began to stir. It felt like despair. I need something to do, she thought as the hazy image of Alexia appeared in her head. She looked at the clock. Quarter to nine. Would many girls be out on Minshull Street yet? Probably not. Her eyes snagged on the suitcase. The bottle of gin was like a beacon inside, emitting a signal she could no longer resist.

'Just a couple – God knows I'll need it where I'm going,' she said quietly to herself, grateful now the decision had been made.

The bottle chinked against the rim of the glass and gin glugged inside. She allowed the level to rise the width of another finger before righting the bottle. The tiny fridge was full, the bottle of tonic nicely chilled. She filled the glass to the top, then took a series of small sips, soon swallowing as much as if she'd given in and gulped it straight down.

Almost immediately the alcohol caused a lifting sensation in her head and without realising it, she let out a satisfied sigh. Now, what to wear? Nothing remotely dressy, that was for sure. She laid out a baggy top and plain trousers then, after sipping the glass dry, set off for the shower room on the first floor.

The train pulled in to Piccadilly and she walked slowly through the station, mentally running through what she'd say. Out on the concourse she looked down the slope towards the road that led into the city centre. The Malmaison Hotel dominated her view, yet now she knew that just a few streets behind a different world existed in the shadows. She broke off from the flow of people marching up to the bright lights of Piccadilly Gardens, headed down a dark side street and emerged into a nearly empty parking lot.

She heard the hoot of a tram as it emerged from the tunnels beneath Piccadilly station. The noise had a desolate note that echoed clearly through the night air. Seconds later the tram nosed into view, trundling round the bend in the hard metal tracks, wheels whining and squeaking in protest. Emotionless faces looked at her from within the bright carriages and then it was gone.

Making her way across the parking lot, she scanned the dark areas behind the trees lining Minshull Street on the other side, and soon caught sight of a lone female figure.

Unsure suddenly of what to say, she walked straight past the woman and found herself being dragged towards Portland Street. She emerged on to the busy road and looked around. A garish bar was on her immediate right and she went in.

The double gin disappeared in no time. She looked in her purse. She didn't have the cash to afford city centre prices, not after spending so much on things for her room. As she swung her knees round to climb off the bar stool, she nearly bumped a man who had appeared at her side, a fifty-pound note in his hand. He was late forties, thinning hair, but nice eyes.

'Sorry,' she said.

'Time for another?' he asked, nodding at her empty glass.

Fiona's mouth opened and shut. She hadn't been bought a drink by anyone other than her husband in years.

'Don't look so surprised.' He tapped the menu card on the counter – until then she hadn't been aware of it. *Thursday night – Singles night! Bottles of bubbly half price!*

His smile revealed a row of white teeth, one canine slightly chipped.

'Sorry.' Fiona shook her head. 'You caught me by surprise.' She felt her hand going up to her face. The cut over her eyebrow was becoming less and less apparent, but it still made her feel uncomfortable.

'Are you waiting for someone else? I mean, I hope I'm not ...'

'No.' she shook her head again. 'I just popped in. I'm on my way somewhere else.'

'Anywhere interesting? I'm only here on business and I haven't a clue where to go.' He lifted a hand to his chin, allowing it to linger, the lack of wedding ring obvious.

'Er, actually, I'm just delivering a message. I shouldn't be long.'

He blinked, trying to work out what she meant.

'If the person's not there, I should be back in five minutes,' Fiona explained, trying not to look at the money in his hand. Thinking of how many drinks it would buy.

'So, maybe see you here in a short while?'

'Yes, hopefully.'

'I'm Martin, by the way. Martin Mercer.' He extended a hand.

'Fiona,' she answered, shaking it and climbing down simultaneously.

Minshull Street stretched off to her side like a dimly lit tunnel. In its murky depths she could see silhouettes of girls caught in the headlights of a slowly approaching car. Before apprehension could take hold, she strode purposefully forwards.

The first girl she got to was dressed in a surprisingly conservative way. Her skirt was a little too short, but the shoes weren't ludicrously high heeled and the jacket looked practical. She had heard Fiona's approaching footsteps and was keeping one eye on her and one eye on the road in front.

As Fiona slowed to a halt, the girl turned to look at her properly. Fiona guessed she was in her late twenties. 'Hello.'

She nodded back.

'I wonder if you could help me. I'm looking for a girl. I've heard she's often around here.'

The woman raised her eyebrows, so Fiona pressed on. 'She uses the name Alexia, but I'm not sure if it's her real one.'

'How come you're looking for someone and you don't even know their name?'

Her voice had a pleasant Scottish brogue and visions of unspoilt glens sprang up in Fiona's mind. How had she gone from there to here? 'Well...' Fiona dried up. The question cut straight through her story of Alexia being a friend's daughter. 'It's a strange story.'

'I bet,' the girl replied looking away. 'Never heard of her.'

Another car was slowly approaching and she stepped nearer the kerb, one hand on her hip. Fiona moved back against the tree trunk until the car had passed. When it had, the girl didn't turn back and Fiona guessed the opportunity for questions was over.

The next girl was older and slightly overweight. She also wore a sensible jacket but it was almost fully unzipped. A white lycra top bulged with flesh underneath. This time Fiona chose a more direct approach. 'Hello, I'm looking for Alexia. Have you seen her around?'

She turned, jaw moving and lips apart as she worked on a piece of chewing gum. Her open-mouthed expression lent her a vacant air. 'You what?'

'I'm looking for a girl called Alexia. Have you seen her?'

The girl scratched at her neck. 'Reddish-brown hair? This tall?' She held a hand up to the level of her ears.

Fiona nodded.

'Not for a bit. Who are you?'

'A friend. Her mum and me are best mates.'

The girl's voice hardened. 'Maybe she doesn't want to see her mum. Not after she sided with the dad over what he did to her.'

Despite the implications of the comment, Fiona felt a surge of excitement. This girl was more than just a casual acquaintance. 'She's sorry. And he's gone now. Her mum just wants her back. Listen, can we go for a coffee and talk?'

Another car was coming. The girl looked at it, then back at Fiona. 'If you're paying. It'll be thirty quid.'

Fiona's hopeful smile gave out. 'I'm sorry. I haven't got that kind—'

The girl cut her off. 'Prime time, love. I can't afford to be sitting in cafés right now.' She stepped towards the kerb and the car slowed to a stop.

Fiona turned away, feeling as awkward as if she was watching another person going to the toilet. She started towards the other side of the road.

The girl opened the passenger door. 'Try Crimson,' she called. 'She might be hanging around there, pocketing the free rubbers.' She got in and the car pulled away.

Crimson? What was that? Fiona started back towards the first girl, but she'd obviously heard the exchange. 'Second on your right, back that way.' She pointed behind Fiona towards the area of Canal Street.

'Thanks,' Fiona replied, turning round.

The side street was like a narrow alleyway, barely wide enough for a car and she hesitated before setting off down it. Black forms crouched menacingly in the doorways and Fiona couldn't be sure they weren't all full bin liners. With her first step, her heels caught uncomfortably on the cobbles. Up ahead people mingled in a pool of soft red light. They were going in and coming out of a doorway. She looked back towards the normality of Portland Street, bathed in brilliant light and she thought about the man in the bar and his bulging wallet.

Chapter 18

Jon was hunched over his pint, enjoying Beth Orton's tremulous vocals when he heard Rick's voice behind him. He looked round, relieved to see that he was dressed casually in a striped shirt that hung outside his trousers.

'Yeah, I'm all right, mate,' Jon replied. 'What are you having?'

'Gin and Coke. Cheers.'

As Rick took the bar stool next to him, a wave of aftershave washed over Jon. 'So, you all set?'

'Ready as I'll ever be.' Jon picked up his pint and took a sip.

They went over the day's progress, or lack of it. Still no one had come forward to report a missing female who matched the third victim's description. Missing reports from all over the country had been checked for matches on fingerprints, DNA and dental records, but with no joy.

All the information about Gordon Dean and the tattoo artist from Affleck's Palace had been entered into HOLMES and a new index on 'Body Art/Piercings' opened. Despite Rick's optimism, it failed to make any cross-connections with Angela Rowlands or Carol Miller.

They saw off their drinks, then headed for Crimson. Down the narrow side street they saw a number of people disappearing into the red glow. Jon thought of moths being drawn into a flame.

A group of three lads – late teens or early twenties – were gathered at the doors. They were wearing jeans, trainers and baseball caps.

'No chance,' Rick said quietly as they got closer.

Sure enough, the bouncers were letting other people in, but not those three.

'Fucking full of poofters, anyway!' one snarled, realising the type of venue they'd stumbled across. They backed out of the bouncers' punching range and began hurling abuse.

Jon automatically increased his pace, keen to get there before things escalated.

Rick put a hand on his arm. 'Let the bouncers sort it.'

One stepped out into the side street and the group shied backwards. They were all mouth. After spitting towards the door and making a last few gestures, the group of three walked straight towards Jon and Rick.

The first held up a hand, face red with excitement. 'I wouldn't bother. It's full of shirt-lifters.'

One of his mates cut in. 'Sharpy, leave it. They're probably a pair of bum bandits, too.'

The lad looked at Rick, his expression rapidly turning ugly. 'You fucking are, aren't you?'

In the periphery of his vision, Jon saw the lad's hand curl into a fist and shoot towards Rick's face in a vicious uppercut.

Jon swung his forearm out in a short chopping movement, knocking the punch away before it even got to chest height. The movement left his hand close to the lad's throat. Before either of his mates could react, Jon grabbed his windpipe, digging his fingers into the ridged cartilage. Then, locking his elbow, he propelled the lad across the alley, putting distance between him and his mates before slamming him into the wall. A jerk of his arm sent him stumbling away, coughing and gasping simultaneously.

He spun round and faced the other two. Air was pumping in and out of his lungs, the oxygen making him feel light-headed. He stepped forwards, waves of energy radiating through him, every muscle in his body singing. And in that instant he wanted – more than anything in the world – one of them to go for him. Knees slightly flexed, he stared at them, picturing the havoc he could wreak on their faces. 'Who's next, then?'

They looked at him uncertainly, neither prepared to make a move. Things hung in the balance as, off to the side, their friend started vomiting down the wall.

'Listen, mate, no bother, hey?' one said quietly.

Jon said nothing.

The other took a step back. 'Let's go.'

His fists still clenched at his sides, Jon watched as they cautiously helped their friend upright and guided him away. With their retreat the adrenalin drained away and he suddenly felt dizzy. He leaned a hand against the wall.

'Why did you do that?' Rick was staring at him, shocked.

'He was swinging for you. Didn't you see?'

'The one you grabbed by the throat?'

Jon held up a thumb and finger slightly apart. 'You were this close to getting chinned. That would have been you flat on your back – the last place you want to be in a fight.'

Rick shook his head. 'Shit. I didn't see a thing.'

Jon dropped his hand and sucked in a deep breath.

'You all right?' Rick asked hesitantly.

He held his hand up again. 'Yeah, just give me a second.' He concentrated on taking regular, slow breaths and after a few seconds his heart rate levelled out.

By now the trio had reached the end of the alleyway. The two who could speak turned and shouted a quick chorus of 'Does he take it up the arse?' before running away.

Shaking his head, Jon pushed himself upright. 'Let's get a beer.'

When they reached the door, the bouncers waved them straight in with a smile, and one of them said, 'Good to see a bit of bashing back, mate.'

Fucking great, thought Jon. They think I'm gay, too.

The upstairs area was dominated by the bar spanning the back wall. The lighting was subdued, small spotlights directed on the swathes of red velvet that hung down the bare brick walls. The same material was draped round marble pedestals on which stood full-length nude male statues. Apart from the figleaves over their groins, they were styled like Michelangelo's *David*. Cascaded over the material at the base of each pedestal were piles of fresh oranges, lemons, apples, tomatoes, melons, grapes and peppers.

'Is that all real?' Jon said, trying to make it out in the half-light as he headed for the bar.

'Absolutely,' Rick replied. 'It's based on this amazing bar in Majorca apparently. The display gets changed every night. I think it helps that Miss Tonguelash's brother runs one of the biggest grocers at Smithfield market.'

As Jon watched, a barman plucked a few lemons from the top of a pile and threw them to a colleague preparing cocktails behind the bar. The place was about half full, with many people heading down a staircase to the floor below.

'What are you drinking?' Rick asked.

'Pint of strong lager,' Jon replied.

They found a space at the end of the bar next to more glass bowls of the same safe sex packs he'd picked up in Taurus. Jon leaned against the counter and looked around. Immediately he spotted a group of transvestites at a nearby table. Seeing their big shoulders, square faces and bad wigs, he remembered an end-of-season party at his previous rugby club where drag was the obligatory costume. The rest of the clientele looked fairly ordinary, though dominated by men. Rick was talking to the barman and Jon had to concentrate to make out their words over the music floating up from downstairs.

'That's great. Thanks for your help.' Rick slid a pint across to Jon.

'What did he say?' Jon asked, ducking his head and taking a massive gulp.

'He remembers Dean. A bit of a regular. Says he often saw him in here chatting to various people.'

Jon knew more was to come. 'What about the night in question?'

'Usual thing, floating around up here, went downstairs for a bit.' Rick smiled. 'But thinks he saw him leaving at the end of the night with a working girl who sometimes pops in to grab free condoms off the bar.'

'Any description?'

'Shoulder-length reddish hair, five feet eight, slim build.' Rick held up his drink and they clinked glasses. 'I reckon if we ask about in here, we could find out more.'

Jon looked around. 'I'll let you do the honours.'

Rick gave a little snort. 'Coward.' He walked over to the

nearest table, the photo in his hand. From the corner of his eye, Jon saw heads shaking.

Five minutes later Rick returned. 'Nothing. You know what this means?'

Jon finished his drink. 'Time to go downstairs.'

There was a small counter at the bottom of the steps. After flashing their warrant cards to the woman behind it, they showed her the photo of Gordon Dean, but she couldn't remember seeing him.

Rick peered through the windows in the double doors before them. 'Not too busy yet.'

Inside was a lot darker. A glitter ball hung over the dance floor and several couples were milling around to 'Dancing Queen'. In the DJ box was a tall figure with a hairdo like Marge Simpson's. She was wearing a satin dress covered in what looked to Jon like a collection of luminous ping-pong balls. As he and Rick made their way round the edge of the dance floor the song came to an end. But rather than another starting up, a beam of light swung across the room and settled on Jon.

Shielding his eyes, he squinted at the DJ box, the figure now barely visible behind the spotlight's glare. 'Fuck me, this one's new in town.' The voice was high, the words drawled. 'Look at the size of him, girls. He can slip up here and butcher my snatch any time.'

As laughs of disbelief at the joke's poor taste erupted all around, the spotlight was cut and the next song kicked in. Despite his embarrassment, Jon recognised the trumpets building in strength before the drumroll started. 'Lola's Theme'. Whoops of delight came from the dancefloor and a group of transvestites started sashaying around singing, 'I'm a different person!'

When he reached the bar, Rick grinned at him and said, 'That was Miss Tonguelash.'

Jon could feel his face was still burning. 'I see how she gets her name.' He looked around uneasily and saw Fiona Wilson staring at him. A slimy-looking creep was standing next to her. She lurched over, her large gin glowing faintly under the ultraviolet light mounted behind the bar.

'Fiona.' Jon nodded. 'Enjoying yourself?'

She raised a forefinger and tapped him on the chest. 'You never checked that room. I spoke to the receptionist. She told me.'

Jon noticed that Rick was looking totally bemused. 'Rick, this is Fiona. She works with my girlfriend. Fiona, Rick, my partner.'

Her eyes slid unsteadily towards Rick. 'You're his what?'

'We're partners,' Rick replied with a grin.

She looked lost.

'In the police,' Jon added.

She started giggling. 'For a moment there I thought you meant—'

'Yeah, I know,' Jon interrupted.

The slimy creep appeared behind her. Jon instantly saw that he was trying to appear friendly and inquisitive but couldn't hide the look of concern that his shag was escaping him.

'Martin Mercer,' he said, extending a hand towards Jon.

'Jon Spicer.' Briefly, they shook.

'Fiona's certainly got an interesting taste in night venues. One minute we're in a place on the main road, next she's dragged me in here!'

Jon looked away from his shining teeth. 'So, Fiona, what are you up to?'

'Trying to find out what happened to that girl. You know, the one you couldn't give a shit about.' She was tilting towards aggression again.

Taking her elbow, he guided her towards the corner of the room, out of earshot of the creep. 'Fiona, Alice mentioned you've been making enquiries. You need to be careful.'

Fiona curled her lips in distaste. 'Someone's got to try and find out if she's OK. No one else is.' She took a large gulp of her drink.

'What did the woman at Cheshire Consorts say?'

'She had an Alexia come and try to get a job with her. But she thought she was on drugs. Sent her packing.'

'And now you're trawling round the red-light district, searching for her? Fuck, Fiona, it's not safe. Specially at the moment.'

Fiona leaned against the wall and rolled the back of her head against it. 'Not just trawling. I was told she comes in here sometimes. But no one's seen her since the night I heard someone being killed.' Abruptly, she tipped the last of her drink into her mouth, spilling an ice cube down her front. 'Bollocks,' she said, leaning forwards and shaking her top so it fell to the floor.

Jon glanced at the creep. He hadn't moved an inch, unwilling to walk away from his claim. 'Who's the bloke?'

Fiona's head lolled in his direction. 'An old acquaintance.'

'Is that right?' Jon didn't believe her.

'See you around, Mr Spicer.' She tottered away.

The salesman whispered something to her, and they moved off towards the stairs. As they went past, Jon pointed at his own eyes then at the man's face. I've clocked you, the gesture said. Next instant, they were gone.

'She's heading for the mother of all hangovers,' said Rick.

'I hope that's all she's heading for.'

'So what was she on about?'

'She's the one who thought she heard a prostitute being strangled in the next room at that motel. She thinks the girl worked for an escort agency and now she's trying to track her down.'

'Sounds dodgy.'

'Exactly,' Jon replied. He looked around. 'I need a piss.'

The red bulbs lighting the toilets made the narrow room disorientating. Jon peered around in the half-light for any urinals, but saw only safe-sex posters lining the walls. He realised there were only cubicles. He took an end one and started emptying his bladder. Halfway through he noticed a waist-high hole in the partition wall between his cubicle and the next. At first he thought it was where the toilet roll holder had been ripped off. But the hole was properly drilled and, besides, the toilet-roll dispenser was mounted on the back wall.

He re-zipped his fly and bent down for a closer look. He could see straight through into the next cubicle, where an identical hole had been cut in the next partition wall. He realised he was looking through a series of holes that ran the entire length of the toilets. The music got louder suddenly as someone entered the toilets. Jon quickly straightened up.

Back in the main bar he was shocked to see Rick sitting at the bar talking to Miss Tonguelash herself. Resisting the urge to flee up the stairs, he walked over and picked up his pint.

'Jon, this is Miss Tonguelash.'

She swivelled round, one leg crossed over the other, a slit running up to mid-thigh. 'Call me Andrea.' Absurdly long eye-lashes fluttered and the back of a hand was proffered, fingers pointing down.

Not prepared to kiss it, Jon grasped it lightly. 'Hello.'

Looking mildly disappointed, she said, 'You've just been holding your penis. I do hope you used the sink afterwards.'

Jon hadn't. 'Of course.' He put his hand in his pocket.

Rick looked amused. 'I was asking Andrea about the night we're interested in.'

'Mmmmm,' she said, sipping her cocktail through a long straw, talon-like nails giving her fingers a more feminine taper. 'He was larking around down here with some little hussy on his arm.'

'A slim girl with brown hair?' Jon asked.

Miss Tonguelash nodded at the people on the dance floor. 'What colour hair do you think they all have?'

Jon looked. Banks of lights flickered on and off, bathing the dancers in a succession of colours. 'OK, I take your point. But you'd say this girl had darkish hair?'

'Girl? I used the word "hussy".'

'OK, hussy, then. But why call her that?'

'I imagine she'd only come in her to help herself to free condoms before her next trick. Looks like this Mr Dean was it.'

'You mean she was a prostitute?'

'Absolutely, darling.'

'And you don't mind prostitutes roaming around in your club?'

'Not if they're in here to pick up condoms. I'm all for safe sex, whatever form it may take. Aren't you, Mr Spicer? In favour of safe sex?' She brushed her lips over the end of her straw and fluttered her eyelashes at him.

Jon gave a businesslike smile. 'Of course. And did they leave together?'

'I can't say for sure, but it seemed pretty likely.'

He looked at Rick. 'Is that all we need?'

Rick nodded. 'Thanks for your help, Andrea.'

'Not at all,' she answered, eyes still on Jon as they turned to the door. 'Oh, one more thing.'

They stopped and turned back.

'You two make a lovely couple.'

Out on the street Jon breathed a sigh of relief. 'Christ, that was embarrassing.'

Rick chuckled. 'I thought you handled her very well.'

'Her or him?'

'Her when she's working.'

'But him at other times?'

'I don't know. Probably.'

Jon shook his head. 'And another thing. The partition walls in the toilets all had these holes cut in them.'

'Glory holes. Surely you've heard of them?'

Jon rolled his eyes. 'Yeah, it's just I've never imagined them to be fitted as standard. What a place.'

'But worth going. Now we know he didn't leave alone.'

'Yup.' Jon took the credit-card company's report out of his pocket. 'From here, he headed to the twenty-four-hour garage up near the Apollo. Two transactions. Cashpoint for £150 and the petrol station itself for £9.99.'

'OK, let's head there.'

They walked up to Minshull Street, Rick looking with surprise at the number of women hanging around. 'Jesus, do Vice realise it's got this busy along here again?'

'I'm sure. But until enough people start complaining, what's the point?'

'Bring on licensed brothels,' Rick said, dismissing a hopeful girl with a wave of his hand. 'Save everyone a load of hassle.'

They hailed a cab on Whitworth Street and pulled up on the petrol station forecourt a few minutes later. Jon tried the door, but it was locked. 'Intercom service after ten,' he said, reading the notice. 'I hate this.'

They held their identity cards up at the cabin window. The bald man inside reached to his left and a small speaker crackled. 'Can I help you gents?'

'Could you let us in? We'll talk inside,' Jon answered.

The man stepped round the counter, crossed the deserted shop and opened the door.

'Cheers,' Jon said, locking it behind him. 'Were you on duty last Thursday night?'

'Yup, I'm on duty every night but Sundays and Mondays. Those nights are my weekend.'

Rick showed him the photo of Gordon Dean while Jon got out the credit-card record. 'We believe this man called in here at 3:08 a.m. and purchased something to the value of £9.99,' Rick said.

The man smiled. 'Yeah, I sold out of three-packs that night.'

'Three-packs?'

'Condoms. Didn't you see the report in the *Manchester Evening News*?' He said proudly, 'Per head of the population, Manchester has more massage parlours than any other city in Britain. And we sell more condoms than any other petrol station in the country. What with the Hurlington over there and all the saunas and working girls around Piccadilly station ...'

'So what costs £9.99?' Jon asked.

The man pointed behind him to a twelve-pack on the shelf. 'There you go. I'd sold out of them by the end of that night, too.'

'Do you remember this man? He'd had his hair cut short and his moustache shaved off.'

He leaned over the photo. 'No, 'fraid not.'

Jon looked at the security monitor. 'Is that CCTV on all the time?'

'Yes. You want the tape from that night?'

'If you don't mind,' Jon replied, impressed by the man's willingness to help.

'There's a VCR in the back office. Can you watch it in there?'

'Sure,' said Jon. He paused at the coffee machine. 'Can I get you a drink?'

'I bring my own flask in, cheers.'

'Don't blame you,' replied Jon, getting a couple for him and Rick.

The tape was dated and timed, allowing them to picture-search through until 3:05 a.m. 'Here we go,' said Jon, sitting back and stirring his coffee.

The camera was set up high, looking down on to the fore-court below. Within seconds the grainy black-and-white footage revealed a Passat pulling up next to the cashpoint built into the wall by the cabin window. Gordon Dean, hair cut short and spiky and wearing a black shirt, got out first.

Then the door on the far side of the car opened. Jon and Rick leaned forward. A woman with dark shoulder-length hair got out. From the way she walked, Jon could tell she was wearing high heels before she came round the back of the car. Now she was fully in the camera's gaze, Jon took in her body. Quite tall, slim hips and a hard, tight arse. His eyes rose to her breasts as she turned. They were high and jutting, the type only pos-sible with the help of surgery or a push-up bra. To his dismay, Jon felt sexual interest stirring in him. The thought of fast and dirty sex in an anonymous hotel. He suppressed the thought by saying, 'Gordon Dean's happily driving round town with a load of champagne in him.'

Rick nodded, eyes on the screen as the woman caught Dean up at the cashpoint machine. She reached out a hand and cupped his buttocks. The entire time he was withdrawing money her face was out of sight, nuzzling at his neck.

Next, she said something into his ear and disappeared back inside the car. He went to the cabin window, handed over his card and seconds later it was returned with a box of condoms.

The tape ran on and they watched as the car moved off, started to indicate right then disappeared out of the picture.

'Is it the girl in the morgue? I reckon it could be.' Rick com-mented.

'Time of death's totally wrong,' Jon answered. 'Victim number three died early to late evening, according to the pathologist.'

'There's always a margin for error. Especially when the body's been exposed to the coolness of the night air.'

Jon rubbed the back of his neck. 'OK, it's a possibility.'

Rick looked at the screen. 'I get it. The £150 from the cash-point is her charge for sex. Then she taps him for the condoms, too.'

'But I thought she snaffled all the condoms she needed from Crimson?'

Rick shrugged in reply.

As they got up, Jon snapped his fingers. 'Shit! We forgot the tape from the Novotel. That woman on reception was keeping it for us.'

'I'll bob in first thing tomorrow morning. Shall we call it a day?'

Jon looked at his watch and saw how late it was. 'Good idea.'

Rick wrote a receipt for the garage's tape and they let them-selves out. The door clicked shut behind them and Rick buttoned his jacket up. 'I'll walk from here, I'm only five minutes away. The cab rank by Piccadilly station is probably your nearest.'

Jon glanced at the traffic. 'No, you're all right. There should be plenty of cabs passing this way. Nice work tonight, mate. I'll see you tomorrow.'

As they shook hands Rick said, 'Cheers for that outside Crimson by the way.'

Jon met his eyes. 'My pleasure.'

Rick let go of his hand and laughed. 'Yeah, I got the impres-sion it was.'

As he wandered off Jon looked down, embarrassed that Rick had witnessed him in the alley spoiling for a fight. He found it hard enough to accept that, rather than fear or anxiety, the pros-pect of violence gave him a jolt of excitement. But he couldn't deny it was there, ready to erupt whenever anger flooded his veins.

He looked up the road, forcing his thoughts back to the in-vestigation. Gordon Dean had signalled to turn right when he left the forecourt. The centre of town and the Novotel were to his left. He stared in the other direction, towards the roundabout and the start of the A57, leading towards the Platinum Inn and Belle Vue.

Even if Gordon Dean had driven the hooker from the CCTV

footage straight to the motel and Fiona Wilson heard her being murdered, time of death was all wrong for her to have been the third victim. But as he shifted from foot to foot, uneasiness was gathering at the back of his mind like the beginnings of a headache.

Chapter 19

It was the angry throb bouncing back and forth between her temples that dragged Fiona from the depths of unconsciousness. She kept her eyes shut, trying to gauge if more sleep might be enough to make it go away. But then other parts of her mind started to function. She heard the sound of traffic passing in a continual stream. The smell of stale sweat and alcohol filled the air. Her eyes were still shut but she could tell it wasn't dark. She tried to turn over onto her back, but her arms were restrained.

Her eyes snapped open, trying to focus. She couldn't see. Something was covering her face and she started to panic. As she tilted her head back the material slipped from her face. A bedside table, the surface bare except for a lamp and a small foil square, almost ripped in half.

She began to wriggle and realised her arms were only caught up in the sheet that had been covering her face. Behind her someone grunted in their sleep. Her eyes went back to the square of ripped foil. It was a condom wrapper. As she sat up and straightened her legs she could tell that she'd recently had sex. She was naked and a wave of nausea welled up. Looking over her shoulder she saw the salesman, his face pressed against the pillow and saliva glistening at the corner of his mouth. Meredith? Mercier? He was asleep next to her, a half-drunk bottle of champagne on his bedside table. Slowly she looked around. She was in a hotel room, her clothes lying in a pile on the floor next to the bed. Carefully she climbed out, scooped them up, let herself into the bathroom and locked the door.

She just got to the sink before violently retching. Two mouthfuls of acrid brown liquid came out and a sour, fruity smell filled her nostrils. She turned on the taps and as water started to wash the liquid away, strings of mucus-like saliva were revealed in it. She retched again.

Her brain felt like it was clenching in on itself, sending waves of pain right down into her molars. She grabbed a glass, filled it with water and started to sip. Her stomach heaved, but it stayed down. The self-loathing that trailed her heaviest drinking sessions, like a rusting old tanker being pulled by a tug-boat, loomed over her. But this time it was compounded by shame. She wanted to curl up and cry, but not here. Anywhere but here.

She climbed into her clothes, careful to keep her head up to minimise the pounding in her temples. A wash bag was on the shelf above the sink. Guiltily, she lifted out his toothpaste and squirted some onto her finger. She smeared it over her teeth and worked it around her mouth. Her tongue soon felt like it was burning and she thought that the pain served her right.

Looking at herself in the mirror, she adjusted her hair and used a tissue to wipe off the smears of mascara. The bathroom door clicked loudly as she opened it. Round the corner, in the main part of the room, she heard movement and held her breath.

'Jesus, what a night,' he groaned.

Fiona moved quickly to the door and let herself out. She eventually found a lift, walked through reception and out on to the street. Wincing in the bright light of day, she looked to her left and right. She was on Portland Street, Piccadilly Gardens and the bus terminal almost opposite. A digital clock read 8:43 a.m., cars filled the road and people hurried by, freshly showered and ready for work. Fiona folded her arms across her stomach and set off towards the bus station, eyes fixed on the pavement in front.

After thirty metres she realised the bar where she first met him was on her right. The doors were shut and a couple of cleaners were clearing the tables of glasses, many half finished. Her stomach flipped over.

The station was filled by a disorderly procession of buses, some trying to pull in and drop off passengers while empty ones queued to pull out. Engines revved, horns blared and exhaust fumes filled the air. Fiona felt like she could die at any moment.

Miserably she approached a noticeboard, trying to work out how to get back to her bedsit.

The bus dropped her off at the top of her road half an hour later. Breathing a sigh of relief, she slid the key into the front door and almost walked straight past the small pile of post with her name on.

Dreading they were bills, she opened her room, threw the envelopes on the bed and headed straight upstairs for a shower. Quarter of an hour later she sat down, a dressing gown on and a towel wrapped round her head. She selected the handwritten envelope first. A card from everyone at the salon, wishing her the best in her new home. Looking at their signatures, a tear sprang up in her eye and she forgot her headache for a moment. But the next letters brought it back with a vengeance. Payment forms for electricity, gas and water. Recommendation to pay by Direct Debit, £5 off if she did. Fiona looked at her purse – she'd barely had enough money for the bus fare home.

Woodenly she got to her feet and opened the cupboard above the sink. There was a couple of inches left inside the bottle of gin. She tipped it into a glass and sat down, tears springing to her eyes as she thought about the last few years of her marriage.

As Jeff's intimidation worsened, she'd started taking the odd nip of gin in the evenings when he was at the pub. Had fear or loneliness prompted it? Take your pick, she thought, raising a silent toast.

The nips became larger and more frequent. Finding the money for new bottles became ever more difficult. She'd got Melvyn to pay her partly in cash, hiding her supplies under the sink or inside the big casserole dish. Places he'd never look.

She hadn't dared consider how much she was growing to need it. Empties were spirited out of the house in her handbag, dropped in shop bins or even the hedge if the street was quiet.

Fiona looked at her glass and a wave of self-pity washed over her. God knows, if anyone deserves a drink it's me. It doesn't mean I have a problem, she thought, gulping the gin down.

Chapter 20

Once again Rick was in before him and Jon felt a slight pang of irritation. 'Up with the chirp of the sparrow again.'

'Where's that expression from?'

Jon thought for a moment. 'My grandpa used to come out with it. Must be an Irish one.'

'Yeah, you mentioned your family was originally from Galway.'

'A little fishing village called Roundstone. Ever visited the west coast of Ireland?'

Rick shook his head.

'You should do. Catch it right and it's the most beautiful place on earth.'

'So have your family always been in the job?'

Jon laughed. 'No, I'm the first. My great-great-granddad moved over here with his two brothers. They all worked as navvies on the Manchester Ship Canal. My great-granddad did, too, only he supplemented his income in another way.'

'Oh, yeah? Doing what?'

Jon couldn't keep the pride from his voice. 'He was a champion bare-knuckle fighter. Made enough from it to get the family out of their slum in Little Ireland.'

Rick grinned. 'Well, that explains a few things.'

Jon felt his face flush as he realised Rick was referring to the confrontation in the alley the previous night. 'Bare-knuckle fighting was a big thing back then. He was a real celebrity. Anyway, never mind that. What have you got there?'

'The tape from the Novotel. The receptionist had it ready in an envelope, bless her.'

'Have you been through it yet?'

'I wasn't in that bloody early.' He stood up. 'Shall we?'

They went through to the side room that housed the VCR unit. Jon immediately opened a window, then picked up an ashtray full of cigarette butts and placed them outside on the windowsill. Rick slid the tape in, turned the telly on and picked up the remote. The tape was time-lapse, comprising of a series of images taken at two-second intervals. The result was infuriatingly disjointed footage of the hotel foyer.

'God, shall I get the paracetamol now?' Jon sighed.

'From the hotel's records, he checked in at two seventeen p.m.,' said Rick, turning the tape on to picture search, making the images seem even more random. After ten minutes of the machine whirring, he hit Play again. 'There he is, still with his moustache.'

They watched Gordon Dean check in, then vanish into a lift carrying one large bag and a protective cover for suits.

Jon went to his notebook. 'Right, he was the last customer at that hairdresser's in Affleck's Palace at about six p.m., and he was eating in Don Antonio's by around seven.'

Rick hit the picture search again, stopping it at 6:15. A few minutes later Gordon Dean appeared at the top of the picture, crossing the corner of the foyer on his way to the lift. His hair was short, his moustache shaved off.

'I'm a different person now,' Rick sang under his breath.

Thirty-five minutes later he reappeared, now in his black shirt.

'OK, so far so good,' said Jon, consulting his notes. 'Now, he's out around town for the next few hours. We know he used his card at the petrol station at Ardwick Green at three oh eight a.m. Next activity is the cashpoint on Miller Street where he maxed out his card at six forty-three. After that he paid for the car park at Piccadilly station at seven oh five. That's another thing that strikes me as odd.'

'What?' Rick pressed Pause.

'That cashpoint is way out of the route you'd take driving from the Novotel to Piccadilly station. What's wrong with the Barclays just up on Portland Street or the ones in the station itself?'

Rick was looking blank.

'Come on, I'll show you.'

They walked into the main room and crossed to the street map of Manchester pinned to the wall. 'Here. Miller Street. Why drive all the way to there?'

'I see what you mean.'

Jon held up a finger. 'Unless you're avoiding city-centre cashpoints because you don't want to be seen.' He waved his finger in a circle over his head. 'Manchester has the most comprehensive network of cameras in any British city. Almost every cashpoint is covered by CCTV. But I'm almost certain that one out on Miller Street isn't.'

'Why the sudden subterfuge?'

'I don't know.'

Rick turned the remote over in his hand. 'How about this? He whisks her off to a rented property somewhere, snuffs her out and removes her skin. Then he dumps her on the grass in Belle Vue. But something goes wrong, making him panic. So he empties his bank account and flees town.'

'Or how about this? He picks up the condoms at the petrol station, and they head back to the Novotel and get down to business. An hour later, she's given him such an incredible time, he thinks, Fuck it all, let's get out a wedge of cash, jump on the train and go off somewhere to enjoy ourselves for a few days. Somewhere remote, no cashpoints anywhere near.'

Rick rocked his head from side to side, weighing the argument up. 'Doesn't explain his shady behaviour. I'd say seven to one my theory's correct.'

'Bollocks,' Jon replied. 'That tenner's mine.'

Rick laughed. 'OK, we need to scan the Novotel tape for when he got in. Some time between leaving that petrol station and visiting the Miller Street cashpoint.'

'That's almost four hours,' Jon said, walking away. 'I'll get the coffees and paracetamol now.'

They'd got to 6:04 a.m. on the videotape when it clicked to a halt. They stared at the blank screen for an instant before looking at each other.

'Shit,' they announced simultaneously.

Rick ejected the tape and looked at the label. 'It runs from six in the morning to the same time next day.'

'So we need the next one. That's bloody typical.'

Rick pointed to the telephone number on the label. 'No worries, I'll phone her.' He got out his mobile and keyed in the number. 'Hello. Can I speak to Kristina, please?' He waited for a moment. 'Hi, Kristina, it's DI Rick Saville. I picked up the security tape this morning … Great … Listen, we need the one from the next day, too. You've got it there still? … Lovely. We'll be there shortly.'

It was strange to walk into a scene they'd been observing as a recording for the past four hours. Kristina was there, the usual smile on her face.

'Hi, there,' said Rick. 'Thanks so much.'

'That is OK,' she answered, blushing slightly. 'Are you, how did you say, seizing it?'

Jon and Rick glanced at each other.

'Tell you what,' said Jon. 'Why don't we just whiz through it in your back office first? We're only interested in the first hour.'

'Oh, yes, of course. Please.' She lifted the counter flap and showed them through. After loading the cassette, she pressed Play and stood aside. Static swarmed the screen, before stuttering frames began cutting in. Then the picture took hold properly. The foyer was busy. Too busy for six in the morning.

Jon pointed to the time frame. 'Six fifty-eight a.m. Where's the first hour?'

Kristina looked crestfallen. 'The night porter must have forgotten to change the tapes over. I'm very sorry.'

Outside the hotel he kicked the base of the wall. 'Fucking typical.'

'So that's it, then. Until something else happens, the trail goes cold.' Rick said angrily.

'There's always the CCTV footage from Piccadilly station,' Jon said reluctantly. 'If we pick them up there we may even be able to work out which train they caught.'

'Of course!' Rick replied.

'Don't look so pleased. My other half got her bag snatched in the station last summer. I've seen the number of monitors in the CCTV control room. Since they redid the station for the Commonwealth Games, you can't pick your nose in that place without it being on film.'

'Surely that's good?'

'Not when you're the mug who's going to be trawling through all the tapes. There must be twenty cameras in the main part of the station. More on each platform.'

Rick sighed. 'When are we interested in? The car was parked at seven oh five a.m., so let's say for the next hour.'

'Call it thirty-five monitors.'

'Thirty-five hours of footage. Surely it would be best to divide that out across anyone who's not on Outside Enquiries?'

'A job that dreary? I'll go another ten quid McCloughlin will give the lot to me – and that means you, too.'

Rick grimaced. 'No, I think I'll pass on that one. If we watch seven hours a day, that's five days in the video room.'

Jon groaned, thinking about the spartan furnishings and smell of old ashtrays. 'Have you got a video in your flat?'

'No, just DVD.'

'We've got one at home. We'll go through it all there.'

Rick nodded, 'So what now?'

Jon looked at his watch. 'We'd better check back in with McCloughlin. But I intend to make the most of the quiet spell.'

Chapter 21

Jon shouldered open the door of Cheadle Ironside's clubhouse and plonked his kitbag down in the bar. A scattering of other players were there, some gathered round a table as one flicked through a copy of the *Sport*, semi-naked girls pouting on every page.

'Hey, Jon! So you are playing – I thought you'd gibbed out.' This from a gnarled old man with bushy eyebrows.

'All right, Heardy. I got a break from work so I thought, Fuck it, it's Saturday, I'll go and sweat blood and tears with the boys.'

'You mean Alice has let you out for a few hours,' a young man with a shaved head called over, fingers curled round a bottle of Lucozade Sport. A chorus of knowing laughter broke out.

'Just wait till your missus gets up the duff, Westy,' Jon replied with a grin.

'I'll have to nip round and service her before that ever happens,' Heardy cut in, and the laughter turned on Westy.

The door to the changing rooms burst open and the captain, already in first-team strip, came in. 'Come on, you bunch of tossers. Kick-off's in forty minutes. Get changed.'

The changing rooms stank of Deep Heat. Jon shrugged his jumper off, loosened his club tie enough to slip it over his head with the knot still intact, then hooked it over a peg. He sat down, opened his kitbag and took his boots out.

The captain crouched in the middle of the room, a pile of rugby shirts at his feet. As he called out a number he threw the shirt at the appropriate player with an accompanying comment.

'Number three, Chico. We want those scrums solid as a rock today.

'Number six, Bamby. I want you leaping like a salmon in the line-outs.

'Number fourteen, Cookie. Have a run at your opposite man – he shat it last time.

'Number seven, Slicer.' A shirt hit Jon in the chest. 'The usual, please. Make them regret ever turning up here.'

Jon nodded, faintly amused that his nickname from when he played for Stockport had finally caught him up. The two players on the bench next to him were sniggering over a camera phone.

'Here, Jon, check this out. Ash's bird's had a tit job. Look at the pair on that.'

The mobile was thrust into his hand, the screen filled with a full-colour image of a young woman. She was smiling proudly at the camera, a mammoth pair of breasts straining beneath her crop-top.

Jon held the phone closer to his face, then looked over at Ash. 'She's really your girlfriend?'

He nodded, beaming, then cupped his hands in the air and wriggled them from side to side. 'B cup to a double D, just like that. The wonders of modern medicine.'

Jon took another look at the phone. 'What do they feel like?'

'Rock-hard mate. Don't even move when she's lying on her back as I'm giving her one. Marvellous, they are.'

A shirt hit him full in the face. 'Ash! Mind on the match, not your bird's plastic tits!'

Jon handed the phone back with a bemused shake of his head. Alice's breasts had ballooned during her pregnancy and, although he found the novelty of it amusing, he couldn't imagine her heaving them around on a permanent basis. To his relief, she had said exactly the same thing.

Half an hour later they trooped back in from the training pitch for the pre-match talk. Studs clattered on the concrete floor as they milled around, sheens of sweat covering their faces. Jon sat quietly in the corner. Breathing deeply with his eyes fixed on the floor, he enacted the first seconds of the match in his head. The need to immediately stamp his authority on his opposite man in order to shake his confidence and upset his desire to even play.

'Right,' the captain announced. 'Get your last-minute pisses out of the way, I want you back here in one minute.'

Jon rested his hands on his thighs and jiggled his knees up and down, thinking forward to the moment the referee's whistle would start the game.

'I want your minds on the match. First ten minutes, boys, we hit them like a fucking steam train. Are we letting this bunch of whining scouse bastards come to our back yard and turn us over?'

A few players growled, 'No.'

'I said: are we letting this bunch of whining Scouse bastards come to our back yard and turn us over?' the captain roared.

'No!' the team shouted back.

By now the captain was prowling up and down the middle of the narrow room, smearing Vaseline over his eyebrows. 'Get up! In a circle!'

Everyone stood, arms going around teammates' shoulders. The captain stood in the middle, rotating slowly. 'Look me in the eye, every one of you. Good, I can feel it, I can see it. You want this. First tackles: make them count. I want them knocked on their arses before they even think about getting a drive on. Right boys, let's get out there!'

As they marched towards the doors in single file, the coach, an ex-Royal Marine with no neck, stepped forward and yanked Jon to one side. Quietly, he said, 'Slicer, you missed the match at theirs, but the open-side flanker did all the damage. He's a dirty bastard, creeping offside, handling the ball in rucks, killing it every time he could. If he even shows a finger on our side of the ball, I want him taken care of. Understood?'

'OK, Senior,' Jon nodded.

The bar after the match was packed with people from both clubs, but the eyes of the Ironsides players were brighter. Standing around in small clusters, they went over the highlights of the match – the try-scoring moments, the big hits, the slick passing.

Jon stood at the end of the bar, a tubi-grip packed with ice covering his right hand. He took another gulp from his pint of orange juice and lemonade, his body still crying out for fluids after the demands of the match.

The captain stepped over to him and nodded. 'Great game today, Jon.'

'Cheers,' he replied, eyes shifting to the other side of the bar where a group from the opposition team were sitting.

The captain saw the direction of his gaze. 'I just had a word. He's a bit groggy, but otherwise fine. That was some punch you gave him.'

Jon shrugged. 'He was asking for it all afternoon.' Despite the casualness of his answer, he felt relieved. He always did what he needed to win a match, but after the final whistle he knew the opposition were ordinary people like him. They also had jobs and families to feed. And they couldn't do that if they were off work with concussion.

'How's the hand?' his captain asked.

'It'll be OK.'

'You ready for a beer?'

Jon glanced down at his near-empty glass. 'No, mate, I need to be going.'

The captain nodded in unspoken understanding. 'See you at training?'

'I'll try and make it. This case I'm on is a bastard, though.' He finished off his drink and slipped out of the side door.

Punch scrabbled to his feet as Jon stepped into the kitchen. Alice and his younger sister, Ellie, were sitting with heads bowed over a magazine. He swung his kitbag so it slid across the linoleum towards the washing machine, then reached out to his dog. Punch immediately sniffed his injured hand.

Jon was marvelling at the dog's ability to sense injuries when Alice said, 'Jesus Christ!'

'What?'

'Your hand. It's like a bloody balloon. What happened?'

Jon held it up, as if noticing it for the first time. 'Oh, someone stamped on it, I think.'

'Oh, yeah, I've heard that one before,' Ellie said with an impish grin. 'Sure someone's face didn't run into your fist?'

Jon shot her a look.

'Why you play that stupid game, I don't know,' Alice sighed. 'There's ice in the freezer compartment.'

Jon opened the fridge. 'Want a beer, little sis?'

'Oh, go on, then.'

'Alice? Anything to drink?'

'No, I'm fine, thanks.'

He took two cans off the top shelf, sprang the tabs a little awkwardly with his left hand and put one on the kitchen table. 'What rubbish are you two reading?' he asked, peering down at the glossy magazine spread out between them.

'It's an article called "Botox Babes",' Ellie replied without looking up.

The text was interspersed with photos of famous females snapped outside the premises of well-known cosmetic surgeons.

'Ha!' said Alice triumphantly. 'I knew she was looking too damn good.'

'You're right,' Ellie answered. 'What was that premiere she appeared at looking dog rough?'

Jon realised he was well and truly excluded from the conversation. He emptied the ice tray into the sink, scooped up a handful of cubes and placed them in a tea towel. Twisting it into a knot, he swung it hard on to the floor. There was a sharp crack and the ice shattered. Punch immediately started to sniff tentatively at the point of impact.

Jon sat down, then reached his left hand across to Alice's swollen stomach. 'How's the wee one?'

'Sleeping at the moment. But he was kicking like a bugger earlier on.'

Jon smiled and sat back.

A page was turned and, pointing at the magazine, Ellie said, 'Oh, I was thinking about going on this diet. It's worked for loads of celebrities.'

Jon cocked his head to look at her. 'You don't need to lose any weight.'

Ellie smiled. 'Aah, thanks.' Her attention went straight back to the page. 'It looks really simple. And you can still have the occasional treat.'

'Alice,' said Jon, 'tell her. She doesn't need to lose weight.'

But Alice was studying the page. 'Yeah, it does look good. Maybe we could go on it together, once the baby's here. I'll definitely need to lose a bit then.'

Jon looked despairingly at Punch. 'Fancy watching *The Simpsons?*'

He'd just settled into his armchair when Alice leaned through the doorway. 'Don't get too comfortable. We're going out, remember?'

Jon made a show of slowly stretching out his legs, racking his brain for what had been arranged.

'You've forgotten, haven't you? Christ, Jon, you can be crap.'

He massaged a non-existent pain in his knee, mind furiously working. 'No, I hadn't.'

'So where are we off to, then?'

Just as the silence reached breaking point, he remembered. 'The parenting class at the health centre. Is it time to go already?'

Alice kept looking at him, suspicion showing in her eyes. 'Yeah, six thirty, just like the last three weeks. You're driving.'

She manoeuvred her stomach back out of the doorway into the hall. Wistfully, Jon put his can of beer on the table. The atmosphere in the meetings made him cringe, something about the happy looks on the organisers' faces as they cheerfully outlined all the trauma ahead. Or it could be the fixed smiles of the parents-to-be, happily grinning but all betrayed by the trepidation shining in their eyes.

'See you later, Punch,' he said, switching off the telly and walking resignedly to the door. Out in the corridor he could hear Ellie clattering about in the kitchen. 'You cooking, little sis?'

'Yeah. Only spaghetti, though. See you in a bit.'

'Good evening. Tea or coffee?' The elderly woman beamed at them as he held the health centre's swing doors open for Alice. After picking up their drinks, they proceeded across the tiles of felt carpet and into the meeting room. The hard plastic chairs were half taken by other couples and a pair of slightly embarrassed-looking women sitting on their own.

Jon glanced around, wondering how many of the other men resented the fact the classes had been arranged on Saturday nights. Quite a few, he guessed, judging from the looks on most of their faces.

He and Alice sat down, nodding hello to the couple beside them. Jon noted the prison tattoos on the man's fingers and wondering how many times he'd been inside.

'Oooof, that's a relief,' said Alice, stretching her feet out in exact imitation of the woman next to her.

'Innit?' she agreed. 'My ankles are so swollen it feels like I'm on a plane the whole time.'

Alice smiled, 'Have you tried any of those soothing creams they do for feet? They're lovely.'

'No, but that sounds a great idea.'

The two women slipped easily into conversation about their shared experiences of pregnancy. Jon and the other man sat back, Jon relieved that the presence of their partners between them prevented conversation.

'Lovely to see so many of you here,' said the health visitor a few minutes later. She started drawing plain blue curtains across the windows. 'This evening we're watching the birth video I mentioned last week. It's not something you get to see on an average night's television, but it's well worth witnessing in advance of your own births I can assure you.'

Jon sipped his tea, realising to his annoyance there was no sugar in it.

'OK,' the health visitor continued. 'Are we all sitting comfortably?' She turned the telly on, then stood to one side with the remote for the video in her hand. Holding it within an inch of the machine, she pressed a button. The screen remained blank. 'Oh, bother,' she said, instantly flustered. 'This was all meant to have been set up. Mary, can you work this thing? The little screen on the video recorder says it's playing.'

Jon groaned inwardly as the woman who had made their tea got up uncertainly. Hooking strands of grey hair behind her ears, she leaned towards the handset, unwilling to actually take it off her colleague. 'I don't know, Marjorie. Did Trevor plug the scat lead thingy in?'

'He said it was all ready. I don't know.' Marjorie thrust the remote at the video recorder again. 'Nothing.'

'Is it on AV?' Jon asked, sitting forward.

'Sorry?' she replied, sounding relieved and instantly offering the handset to him.

Jon stood up and, after checking the leads were properly in at the back, pressed the TV/AV button. Immediately the screen was filled by a close-up of the view between a woman's legs and a fast panting filled the room. 'Unless this is one of Trevor's private collection, I think we're in luck.'

'Quite, thank you,' Marjorie replied, a tight smile on her face as a couple of the men suppressed snorts of laughter.

Jon sat down, only to receive a sharp jab in the ribs from Alice.

Screaming started and a bulbous blue lump started trying to push its way out of the woman. Blood and slime were smeared across her inner thighs.

'We've missed the first bit, but never mind,' announced Marjorie. 'As you can see, the baby's head is just showing. The mother has been in labour for five hours and is fully dilated. Everything's in the right place.'

Her screams faded into sobs and a voice off-camera said, 'That's brilliant. You're doing brilliantly, Karen. Tell me when you feel the next contractions coming. Have some gas and air if you like.'

The camera panned upwards, revealing the distended belly, then the head and shoulders of a wild-haired woman. Jon was shocked to see she was totally naked, enormous and swollen nipples pointing off to the sides.

An ashen-faced man was sitting by the head of the bed, holding a plastic mask over her face. When he saw the camera was on them he tried to arrange the sheet across her breasts. As soon as they were covered she yanked it off again, eagerly gasping away behind the mask. He tried to take it off her face after a few more seconds and her hand clamped instantly over his, fingernails biting deep into his flesh.

'Karen here opted for a natural birth. At first. By the time she changed her mind, it was too late for an epidural,' Marjorie intoned.

Alice angled her head towards Jon. 'I want every drug they've got. Understand?'

'You've got it.'

'Oh God, oh God, oh God,' the woman on the screen started repeating.

Jon saw the muscles in her thighs snap tight. 'Oh Jesus, this is worse than that scene in *Alien*,' he whispered, making Alice choke on her sip of tea.

On the screen a pair of hands reached out and grasped the top of the baby's skull. 'OK, push Karen. This is it. Push!'

There was no way the head could fit through, Jon thought. A nerve-shredding shriek erupted and suddenly the head popped out. A glistening blue body laced with a waxy substance quickly followed, releasing a gush of bloody fluid behind. Unable to watch any more, Jon shut his eyes and heard the health visitor say, 'Now, as you can see, Karen is bleeding quite heavily from a tear here, but the hospital staff are waiting for the afterbirth to emerge before giving her some internal stitches.'

Jon thought of the cold can of beer on his living-room table. The film ended a few minutes later and he was able to open his eyes again.

'So,' said Marjorie, pulling back the curtains, 'you've now seen one of the most incredible things Mother Nature has to offer. And soon you'll be witnessing it for yourselves.'

She smiled at a room full of grey faces.

Jon took Alice's hand and gave it a reassuring squeeze. 'I'll be there for you, Ali,' he whispered.

She looked up at him and murmured, 'You might want to wear gardening gloves to the delivery.'

'What do you mean?'

She sank her nails into the soft skin on the back of his injured hand. 'If my birthing's any where near as horrendous as that, I fully intend you to share in the pain.'

Jon tried to extricate his hand, but she dug a little deeper, the sweetest of smiles on her face.

Chapter 22

Jon was buttoning up his shirt in front of the bathroom mirror when the doorbell rang.

'Ali! That'll be Rick. Can you let him in?' he called down.

He heard the front door open and a man with a foreign accent started speaking.

'Cheap videos! Latest Hollywood blockbusters! Three quid each.'

He peered down the stairs to see Rick standing on the front door step, a stack of cassettes in his arms.

'You must be Rick.' With a smile, Alice stepped back to let him in.

'Hi, there,' he said in a normal voice, adjusting the videos so he could shake her hand. 'And you're Alice?' His eyes dropped momentarily to her stomach. 'How long before the baby's due?'

Self-consciously, Alice placed a hand over her bump. 'Around six weeks.'

'Well, you look great. You've got that lovely glow no amount of make-up and sunbeds can achieve.'

Alice's smile widened and she glanced up at Jon. 'Thanks. Could you give my partner a few tips about paying compliments?'

'Yeah, mate, very smooth,' said Jon, sounding like a stampeding elephant as he came down the stairs.

Alice rolled her eyes. 'Right, I've got a train to catch. Enjoy the blockbusters,' she said to Rick, before turning to Jon and giving him a kiss. 'See you later.'

The door shut and Jon showed Rick towards the front room. Punch stood in the doorway, an inquisitive look on his face. Rick hesitated.

'That's Punch, my stupid mutt. Don't worry, he's soft as shite.'

Rick stepped forward and Jon watched as he gave the dog a cursory stroke with just the tips of his fingers. He moved into the front room.

'Want a brew before we get started?' asked Jon.

'Yes, thanks,' Rick said, looking at the photos of Jon, Alice and Punch in various outdoor settings. 'Who's she?' Rick asked, pointing to a younger girl who shared Jon's bright blue eyes.

'My little sister, Ellie,' Jon answered, watching him from the doorway.

Rick stepped across to the CD collection. The mix was fairly eclectic, including Miles Davis, Paul Weller, Radiohead and the Smiths. He searched in vain for anything more lively. 'Don't you have anything you can dance to?'

'Like what?'

Rick ran a finger along the collection. 'I don't know. Diana Ross, Kylie, Madonna?'

'Oh, you mean gay stuff?' Jon replied with an innocent smile. 'I think Alice has got a copy of *Saturday Night Fever* somewhere.'

Grinning, Rick held up two fingers as he placed the videos by the machine.

When Alice got in at six they were still sitting there, dirty cups, plates and the remains of a packet of digestives on the table. Punch was stretched out next to an untidy scattering of videos on the floor.

'Mind if I let some air in, you stinky boys?' Alice asked, her nose wrinkling.

Rick looked mortified.

Jon hit the Stop button and stretched his legs out. 'What a nightmare.'

Alice undid the window latch and Punch's head was suddenly jerked up by the shift in scents as outside air blew in. 'Any luck?' she asked.

'Not a glimpse,' Jon yawned. He looked at the heap of videos beside the machine. 'We've been over seven platforms. Only another six to go. If we find nothing there, we start on the recordings taken from inside the main part of the station.'

'How about some tea? Rick, would you like to stay for some food?'

Rick glanced uncertainly at Jon, who was still staring mournfully at the pile of untouched videos. 'Er, thanks, but I've got something else already arranged.'

'No problem. How about tomorrow if you're carrying on with this?'

'Yeah, thanks, that would be great.'

'Good,' said Alice, heading off to the kitchen.

Rick turned to Jon. 'We're narrowing it down at least. Only platforms eight to thirteen to go.'

Jon nodded. 'Trains for Manchester Airport leave from platform eight upwards.'

'Yeah, but there's no record of him on any flights from that day.'

'And the trains out to Liverpool and up to the Lake District usually go from platform thirteen.'

'Which would fit with your theory of him being holed up in some remote beauty spot.'

'True,' Jon replied. 'But something doesn't feel quite right.' An image of Pete Gray popped up in his head. He'd still be on the daytime shift, due to finish at eight in the evening.

He was wondering whether to mention his visit to Stepping Hill hospital when Rick began clearing up the mess on the table.

'Don't worry,' said Jon, only just noticing it. 'I'll take care of it.'

Rick straightened up. 'Same time tomorrow, then?'

'Same time tomorrow,' Jon replied grimly.

Once Rick had left, Jon called down the corridor. 'Alice, have I got time for a quick you-know-what?' he said, knowing that if he uttered the word 'run', Punch would start leaping all over the place.

'Whatever,' Alice called back.

Her offhand tone of voice set off a small alarm at the back of his head as he poked his head into the front room. 'Punch, fancy going for a run?'

The dog arched its back and seemed to bounce on to its feet in a single movement. Jon climbed the stairs, the mess on the table forgotten behind him.

They ate in silence, Jon faintly aware of the pile of plates and cups Alice had carried through from the front room and left by the sink.

He wolfed his food down, then mopped up the remains of sauce with a hunk of white bread. 'So what did you think of Rick?'

'Nice,' Alice replied, sounding distracted.

Jon stopped chewing for a moment to study her. 'Just nice? Doesn't sound like you, Ali.'

She sighed and turned slightly in her seat. 'How old is he?'

'Almost thirty, I think.'

'He's doing well, then.'

'Accelerated promotion scheme. Graduate and all that. This is just a stint with us at FMIT. He'll be moved to another rotation in a few months, in between taking tests.'

He cleared their plates and carried them over to the others at the sink, noticing the time as he did so. 'Oh shit, babe, there's something I need to check out quickly.'

'You what?'

But he was already heading down the corridor to the front door. 'Shouldn't be long.'

He only just made it to the car park at Stepping Hill before Pete Gray emerged through the doors. Again he went straight home and Jon watched his hazy form as it moved around behind the frosted glass of the bathroom window. He was shaving, getting ready to go out. Thirty minutes later he emerged through the front door, wearing brothel creepers, black jeans, a white shirt with metal collar tips and with his hair arranged in a glistening Elvis quiff.

Jon eased his car out behind the minivan as it set off towards the centre of town. They parked on a side road near Piccadilly station, and Gray hurried across the road and into a pub with faded curtains hanging behind its dirty windows.

Jon waited a couple of minutes, then jogged over the road. The poster behind one of the grimy panes of glass announced, *Karaoke Night. Singles Welcome*. Dotted round the poster were little stars with names written inside: the Beatles, Frank Sinatra, the Stones, Fleetwood Mac, Elvis.

Obviously aiming for an older crowd, thought Jon, slipping through a side door and making straight for the end of the bar. He kept his head down, aware of several glances in his direction. Safely in the shadows he looked around, assessing the atmosphere. A veneer of jolliness just succeeded in holding a feeling of nervous desperation at bay. More alcohol was required for things to improve. Luckily, doubles with mixers were half-price all night.

Pete Gray was sitting on his own at a table near the karaoke machine. A middle-aged woman was up on stage, ruining something by Alicia Keys. She reached the last line, flabby skin swaying slightly as she flourished her arm. A wave of applause washed weakly across the bar and her semi-embarrassed bow revealed a deep and doughy cleavage. As she stepped off stage Pete stood up. His body language was enthusiastic, short hand movements indicating how impressed he was. The gesture merged into a wave towards the bar, and the woman accepted with a smile that etched the crow's feet deeper into the skin round her eyes.

Jon hunched lower on his stool, eyes on the cocktail menu in front. Two drinks were ordered and Pete led her back to his table. After twenty minutes he returned for two more, but Jon noticed the barman only put vodka in hers.

The compère announced an Elvis song and Pete duly took the stage. It was a rendition of 'Love Me Tender', complete with wavering end notes achieved with a slight curl of his upper lip. Most of the song was directed at the woman. He even braced his legs and gave it a couple of pitiful hip shimmies. Jon wanted to gag but, from the size of her smile, the woman seemed mightily impressed.

Warding off the applause, Pete sat down again and quickly made his move. He put a business card on the table, then his hand slid across to hers and their fingers entwined. He leaned his head closer and said something to make the woman instantly stiffen. She leaned back, putting distance between them, and her eyes started cutting around the room. Somehow Pete had blown it. A minute later she got up and made her way to the ladies'. Clearly irritated, Pete picked up a straw and stabbed at the ice cubes in his drink. When it became obvious she wasn't coming back, he pushed both glasses away, retrieved his card and left. With Jon trailing along behind, he drove straight home. Seconds after going inside, the glow of a TV showed from behind the bedroom curtains.

Checking his watch, Jon saw it was just after ten at night. It was past the reasonable time for a phone call, but he couldn't resist. He opened his notebook and looked at the phone numbers at the front. Deciding that it wasn't fair to rouse Mrs Miller, the elderly mother of the second victim, he called the mobile of the first victim's daughter instead.

It was answered after a few rings, the sounds of a bar loud in the background.

'Lucy here. Who's this?'

'Lucy, it's Detective Inspector Spicer. I'm working on the investigation into—'

'I remember you.'

'Good. Sorry to call this late, but I needed to ask you something. Do you have a minute?'

'OK.' The two syllables were heavy with caution.

'You mentioned that you took your mother to a few singles' nights in town.'

'That's right.'

'Did you ever take her to a place near Piccadilly station called the Coach and Horses?'

'Yes – it was pretty much a disaster.'

'Pretty much? Did anyone make a pass at her?'

'No. Well, no one nice. There was this one guy who gave her his card. But he was such a creep I made her promise to never ring him.'

'What makes you say he was a creep?'

'Just his general attitude. I didn't want my mum being added to his list of cheap one-night stands.'

'What did he look like?'

'I called him the Fat Elvis.'

Jon looked across at Pete Gray's bedroom curtains and the blue light that flickered there.

It was almost eleven by the time he let himself back in through the front door. To his surprise Alice was still up, sitting reading a magazine in the front room, with the telly on low.

'Hiya, babe. Just getting a glass of water.'

Ruffling Punch's ears, he walked down the short corridor into the kitchen, noticing that the vacuum was back in the cupboard under the stairs. The carpet was spotless. In the kitchen he grabbed a glass from the cupboard and had half filled it before realising all the plates and cups had been washed up and put away.

He went into the front room and sat down in his armchair. 'You've done all the clearing up. I was going to do that.'

Alice sighed. 'When?' Her voice was flat and she didn't look at him.

'Tonight. Now.'

'I got tired of waiting.' She looked up and he saw her lips were pale and thin. The alarm bell that had started ringing earlier on returned, much louder now. 'You'd have started vacuuming at this time of night? I'm usually in bed by now.'

'Maybe tomorrow morning, then.'

'Or maybe fucking never!' She slammed the magazine on to the table.

'Where's that come from?' Jon said, surprised by her anger. From the corner of his eye he saw Punch slinking out of the room and he wished he could do the same.

She struggled to get off the sofa. 'Where's that come from? God, you're a prat at times, Jon Spicer.'

He stared at her thinking about how the investigation was floundering. McCloughlin was getting more wound up by the day, and his prowling round the incident room was making everyone tense. 'Ali, I'm not a bloody mind reader. I didn't do the washing up. Is that what this is about?'

She glared at him for a moment longer. When it became obvious that was the best he could come up with a cry of frustration escaped her. She swung her stomach round and waddled out into the corridor.

Jon remained seated for a few seconds, irritation washing over him. 'We're trying to catch someone before he strips the skin off another victim, Ali,' he said, getting up and crossing the room to the door. 'You know the score with my job. Murderers don't tend to work office hours.'

She'd managed to get halfway up the stairs, one hand clutching the banister. He watched her shoulders rise and fall as she tried to get her breath.

'You're also about to become a dad. I'm struggling here. Struggling with this pregnancy, struggling with my job, struggling to keep this place clean for when the baby arrives.' She turned around and pointed down at him. 'I won't have you messing it up. And another thing. That bloody nursery isn't finished yet, Jon, and you promised – you bloody promised!'

A tear broke and she wiped it away furiously. Jon suddenly saw how vulnerable she was, saw how hard she was fighting to keep it together. The knowledge that he was responsible for her distress tore a hole in him.

'And don't ever bring details of your work into this house. That's a rule you made with me, remember? So don't fucking break it to try and justify your shit behaviour.'

Jon opened his mouth but couldn't think of anything to say. She turned and laboriously climbed the rest of the stairs. The bathroom taps came on.

He walked slowly into the kitchen, mind going back over the last few days. He tried to remember when he'd last cooked, cleaned, tidied or thanked Alice for covering for him. He looked down at Punch, who stared up at him with sad eyes. 'I've fucked up big time, haven't I, Punch?'

The dog looked back at him in silence.

He climbed the stairs two at a time, knocked on the half-open bathroom door and looked in. She was brushing her teeth hard enough to remove their outer layer.

'Sorry, Ali.'

Still scrubbing, she looked in the mirror and he saw her eyes were wet. Guilt mushroomed in his chest. He stepped across to the sink, curled a forearm around her stomach and gently gripped her wrist in his other hand, stopping the toothbrush moving.

Leaning his forehead on her shoulder, he whispered, 'I've been a complete prick. I'm sorry. I didn't realise.'

The hand gripping her toothbrush lowered. 'I want this pregnancy to be a good experience. I don't want to be stressed and crying with our baby inside me.'

'I know,' he murmured, eyes shut. 'I'm going to make sure it is.' Gently, he began to kiss her neck, feeling her posture slowly soften.

After a few more moments she whispered his name.

'Yeah?' he said, head still bowed.

'I think I've got rabies.'

'What?' His eyes snapped open and he saw the white foam at the corners of her mouth.

'Grrrrr,' she smiled and, seeing her playful look, he felt his heart actually leap in his chest.

He turned her round. 'I promise, Ali, I'm going to—'

She cut him off by pressing her lips against his. He kissed her back, using his tongue to lick the minty mess away.

He felt one of her hands settle on his thigh and he leaned forwards, tracing his fingers hopefully towards her swollen breasts. His hand was lightly gripped and he opened his eyes to see her looking at him with her eyebrows raised. 'Right now, I'd rather scrub the toilet than do what's on your mind.'

Jon sighed. 'Not even a—'

'No way,' she replied with a grin, extricating herself from his arms and leaving the room.

Jon leaned his hands on the sink and stared at himself in the mirror, trying to remember the last time they'd had sex.

Chapter 23

Dawn Poole leaned forward and gently applied a finishing touch of mascara to the patient's eyelashes. 'There, you look wonderful.'

'Really? How bloodshot are my eyes?'

The bedside mirror had been moved, so Dawn didn't lie. 'They're not clear yet, but compared to a few days ago, they're so much better.'

The patient's head fell to the side, face bandages rasping lightly against the pillow. The front doorbell went.

'That'll be him!' Dawn jumped to her feet and hurried from the room.

As soon as the bedroom door shut a whir of wings came from the window. The robin sat there, head cocked, expectantly looking in.

The patient reached slowly for the biscuit on the bedside table, broke off a piece and crumbled it on the bedcover. With a hop and a flutter, the bird alighted centimetres from the red fingernails. It pecked a fragment, looked up and around, then pecked another.

Apart from the occasional blink, the patient could have been a statue. Or a corpse.

Footsteps were coming up the stairs and the bird stopped feeding to listen. As soon as the door began to open, it darted back out of the window.

Dawn stood aside, allowing Dr Eamon O'Connor to step into the room. The patient tried to smile.

Dr O'Connor walked slowly round the bed, brushed the crumbs off the cover and sat down. 'OK. Let's get these bandages off and see how your face is mending.'

'Will it hurt?' the patient said, fingers fluttering at the collar of the nightie.

'Not at all,' O'Connor said, opening his briefcase. After methodically cleaning his hands with an antiseptic wipe, he took out a pair of stainless-steel scissors. 'Now, hold that pretty head still and I'll just snip your bandages.'

The blades of the scissors came together and the outer layer of gauze fell away.

'Good,' O'Connor said, laying the scissors down. He took a loose end and slowly unwound the layers obscuring the patient's lower face.

As he reached the final lengths watery brown liquid had stained the material. 'You still have some discharge from the wound, but that's to be expected. Keep taking the antibiotics I prescribed.'

Carefully he eased away the final strip, revealing an oval face marred by a thin laceration running along the entire length of the jaw. More bandages held a couple of splints in place down each side of the patient's nose. The wounds on the jaw were held together by a thicket of incredibly fine stitches.

Dawn stared with affection at his face. The masculine edges had been almost totally smoothed away. She thought the feminine look suited him far better.

O'Connor leaned forwards to survey his handiwork. 'Excellent, if I say so myself.'

The patient's eyes were wide. 'Will there be any scarring?'

O'Connor shook his head. 'With sutures applied this well? Keep out of direct sunlight and use the cream I give you, and no one will be able to see a thing. Now, my dear, let's take a look at your nose.'

He took a pair of tweezers from his briefcase and used them to prise away the gauze. Then he slid the lower blade of the scissors beneath and carefully snipped upwards. The patient sat rigid in the bed, eyes tightly shut.

Gently, the doctor pulled the covering away, easing out the little splints and eventually revealing a swollen nose, the skin stretched so tight it shone. Ugly bruising spread away from it, staining the skin beneath the patient's eyes a purplish yellow.

'Hold still. We're nearly done.' O'Connor took a pencil torch from the briefcase, bent forward and shone it up the patient's nostrils. 'Can you breathe through your nose?'

'Just. But the left nostril feels blocked.'

O'Connor nodded. 'It looks like dried blood to me, not how the cartilage has settled. Dawn, can you fetch some warm water and a towel?'

She jumped to her feet and went into the bathroom.

'So I'll be OK, Doctor?'

He smiled at the frightened-looking figure in the bed. 'Of course. We talked about how the process of becoming who you want to be will have its ups and downs, didn't we? You're doing well and I'm certainly happy with how things are going.'

Dawn came back into the room. 'Here you are, Doctor.'

'Thank you.' He arranged the towel like a bib over the patient's chest, tested the water with a forefinger, then removed a cotton bud from a small pot and dipped it in the bowl. He inserted the end into his patient's left nostril and rotated it very slowly. It came out stained dark brown with dried blood. 'Any pain?'

'No,' the patient whispered.

He turned the cotton bud over and repeated the action, slowly dissolving away more blood.

'Very gently now, try breathing in through your nose.'

The patient did so, eyes opening wide. 'I can.'

'Well, thanks for sounding so surprised,' O'Connor said, standing up.

'I'm sorry.' The patient tried to smile.

The doctor clicked his briefcase closed. 'I'll be back to remove the sutures in a few days. In the meantime, keep taking the antibiotics and don't, whatever you do, start to pick.'

The patient nodded meekly. 'Doctor, what about my other pills?'

'Absolutely not, I'm afraid. Not until you've completed the course of antibiotics. Don't worry, no appreciable differences will manifest themselves before then. You can go back on them soon enough.'

Chapter 24

The call to the incident room came in at just before six in the evening.

Barely controlled hysteria created cracks in every word the woman uttered. 'We've just seen the local paper. My daughter isn't here. She's not here. There's post in our hallway.'

'Please slow down, madam. What's in your hallway?'

'Post. We've been away in Lanzarote and she's not here.'

'Can you give me your name and address?'

'Debbie Young. Her name is Tyler. She has shoulder-length brown hair.' She dissolved into sobs and a man came on the phone, voice as flat as the fens.

'We live at 61 Rowfield Road, Stretford.'

'Thank you, sir. Was that your wife just speaking?'

'Yes.'

'And you say you've just got back from holiday?'

'We've been in Lanzarote for the past ten days. Tyler was meant to come with us, but there was an argument and she stayed at home. She's eighteen. About five and a half feet tall.'

'Does she have any distinguishing features you can tell me about?'

'Piercings in her ear, her right ear. And a tattoo.'

'What sort of tattoo, sir?'

He paused, having to force the next words out. 'It's of Betty Boop. Just near her hip.'

'Confit duck leg with grilled spiced fig?' the waiter asked, tendrils of steam rising from the plate in each hand.

'That's for my wife.' The man gestured across the immaculate white linen.

'And slow-braised lamb with sweet pepper mash for you,' the

waiter replied, setting the other plate down with a smile. 'Enjoy your meal.'

He backed away, leaving the couple to examine their food, anticipation making their eyes shine.

'This smells lovely,' the woman said, picking up her fork and spearing a fig. She popped it into her mouth and bit down, eyelashes lowering in appreciation of the flavour.

'Good?' he asked, teasing a strip of meat from the cut on his plate.

She nodded, leaning back and staring across the choppy waters of the Manchester Ship Canal to the dramatic silver angles forming the Imperial War Museum North. 'You know, from here,' she commented, dabbing the corner of her mouth with a napkin, 'you can really see the meaning of Daniel Liebeskind's design. The Earth shard, the Air shard and the Water shard, all interlocking. The three different arenas of twentieth-century conflict.'

Her husband sipped from his glass of Cabernet Sauvignon and nodded. 'He doesn't win the world's most prestigious building projects for nothing I suppose.'

Her eyes trailed back across the water, savouring the setting and atmosphere. Then they stopped, attention drawn to a large, pale object in the water directly below. A seagull was perched on top of it as it drifted slowly past, sharp beak tearing at the eye sockets of the corpse's hideously puffed-out face.

Jon stood motionless, staring at the body of Tyler Young. She'd left school at sixteen, flitting between several McJobs, bored, restless, convinced the world had to be a more exciting place. When she was younger, she'd won a beauty competition and she'd aspired ever since to be a catwalk model.

But her height had never progressed beyond five feet seven, a world away from the Naomis, Giseles and Carmens. More recently she'd been to Tempters, hoping to get work as a top-less barmaid, hungry for paid recognition of her beauty. But the management had turned her away, with the advice that she needed to go up a bra size or two if she wanted a job.

That's what had caused the row. Tyler said she'd prefer to

spend the money her ticket to Lanzarote had cost on plastic surgery instead. They'd refused to entertain the idea and she'd stormed out of the house.

Jon looked at her chest now, the skin of her breasts removed, pectoral muscles showing through the waxy layer of fascia. Could Pete Gray have done this? Tyler Young wasn't the same as the first two victims. For a start, she was over twenty years younger. The only way someone like Pete Gray could get access to a girl like Tyler was if he paid for it. Had she gone on the game to fund her operation?

He tapped a finger against his chin, arms pressed close to his chest in the cool air of the mortuary.

Or was she the prostitute from the CCTV footage of Gordon Dean?

He shut his eyes, trying to sift through his thoughts.

A door opened somewhere and he heard metal clang as a trolley was wheeled down a corridor. Soon the plastic curtains parted and the gurney entered the room, two technicians behind it. Jon glanced at the fibreglass shell coffin as they came to a halt by a stainless-steel autopsy table.

'If you're staying in here, you might want to hold your breath.' This from the pathologist, who entered the room in full protective clothing.

'What is it? Jon asked.

'He bobbed up in the Manchester Ship Canal, right outside the Lowry theatre's terrace restaurant. Ruined a lot of pre-performance dinners he did.'

'A floater?' Jon said. 'I think I'll head for the goldfish bowl.'

'Good move. He's been in a good week or so, I'd say.' The pathologist nodded towards Tyler's corpse. 'Can we put her away?'

'Yes. Thank you.' He stepped out of the theatre area and into the viewing room, wondering how to tell Rick that he'd been following Pete Gray.

In the theatre, the technicians opened up the shell coffin and hefted a large plastic sheet containing the body on to the autopsy table.

The pathologist prepared his implements on a side counter while one of his assistants cut through the adhesive tape sealing the sheet. Then she peeled away the folds to reveal a monstrously bloated corpse, the yellow skin marbled with a network of bluish lines. He was in a foetal position, ankles and wrists bound together.

Oh Jesus, Jon thought, never failing to be shocked at how death could turn the human body into a gruesome parody of its former self. He watched with a grimace as she carefully removed the plastic evidence bag the pathologist had placed over the victim's head. The neck was twisted round, the eyeless face a blob of marshmallow, short brown hair on top of his head looking like a skullcap.

That was enough. Jon started to walk out, but paused, eyes drawn to a red mark on the corpse's buttock. He pressed the intercom button and his voice came through the speaker in the theatre. 'Excuse me. Could someone take a closer look at the mark on his arse?'

One of the technicians stepped round and leaned over the body. 'It's a tattoo of a red devil, I think. A small figure holding a trident.'

A jolt shot down the length of Jon's spine. 'I can't see from this angle, but is there another one on his shoulderblade?'

She moved to the head of the table and peered down. 'Yes. The skin's distorting it pretty badly, but it looks like a ladybird.'

'Thanks.' Jon got his mobile out and called Rick. 'You can let McCloughlin know that Gordon Dean's just surfaced.'

'So the pathologist reckons he'd been in the water for about ten days?' said Rick, sipping his gin and Coke.

Jon put his pint down on the table. 'Yup.'

Rick's lips moved slightly as he counted out a sequence. 'That still puts him in the time frame for Tyler Young's murder. Maybe he killed her then, for some reason decided to top himself.'

Jon shook his head. 'You're not having that tenner. With his wrists and ankles bound as they were, it couldn't have been suicide.'

Rick rubbed his temples. 'But if he didn't kill Young we're no closer to catching the Butcher.'

'Actually, that might not be the case.'

'Why not? What do you mean?'

Jon flipped a beer mat over, but failed to catch it. He looked Rick in the face. 'We've still got the Pete Gray lead. I've been following it up.'

Rick crossed his arms and sat back. 'When have you found the time for that?'

Jon shrugged. 'Evenings. I've only caught him coming off his shift a couple of times. Followed him to a bar the other night.'

'When were you planning on letting me know?'

'I was about to when Gordon Dean's body was wheeled in.'

'Really?' Rick asked sarcastically.

Jon met his eyes. 'I was. He went to a singles' karaoke night dressed like Elvis. Got chatting to a woman there, looked like he was about to pull. Gave her his card, then said something to scare her off.'

Rick was looking more and more pissed off. 'You did all this behind my back?'

'I didn't think you'd be interested in shadowing Pete Gray after the amount of hours we've been putting in during the day.'

'Don't give me that shit. You didn't even ask. We're meant to be working this together.' He drained his drink and stood up to go.

'We are. Just hear me out, will you?'

Rick remained standing.

'I rang Lucy Rowlands, the first victim's daughter. She said a guy gave her mum his card at a singles' night one time. It was in the same bar I followed him to the other night. Lucy said the guy was a total creep, called him The Fat Elvis.'

'Did you speak to the woman he scared off?'

'No, because by the time I got back to the bar after following him home, she'd gone. But it means he could have had contact with Angela Rowlands and Carol Miller.'

'Good work. I'll let you fill in McCloughlin.' Rick walked out without another word.

Jon sighed, then took a mouthful of beer. It didn't make him feel any better.

His mobile started buzzing in his pocket. Nikki Kingston, the crime-scene manager's name showed on his screen.

'Hi, Nikki. How are you?'

'Good, thanks. Why're you sounding depressed?'

'Long story.'

'Good. You can tell me over those drinks you owe me. Where are you?'

He'd finished his pint by the time Nikki walked in to the Bull's Head, a small briefcase under one arm.

Jon waved her over. 'So what news have you got?'

'Uh-huh.' She held up a finger. 'Drinks first.'

Jon smiled and got to his feet. 'What'll it be?'

'Gin and dry martini, thanks.'

Jon returned with their drinks and sat down.

Nikki was checking the ashtray for recently stubbed-out butts. 'Still not smoking?'

'Yes,' Jon protested.

She looked provocatively at him out of the corner of her eye.

'What?' he laughed, holding out his hands. 'What do I have to do to convince you?'

Looking at the ashtray, she said, 'There's only way I could really tell none of these were smoked by you. But the night's a bit young for that.' She moved the ashtray to another table. 'So what's the long story?'

Jon's smile disappeared. 'That guy I'm working with, Rick Saville?'

'Oh yes?' Nikki took a sip, looking over the rim of her glass.

Jon remembered the glance that had passed between them at Tyler Young's crime scene. The pang of jealousy returned and he found himself saying, 'Liked him, did you?'

She smiled. 'He's not bad. Doubt I'm his cup of tea, though.'

Her answer confused him.

Nikki gave his hand a sympathetic squeeze. 'I think he's gay.'

Jon's mouth dropped open. 'He is.'

'No shit, Sherlock? How long did it take you to figure that out?'

'A bit. How did you know?'

'Call it feminine intuition.' She paused, then looked at him. 'Was that a glimpse of the little green monster I just saw?'

'No.' He felt a blush creeping up his neck. Shit!

'It was,' she smiled, a note of triumph in her voice. 'You were feeling jealous! Even if he wasn't gay, he's not my type.' Her eyes went to Jon's scarred hands, travelled up to his lips, then his eyes. 'I like my men a bit rougher at the edges.'

Jon looked away. 'I've been following up a bit of a lead, but in my own time.'

'So?'

'I didn't let him know. Or rather, I just did let him know and he spat his dummy out.'

'Well, there you go. Gay men can get a bit emotional.'

Jon sprang to his defence. 'No, it was fair enough. I wasn't being straight with him.' A look bounced between them. 'If you know what I mean.'

'I think so,' she smirked.

Jon took a gulp of his drink. 'Actually, the lead has to do with the tests I asked you to run. So come on, what's this hot news you have for me?'

She reached for her briefcase. 'You asked me to run an ACE-V on the fingerprints and a DNA analysis on a plastic cup.'

'That's right.'

'I didn't come back with anything conclusive on the fingerprints.'

'You said you'd recovered a partial from the inside of that glove we found by the third victim's body.'

'Yes, but it was only a partial. Comparing it to the couple on the cup you gave me resulted in, as I said, nothing conclusive. A couple of points matched, but that's nowhere near enough, as you know. However, I ran the print through NAFIS. You do know the owner has a record?'

'Yes, don't worry.'

'OK. Are you ready for the good news?'

'Go on.'

'The DNA test from the plastic cup was successful, although not with anything from the scene of the third victim.'

'But?'

'You still owe me another drink, yeah?'

'Yes! Come on, what is it?'

'I ran it against the DNA samples recovered from Carol Miller and Angela Rowlands.'

'And?' Jon crossed his fingers.

'It matches the DNA found on the vaginal swab from Angela Rowlands.'

Jon clenched his fists tight as he leaned forwards. 'Yes! This means a guy I've got my eye on has been in contact with two of the Butcher's victims. Nikki, I could kiss you.'

Before he could move, she brought her lips up against his. A hand slid along his jaw, round the back of his neck, and he felt the softness of her tongue probing his lips. For a second he remained still, his nerves zinging. Then he pulled back.

Her eyes slowly opened. 'You really haven't been smoking.'

'I'd better get those drinks,' he whispered hoarsely.

Nikki smiled.

He stood at the bar, mind racing. A raw desire for sex was threatening to overwhelm him and he knew that staying for another drink would lead to the point of no return.

The barman came over. 'Same again?'

Jon hesitated, hand on the fiver in his pocket. 'Yes, please.'

As the drinks were poured, Jon tried to focus on Nikki's revelation. It had to make Pete Gray the prime suspect. They had enough to haul him in there and then. He paid for the drinks and carried them over to the table. But the look of hurt on Rick's face refused to fade in his mind. After putting the drinks down, he said, 'Nikki, I'm really sorry to do this, but I've got to catch Rick up and let him know the news.'

She looked at him, a half-smile on her face. But when she saw he was serious, her expression turned sour. 'Go on, then, off you run,' she said, waving a hand dismissively towards the door.

Chapter 25

In the glow of the streetlights the drizzle swirled in the air like pollen. It drifted helplessly, pushed and pulled by erratic currents of air, finding its way beneath the umbrellas of the few people walking the pavements, coating their clothes in a damp layer.

Fiona paused long enough outside the bar to scan its windows for drink offers. Then she rounded the corner into Minshull Street. A couple of girls were out and she walked towards the first, who was sheltering under the overhang of a seventies office building, the doorway of which stank of piss.

After listening to Fiona's question, she sucked deeply on her cigarette and shook her head. Fiona thanked her and set off towards the other girl. She was huddling in a doorway on the other side of the street.

Fiona was halfway across the road when she noticed a car rapidly approaching. She had to jump over a large puddle to make it on to the pavement in time. A split second later it drove into the water, sending a cold sheet splashing against the backs of her legs.

'Whore!' a male voice yelled through the vehicle's open window as it sped away.

'Fucking wanker!' the girl screeched back, jabbing her middle finger up.

Fiona tried to brush the worst off, but her trousers were soaked.

'You all right?' asked the girl.

'I'll survive,' replied Fiona a little shakily. 'I was coming over to have a word. I'm looking for Alexia.'

'You just missed her. She's had enough for the night, said she was off to the bus station to get some chewing gum, then going home.'

'Really? A girl around my height, about twenty, reddish-brown hair?' Fiona asked, already setting off towards Chorlton Street.

'Brown, red, bleached – she changes it all the time.'

Fiona half jogged along the side street. Soon the bright lights of the recently revamped bus station came into view. A couple of National Express coaches idled in their bays behind the barriers, a miserable clutch of passengers waiting to be let on.

She approached the doors, eyes scanning the main hall. The newsagent's was long shut and Fiona was afraid she'd missed her quarry. But then she saw the vending machines in the corner. A young girl was standing at them, counting out change in the palm of her hand.

She was taller than Fiona, but wearing heels and a miniskirt. Her thin legs were mottled with bluish marks, the same way Emily's had been whenever she got cold. Fiona could see she was shivering, her hair soaking wet with rain.

'The ten twenty-eight National Express service to Glasgow Buchanan bus station is now ready to board. Please proceed to bay number four.'

Fiona was right behind the girl as she pushed coins into the slot and pressed the buttons. A coil of wire rotated forward, releasing a packet of gum into the abyss. It clattered into the tray at the bottom of the machine and the girl leaned forward to pluck it out, one knee bending more than the other. As she turned around their eyes met and the girl began to move past.

'Alexia?' Fiona said in a whisper, having to hold back the torrent of apologies trying to escape her.

The girl paused. 'Huh?'

'I was in the next room at the Platinum Inn. I heard you being attacked. Oh God, I'm so sorry I did nothing to help.' Tears made her vision swim. 'Are you OK? I was so afraid, so afraid for you ...'

The girl was frowning. 'What the fuck are you on about?'

'Room nine of the Platinum Inn. I was there, Alexia.'

'Alicia, not Alexia. And it's not even my real name, anyway.'

Fiona stiffened, remembering the mix-up of names with the

owner of Cheshire Consorts. 'You worked … Did you work at the Hurlington Health Club?'

Her face was becoming suspicious. 'What if I did?'

'I'm trying to find a girl called Alexia. I think something terrible might have happened to her.'

She was moving away now. 'Yeah? Tell me something new.' The bitter laugh should never have come from someone her age.

Fiona crumpled into one of the plastic seats. Her surge of optimism had been sucked away, leaving her with a dry despair. Looking at the time, she got to her feet. The twenty-four-hour Spar was only five minutes away – she was sure they sold alcohol right up until eleven.

Twenty minutes later Fiona pulled up outside the Platinum Inn. The car park had three other vehicles in it. She walked towards the doors, her handbag heavy in her hand. Dawn's smile faltered when she saw Fiona's expression. She looked like she couldn't decide whether to scream or cry. 'Are you OK?'

Fiona lifted the neck of the bottle of gin clear of her handbag. 'Fancy a nightcap? I really need one.'

They sat side by side, each holding a full glass in one hand and a lit cigarette in the other. Dawn watched the twin streams of smoke twisting up from their fingers. 'So it was all a mix-up of names?'

Fiona sighed, took a long sip and sighed again. 'I don't know. But yes, it seems that I've been chasing a girl called Alicia, not Alexia. The owner of Cheshire Consorts was a bit confused about what the girl she interviewed was called.'

'But didn't the card you found here have "Alexia" written on the back?'

'Yes.'

'So surely an Alexia visited her?'

'Not necessarily,' Fiona replied, dragging on her cigarette. 'The owner said there's loads of her cards floating around town. The one I found could easily have belonged to a punter.'

'What about the Hurlington Health Club? The woman there gave you the same description.'

'The woman there didn't listen to a word I said. She wouldn't even turn the bloody vacuum cleaner off to talk to me properly. There is an Alexia out there somewhere, but who knows what she looks like? What a mess.' She took another drag and breathed out in exasperation, a veil of smoke spreading before her.

Dawn clinked her glass. 'You did your best. Can't ask for more than that.' She regarded Fiona, waiting for a reaction.

Fiona stared miserably at the other wall, her bottom lip slightly red from where she'd been worrying it with her teeth.

Dawn's eyes travelled to the cut that emerged from Fiona's eyebrow. Despite the expert application of make-up, she could see it would leave an ugly scar. 'How's your eyebrow? Still sore?'

Fiona continued staring straight ahead.

'Fiona, hello! Anyone in?' She waved a hand in front of Fiona's face.

'Sorry. What?' Fiona blinked.

'Your eyebrow. Will you get a professional to look at it?'

Fiona smiled bleakly. 'A private hospital? I could never afford that.'

Dawn stubbed her cigarette out. 'There are other options.'

'Like what?'

Dawn shrugged. 'You know I mentioned the person I'm with?'

'Your companion?'

'Yes,' Dawn smiled. 'My companion. Our relationship, it's quite complicated. He's having surgery to change his ... appearance. He's never been comfortable with how he is. I'm sure you'll meet him one day.'

She cleared her throat and waved a hand weakly, not prepared to elaborate. At least, not yet. 'Anyway, what I'm trying to say is, the doctor treating him does it all for cash. And cheaply, too. I think he enjoys the challenge.'

She registered Fiona's sceptical look. 'He's no quack. He has his own clinic and really knows his stuff.' She winked at Fiona. 'Pretty dishy, too, in an older-man sort of way.'

'How old?' asked Fiona, looking more interested.

'Late fifties, I suppose. Why don't you ring him, explain

your circumstances? I honestly believe he'd treat you. Probably even let you pay him when you can. It's worth a try, don't you reckon?'

Fiona traced a finger over the raised line of damaged tissue. 'He can get rid of something like this?'

'God, yes,' Dawn said eagerly. 'I've seen what he can do. It's amazing.' She got up, stumbling as the alcohol pulsed in her head. 'He's called Dr O'Connor. I'll write his address down.'

Fiona drained her drink. 'OK. No harm in just popping in, is there?'

The next morning Fiona turned over in bed and looked around. To her relief she found herself in the tiny room that was home. The bottle of gin on the table acted like a magnet on her eyes. Immediately she started to fret about the fact that she didn't have enough money to buy another. Kicking the duvet off, she pulled her dressing gown on and shuffled over to the door. Peeping out into the hallway she saw some post on the shelf. Two letters for her, both looking ominously official.

Back in her bedsit, she made herself a coffee and sat at the table. The letters lay at her elbow, but she didn't dare open them in case they were demands for money. Chin resting on the heel of one hand, she watched the curls of steam rising from the coffee. There was no milk in the fridge, her bread had run out the day before, and her packet of cigarettes was empty.

Her mind went back to waking up in the salesman's hotel room. She finally admitted that she'd only slept with him because he was a way of procuring more drink.

Was it so bad? She'd had a great time, forgotten all her worries for a while.

Far better, in fact, than any time she'd spent with her husband in years. Bitterly, she thought about their marriage. How many times had she endured sex with him through no will or desire of her own? And for what? A stifled existence behind the façade of a respectable house, her money rationed and her movements controlled.

Christ, the night with the salesman was a pleasure in comparison. At least he'd treated her with respect.

She stared at the empty gin bottle then picked up her purse. There at the back was the number for Cheshire Consorts. She remembered Joanne's phone conversation with the escort girl. A hundred and fifty quid an hour. It seemed so respectable, so above-board. They met in hotels and the men paid by credit card, for God's sake. There was a world of difference between that and the poor wretches she'd seen working Minshull Street in all weathers.

She tried to turn her mobile on but remembered the battery had died days ago. Searching in her purse, she found just enough money for the payphone in the hall.

'Hello. Joanne? It's Fiona Wilson here. I came to see you just over a week ago ...'

'Yes, I remember. What can I do for you, Fiona?'

She took a deep breath to quell the tremors in her throat. 'Well, when I saw you, you mentioned that when I'd sorted myself out ...'

'I did. And have you? Is the bruising on your face gone?'

'Yes,' Fiona whispered, fingers touching the cut on her fore-head.

'How about your wardrobe?'

'I've been home and collected all my clothes.'

'So you're in your own place now?'

'Yes.'

Silence for a second. 'Then I'd like you to come and see me.'

Fiona said nothing.

'Fiona? Are you still there?'

'Yes.'

She heard Joanne light a cigarette. 'Fiona, the girls who work for me have made a rational choice to do so. They're paying their way through nursing college, saving the fees for law school, getting together a deposit for a house. It's not a permanent job, it's a stepping stone to something better. They are in control at all times and they most certainly are not whores.'

She arrived just before lunch, having made herself up and put on a simple black dress that suited casual or more formal occasions.

Joanne opened the door and smiled. 'Well, that's some change from the lady I saw two weeks ago.'

Fiona smiled back, trying to look confident and relaxed.

'Don't worry,' Joanne said, showing her inside. 'A lot of men find a touch of nerves very attractive.'

Chapter 26

The enquiry room was hot with bodies. Much longer like this and the condensation will start dripping from the ceiling, Jon thought as he opened a window.

The hum of voices started to die down as McCloughlin's door opened. He stepped out, followed by a thin man with long strands of greying hair swept across his head. Perched on his nose was a pair of rimless glasses that gave a clear view of his feminine eyelashes. Dr Neville Heath. Jon thought back to last summer and concluded that he should have stuck with the black frames he'd had then. After the two men had passed his desk he whispered to Rick, 'Thought it wouldn't be long before this guy got involved.'

Rick swivelled in his seat to regard McCloughlin and his companion, who took up position side by side at the top of the room. McCloughlin glared at the last two officers still speaking. Their conversation withered under his gaze.

'Right, people, as you all know, Gordon Dean's body was discovered yesterday. However, there is nothing to prove he killed any of our three victims, so this investigation is very much ongoing.' He waved the murmurs down. 'In fact, I want you to assume Gordon Dean wasn't the killer. Which means we have to redouble our efforts until we find out who is. To this end, I'd like to introduce Dr Neville Heath. He's a criminal psychologist and has been lecturing at Manchester University since some of you were in primary school. Dr Heath has been over all the information we've gathered so far. He isn't aware of any suspects we're pursuing – alive or dead – so whatever profiles he produces are not biased by our own suspicions. I think you'll agree he has some interesting thoughts to share.'

Jon's eyes turned to the doctor. If you've been lecturing for so long, he wondered, how can talking to us lot make you look so uncomfortable? This isn't the sort of case for someone with a nervous disposition.

'Hello,' the doctor said, looking down at his notes, failing to make eye contact.

The room remained silent.

Dr Heath glanced anxiously at McCloughlin. 'Actually, I haven't produced any profiles quite yet. More a number of observations that could be helpful.'

McCloughlin nodded politely, his expression saying: get on with it.

Registering the look, Dr Heath turned to the room. 'OK,' he said. 'The first thing I'd normally do in a case where more than one crime is being carried out by a person is map the locations where the attacks have occurred and draw a circle round them. It's been frequently found that the criminal lives within that circle, often towards its centre. That's because criminals – especially burglars, rapists and murderers – usually start offending in their own neighbourhood, where they're familiar with their surroundings, before moving further afield as their confidence grows.'

Jon could see people beginning to lean forwards and the doctor's confidence appeared to increase as a result.

'The problem with this case is that we don't know where the mutilations and killings were actually carried out. However, we can say where the victims came from. Number one, Angela Rowlands, lived in Droylesden. Victim two, Carol Miller, in Bredbury. From this we can extrapolate a midpoint around Denton, where the Hyde Road intersects the M60.'

'Hyde Road's the A57,' Jon muttered to Rick.

'Now, I realise this is close to where the bodies are being dumped, but I don't think it's where our killer lives. And here's why. When we add in the address of Tyler Young, which is in Stretford to the west of the city, our circle expands to cover the whole of central Manchester with a midpoint around Didsbury and Fallowfield. This is a far more likely area of residence, for reasons I'll come to in a minute.'

He flipped his top sheet of notes over and took a shallow

breath. 'Now, studying our killer's temporal patterns reveals a bit more about him. Our victims were all discovered on different days – a Tuesday, a Thursday and a Saturday morning. Times of death suggest they were all killed at some point during the evening before, so he's killed on a Monday, a Wednesday and a Friday. Angela Rowlands was last seen when she left her office in central Manchester at lunchtime. Carol Miller dropped her infant son at her mother's house in the late afternoon, and Tyler Young we're unsure about. Taking Angela Rowlands, there was a gap of about six hours between her last sighting and her time of death. This suggests to me she had initial contact with the killer during the office hours of a weekday.'

He took his glasses off and rubbed tiredly at the red marks on each side of his nose. Come on, Jon thought. The whole bloody room is hanging on your next comment.

With his eyes shut, the doctor continued, 'We can therefore suppose our killer isn't constrained by normal working hours.' Glasses back on, he opened his eyes and had to blink a couple of times to regain his focus. 'He has freedom of movement during the day to control his own movements. Keep that thought.

'Next is what he's doing to his victims. These aren't, to use the term our colleagues in America prefer, disorganised killings. They haven't been carried out in a fit of uncontrolled rage. They're careful, meticulous and unhurried. He needs a private place to carry out his work, somewhere he has no chance of being disturbed. Therefore he's probably a property owner or has access to commercial premises.

'He's organised and, judging from the mutilations themselves, skilled. I would also guess these characteristics apply to him in general. He's in a professional occupation, probably supervising his own movements during the day. Possibly self-employed in some capacity.'

Rick paused in his note-taking and held his hand up. Christ, thought Jon, does he think this is a classroom? The doctor nodded at Rick.

'Why do you assume he's got a job?'

The doctor lowered his notepad. 'Well, the bodies are turning up on waste ground in Belle Vue, having been moved there from somewhere else. That suggests he owns a car or has access to a commercial vehicle. It needs to be big enough for him to stash a corpse in it quite comfortably. It takes money to run any vehicle – hundreds a month if you build in the purchase price or cost of loan repayments. He needs a regular wage for that.'

'Like a salesman of latex gloves,' Rick whispered.

Jon shrugged, thinking of Pete Gray's van.

'I would also expect our killer to be very organised in his personal life. His place of work will be neat and orderly, as will his appearance – fastidious, even. Given his professional role, I would say suits for work, smart dress outside it. Shirts, leather shoes, trousers, not jeans. We're not looking for a dishevelled, wild-eyed maniac. Unfortunately, we rarely are. We're looking for a quiet, unassuming, individual. One with an understated type of charm. Think Jeffrey Dahmer. Unobtrusive, able to merge in without making much of an impression. Probably regarded as "nice" by his neighbours.'

While Rick eagerly noted down the doctor's words, Jon sat back and mulled the information over. Pete Gray drove a van with blacked-out windows. And God knew why, but it seemed some women believed he had a certain charm.

'How is he selecting his victims?' the doctor continued. 'They're from three different parts of the city. The first two mentioned they were going somewhere specific before disappearing. A liaison with our killer, but for what? A date? An appointment? They've made the decision to meet him. Has there been prior contact? If you haven't done so, check all three victims' neighbours for any recent visits. I don't mean by trades people such as window cleaners – too menial. Someone flogging conservatories, satellite TV, free holidays. Professional salespeople basically. As I said, he can turn on the charm when required.'

Jon glanced over and saw Rick shooting him a look of triumph.

'What is he trying to achieve through his murders? I'm not sure, but he's certainly settling into it. More flesh is being removed and, in the third instance, the face and teeth as well. I'm assuming the surgical avenue is being treated as a priority?'

McCloughlin gave a tight nod.

'It wouldn't surprise me if the next victim were to be completely stripped of her flesh.' The atmosphere in the room tightened perceptibly and the doctor flushed red on realising his gaffe. 'If he isn't caught before, of course. But he's getting more careful. Removing the third victim's face and teeth is a way of preventing identification. He's covering his tracks in order to carry on. This also links into the general lack of evidence recovered so far. He's wearing gloves, probably a facemask and gown. Of course, that suggests medical knowledge, but it also suggests forensic awareness. So he may well have a record for similar, more minor crimes. Mutilating pets, for instance.'

'What about sex crimes?' a female officer asked from the back.

The doctor shook his head. 'I don't think so. All three victims were discovered with their underwear on. There's no sign of sexual activity, forced or otherwise. Of course, they might have believed they were meeting him for that. But it's not his motivation. Mutilations of this nature are often ritualistic, and in ritualistic killings the genitals are frequently the focus of mutilation. But not here. He's seeking to achieve something else here.

'Another point to consider is this. Why is he choosing Belle Vue as his dumping ground? It suggests to me that he has good familiarity with the area, but I don't think he lives there. More likely is that he regularly passes through, perhaps to and from a place of work. As I mentioned earlier, given his likely professional status and the level of house prices in Didsbury, I suspect that is his area of residence. Taking into account the need for privacy, we should be considering detached houses.'

Wrong! Jon had to make an effort to stop his head from shaking. Pete Gray worked at Stepping Hill hospital and lived in a terraced house near Davenport train station. Neither was particularly close to Belle Vue. He'd chosen the area for another reason.

'Also, he has to get the bodies into his vehicle and then dump them in Belle Vue. Perhaps he has a drive-in garage or a garden with a screening hedge. My final comment is this. From the intervals between his first three killings, we can unfortunately expect him to strike again any day.' He lowered his notes, stepped back and looked at McCloughlin.

Taking the cue, McCloughlin nodded. 'Thank you for that, Doctor.' He turned to face the room. 'A summary of Doctor Heath's observations will be coming round. In the meantime, we focus on Tyler Young – victim number three and a whole new avenue to investigate. You all know her details; now we need to start delving into her life. Her parents told us she was angling to get a job in Tempters, that topless bar in the centre of town. I want the management and all the staff questioned – barmaids, cleaners, glass washers, the man who stocks their condom machines, the lot. Gavin, your team can handle that?'

'Certainly, sir,' the DI replied. Jon could almost see the team rubbing their hands with glee at the prospect of interviewing the barmaids.

'We need to map out her last twenty-four hours. Usual routine – friends and family first. Obviously Mum and Dad were abroad on holiday, but she has two aunts living nearby. The reason they didn't come forward was because they thought she was on holiday with the parents. Nevertheless, we still need to talk to them. She didn't have a boyfriend as far as her parents knew, but we need to verify that with her mates.

'Vanessa, that's your team's shout. I also want you to get over to the family home and have a good look through her stuff. The mum doesn't think she kept a diary, but you know how it is with teenage girls. Go through her bedroom, check the backs of her drawers, under the carpet – you probably know better than me where she might hide stuff. We'll need the family computer, too, to see what email she's been sending or receiving.'

As Jon watched the young DI brush her hair off her face, he wondered what McCloughlin had in mind for him and Rick.

'Andy, I want your team to continue with your TIEs on the members of the dating agencies Angela Rowlands met up with. How many have you got left to trace?'

'She was sent the profiles of twenty-seven men. It seems she had contact with sixteen of them. So far we've traced, interviewed and eliminated twelve.'

He turned to another officer sitting at the front. 'Simon, how's your team going with the surgeons?'

'Not bad, boss. We've just got to check the alibis for three who have contracts with the Paragon Group.'

'Good. Keep going.' He held up a sheaf of photocopies. 'The most recent photo of Tyler Young her parents could find. Help yourself.' He dropped them on the table and was turning back to his office when he said, almost as an aside, 'Oh yes, Jon and Rick, keep trawling through those videos from Piccadilly station. We need more footage before we can categorically say the woman with Gordon Dean wasn't Tyler Young.'

Jon uncrossed his arms, trying to keep the irritation out of his voice. 'Sir, doesn't it now appear that Gordon Dean's murder is unconnected to the Butcher investigation? I was hoping to invest our time in following up the Pete Gray lead Rick and I unearthed.'

'Rick and you unearthed?' McCloughlin replied sarcastically. 'Pete Gray is not a priority at this time. The whereabouts of that prostitute is. I want her tracked down.'

He ushered the doctor back to his office.

Shit, Jon thought, how do I let him know Gray's DNA showed up on Angela Rowlands's body? McCloughlin has enough doubts about my working methods without me announcing that I've run an illegal and unauthorised DNA test on a suspect. He pursued them into his boss's office. 'With respect sir, Pete Gray is definitely hiding something. He has free access to the type of latex glove found at the crime scene of Tyler Young, he works odd shift patterns, he drives a van with blacked-out windows, he's a regular at singles' nights around town. Surely that's grounds to at least ask the man for a voluntary DNA swab?'

He glanced at Dr Heath, who was peering at McCloughlin over his glasses, one eyebrow raised.

But McCloughlin's face had drained of colour. 'DI Spicer, there are many more avenues to this case than the ones you see fit to create. As SIO, it's my job to prioritise them. You'll go through that footage if you want to stay on this investigation.'

'And once we've been through it all?'

'If there's no sign of her, you can question Pete Gray. Now get out.'

Jon stepped out of McCloughlin's office and into a mass of excited conversations. He went back to his desk and slumped down in his seat, wondering how to get out of the mess he was in.

Rick looked across at him. 'Did you tell him about your dodgy DNA test?'

'Christ, no! I'd be off the investigation by now if I had.'

Rick whistled. 'You're sailing very close to the wind. Though personally, my money's still on Gordon Dean.' He put a few finishing touches to his notes, swivelled the pad around and pushed it across the desk.

Reluctantly, Jon started reading. *Works to his own schedule. Skilled or professional role, probably 'high end' of sales. Has his own vehicle. Fastidious in terms of organisation and personal appearance. Familiar with Belle Vue.* Rick had a satisfied look on his face. 'Gordon Dean fits all those criteria – every time he had to get to Protex he'd have driven through Belle Vue.'

Irritation itched Jon's scalp. 'It wasn't him.'

'On what basis exactly?'

'This,' said Jon, pressing his fist into his sternum. 'I can feel it in here. He's not our man.'

'Great! Discard all the techniques of twenty-first-century policing and go on good old gut instinct.'

Jon hooked a forefinger under Rick's pad and flipped it over. 'There's more to this job than treating it like some frigging university course.'

Rick retrieved the pad and stood up. 'I'm getting a coffee.'

Jon watched him go, waiting until he was out of earshot before saying, 'Fucking little smart-arse.'

Chapter 27

The lines of halogen spotlights came on and he crossed the concrete floor, the low cellar ceiling muting the sound of his footsteps.

On the other side of the small room he stood before a counter lined with his collection of surgical instruments. He surveyed the rack of scalpels before picking one out and examining its blade, eyes narrowing under the bright light glaring down from above.

With a deft movement he released the blade from the metal handle and disposed of it in a flip-lid bin that was spattered with specks of red. Then he lifted a small foil wrapper from a box labelled: *Carbon steel. Sterility guaranteed if packet unbroken.*

He tore the foil open, lifted out the new blade, fitted it to the handle and replaced the scalpel on the rack.

Shutting his eyes, he breathed in. Unable to escape the airless room, the coppery tang of blood hung heavy around him.

So many to choose from, he thought, opening his eyes and looking at the sheets of paper beside him. Women's names, addresses, hopes and desires were all listed there. He lifted the top sheet and ran his eyes over the form.

Should he select one of these? After a few moments' contemplation, he decided against it. None of them felt quite right. He wanted his next job to be really special. Something that would leave the crowds of imbeciles gaping with shock.

Another woman would come along soon. They always did.

As he put the forms back his eyes shifted to the collection of human teeth in the test tube. The corners of his mouth twitched with anticipation.

Chapter 28

Jon and Rick sat in the front room. Still treating each other a little warily after their argument the day before, they had now waded through the footage from every platform without success. Rick loaded the first tape from the main terminal building and sat back on the sofa with a sigh.

Jon couldn't concentrate on the screen. 'He's fucking sidelined us. This is a wild-goose chase and he knows it.'

Rick half turned his head, one eye still on the screen. 'Jon, we can do this in less than three days if we keep going.'

'Three days! We could crack this case in hours if we go after Pete Gray.' He began picking at the frayed armrest. 'Look, this is a waste of time, right? Gordon Dean pops up in the Manchester Ship Canal. So why are we looking for him catching a train out of Manchester? Someone else dumped the car at Piccadilly station to make it appear like Gordon Dean had eloped. Probably the prostitute's pimp.'

Rick was trying to watch the footage.

Jon sat forward to get in his line of vision. 'Whatever that prostitute's involvement in Gordon Dean's murder, it's a separate case from the Butcher. Tyler Young was killed and her flesh stripped off early in the evening. Dean and that prostitute are together on the CCTV film from the petrol station hours later that night. Tyler Young and that prostitute are different people.'

'That's not to say Dean isn't the Butcher. He skins Young, then goes out celebrating with the mystery girl from the CCTV. Later, he ends up in the Manchester Ship Canal. We still need to track her down and find out what happened.'

'OK, I agree the prostitute holds the key to Dean's death. But I bet she'll still be in Manchester, back on her old patch in all likelihood. What I'm saying is Dean isn't the Butcher. When could he have skinned Young? We have his movements mapped out from early afternoon until three in the morning.'

Rick stopped the tape and gripped his head in his hands, growling in frustration. 'So what do you suggest?'

Jon waited for him to look up. 'We fuck those tapes off. Let's tell McCloughlin we split them in two. We phone him later to say we did half each and there's nothing on any of them.'

Rick fiddled nervously with the remote control. 'And what do we do in the meantime?'

'Check out Pete Gray. Ask him for a voluntary DNA swab, maybe put some questions to his colleagues at Stepping Hill hospital.'

Rick remained silent and Jon could tell he was wrestling with the decision to actively deceive his SIO. Finally he said, 'I'll agree to take a break from these bloody tapes, but on one condition.'

'Go on.'

'We go back and talk to that tattooist in Affleck's Palace first. We take the photo of Tyler Young and see if it's the girl Gordon Dean spent time waiting with. I still reckon he's the Butcher.'

Jeff Wilson walked past Melvyn's salon, glancing quickly in. Where the fuck was his wife? He knew she wouldn't have been able to cut off all contact with her friends there. They must know where she was. The vacant-looking girl who seemed to have only just started was sitting at the reception desk, chewing a pencil. It seemed like no one else was there.

Looking at his watch, he realised he could only stay for another fifteen minutes. A business meeting beckoned. Suddenly he saw a way of finding out where Fiona was hiding. With a bit of luck, it might just work. And then he could teach the bitch a lesson for trying to leave him.

He crossed the road to a florist's and ordered a big bouquet of flowers. Once the girl had curled a sheet of cellophane round them, she asked if he'd like a message added.

'Actually, the lady doesn't even know me. But we got talking once in the queue for the sandwich shop and, well, it sounds silly I know, but I think I've found my soulmate.' He feigned embarrassment and was pleased to see the girl's face soften. Would the stupid cows ever give up on their absurd faith in fairytale romance? 'I was wondering, could you carry them to that beauty salon across the road for me? I'll pay your standard delivery costs.'

She looked over his shoulder, an intrigued expression on her face. 'To that one? Melvyn's Salon?'

'Yes, that's where she works. I've been plucking up the courage to do this for days.'

'OK,' she smiled. 'But you do know it'll be £12.50?'

'A small price to pay, believe me. The lady's name is Fiona. Fiona Wilson.'

After writing down his message, she carried the bouquet across the road and into the salon. When she walked in, Zoe's eyes widened in hope at the huge spray of flowers.

'Hi, there,' the florist announced cheerfully. 'A bouquet for Fiona Wilson.'

Zoe looked disappointed. 'She's taking some time off work.'

The florist's shoulders slumped. 'Oh. Well . . . that's a shame.' She turned towards the door.

'Hang on!' Zoe exclaimed. 'Her home address is here somewhere.' She opened the appointments book and turned to a load of loose bits of paper at the back. 'Yes, I thought it was. They can go to Flat 2, 15 Ridley Place, Fallowfield. Here, I'll write it out for you.'

'Thank you.' The florist took the piece of paper.

Back in her shop she felt a surge of sympathy over her customer's concerned expression. 'Don't worry. She's off work for a while, but I've got her home address.'

'Really?' Jeff Wilson replied. 'That's smashing.'

When they walked into the tiny tattoo parlour, Jake was sitting behind the desk, blowing smoke rings at the ceiling. Jon hooked a finger through one and then withdrew it, the gesture making the pale loop bend and waver.

'Gents, good to see you again.' Jake sat up, not bothering with any clever comments. Jon stood aside to allow Rick up to the desk.

'Jake, we won't take up any of your time. The girl who picked the Betty Boop tattoo on the same day as Gordon Dean was in here getting his ladybird. Is this her?'

He laid the photo on the desk.

Jake leaned forwards and studied it. With his head still bowed, he said, 'She's the Butcher's third victim, isn't she?'

Jon and Rick said nothing and he looked up. 'The papers said she had a distinctive tattoo on her lower abdomen. It's her, right?'

'We're not at liberty to say,' Rick replied, voice tight.

Jake's eyes narrowed and moved to Jon. 'It is. That's heavy shit.' He let out a whistle and picked the photo up. 'Yes. I'm pretty certain that's her. She's got the line of earrings and everything.'

'What happened that day?' asked Rick. 'Think back. You finished the Maori armband. You showed the customer out. Gordon Dean and this girl are sitting here.' He pointed to the two stools. 'Their thighs must have been practically touching. What did they say?'

Jake shut his eyes and started twiddling the rod in his nose. 'Nothing. I took the armband guy's cash and then said Gordon Dean was next. He stood up, squeezed round her knees. She smiled and wished him good luck.'

'And what did he say?'

'Just thanked her, I think.'

'And afterwards? You've completed Gordon's ladybird tattoo. You show him back through the curtains ...'

'Yeah, she's still sat there.' Jake opened his eyes and looked at the empty stool. 'Dean pays me, says he'll call again soon. Then he wishes her luck, says she's made the right choice, and walks out.'

'The right choice?' said Jon, pushing himself clear of the doorframe.

'Yeah, the right choice.'

Despite the street being bathed in cold sunshine, a flurry of raindrops started to fall around them. Squinting, Jon looked up but could only spot a few tiny clouds in the sky. Then a breeze whipped up from nowhere and the air abruptly cleared. Jon looked back down, thinking that nothing felt quite right.

'There's something in this,' Rick said, holding up a hand and testing the texture of the air between a forefinger and thumb.

Jon kept silent, desperate to get over to Stepping Hill hospital.

'"The right choice". What did that mean? Tattoo? Job? Decision to see him again?' Rick frowned. 'I want a word with that Dr O'Connor. He seemed fairly friendly with Dean.' He set off towards the Rochdale Road.

Just give it up, will you? Jon thought, following along behind.

As they reached the Beauty Centre, the door opened and a woman who appeared to be in her late thirties stepped out. She looked like someone had just punched her mouth and, on seeing Jon's stare, she raised a self-conscious hand to her swollen lips. She hurried past and Rick caught the door before it could shut, while Jon buzzed the intercom. 'Dr O'Connor, it's DI Spicer and DS Saville. Could you spare us a couple of minutes?'

'Of course. Please come up.' The lock clicked uselessly. Halfway up the stairs, Rick tapped a photo on the wall. 'Her with the trout-pout we just passed? That's what she'd had.'

Jon looked at the image of a woman with puckered, glossy lips. The words below read, *Softform. For enhancing lips and eradicating deep wrinkles.*

Jon shuddered. Why did women feel the need to do this to themselves? If it was to attract men, it did nothing for him.

O'Connor rose to his feet and extended a hand across his desk as they entered his office. After they'd shaken, he gestured to the pair of chairs and sat down. 'Officers, how can I help?'

Rick reached into his pocket. 'Doctor, we're still following up leads regarding Gordon Dean's disappearance.'

The doctor crossed his legs. 'Any progress?'

'The investigation is ongoing,' Rick replied. 'However, we're still trying to fill in some of his movements after he last saw you.'

At that moment they heard the door across the corridor open, and a woman came into the room. Mid-forties, hair tied back.

Poking out from beneath her coat was the hem of a starched white dress. 'Sorry to disturb you, Doctor. Everything's locked up.'

'Good, then I'll see you tomorrow,' he smiled.

'See you tomorrow.' She disappeared down the stairs.

'Jenny Palmer,' said O'Connor, 'my nursing assistant. Wonderful woman.'

Rick nodded. 'Did Mr Dean ever mention any lady friends in Manchester?'

The doctor frowned. 'No. But wasn't he married?'

'Yes,' Rick answered. 'But perhaps not as happily as he might have been ...'

The buzzer sounded on the wall. Rick waited but the doctor waved it away. 'Kids, I imagine. I have no further appointments this morning.' The buzzer sounded again and he leaned forward. 'You were saying?'

Jon got up, went over to the window and looked down at the street below. The receptionist from the Platinum Inn was staring up. On seeing Jon, her eyes dropped and she scurried off down the street. He was about to ask O'Connor what was going on but changed his mind, sensing that, for the moment, it might prove more useful to keep what he'd seen to himself.

'You seemed quite friendly with Mr Dean. Did he ever mention a girl fitting this description?' asked Rick, putting the photo on the table.

O'Connor took it. 'No, I'm afraid not.' He glanced at the image again. 'Pretty young thing, though a bit too young for Mr Dean, don't you think?'

Rick took the piece of paper back, disappointment obvious on his face. 'Well, thanks, that's all.'

They stood and shook hands again.

'Please let me know if you hear anything about Gordon,' said the doctor.

'Will do,' Rick answered after a moment's hesitation.

Jon waited until they were outside before saying, 'The buzzer, it was the night receptionist from a motel in Belle Vue called the Platinum Inn.'

'How do you know that?' asked Rick.

'Because I spoke to her a few days ago. Favour to that friend of my girlfriend – the one who thought she heard a prostitute being killed in the next room.'

'Oh, yeah, the one who gave you that business card? What was the name on it? Alexia?'

Jon nodded. 'What was she doing here, I wonder? She practically ran off when she saw my face in the window.'

'Don't know. But Tyler Young and Gordon Dean definitely had an association. I think we should get back to those tapes.'

Jon held up his hands. 'Hang on. We agreed to pop over to Stepping Hill and ask Pete Gray for a voluntary DNA swab.'

Rick looked away, tapping his foot against the pavement. Eventually he turned back. 'One hour, OK? No more.'

At Stepping Hill hospital a grey-haired porter looked at Jon's warrant card then tapped his tunic. 'Twenty years in the Transport Police, me.'

'Really?' said Jon. 'When did you retire?'

'Twelve years ago. Trouble with the ticker. Mind you, I'm glad I got out, reading about how things are going for you nowadays. Can't touch those little yobs for fear of legal action, isn't that right?'

'There's ways and means.' Jon gave the old boy a wink and got a knowing smile in return.

'What's that pepper spray like? Does it drop them like flies?'

'Never used it myself, but the uniforms certainly like it.'

'Wouldn't have minded a can of that in my day. So, who are you looking for?'

'Pete Gray. Is he around?'

'It's his day off.' The porter put a couple of boxes of medical supplies on a small trolley.

'Could we ask you a few questions instead?' Jon asked.

'Certainly, if you don't mind talking on the move. I've got to get this lot over to the surgical ward. A rare trip for me.'

'Is that so?' Jon set off alongside the man, Rick just behind.

'Pete usually delivers everything to the surgical wards. He's very possessive about it.'

'Latex gloves, for instance?'

'Everything. He wheels everything over there.'

'Why's that?'

'He loves the surgical ward. Says he'd have been a surgeon if he'd had the education.'

The back of Jon's neck started to tingle. 'Really? I thought he was more into learning the lyrics of Elvis songs.'

The man laughed. 'You mean his karaoke stuff? Yes, he's certainly a bit of a ladies' man. In fact, I reckon the real reason he always delivers to this ward is because he fancies the medical secretaries.'

Jon smiled. 'A bit of a skirt-chaser, then?'

The porter nodded. 'Oh aye. I don't believe in bragging about your love life. But then I've been married for forty years, so I don't have one.' He laughed at his own joke. 'Bachelors like him? I suppose it's different.'

Jon thought about Gray's record of violence against his first wife. 'So he's never given marriage a go?'

'Pete? No. Says he's not the marrying kind. Not his thing.'

Jon flicked a glance at Rick walking just a pace behind. 'Are there many ladies he talks about?'

'If you believe everything he says, he's had more than I've had hot dinners. It's those singles' nights he goes to around Manchester. Always a new story to share with us on a Monday morning.'

'He never mentions regular girlfriends?'

'Too busy having fun for that, according to him. Not that I believe he's truly happy. Still sowing your wild oats at forty odd? There's only one hole he's filling at weekends, and that's the great big one in his life.'

By now they'd reached the doors to the surgical ward. Jon held them open and the porter wheeled the delivery through.

'No Pete today?' asked the woman behind the reception desk.

'Day off.' He pointed at the boxes. 'They're only light things. Shall I leave them here?'

'That's fine,' she replied, coming round the counter.

Jon helped him lift them off the trolley. As the porter made for the doors Jon said, 'Thanks for your help.'

'You're finished with me, then? Rightio.' The door swung shut.

Jon produced his warrant card and showed it to the receptionist. 'DI Jon Spicer. Could I ask you a question or two?'

'Yes?'

'It's about Pete Gray who you just mentioned.'

'Pete?' She looked amused, but her voice held a note of caution. 'Has he done something wrong?'

'Nothing like that,' Jon assured her. 'The other porter mentioned he has quite an interest in the surgical ward.'

'Oh, does he! You need to speak to Mr Anderson. He's let Pete observe him in the theatre once or twice.' Suddenly she looked concerned. 'That's not illegal, is it?'

'Not as far as I'm concerned.'

She smiled with relief.

'Is Dr Anderson in today?' Jon asked.

'Mr Anderson,' she corrected him. 'You call consultant surgeons "Mister". Yes. He's performing a laparotomy. Very busy.'

'Could you find out if he'd object to me asking him one or two questions?'

'What, now?'

'It's extremely important.'

Ten minutes later, Jon was standing at the end of an operating table, wearing green overalls, a facemask and surgical goggles. While a young man held apart flaps of flesh with retractors, the surgeon was delving around in someone's stomach. Blood was being sucked away down a tube with the same sound as a child finishing a drink through a straw.

The surgeon turned to the scrub nurse. 'Number fifteen scalpel, please, Ruth.'

She handed it to him and he leaned forward to slice something within the wound. The vicious-looking scalpel was dropped with a metallic clink into a stainless-steel kidney tray and he straightened up. 'Pete Gray? Harmless enough fellow. Approached me in the canteen one time. Bit of an odd request, but whoever's fault it was he left school so poorly qualified isn't my concern. I was just pleased to see the fellow taking an interest. Yes, he's sat in on quite a few operations, even borrowed a few of my anatomy books.' His eyes narrowed above his facemask. 'Still got my *Gray's Anatomy*. Must remember to ask him for that back.'

'And what sort of operations has he observed you performing?'

'Oh, removing bowel cancers, mainly. Clearing blockages in lower intestines. Couple of abscesses, too.' He picked the scalpel up and began cutting again.

'Does he ask questions?'

'How do you mean?'

'Regarding surgical techniques. How you make incisions, that sort of thing.'

'Yes. Lots. In fact, it was usually easier for me to give a running commentary.'

Jon had heard enough. 'Thanks very much for your help.'

As soon as he was out of the operating theatre, he yanked off the surgical clothing.

'Well?' said Rick expectantly, as Jon entered the reception area.

He kept his voice down and tried to keep the flow of words under control. 'He's been in there watching all sorts of stuff. Observing the surgeon as he opened people up, asking questions about how he does it, borrowing books on anatomy.'

'Jesus Christ.'

'Now do you believe me?'

Rick coloured slightly. 'Yeah, I think you could be right.'

'Come on, let's get round to his house.' Jon set off towards the double doors.

'What about the boss?' Rick called after him.

Jon fished out his mobile phone. 'DCI McCloughlin please. It's DI Spicer.'

A moment later McCloughlin came on the line. 'Got some interesting news for me, Spicer?'

'Yes, I have, sir. Very interesting. Pete Gray has been sitting in on operations at Stepping Hill hospital, watching the surgeon perform. Only observing, but he's also borrowed books on anatomy.'

'What the hell are you doing there? I instructed you to go through the CCTV footage from Piccadilly station.'

Jon shot a guilty glance at Rick. 'We've been through them all sir. DS Saville and I split the tapes. Went at them most of the night and all this morning. Not a thing sir, no. I think it was a ruse. The car was parked there to make it appear Gordon Dean had fled.'

'So where is this prostitute? We need to trace her.'

'Rick and I believe the prostitute is still in the area. I'm sure, given time, we'll find her. But as regards Pete Gray, I think it's imperative we talk to him and request a DNA swab to eliminate him from the enquiry.'

'And don't tell me, you just happen to have a chance of speaking to him now?'

'As it happens, we have, yes. We're about ten minutes from his house.'

'A chat, Spicer. And a polite request for a swab. No more, do you understand?'

'Absolutely. Thank you, sir. We'll keep you informed.' He snapped the phone shut, looking relieved. 'We've got the go-ahead.'

As they walked up the short drive Jon pointed out the stickers on the rear window of Pete Gray's van, *Shaggin' Wagon* and *If it's a-rockin', don't come a-knockin'*.

Rick raised his eyebrows. 'Classy.'

Jon pressed the doorbell and stepped back. They heard the jangle of keys a few moments later and the door swung open.

Pete Gray looked out at them. His hair was messed up, great greasy strands of it hanging down over his face. Nervously, he swept it back over his head.

'Mr Gray, DI Spicer and DS Saville. We spoke to you—'

'Yeah, I remember. What do you want?'

'Could we come in for a quick word?' Jon took a step towards the open door.

Gray shifted back and glanced over his shoulder into the house. 'Er, can you call later?'

'It really won't take long.'

Gray rubbed his unshaven jaw with the knuckles of one hand. 'It's not a good time.'

'As I said, we'll be out of your hair in two ticks.' Jon placed a hand against the door frame.

He glanced at it. 'Are you arresting me?'

'Why would we do that?'

'I don't know.' His eyes shifted to Jon's hand for a second time. 'OK, come through to the kitchen.'

The kitchen was at the end of a short corridor directly ahead. Before that were two doors, one on each side. Jon knew the one on the right led into the TV room, its shelves stacked with books. Pete Gray pulled the one to his left shut as he walked down the corridor.

Jon pointed to the closed door. Then he stepped into the house and walked into the TV room on the right.

Gray whirled round. 'Hey! The kitchen's down here.'

Jon was in the centre of the room, looking at the bookshelves. 'Sorry?'

Gray walked angrily into the room. 'You heard me. The kitchen, it's down—'

He heard the door across the corridor being opened and realised he was caught in between the two men.

Jon read out some of book titles. '*The Anatomical Drawings of Leonardo da Vinci. Andreas Vesalius: The Work of a Master. Clinical Anatomy for Medical Students*, Richard S. Snell. *Gray's Anatomy*. What a strange collection. What would you want with books like these?' He took *Gray's Anatomy* off the shelf.

'What? Put that down.' He looked towards the other room. 'Get out of that fucking room. This is illegal!'

'I'm sorry, sir, but you invited us in.'

'Jon, in here.' Rick's voice was thick with suppressed emotion.

Jon kept his eyes on Pete Gray. The man was highly agitated, but there was still red in his cheeks. Jon knew if he was about to fight or run his face would be white, the blood rushing into his arms and legs. 'After you, sir.' Jon extended a hand towards the corridor.

They went into the other room. Rick had a folder open on

the dining-room table and was spreading out colour photos. What struck Jon at first was the redness of the bodies; torsos completely stripped of their flesh, skull-like faces with eyeballs exposed, lips missing and teeth bared to the world.

Chapter 29

Dawn Poole paused before the bedroom door, took a slight breath in and pushed it open.

The patient was sitting up in bed staring across the room. Rows of stitches along the jaw were merging with a light covering of stubble. The nose was still swollen from where Dr O'Connor had broken it, shaved down the bone, then reset it. Bruising lay heavy beneath the eyes. 'Did you get them?'

Dawn shook her head. 'I couldn't. That policeman was there, the one who came asking questions at the Platinum Inn.' She realised that she was still in the doorway, nervousness rooting her to the spot. 'He saw me and I had to walk off. What's going on? Why was he there?'

But her questions hadn't been heard. The top of the sheet was being twisted in a knot, red fingernails digging deep into the folds of material. 'I need fucking Androtone. Look at me! The hair's coming back. I'm disgusting.'

Meekly, Dawn stepped forwards. 'You've been in bandages for days. When I had my leg in plaster for a while it was covered in hair when the cast came off.'

'Your leg, not your face! Jesus!' The patient looked wildly around, scratching at the spiky hair on his head. 'My bust's shrinking, too. He can't deny me my tablets. I must have Progesterone!'

'They're not shrinking darling,' said Dawn, looking at the swelling under his nightgown.

'You're lying! In there.' A hand flapped towards the chest of drawers. 'Second drawer down.'

'Alex, you're scaring me.'

His eyes met hers. 'Listen, it's not my fault. It's the testosterone. It's flooding me like poison.' Wretchedly, he clutched a

243

hand between his legs. 'Oh God, the sooner we go to Holland and I get the full operation ... Now, please, the drawer?'

Dawn took a few more tentative steps into the room, increasingly alarmed at the aggressive way he was ordering her around. It had never happened before. At the start of their relationship she'd found things awkward, not knowing if they were stumbling towards something that would involve sex. Then, one night, he had gently resisted her hesitant advance, telling her that, although he loved her, it was as a soulmate. More than friends, but not quite lovers.

She was just glad to know one way or another, and actually quite relieved they could continue together as companions without the confusion. As the trust between them grew, he'd begun to describe his dream of being more than a transvestite, of becoming an actual woman.

She'd been shocked and worried. Was the operation dangerous? Would he want to leave her once the transformation was complete? But she soon realised that, in many ways, he needed her more. As a physical carer after each painful stage of surgery and as an emotional carer as he struggled with feelings of self-doubt and despair.

Cost was the hardest part. He'd never had more than the most basic jobs, same for her. She'd reacted with horror to his suggestion that he go on the game. But he told her that he'd done it before. He'd worked as a rent boy for spells during his teens and early twenties. He knew there was a thriving market for transvestites and pre-op transsexuals. Knowing his happiness depended on changing sex, she eventually accepted the idea.

The first night he went out in full drag she'd been terrified for his safety. But he reappeared the next morning with hundreds of pounds. Within a few more nights he'd earned enough money to pay Dr O'Connor for his cheek implants. So the process began. Alex selling himself to pay for the next stage of surgery, lying in bed being cared for by her as his wounds healed, then going back on the game to finance his next visit to O'Connor.

Of course, there were times when he was angry, hurt by punters' scathing remarks or cheated out of payment after servicing their needs. Her mind jumped to the night Fiona had thought she heard someone being killed. 'Alex, the night before Dr O'Connor operated on your nose and jaw, you were working, remember? You brought a punter back to the motel in the early hours. Did you end up in room nine?'

'Second drawer down!' A sudden falsetto scream.

She flinched, then hurried across to the chest of drawers. On top of it was a mannequin's head, covered by a chestnut-brown wig shot through with strands of red. Dawn opened the drawer and gaped at the pile of cash inside. 'Where did all this come from?'

'Take two hundred. Get over to Annabella's. Tell her I need a fortnight's worth of Androtone, two hundred and fifty mg a day. And Progesterone, five-mg pills, all she's got. Now go!'

Dawn peeled off four fifty-pound notes and almost ran from the room.

The patient sat back, arms over the covers, palms upwards. After a few seconds the robin flew in. It perched on the end of the bed, peered at him, then flew halfway up and landed by his hand. He watched it impassively until it alighted on his palm. Then his fingers clamped inwards, crushing it to death.

Chapter 30

'You've done what!' McCloughlin exploded.

Jon kept his voice calm. 'Sir, he tried to run. We had no choice.'

McCloughlin looked at Rick for confirmation.

'It's true, sir. He saw me with this lot and went for the door.'

'At which point DI Spicer body-checked him so hard, he's claiming that his shoulder's dislocated.' McCloughlin voice was brimming with contempt.

'It's not dislocated, sir. Believe me, he'd have been squealing a lot louder if it was,' Jon answered.

'Shit,' said McCloughlin. He looked down at the clear plastic bag and the collection of images inside. 'So what the bloody hell are these?'

Rick stepped forward. 'It's the work of a German anatomist called Gunther von Hagen, sir. He's pioneered a process called plastination. Basically, he takes the corpses of people who've left their bodies for medical research, strips them of their flesh, dissects them to expose the internal organs, preserves the whole thing and puts them on display.'

McCloughlin was shaking his head. 'Yes, I remember there was a documentary on TV. I switched over after a few minutes.' He stared at a photo of a corpse, its own skin draped over its outstretched arm. Another of a man holding a basketball in one claw, tensed and ready to leap, all his muscles exposed, mouth open in an eternal gasp for breath. 'Where are these monstrosities put on show?'

'He has an exhibition called *Body Worlds*. It travels all around the world. These images are from when it came to London earlier this year. Loads more are for sale on the web site, too.'

McCloughlin pushed the images away. 'So Pete Gray was there. OK, go and interview him. I'll be watching.'

Jon and Rick sat down opposite Gray. He stared back at them in silence as the Neal twin-deck tape recorder whirred away.

'Strange hobby you have there. Collecting pictures of dead people, poring over anatomy textbooks. Why don't you talk us through it?' asked Jon.

Gray shrugged. 'You think I'm a ghoul.'

Jon stared back at him, thinking, too bloody right you are.

'If I were a medical student studying to be a doctor, you wouldn't be looking at me like that. You'd be full of respect at my desire to learn how the human body functions.'

'But you're not.'

'Why should that matter? Why should knowing about the secrets of our insides be confined to the medical establishment? Why should the Royal College of Surgeons deny people like me access to autopsies through their secretive Fellowships? We are all human, we're all entitled to understand how our bodies work.'

'Why?'

'Because it's fascinating. At least, I happen to find it fascinating. But, because I'm not a doctor, you think I'm a ghoul. If it helps you to understand, I wanted to be a surgeon when I was younger.'

'You wanted to be a surgeon? Why? Did some relative of yours write that *Gray's Anatomy* textbook?'

'No.'

'Was your father a surgeon?'

'No. He was a printer.'

'Was an uncle? A relative? A friend? You don't just take a fancy to being a surgeon.'

'I did. Leonardo da Vinci did, and he's regarded as a genius.'

Delusions of grandeur, Jon thought. The trait of a psychopath. He placed the plastic bag of *Body Worlds* images on the table. 'These pictures you had in your house. Why are you collecting images of corpses stripped of their skin?'

'They show the true workings of the human body in all its glory.'

'Like the corpses of Angela Rowlands, Carol Miller and Tyler Young show the true workings of the human body in all its glory?'

Gray looked disgusted. 'I've got nothing to do with them. Whoever did that is sick.'

'Paying to see skinned people and collecting photos of them isn't sick?' Jon lifted the bag and let it fall with a slap on to the table.

'Maybe you should be interviewing the other people who attended that exhibition, then. There were over eight hundred thousand of us.'

He was too glib, too well rehearsed. Time to shake him up. 'So when did you meet Angela Rowlands?'

Gray flinched. 'How do you mean?'

'I mean, when did you meet Angela Rowlands? It's a simple question.'

'Did I?'

Jon leaned forwards, aware that his next comment was about to leave him wide open with McCloughlin. But he was so close to nailing the bastard sitting opposite him, he didn't give a shit. 'How else did your sperm get inside her?'

'How do you ... ?' The sentence faded out.

'You've got a fucking record, man!' Jon shouted. He remembered McCloughlin was listening, and lowered his voice. 'Kicking the crap out of your wife and then two other girlfriends, remember?'

'But I never gave a DNA sample. I don't understand.'

Jon's eyes flicked briefly to the mirror window at his side and he imagined McCloughlin's face. 'We know everything about you. Now, tell me what happened!'

Gray's shoulders collapsed. 'It was at a singles' night in town.'

'Which one?'

'The Coach and Horses, near Piccadilly station.'

'And?'

'We talked, I gave her my number. I didn't think she'd call, but she did. Obviously didn't take her young friend's advice.'

'That was her daughter.'

Again Gray's face showed complete surprise at Jon's knowledge. When he proceeded, it was a lot more cautiously. 'She rang me about a week later. We met, she came back to mine and we had sex.'

'Just the one night?'

'Yes.'

'Any talking involved? Chat to her about your interest in human anatomy?'

'No! Look, I know you think I killed her. And you think I saw Carol Miller, don't you? I didn't. We talked on the phone about that bloody rowing machine, but she didn't ever come round to see it.'

'On the night she disappeared she was off to see someone about something.'

Gray started biting a thumbnail. 'Listen. When you came asking about Carol Miller that time, I didn't lie. I've never met her. But I had seen Angela Rowlands. I thought if I told you that, you'd haul me in. And sure enough, here I am.'

Jon found himself scowling. The interview wasn't going as he'd hoped. 'How long before we find the link between you and Tyler Young? There are officers searching her home now. Will they find one of those cards you like to hand out at karaoke nights?'

'You've been following me!'

Jon ignored the remark. 'When did you meet Tyler Young?'

'How would I ever come into contact with a girl her age? Look at me.' He glanced down at his paunch. 'I'm a fat forty-three-year-old who does Elvis impressions.' He looked up, and Jon was shocked to see a tear running down his cheek. 'I'm a fucking hospital porter, for God's sake. I'd have as much chance of pulling a girl like Tyler Young as I did with Angela Rowlands' daughter.'

'You tried it on with Lucy Rowlands?' Jon asked emotionlessly.

By now Gray was openly crying. 'Yes, when her mum had gone to the toilet. She told me to fuck off.'

Jon kept at him. 'You'd have plenty of chance with Tyler Young if you were paying for it.'

Gray hauled himself up in his seat. 'I've never paid for it. Ever.' Defiance rang in his voice.

The silence stretched out until Rick nudged Jon and made a T shape with his hands.

Reluctantly, Jon reached over to the tape machine. 'OK, interview suspended at three fifty-two p.m.' The tape clicked off and he got up.

'Cup of tea?' Rick asked gently.

'Three sugars,' Pete Gray replied, wiping the tears from his cheeks.

Jon was halfway down the corridor when McCloughlin's voice rang out behind him, 'Have you been following that man?'

Jon stopped. 'I was in a pub one night, sir, and observed him making a pass at a woman.'

McCloughlin gave a snort of disbelief. 'What was that about finding his DNA in Angela Rowlands?'

Jon bowed his head. 'After speaking to him in the hospital canteen the first time, I had a test run on the cup he'd been drinking from. We got a match from that.'

Fury made McCloughlin's voice squeak. 'Who the bloody hell do you think you are? I didn't authorise it, you arrogant prick. You knew it went against regulations.'

Jon turned. 'No one ever need know, sir. Now he's under arrest, we're entitled to take an evidential mouth swab from him. We'll get our match from that.'

'He's not under arrest – you're to release him without charge immediately.'

'What?'

'You've badly jumped the gun on this one, Spicer. He hardly had the look of a guilty man to me.'

'He's had a sexual encounter with one victim, phone contact with another, and we haven't even started looking into who the third victim was involved with.'

'Pretty much the same could be said for over a dozen men Angela Rowlands met through her dating agency. We haven't arrested any of them.'

'I doubt they have photos of skinned corpses in their homes.'

'So your little vendetta – which is what it looks like to me – should suddenly take precedence in this investigation?'

'I'd say it's a very promising lead.'

'A very promising lead,' McCloughlin sneered. 'DI Spicer, with Tyler Young's identification the incident room has turned into a fucking spaghetti machine. There are very promising leads oozing out all over the place. I've got three extra indexers and they still can't enter the information into HOLMES fast enough.'

Jon fought to suppress his rage.

It must have shown on his face because McCloughlin paused to let out a dry laugh. 'I'll give you one thing, you're a tenacious bastard, aren't you? The only reason you found those photos is because you barged into his home without a search warrant. And the only reason you know he had sexual relations with Angela Rowlands is because you obtained a sample of his DNA in a manner that will be laughed out of court. Now, in keeping with PACE procedures, you can put his mouth swab in for DNA analysis. It can join the queue along with our many other suspects'.'

'It could be days before we get a result.'

'So be it. I've got plenty of other leads you can be following up in the meantime. Now, process him, let him go and then report upstairs. It's time you fitted in with this investigation just like everybody else.' He brushed past.

As soon as the door to the stairway shut behind him, Jon spun round and slammed the heel of his hand against the nearest door. 'Fuck!'

Rick kept his distance. 'Easy, Jon. He isn't getting away – he's just got a stay of execution before we haul him in again.'

'Yeah, by which time he'll have destroyed any evidence in his house, had the inside of his van steam-cleaned, and thoroughly prepared his story.' He took several deep breaths. 'McCloughlin's got it in for me and it's tainting his judgement.'

Rick leaned against the wall. 'Let's just play it cool. There's time yet.'

'I need some air.' Jon strode down the corridor and out through a side door into the car park.

The scent of cigarette smoke wafted over him and he looked around. A couple of uniforms were standing there, puffing away. Before his conscience could stop him, he stepped towards them. 'Could I ponce a smoke off you?'

'No problem. You look like you need one.'

He put the cigarette in his mouth, bent towards the lighter's flame and drew the smoke deep into his lungs. Then he leaned back against the wall and shut his eyes. Six months without a cigarette. Bollocks to it all, he thought, breathing out and immediately taking another drag. His boss, the case, the prospect of fatherhood; everything was getting to him. He thought about having to let Pete Gray back out on to the street and exhaled smoke in disgust.

When Jon and Rick walked into the incident the room an hour later the place was full of excited faces. Glancing at the windows of McCloughlin's little office, they saw it was jammed with senior officers. They headed over to the receiver's desk.

'Hear you dropped a bollock with a suspect,' he said.

'We'll see,' Jon replied, lips tight. 'Why all the commotion?'

'DI Gardener's team found Tyler Young's diary in her bedroom.'

'Really?' said Rick. 'And what was in it?'

'Quite a few names.'

'Was there a Pete Gray mentioned?' Jon demanded.

The receiver looked down at a sheet of paper. 'I'm putting together a list at the moment, but no, I can't see him.'

'How about Gordon Dean?' Rick's voice was full of hope.

'No, we've looked for him already. Have a word with Sergeant Evans – he's ready to give out the first actions now.'

Jon and Rick drifted across to the allocator's desk, where a few members from the team tracing Angela Rowlands' contacts from the dating agency were already waiting.

'Tracked them all down, then?' Rick asked one of them.

'No. McCloughlin's given the Tyler Young leads priority.'

Jon glared out of the window, noting that the day's brightness had died. While they'd been in the cells a layer of grey had silently closed in over the city. In the distance he could see dark ribbons of fine drizzle drifting down. The cooler air that crept through the window had a musty smell, like that of a dank cellar.

Behind him the allocator announced, 'OK, you lot, come and get an action.'

Rick joined Jon a few seconds later, a piece of paper in his hand. He read it through and then looked up, bewilderment on his face.

'What is it?' asked Jon, turning away as the first droplets began hitting the glass and burrowing their way downwards.

'We're being sent to the Beauty Centre. Tyler Young had made enquiries with Dr O'Connor about lip implants. Then he told her he could do breast implants, too. Quoted her an amazingly low price if she could pay cash.'

Chapter 31

'I'm sure I could help with that,' Dr O'Connor said. 'Why don't you come in and see me?' He paused, a pencil balanced in his fingers. 'Tomorrow afternoon is good for me, too. I have a slot at three thirty ... OK, that's grand. And the name was? ... Fiona. Fiona Wilson.' He wrote it in his appointments book. 'See you tomorrow, Fiona.'

After replacing the phone, he pressed a button at the top of the unit and looked at the woman on the opposite side of his desk. 'Sorry about that. I've turned the thing off. Now, where were we?'

She crossed her legs. 'I was saying that I haven't discussed this with anyone.'

'I usually advise all my patients to seek the opinions of family or friends before embarking on any procedure,' O'Connor replied.

She shook her head. 'I want it to be a surprise, that's the whole point. I'm telling everyone that I'm going on holiday, then I'll turn up as the new me.'

'You haven't even let your partner know of your plans?'

'I'm single,' she replied. Moisture glistened in her eyes, but she blinked back the tear and sat up straight in her seat.

Yes, O'Connor thought. You've been through a traumatic experience, in all likelihood created partly by a fundamental flaw in your character. Perhaps you were too jealous. Maybe insecure. Probably just plain dull. And now, rather than address the real reasons for why things went wrong, you're going to reinvent yourself by taking out a bank loan and paying for a few cosmetic procedures. Probably treat yourself to a new hairstyle, too. And that's it, the new you will carry on exactly as before because you really haven't changed a thing.

He shifted slightly in his seat, the ache in his bad knee bothering him as usual. He looked down at the patient form on the desk, and moved straight to the last section. 'Could I ask how you heard about the Beauty Centre? Were you recommended by word of mouth or did you see an advertisement?'

'I saw your advertisement in the 'Health and Beauty' section of the local paper. When I realised you were near my office, I thought I'd pop in.'

O'Connor nodded.

'So does this mean you'll treat me?' she said, as he began filling in the form.

'Well, let's start by assessing you. Which parts of your face are you unhappy with?'

She raised her chin and looked at him. 'My eyes are sagging, especially the skin below them. And I'm developing these lines above my upper lip. My throat bothers me, too. The skin there needs tightening.'

O'Connor gazed at the face of a perfectly normal forty-five-year-old. Apart from the slight bagging off the skin below her eyes, which could be easily rectified with a blepharoplasty, she didn't need any treatment. Apart from reasons of pure vanity, at least. 'Well, I can certainly perform a couple of procedures to address those issues—'

'And my skin in general,' she interrupted, warming to her theme. 'It just looks tired, no matter how much I exfoliate and moisturise. I noticed on the stairs that you offer those lasers. How do they work?'

Her bleating had started to aggravate him, and keeping the pleasant lilt in his voice was becoming more of an effort. 'Just out of interest, how much do you spend on moisturisers?'

'Well, I use a Clarins programme. Let's say it's not cheap.'

'Anti-wrinkling properties in the treatments?'

'Of course.'

He nodded. 'I can save you that money. After all, why use anti-wrinkle treatments when you have no wrinkles to treat?'

She gasped. 'I'd never thought of it like that!'

Smiling, O'Connor swivelled the lamp on his desk so it shone directly at her face. He scrutinised her for a few seconds then

said, 'Well, we offer Cool Touch laser. It works by stimulat-
ing cells to produce natural collagen, the supporting framework
beneath your skin. That would take about twenty minutes. The
pinkness fades very quickly and you could be back at your desk
within an hour. You really haven't mentioned your visit to any
of your colleagues?'

Smiling, she shook her head. 'I can't wait to see them when
I walk back in.'

'But in your case I think we should opt for what used to
be crudely known as a skin-peel. It's actually called laser skin
resurfacing and I would admit you as a day case in order to
perform it. Your skin will feel tender for about a week, but the
results last much longer. You could forget about your monthly
expenditure on Clarins – I'd prescribe you a moisturiser that's
far less expensive.'

'That sounds better to me. And will it sort out these marks?'
She held a finger to her forehead.

He leaned forward. 'Are they old acne scars?'

'Yes. They've bugged me ever since I was a teenager.'

He sat back. 'Everything would be removed.'

Eagerly, she probed her upper lip. 'What about these awful
grooves that are appearing?'

Would she ever shut up? 'Well, we could eliminate those
with filler. I favour Dermaleve. It involves a few injections, and
the whole procedure would take half an hour. There's really
very little impact on your time. If you like, I'll show you the
treatment room. Then I can conduct a proper assessment prior
to arranging a convenient date for your treatment.'

'Yes, I'd like that.'

He got up, straightened his stiff knee and limped round the
desk. 'OK, this is where it all happens.' He unlocked the door
to the treatment room. On the far side was an adjustable bed, a
large roll of blue paper mounted behind it. By its side was what
appeared to be a small printer or photocopier. Grey plastic and
a few buttons on the top. Cupboards lined two of the walls,
and a small sink was in one corner. Next to that were several
cupboards with all their doors closed. O'Connor hobbled across
the shiny floor to the grey plastic machine. 'Cool Touch laser.'

She had sidled across to a poster of a smiling woman with immaculate skin. 'Doctor, you mentioned that you could do my upper lip in twenty minutes and I could go straight back to work.'

Nurse Palmer wasn't due in until the next day. Their privacy was assured. No one knew she was here. O'Connor saw the opportunity presenting itself. 'Yes. There would be a bit of pinkness and a slight numbness from the anaesthetic. I suppose if we perform the procedure now, we could fill out the rest of the form while your skin settles down.'

'How much would it cost?'

He waved a hand. 'Seventy-five pounds. But I'd only charge you once all your procedures had been successfully completed.'

'Oh,' she smiled. 'In that case, could you do it for me now?'

God, will your incessant whining never stop? He imagined how her voice box would look when the skin covering it had been stripped away. He pulled the roll of blue paper until a length of it covered the treatment bed. 'Hop up.'

She removed her coat, climbed up and sat back. 'Will it hurt? Needles really bother me.'

O'Connor flicked on the examination light hanging down from the ceiling. Then he turned on a tape recorder. As the sound of soothing pan pipes filled the room, he unlocked a cupboard. It was filled with bottles and boxes. He took out a pre-prepared syringe, the needle only centimetres long. Inside was a clear, gel-like substance. 'Here it is, five millilitres of Dermaleve. And no, you won't feel a thing. I'll apply some anaesthetic cream first.'

'That's a relief.' She sat back.

He moved out of her line of vision then took an empty syringe from the cupboard. Next he removed a tiny vial of Propofol from the shelf, washed his hands in the sink and dried them. After smearing her upper lip with cream he said, 'OK, I'll get everything ready back here while that takes effect. You just relax.'

He pulled on a pair of size eight latex gloves, picked up the syringe and sucked the Propofol into it. He placed it in a stain-less-steel kidney tray, put that on a small trolley and wheeled it over. Sitting down on a stool by the top of the treatment bed, he leaned forward. 'How does that feel?'

'I don't think it's ...' she mumbled. 'Oh, my mouth won't work properly.' She tried to smile, but her upper lip wouldn't respond.

'Perfect. Now close your eyes and lift your chin up slightly.' Visualising what was beneath her skin, he traced the facial vein as it crossed the submandibular salivary gland and branched off beneath the skin of her upper lip. He slid the needle in and injected half the Propofol directly into it. He knew the anaesthetic would render his patient immobile in seconds.

Calmly, he returned the syringe to the tray and walked back over to the cupboards. 'How does that feel?'

She didn't reply. He returned to the treatment table and looked at her. Her eyes were fixed open and he lifted a hand to shield them from the harsh light above. Gradually her pupils widened a fraction. 'Good, you can hear me but you can't move.' He sat back on the stool and, keeping the soothing, doctorly, tone in his voice, took her hand. 'I want you to know that I despise you.'

Flecks of panic flew from her irises, though her breathing stayed steady and slow.

Needing time to quell the bile in his throat, he listened to the music for a few seconds. 'Don't worry, my skills are far superior to injecting bloody filler.' Angrily, he looked around the treatment room, then began breathing deeply. When he spoke again, his voice had a melancholy note. 'Not here. We're going to a place where I won't have to hurry. Mine is a delicate art, one that we don't want to rush.'

He lifted the half-full syringe, turned her head slightly to the side and injected the remaining Propofol directly into her external jugular vein. Her eyelids slowly lowered and she slipped from consciousness.

Chapter 32

'I'm afraid she wasn't in, Alex,' Dawn said miserably, taking off her soaking wet coat and laying the cash on the end of the bed.

He dropped the mirror on the bedsheet and started to sob. 'Oh God, look at me. I'm vile, absolutely vile.'

'You're not,' Dawn insisted, trying to take his hand. 'You're beautiful.'

She peered at him, always slightly amazed at how different the person she had fallen in love with now looked. When they'd met in Boots his blond hair had been long and swept back from a face which, although unmistakably masculine, had a curious delicacy. She sometimes thought that maybe there'd been a woman in there all along.

Gradually his appearance had then altered. Superficial changes like the removal of his hair were immediate. A simple laser treatment and female hormones saw to that. Then came the operations. His angular cheeks were smoothed over and filled out, his chin reduced and rounded off, his lips enlarged. Now his square jaw was gone and his nose had been turned into something dainty and petite.

When his breasts were inserted last year the switch in genders became startlingly real. But still he refused to let her call him 'she'. Only once they'd been to Amsterdam for his vaginoplasty. Then he'd be a real woman.

He picked the mirror up again and started to probe his Adam's apple. 'I need the tracheal reduction to get rid of this.'

'You can, Alex. You just have to be patient. You've come so far.' She reached out and embraced him, running her fingers through his short hair until he calmed down.

She'd never seen him like this before. However difficult

things had got for them in the past, it had only made her more determined to stick with him. This rage was something new. The way he'd started shouting at her. It reminded her of previous relationships. Ones that had ended in her being beaten up and eventually having to flee.

Gently she said, 'That woman I told you about. Fiona. She called in at the motel again. She thinks the name of the girl she heard being attacked in the motel was Alexia. She's searching everywhere for her, trying to find out if she's OK. She won't give up. It's like an obsession.'

He raised his head to look at her. A muscle had gone into spasm at the corner of his mouth and he looked like he was repeatedly attempting a particularly miserable smile. 'What do you mean, searching everywhere for her?'

Dawn shivered. 'She lost a daughter years ago and now this Alexia is part of that guilt. It's like she believes that if she can find her and make sure she's safe, her own life can move on. So she's up and down Minshull Street talking to all the girls. Someone said she'd find her in Crimson, so she's been going there, too.'

'And she's been talking to a policeman about it?'

'Yes, the one I saw at Doctor O'Connor's surgery. Alex, do you know what this is about? That night in the motel—'

He slammed the mirror down on the bedside table, cracking the glass. 'Give me her address.'

'Why?'

He sat on the edge of the bed, knees sticking out from under the hem of his nightie. 'Gordon Dean was a pervert.'

Dawn stared at him in silence.

'He wanted to tie me to that bed, wanted to perform his sick fantasies on me.' He glanced at her. 'He wanted to humiliate me.'

Dawn's hand went up to her mouth. 'What are you saying?'

'God knows, he'd have tried to kill me if I'd let him bind my hands. But I asked to tie him up first. He liked that. He was the same as the others, not interested in me as a woman. Just interested in me as a freak.' His hand went to his groin and he grabbed his penis through his nightie. 'If this was gone, he wouldn't have been interested. Yes, I killed him and took his money.'

Dawn turned slowly to look at the fifty-pound notes on the bed. 'You killed him?'

'Dawn, we're so close to getting out.' He held his hand up. 'It's within reach. You and me, living together in Amsterdam. No fear of persecution. We'll be so happy together. But this Fiona's determined to ruin it for us. I need her address. What is it?'

'What will you do?'

'Just talk to her. Explain that I'm Alexia. Show her that I'm all right and ask her to leave us alone.'

He got up and pulled a purple tracksuit on over the nightie. 'Her address, Dawn. Give it to me please.'

Dawn was hunched over, gently rocking herself back and forth. 'You killed him?'

He regarded her for a second, then turned to the mirror and starting applying make-up, vainly trying to mask the bruising around his nose and below his eyes. After that he put the wig on, teasing strands of hair forwards so they hung over his eyes. Next he took a chiffon scarf and wrapped it round his neck, fluffing the folds of material up so his jaw was hidden. 'The address, Dawn.'

The room was silent.

He put on a pair of high heels, then turned round. Her handbag was on the bed. His footsteps were loud as he stepped across and picked it up. Her address book was in there and he began flicking through the pages. There weren't many entries.

Finally Dawn looked up. 'No, you mustn't! Give it to me.'

She made a feeble lunge for the book but he batted her hand away. 'Is this her? Fiona Wilson? It is, isn't it?'

'Leave her alone!' She tried to stand but he shoved her back on the bed. The first time he'd ever used force against her. She curled into a ball as he ripped the page out and strode from the room.

The buzzer made Fiona's hand jolt. She grabbed a tissue and wiped off the bit of misapplied lipstick. Then she looked towards the door. No one had arranged to come round. Besides, she had to be at the hotel airport in under an hour: her first client was expecting her.

The buzzer went again.

This time Fiona replaced the lipstick in her make-up bag and stood. She straightened her dress and walked over to the door. As she peered out into the hallway the buzzer went yet again.

She padded across to the outer door and looked through the peephole to the street. All she could see was rain drifting down and a huge bunch of flowers.

Joanne Perkins, she thought: It must be a good-luck gesture. Something she does for all her escorts before their first date. How sweet.

She opened the door and looked out. The flowers dropped to the doorstep and her husband's dripping face leered at her. 'Found you, you fucking bitch.'

The sour stink of whisky hit her in the face.

Fiona tried to slam the door, but he jammed his foot into the gap. Knowing she'd never get her bedsit door locked in time, she whirled round and darted for the stairs. As she raced up them his footsteps were heavy behind her. She ran into the bathroom and slid the heavy brass bolt shut. The window was half open when he started kicking the door. Climbing out on to the windowsill, she reached an arm round the wet drainpipe. Her car was parked directly below, spare key hidden in the gap between the bricks.

Chapter 33

'Can I remind you this is a murder investigation?' Rick shook his head disbelievingly at Jon. 'That's right, the investigation is on-going ... Yes, you go and check with someone more senior.'

He cupped a hand over the phone mouthpiece. 'Incredible. The General Medical Council. Protecting patients and guiding doctors, according to their web site. More interested in looking after their own, if you ask me.' Abruptly he took his hand off the mouthpiece. 'Yes, it's extremely urgent. Call it a matter of life and death if you like – the Hippocratic oath has something to say about that, doesn't it? ... Thank you. Email is perfect.'

A message pinged on Rick's computer ten minutes later. He printed the documents out and sat down.

'Jesus Christ,' he whispered. 'He's a bit more than the plain old Dr O'Connor written on that brass plate outside the Beauty Centre.'

'Go on,' said Jon, leaning forward, elbows on the table.

'Try Dr Eamon O'Connor BDS, MB Bchir, FDSRC (Eng), FRCS (Eng), Phd. He's an oral and maxillofacial surgeon.'

Jon stared at him blankly. 'What's that?'

'Fucked if I know,' Rick replied, scanning down the top sheet. 'Born 5 August 1948, Dublin. Spent five years at dental school there, then two years training as a surgical dentist at Bart's in London. Then he took a postgraduate qualification at the Royal College. Passed it to become a Fellow in Dental Surgery.'

'So he's really a dentist?' Jon asked, thinking about Tyler Young's missing teeth.

'I haven't even started yet. Then he went back to medical school as an undergraduate. Four years at Cambridge, emerg-ing as Dr O'Connor. One year as a junior houseman at Guy's, where he spent six months training in general surgery and six months training in general medicine.'

'General surgery?'

'Wait,' said Rick. 'There's plenty more. Next he spent two years doing a Basic Surgical Training Rotation. Six months at the Accident and Emergency at St Thomas's, six months in their cardio-thoracic unit, and finally one year learning plastic surgery at University College London hospital. Then he took another exam to become a Fellow of the Royal College of Surgeons. After that he spent five years as a registrar at Guy's. He got a consultant's post there, and he started specialising in cranio-facial surgery.'

Rick read the next paragraph in silence, shaking his head all the while.

'What?' Jon demanded.

'Get this. It says that while he was a consultant at Guy's he reconstructed a lot of faces that had undergone major traumas. Even worked on a couple of casualties from the Falklands conflict. But his particular area of expertise, and one that he pioneered new techniques in, was removing sections of patient's faces to allow neurosurgeons access to tumours located at the base of the brain.'

Jon got up. 'You're serious?'

Before he could walk round and look at the documents himself, Rick tossed the top one across the desk.

Jon sat back down and flicked through it, stopping at the last page. 'It says here that, in 1989, he attended a hearing of the Professional Conduct Committee. Something called an FTP.'

'Fit to Practise,' said Rick, consulting another sheet. 'The committee judged that his FTP was impaired due to mental ill health resulting from a drug dependency. He botched an operation and left a patient with brain damage.'

'What was he taking?'

'Diamorphine.' Rick whistled. 'He got addicted to smack. Mitigating circumstances according to this. He smashed his knee in a road traffic accident and that led to his dependency.'

Jon snapped his fingers. 'The strange footprint! He's never

emerged from behind that bloody great desk of his. We've never seen him walk.'

Rick traced a finger down his sheet. 'So they suspended him from the medical register. Then, three years later, they allowed him to practise again, but with conditions on his registration.'

'Don't tell me,' Jon said, dropping the print out on the desk. 'He's not allowed to perform surgery.'

'Exactly,' said Rick. 'He moved to Manchester and set up the Beauty Centre in 1994.'

They parked in the side street by the Beauty Centre.

Jon looked into the rear yard of the building. 'The Range Rover's there. He must be in.' Then he glanced up at the heavy sky. 'This is coming in off the Irish sea. It won't stop for a while yet.'

They hurried round to the front entrance of the blackened building and rang the buzzer. After waiting a couple of minutes, Jon stepped back out into the rain and looked up. Doctor O'Connor tried to shrink back from the window, but their eyes had met.

Jon held a finger to his chest, then pointed upwards. Seconds later, the lock on the door clicked open.

They moved quickly up the stairs, Jon anxious to close down his time to think. When they entered his room, O'Connor was sitting behind his desk removing the skin from another tangerine. 'Gentlemen? You caught me just as I was about to lock up.'

They shook hands again and sat down. Jon glanced at Rick, a cue for him to begin.

'We don't want to keep you,' said Rick.

'Go ahead.' The doctor smiled and sat back, the leather of his chair creaking slightly. 'News about Gordon Dean?'

'No.' Rick slid the photo of Tyler Young from his jacket and laid it on the desk between them.

Jon studied O'Connor's reaction. He looked down, put the half-peeled piece of fruit aside, then extended a forefinger and rotated the photo so it was in perfect alignment with the edge of his desk. As usual he kept a poker face, not a hint of emotion on it. He looked up and raised his eyebrows questioningly, the skin on his forehead barely wrinkling.

'Have you ever seen this woman?' Rick asked.

The doctor didn't look at the photo. 'No.'

'You've never spoken to her?'

'How could I say? I get a lot of telephone enquiries. I could have spoken to her, but I wouldn't know what on earth she looked like. To what is this in relation?'

'According to her diary, she was discussing lip implants with you. Then you mentioned breast implants, too. Your prices were extremely competitive.'

O'Connor interlinked his fingers over the photograph, concealing the smiling face below. 'That's impossible for two reasons. One, I only perform non-surgical procedures. Two, she's clearly under twenty-five and I've made it a condition of the Beauty Centre not to offer treatment to anyone below that age.' He slid a brochure across the desk. 'Here, you'll find it in my introduction on page two.'

Jon got up and walked over to the shelves of books behind the doctor. O'Connor clearly found his presence there unsettling and partly turned in his seat.

Rick ignored the glossy booklet and nodded at the photograph. 'The body of Tyler Young was recently found with her breasts, face and large amounts of her flesh removed. Have you ever spoken to Carol Miller or Angela Rowlands? Their bodies were also discovered not long ago with most of their skin missing.'

O'Connor turned his attention back to Rick. Still his expression was neutral. 'Of course I haven't.'

Jon spoke. 'Interesting collection of books you have here. Tell me, Doctor O'Connor, you only perform cosmetic procedures?'

'Aesthetic medicine, I prefer to call it.'

'So why have you got a copy of this?' He didn't identify *Gray's Anatomy* or take it off the shelf, trying to oblige the doctor to get out of his seat.

But O'Connor leaned forward and peered round Jon. Before answering, he looked at Rick, then back at Jon, his eyes calculating. 'Would you mind sitting down? I can't speak to you

266

and your colleague if you're hovering behind me.'

Jon shrugged and took a seat, pleased to have rattled the doctor's apparent calm.

'I used to perform surgical procedures. Facial reconstructions for people who'd developed brain tumours or for the victims of car crashes and suchlike. Then, rather ironically, I was involved in a crash myself. My left knee was badly damaged and I developed an addiction to painkillers.'

'What sort of painkillers?' asked Rick.

O'Connor's eyes filled with shame. 'Diamorphine. I had free and easy access to it through my surgical work. Eventually it had a detrimental effect on my ability to perform. I was investigated by the General Medical Council and my licence was suspended. After attending a rehabilitation course, I was allowed to practise again – but with the condition I didn't perform surgery. That book is a leftover from my earlier career.'

The room was silent for a moment. Then Jon looked around and said, 'For a business, this place is always very quiet. When do you actually treat people?'

'Normally I use Thursdays and Fridays as my treatment days. It gives customers the weekend to recover. The rest of the week is given over to fielding enquiries, conducting consultations and, if I think it's appropriate, booking in customers for treatment.'

'So if those days are for, essentially, drumming up business, why did you ignore the door buzzer on our previous visit?' Jon stood up again and went to the window.

The doctor shifted in his seat. 'Probably because I was talking with you.'

'On our last visit I looked out of this window, like I'm doing now, and saw that your caller was a woman I recognised. She works in a motel on the A57. When she saw me looking down she couldn't walk away quickly enough. Why do you think that was?'

The doctor raised one shoulder a fraction. 'Perhaps she was coy about the fact she was considering aesthetic medicine. There's still a surprising amount of stigma attached, though it's lessening all the time, thanks to the exemplary lead provided by our celebrities.'

Jon thought he heard a cynical note in the doctor's voice. He walked over to the doorway and pointed across the corridor to the treatment room. 'Would you mind if I look around? Is this where you carry out your procedures?'

The doctor kept his seat but leaned forward, agitation finally showing. 'I'm afraid that room is locked.'

'Surely you have the key?'

'I've left it at home. My nurse has the other, but she's only here if we're treating customers.' He licked his lips.

Jon stared at him, sensing the man was telling lies. The blank expression was still clamped on the doctor's face, but a faint sheen of sweat glistened on his forehead. Jon's hand was outstretched to try the door handle. Instead, he crossed the room and, like a predator closing in for the kill, leaned in towards the doctor's face. Small beads of sweat oozed out of the shiny skin and began to run down his forehead.

'You're sweating, Doctor. Or can't you feel that? Perhaps you've been using Botox a bit too much. It wouldn't be the first time you've self-administered, after all.'

The doctor angrily wiped a hand across his forehead. 'I resent that insinuation and I don't like the direction this discussion is taking. I'm not prepared to say anything more without my solicitor present.'

'That's probably a good idea,' Jon replied.

O'Connor stood up and walked to the door: they saw that he had a pronounced limp. 'Good day, officers. You can show yourselves out.'

As they passed him, Jon smiled. 'I'm sure we'll be speaking to you again very soon, Doctor.'

When they emerged on to the street, the drizzle was still falling.

'Why didn't we just arrest him?' asked Rick.

Jon kept walking. 'After what happened with Pete Gray? The top of McCloughlin's head would blow clean off.'

'The man's bullshitting us! It's as clear as day.'

'I know.' Jon unlocked the car. 'Let's wait here and see what he does next. He's rattled. My bet is he'll be off like a shot.'

They moved further down the street and swung the car round. While they waited Jon watched the giant cranes looming out of the haze shrouding Ancoats. One was silently turning, a load of girders suspended from its end. Jon was reminded of a gentle animal, quietly grazing. But it was a harsh clanging that carried from behind the buildings in front. The noise seemed more akin to destruction, as if that part of the city was being demolished, not rebuilt.

O'Connor's Range Rover appeared ten minutes later. He drove up to the junction with the main road and turned right. With their windscreen wipers on their fastest setting, Jon and Rick followed him as he headed along Great Ancoats Street, passing the black glass of the old *Daily Express* offices and assorted derelict industrial buildings. Soon he got to the junction with the A57, just up from the Hurlington Health Club. He turned left, away from the city centre and towards the Platinum Inn. The streetlights flickered to life as the sky darkened above them.

'We're right in the Butcher's dumping ground. It's him. It has to be him!' Rick whispered excitedly.

Jon kept a couple of cars behind. They passed the motel and the greyhound stadium, then crawled through Gorton, failed shops and the occasional massage parlour lining the road. When they reached the roundabout for the M60, the Range Rover took the final exit, heading south, keeping in the slow lane, speed never creeping above seventy miles per hour.

'The turn off for Didsbury is in two junctions' time,' Jon said, remembering Dr Heath's report.

But O'Connor took the next exit. They dropped back and shadowed him along the A560, passing a Safeway and then a boarded-up building with the name Quaffers just visible above the entrance.

Five minutes later they were driving through the centre of Romiley, one car behind him. The high street petered out, shops replaced by terraces of housing. Soon they changed to semi-detached, then finally detached as countryside opened up on the left of the road. Farm lights dotted the dark hills in the distance. After a couple of hundred metres the Range Rover's brake lights lit up and it swung into a driveway closed in by large fir trees.

Jon and Rick pulled up on the verge. A privet hedge shielded the house from the road and they squeezed through the soaking branches into O'Connor's garden.

Crouching behind a rhododendron bush, they saw him hobble up the steps to a large Victorian house with wooden gables and a band of decorative brickwork running above the ground-floor mullioned windows. The exterior light came on and he set his briefcase down at his feet in order to unlock the front door.

The hallway lights went on. He came back outside and walked over to the rear of the Range Rover. After glancing down the drive, he opened the boot. He leaned in and, with some effort, straightened up. In his arms was a large object wrapped in a sheet.

'Christ almighty!' Rick whispered as the material slipped and a pair of feet wearing women's shoes were revealed.

'Oh, my fucking God,' Jon said, straightening up.

He felt Rick pulling him down as the doctor plodded up the steps into his house and shut the door behind him. 'Wait, Jon. We've got to call for back-up.'

Jon shook his head. 'They'll take half an hour, easily. She could be dead by then.'

Squinting at the placard beside the front door, Rick scrabbled for his phone. 'DS Saville here. We need back-up. We have a potential hostage situation at The Briars, Compstall Lane ... Yes, Armed Response Vehicle, everything. You'll see our car parked on the side of the road. It's a dark-blue Volvo, registration mike, alpha, zero, two, hotel, tango, foxtrot.'

He lowered the phone. 'They're on the way.'

A light showed in a tiny window at the base of the house, just above ground level.

'He's got a cellar,' Jon whispered. 'He's taken her down into the cellar. He's skinning them down there and then driving back into Belle Vue to dump their bodies.'

Keeping low, he splashed through the shallow puddles dotting the lawn, slowing when he reached the driveway. Carefully, he crossed the tarmac and crouched against the wall.

Rick emerged from the gloom and squatted down beside him.

Jon lay on his stomach and tried to look through the filthy pane of glass. A shadow moved across the room below and he was just able to hear a door open. 'He's down there. Taken her into a side room, I think.'

A car passed on the road. As the noise of its engine died away he heard a metallic clink. It was exactly the same sound as when the consultant at Stepping Hill hospital had dropped the long-bladed scalpel in the kidney tray. 'Oh, sweet Jesus. Rick, we can't wait. He's going to start skinning her.'

'You can't go in! We've got to wait.'

Jon got to his feet and went to the front door. It was made of solid-looking wood with two panels of stained glass running down it. He pressed the bell and heard it ring deep inside the house.

He counted to thirty, then pressed the bell again and kept his finger on it. Eventually he saw movement behind the glass. There was a rattling of a chain and the door opened a few inches. The instant O'Connor saw Jon outside he tried to slam the door shut.

Jon crashed his shoulder against it, just managing to prevent it clicking back on to the latch. The doctor pushed from the other side and for a few moments they were cheek to cheek, just the layer of wood separating them. Jon felt his strength begin to show and the door started inching inwards.

Abruptly the resistance disappeared and the doctor fled down the corridor, surgical gown flapping behind him.

Jon took a step back and kicked the door open, part of the security chain spinning across the hallway tiles.

He raced down the long corridor and into the kitchen. The doctor's briefcase lay partly open on the floor, files spilling out of it. Jon looked around. The door leading down to the cellar was in the opposite corner and it was slightly ajar.

He heard a voice behind him. 'Where is he?'

'Down there.' Jon pointed to the door and then whirled round. Against one wall stood a Welsh dresser and next to it was a wicker basket containing walking sticks and umbrellas. Jon grabbed a thick walking stick with a V-shaped split at the top and approached the cellar door.

He pushed it fully open with the end of the stick and looked down. A flight of bare wooden stairs led to a concrete floor. He started downwards, holding the stick before him. A shudder caught his shoulders and then snaked down his back as the air grew noticeably cooler. The cellar's central area was lit by a single bulb and three plywood doors led off from it, light shining from beneath two of them.

Jon stood listening.

To his side, an ancient-looking boiler came to life, a line of blue flames flaring behind a soot-speckled panel of glass. The row of pipes fastened to the bare brick wall above it started to creak and tick.

'Doctor O'Connor, there's no means of escape down here. Come out now.'

No reply.

Jon stepped up to the door for the unlit room and kicked it open. A dark and narrow space was beyond, the floor knee deep in coal.

He kicked open the next door. A larger room, lit by another single bulb which revealed stacks of medical journals, a pristine mountain bike, some folded-up deckchairs. At the back was a pile of clothes and women's shoes.

He turned to Rick and pointed at the last door.

Rick shook his head furiously and mouthed, 'Wait.'

The flames of the boiler went out and, as the cellar became silent again, they could hear a faint, wet hissing sound as if someone was blowing a thin stream of air through their teeth. They looked questioningly at each other, then Jon bowed his head and listened.

As he did so, a trickle of blood began to creep out from under the door. He jumped backwards, lowered his shoulder and charged. The door splintered off its hinges and he nearly fell into the room beyond. A cluster of halogen lights shone down, adding a glare to bright white walls that were spattered with dry blood. In the centre of the room was a concrete block, topped with a layer of what appeared to be marble. Stretched out on it was the woman, still partly wrapped in the sheet. Jon could see that she was still fully clothed.

The hissing was coming from the side of the room and Jon turned his head.

O'Connor was sitting with his back against the wall. His hands were slick and red and he was clumsily trying to pick up a scalpel caught in the blood-filled folds of his surgical gown. Blood spurted from his neck, each little jet hissing like a snake as it erupted into the air.

Rick came in. 'Oh my God, we need ... we need cloth. Something to stem the bleeding.' He grabbed the corner of the sheet wrapping the woman and tried to tear it.

O'Connor at last got a grip on the scalpel with his right hand. He turned his left wrist upwards and moved the tip of the blade towards it. Jon lifted the walking stick and brought the V of it down on to the doctor's right hand, pinning it in the puddle spreading out beneath his legs.

He told Rick, 'Leave it. The woman's our priority. Has she got a pulse?'

With shaking hands, Rick felt her neck. 'She's alive.'

'Then get upstairs and find out where the paramedics are. Now!'

Rick's mouth opened and shut. He pulled his mobile phone out and hurried back up the stairs. Jon looked around. Next to the woman was a small trolley. In a stainless steel tray on top of it were two syringes and a pair of latex gloves. Medical instruments lined the back wall. More scalpels, blades becoming ever more thin and cruel. Next to them were saws, clamps, retractors, hammers, chisels. A drill with a shiny silver bit. His eyes were caught by a test tube filled with what appeared to be human teeth.

He felt the walking stick shift and he looked down. The doctor was feebly trying to lift his scalpel hand.

Jon leaned on the stick. 'You're not taking the easy way out. Not before you tell me why.'

The doctor slumped back against the wall and raised his eyes. Even under the harsh lights their shine was fading, and Jon knew he hadn't long left. The little jets coming from his throat were getting smaller, weaker.

'Why?' Jon repeated. 'Why did you do it?'

O'Connor's eyes swivelled to Jon's hands and his voice sounded like wind in a cave. 'Enjoyable, isn't it?'

'What?' Jon demanded.

'Playing God, controlling whether I live or die.'

Jon looked at his knuckles, saw they were white with the pressure he was exerting on the end of the stick. He took his weight off. 'I'm not like you, Doctor.'

O'Connor's lips stretched in a faint smile as his head sagged forward and his eyes slowly shut. The blood now just trickled from his throat.

Jon knocked the scalpel from O'Connor's hand and rammed the V of the stick against the man's forehead, cracking his head against the white plaster. 'Why? Tell me why!'

The tiniest slit opened between the doctor's eyelids and a faint whisper emerged from his bloodless lips. 'We're just the same underneath.'

Violently Jon shook his head. 'No. No, we're not. Tell me ...'

His words faded to a whisper. The doctor had gone.

Jon stepped away from the pool of blood which was moving slowly across the floor like a living thing, easing itself into the gutter that ran around the table, dripping through the slats of the rusty drain.

He lifted the woman clear of the cold stone and carried her out of that terrible room with its cloying aroma of blood, both fresh and old.

Up in the kitchen he laid her on the table, lowering her head gently to the oak surface, tilting it back to make sure her airways were clear. He could hear Rick talking on the phone out on the front step. He sat down at the table, as if starting a vigil at the woman's side.

The doctor's briefcase and files still lay on the floor. Jon's eyes settled on the uppermost folder and the name written on its front: 'Alex/Alexia Donley'.

Alexia. The name of the prostitute Fiona Wilson was so desperate to find. He picked the file up and opened it.

A patient profile, Polaroid photo of a man in the upper right-hand corner. He was staring at the camera, self-conscious in its uncompromising gaze.

Alex Donley
Age: 34
Initial assessment: 3 /3 /01
Patient background: Alex came to me in a state of considerable agitation. In the last few years he has come to believe that he is a transsexual and has been seeking a gender reassignment through the NHS. His GP 'reluctantly' (to use Alex's word) referred him to the gender identity clinic at Charing Cross hospital. After fully assessing him, a consultant psychiatrist there judged that Alex wasn't a genuine transsexual. Alex scathingly told me that the consultant thought Alex is interested in becoming a woman because he believes it will resolve the violent outbursts to which he is susceptible. I questioned Alex more closely on this and he expressed his opinion that, once his testes have been removed and oestrogen prescribed, his masculine traits (which he sees purely in the form of aggression) will be replaced by feminine traits (which he sees purely in terms of compassion). Despite this obviously simplistic belief, Alex presents a rare and challenging case.

Jon heard footsteps in the hallway. He looked up to see Rick and a couple of armed officers trooping towards him.

'Where is he?' the one in front asked.

Jon nodded towards the cellar door. 'Down there, but you needn't worry, he's dead. It's a crime scene now, so best keep out.' He turned back to the file on his lap, the voices around him fading away.

I explained to Alex that I do not have the expertise or facilities to perform a vaginoplasty – recommending that he pay privately for the operation in Holland. Despite this, he was keen for me to perform facial surgery in order to feminise his features. We agreed that he should start a course of hormone therapy in order to develop breasts, redistribute fat around his hips and thighs, soften his body and facial hair and lift the pitch of his voice.
In terms of facial reconstruction we agreed on the following areas:

Octoplasty (to reduce the protrusion of his ears)
Rhinoplasty (to create a thinner nose)
Thyroid chondroplasty (to reduce the prominence of his Adam's apple)
Mandibular osteotomy (to reduce the squareness of his jawbone)
Dermal implants to cheeks, chin and lips (to round out his face)
Laser hair removal (back of neck, chest, nipples, underarms, forearms and hands)
Breast augmentation (C cup)
Alex appreciates that the treatment is on an unofficial basis and that the prices I charge reflect that. He has stated that he will pay for the procedures on a stage-by-stage basis as the necessary funds become available to him.

A hand shook Jon's shoulder and he looked up at the officer who'd spoken earlier.

'I said, how is she? What's he done to her?'

'Sedated her somehow.' Jon held a finger to her neck. 'Her pulse and breathing are regular. Where are the bloody paramedics?'

'On their way.'

Cursing, Jon returned to the file and flipped the page. A photo of Alex with bandaging around his ears, cheeks swollen and red. *16.7.01 Octoplasty and cheek implants. Paid cash.*

On the next page Alex was pouting at the camera, make-up and mascara on. *23.3.02. Breast augmentation, lip enlargement and laser hair removal. Paid cash.*

On the next he was wearing a wavy red wig. *5.12.02 Chin implant.* Jon realised he was looking at the woman from the garage forecourt CCTV footage.

His mind started ticking. The false eyelash in the boot of Gordon Dean's car. The last withdrawal on his credit card from a cashpoint that wasn't overlooked by CCTV cameras. Gordon Dean's car turning right as it left the garage forecourt, heading towards the Platinum Inn.

The pieces were coming together.

Alex Donley had killed Gordon Dean in that hotel room and put his body in the boot of the car. Then he'd driven to the Manchester Ship Canal and rolled the corpse in. After that, he'd cleaned out Dean's credit-card account and left the car at Piccadilly station to create a false trail.

Fiona Wilson had indeed heard a prostitute and a punter in the next room – but the person choked to death wasn't Alexia, it was Gordon Dean.

Jon turned the page and felt his scalp contract. There it was. *3.3.03* – the day after Gordon Dean had disappeared. *Rhinoplasty and mandibular osteotomy. Paid cash.* Alex Donley had funded the procedure with the money he'd taken from Gordon Dean's bank account the night before.

Rick sat down next to him. 'Just spoke to McCloughlin. He's on his way, though it nearly choked him to say it.'

Jon reached for his mobile, then realised he'd left it in the incident room. 'Give us your phone a second.'

Rick flinched at his abrupt tone but handed it over.

'Keep a check on her breathing,' Jon said, whipping out the notebook from his jacket. He flicked through to Fiona's mobile and rang it. Answerphone. He cut it off and thought for a second. It was evening opening at the salon. By the time Alice answered, he was standing on the front steps, noting with relief that the night was now clear. 'Ali, it's me. Your friend Fiona, where did you say she is?'

'She moved into a bedsit near Manchester City's old ground.'

'She still trying to find Alexia?'

Alice sighed. 'She thought she had the other day. But it was a mix-up of names. Yeah, she's out most nights I think.'

'I need her address, Ali. Have you got it there?'

'Jon, I'm with a customer. Can't it wait?'

'Alice, she's in real danger. I need it right now.'

Jon heard her making apologies to her client. Movement as she left the room.

An ambulance pulled into the driveway. The driver cut the engine and Jon heard the rear doors being opened. A moment later two paramedics appeared.

'Straight down the corridor into the kitchen,' Jon told them.

At the other end of the line he heard Alice call out, 'Has

someone moved Fiona's address? It was in the back of the appointments book.'

A female voice just audible. 'Oh, sorry, it's by the till. I had to give it to someone trying to deliver her some flowers.'

Alice again. 'You what? Who did you give it to?'

'A woman. She had a bouquet for Fiona.'

'When was this?'

'Earlier today. Lunchtime.'

'Jesus Christ, Zoe, that address was a secret. Jon?' Her voice was louder now. 'It's Flat 2, 15 Ridley Place, Fallowfield. Can you get over there now? I think her husband may have tracked her down.'

He turned and shouted down the corridor, 'Rick! I've got to go, that friend of Alice's is in serious trouble.'

Rick strode towards him, astonishment on his face. 'McCloughlin isn't here yet.'

'I know.' Jon handed back the phone. 'I'll let you fill him in.'

Rick's hand was still out, the phone resting on his upturned palm. 'You're not serious?'

But Jon was already jogging down the garden path, pulling the car keys from his pocket.

Chapter 34

Alex Donley paused at the front door of 15 Ridley Place. A huge bouquet of soaking flowers lay on the top step. The card read, *Together for ever.*

As he adjusted his wig and pulled the chiffon scarf up to hide the stitches running along his jaw, he noticed the door was slightly ajar.

With the tips of his varnished nails he pushed it open. The hallway was deserted. He could hear loud music upstairs. He looked at the doors in front of him and saw that number two was slightly open as well.

His heels clicked lightly as he stepped across the plastic tiles. Silence from Fiona's flat. Carefully, he pulled the kitchen knife from his handbag and eased the door open.

Thick fingers grabbed him by the wrist and he was yanked into the wrecked room beyond. A big man, growling with fury, swung him against the wall. The tip of the knife struck a radiator and was knocked from his grip. Another hand locked on to his jaw.

Alex smelled whisky as the man looked him up and down before saying, 'What sort of a fucking freak are you?'

He tried to escape the man's disgusted stare by turning his head, but the man yanked his chin round. Sharp pain shot along his stitches.

'I said, what sort of a fucking freak are you?'

'Let me go.'

But the man's grip on his face was steadily increasing. He felt the stitches starting to tear. Rage erupted in him like a geyser going off. He brought his hand up between the man's legs, grabbed his scrotum and twisted as hard as he could. The hands clamped on his jaw and wrist instantly released. Alex's free hand came up under the man's chin, preventing him from doubling over. Their eyes met for an instant, then Alex crashed his forehead against the man's nose. He dropped to the carpet as if taken out by a sniper.

Alex felt his face. His fingers came away covered in blood. The pain, the days spent in that bed, all for nothing. 'You fuck!' He stamped on the man's face, high heel snapping off as it connected with his teeth. 'You fuck, you fuck, you fuck!' he screamed, bringing his foot down again and again and again.

As he turned away he spotted a hand mirror on the shelf. When he looked into it he saw that his wig was hanging off one side of his head, an eyelash was missing and a four-inch slit had opened up along his left jaw, blood streaming down into the folds of his scarf.

'You piece of shit,' he said to the prone form curled on the floor, aiming one last stamp at the man's blood-filled ear.

He took out his mobile phone, waited until his breathing slowed down. 'Dawn, she's not here. Where else might she be? Didn't you mention a sal—'

Dawn cut in. 'She's here.'

'What, now?'

'Yes. She's asleep in one of the upstairs rooms. She turned up around half an hour ago and drank half a bottle of brandy straight down.'

'What did you tell her? Did you tell her about me?'

'No, I hardly said a word. She was going on about her husband finding her. Alex, what are you going to do?'

'Don't let her out.' He kicked the bouquet into a bush and staggered down the steps.

Ten minutes later Jon slipped cautiously into Fiona Wilson's flat and looked down. A large man with tight grey curls lay on the floor, face bruised and swollen, blood oozing from his nose, mouth and ears. Jon couldn't tell if it was Jeff Wilson or not. Next to his head was the broken-off heel of a woman's shoe.

Jon crouched down and started to put him in the recovery

position. An eye opened, slit-like in the puffy flesh.

Jon tensed, unsure of what the man might do. 'Can you hear me?'

'Bitch,' he mumbled through thick lips, blood bubbling out of his nostrils.

'I'm a police officer. Can you tell me your name?'

'Red-haired bitch.'

Jon opened his jacket, removed a mobile phone and wallet. He glanced at a bank card. Yes, it was the husband. 'Mr Wilson. Jeff. Can you hear me?'

The man coughed a few times and the eye swivelled round a bit.

'Where's your wife, Mr Wilson? Have you seen her?'

'She's gone.'

'Who did this to you?'

'Red-haired bitch.'

Jon's mind went to the person with Gordon Dean at the petrol station's cashpoint. 'A woman with red hair? About five feet eight or so?'

'Red-haired bitch.' His hand moved to his crotch and he winced with pain.

Jon got up. 'Don't try to move. I'm calling you an ambulance.' Fumbling through the unfamiliar menu on the phone, he called for help. Then he rang Alice. 'It's me. I'm at Fiona's place but she's not here. Where else might she be?'

'I don't know. Patrolling Minshull Street, maybe. That's where she's been looking for Alexia.'

Jon shut his eyes. 'Where would she go if she needed somewhere to stay?'

'Well, she just moved out of that refuge. Maybe back there?'

Jon ran upstairs and hammered on the door of the flat playing loud music. It opened on a dingy interior, a student blinking stupidly out at him from a haze of cannabis smoke. His eyes nearly popped out of his head when Jon thrust his warrant card in his face and demanded, 'What's your name?'

'Er, er ... it's Raymond. I can explain.' He waved at the thick fumes flooding out from his flat. 'I'm a student here at the university. But I also went to—'

'Raymond, shut up. I need you to look after a casualty until the ambulance arrives.'

Jon drove round to Stanhope Street, got his warrant card out and knocked on the door.

A very wary-looking woman answered. 'Hello?'

'I'm looking for Fiona Wilson. Has she turned up here this evening?'

'No. I'm Hazel, the manager. She moved over two weeks ago.'

'Do you know where to?'

'No, she didn't say.'

'OK, thanks.' He walked back to his car. Somewhere in the distance a burglar alarm let out an insistent wail into the night. He called Alice again. 'Think. Where else could she be?'

'What about the motel in Belle Vue? She mentioned the woman who runs it. I think they've become quite friendly.'

Dawn Poole stood behind the reception desk of the Platinum Inn, twirling a strand of hair round and round.

She'd run to the bathroom and vomited as soon as the front door had banged shut. Then she'd just sat on the bed for a while. None of this was happening. Her dreams of a life with him were falling apart.

Had he really killed that man? No. Coming off his hormones, and the business with Fiona, had upset him. Made him tell a load of lies.

So why are you packing your suitcase? she'd asked herself, pausing to look around their bedroom.

She stopped, a pair of jeans in her hand. Her usual response to violence was to curl up until it was over, then run away. But the thought of being alone again terrified her. She couldn't abandon everything with Alex so abruptly. Her mind swung back to how he'd pushed her. No. He wasn't really a violent man. She couldn't accept she'd got involved with one yet again.

Glancing at the half-packed suitcase, she'd had a desperate desire to talk to him. Unable to decide what to do, she'd caught the bus and gone to work as normal.

A gasp of shock escaped her as Alex tottered into the foyer. 'What have you done to your face?' she said, opening the counter flap and hurrying to him. 'You're bleeding!'

Alex slapped her hand away. 'Which room is she in?'

Dawn's voice faltered. 'Alex, you're making me so scared. What's happening?'

'Listen,' he hissed, bringing his face close to hers. 'Do you want her to ruin our future together?'

'No.' A tear started down Dawn's face and she bent her head.

'Good. We've got enough cash to get out of this country right now. Tonight. We'll make a new start together. You and me, Dawn. Just us. But this woman will wreck it all. She will. Now give me the fucking room number.'

Dawn's shoulders were drooping as she tried to control her sobs. 'What will you do to her?'

Alex slammed her up against the counter. 'Which fucking room!' he shrieked.

No. Oh God, no, it was happening again. She shut her eyes and heard a long moan coming from deep inside her. Be small. Don't do anything to make it worse. It will end soon.

His open hand crashed into her face, snapping her head back. 'The room!'

'Twenty-three – she's in room twenty-three. Please don't hurt me.' She fell to the floor as Alex kicked off his shoes and stormed towards the stairs.

Jon could see the motel foyer was empty as he raced towards the doors. He burst through and spotted a pair of woman's shoes on the floor. One was splattered with blood and missing a heel. Immediately he ran to the double doors on his right and scanned the corridor. Empty. The sound of sobbing was coming from the back office. He vaulted over the counter and went in. Dawn Poole was huddled in the corner, arms wrapped tightly round herself. A nearly empty bottle of brandy was on the floor at her feet, sodden tissues strewn around.

'Dawn, it's DI Spicer,' he said, crouching in front of her and looking into her face. 'Are you all right?'

She couldn't control her crying, her whole body convulsing with sobs.

Jon took her gently by the arms. 'Easy, Dawn, easy. You're OK.'

Her eyes were tightly closed.

'Dawn, can you answer me? Is Fiona Wilson here?'

He felt her stiffen.

'She's here, isn't she? Her husband found her flat. She came here because she had nowhere else to go. I'm right, aren't I?'

Dawn took in a shuddering great breath.

'Dawn, is Alex Donley here? Alexia, the red-haired prostitute?'

She started to shiver. 'He said he'd never hurt me. Oh God, it's all gone … it's all gone wrong.'

Jon frowned. 'Who said that? Alex?'

She nodded.

'Alex is your partner?'

'He said he was different. Said he'd protect me.'

Jon gently squeezed her arms, aware how painfully thin they were. 'Dawn, none of this is your fault. Do you hear me? Dawn, open your eyes. Look at me.'

She took another breath and her eyes slowly opened.

Christ, he thought, seeing the look of utter defeat in them. 'I know people have made you a victim in your life. But you can put a stop to it now, do you hear me? You can put a stop to all of this by telling me where Fiona is. Please tell me before she gets hurt.'

She shut her eyes and Jon thought he was losing her. But she lifted her chin and said, 'Room twenty-three.'

He jumped to his feet.

She started to cry again. 'He's up there already. You must stop him – he's going to do something terrible.'

The door at the top of the stairs opened on to another empty corridor. Jon looked at the first door: fourteen. He crept forwards, passing fifteen on the other side. Seventeen, nineteen, twenty-one. Twenty-three. The door was shut. He listened, but no noise came from inside. Slowly he turned the handle and opened it a crack.

'You stupid cunt.' A man's voice, straining with effort. 'This is what happens to stupid cunts like you.'

Jon slipped inside, moved past the bathroom and looked into the room beyond. Alex Donley was straddling the chest of Fiona Wilson, pressing a pillow into her upturned face. Fiona's hands were scrabbling around, feebly trying to get a grip on the thing smothering her.

One step took Jon to the edge of the bed. 'Hey!' he barked, swinging with all his might.

Alex's head whirled round, streaks of long red hair flying out. Jon's fist caught him full in the mouth, lifting him clean off Fiona and sending him somersaulting backwards to the floor.

Jon plucked the pillow from Fiona's face, heard her gasping in air. He looked over the end of the bed.

Alex Donley lay crumpled and unconscious on the floor, both lips burst open, the upper one split right up to the base of his nose.

Chapter 35

Officers were clearing their drawers, packing files and personal effects into boxes. Rick held up a batch of reports and tapped their lower edges on the desk to square them off. 'How did you track them down?'

'I pulled all the reports for credit cards that had been lost or stolen in the city centre in the three days prior to Alex Donley paying for a new surgical procedure.'

'Quite a few, no doubt?'

'A few dozen. From those, I selected all reports made by men. Next I took the cases where money was withdrawn from a cashpoint after the card's disappearance had been reported. That narrowed it down massively, since you need the card's PIN to make a cash withdrawal. After that it was just a case of contacting the card owner, explaining it was a murder investigation and asking whether they'd lost their card in the vicinity of Canal Street.'

'I bet that got a few evasive answers.'

Jon smiled. 'It certainly did. But I explained that it was all confidential and they soon admitted involvement with a certain red-haired individual going by the name of Alexia.'

Rick shook his head. 'So who were these people?'

'All sorts. An immigration officer from Gatwick doing a placement at the airport, a builder working on the new apartments going up, and an out-of-towner who was in Manchester for the weekend.'

'What I don't understand is how he got access to all their bank accounts.'

'I've been thinking about that, too,' Jon replied. 'Remember the garage forecourt? He was snaking round Gordon Dean at that cashpoint. I reckon he skimmed the guy's PIN then.'

Rick rubbed his forehead. 'The sneaky bastard. So he'd rob someone, then go straight to Dr O'Connor and use the money for his next stage of surgery.'

'Exactly. There's a gap of several months between his visits to O'Connor. As soon as the wounds from one operation healed, he'd go back on the game and rob another punter. What I want to know is why he took the step of actually killing someone. What's the score with him? Has he spoken yet?'

Rick shook his head. 'Still scrawling on his little pad that he can't talk. They'll do a psychiatric assessment once his mouth's sorted out.' He glanced at Jon's bandaged right hand. 'That must have been some punch.'

Jon said nothing.

'In the meantime,' Rick quickly continued, 'Dawn Poole's proving extremely helpful.'

'She still under arrest?'

'No. We're putting her up in a hotel for the time being. Obviously she knew Alex was earning money by turning tricks on the ladyboy circuit, but McCloughlin's happy she had no idea he had murdered a punter.'

'Good,' Jon said. 'She didn't.'

'And Fiona Wilson?' Rick's question hung in the air.

'She's moved back in with her parents and is talking to the Domestic Violence Unit. I gather from Alice that she's pressing charges against her husband. The refuge has got photographic evidence. She's divorcing the prick, too. He's been on a decent salary for years, so she'll be fine from a financial point of view.'

Rick looked around. There were only a couple of other officers left. 'Good. Coming for a drink? McCloughlin's put a couple of hundred behind the bar, apparently.'

Jon thought of how McCloughlin had rubbed his nose in it about getting it so wrong with Pete Gray. He got up, a half-hearted smile on his face. 'I don't think so. Tell the lads I'm on painkillers. No alcohol allowed.'

'A Coke, then?'

Jon raised his eyebrows. 'Be serious. No, I'll pass.'

'Another time, then. The Bull's Head, perhaps?'

'Definitely. So where's your next stint?'

'I've got some time off to think about it. I'm not sure if the front-line stuff is really my thing. Maybe I'll head back to Chester House. There's something I could do on discipline and complaints.' He looked at Jon for his reaction.

'You've been excellent to work with, Rick. You're bloody sharp and you're meticulous with detail.'

'Thanks. But I froze at O'Connor's house. I didn't want to go in there. If you hadn't led the way ...'

Jon shrugged. 'Another thing about that cellar. He had two syringes in the tray by the stone slab. Did you find out what they were?'

'Yup. Propofol, to keep her sedated. Diamorphine for him.'

'He'd started using again?'

'That psychologist, Dr Heath, reckons he was using it as a disinhibitor. To allow him to do what he did.'

Jon picked at the edge of the box of files.

'What's on your mind?' Rick asked.

'Any theories from Dr Heath on why he was doing it?'

'Only the usual ones – the thrill of playing God, that sort of thing.'

Dr O'Connor's final words echoed in Jon's head. Deep inside a little part of him agreed that there was a thrill in holding another man's life in his hands. The sensation, he realised, hadn't been a lot different from swinging his fist into Alex Donley's face.

'Come on, mate, spit it out,' Rick said.

Taking a deep breath, Jon quietly spoke. 'Down in that cellar, after you'd gone upstairs to check on the ambulance, he said something to me.'

'Really? What?' Rick hunched forwards to hear better.

Jon caught Rick's eye for an instant. 'I let him die down there, Rick, and he smiled and said, "We're just the same underneath."'

His eyes dropped to his watch and he kept them there as the seconds ticked silently past.

Finally Rick said, 'Two things. You didn't let him die. He'd just about bled out by the time we got there. He'd gone through an artery. I doubt a team in an operating theatre could have saved him.'

Jon tried to smile. 'But I was happy to not even try. What's your second point?'

'"We're just the same underneath". Are those his exact words?'

Jon nodded.

'I don't think he meant we as in you and him. He meant we as in all of us. We're all the same underneath. Maybe that's what he was trying to show by skinning his victims. It was a demonstration, a display. Perhaps a protest against the way his art – one that took him years to acquire – is being debased and exploited to satisfy people's vanity.'

'You think so?'

'Yes.' Rick got up and came round their desks. They faced each other a little awkwardly. He held out a hand.

Jon glanced down at his bandaged fingers. Unable to shake, he raised his left hand instead and clapped it on Rick's shoulder. 'Good working with you, mate.'

'Likewise.'

They embraced, each slapping the other's back – a ploy, Jon knew, to keep up the required level of manliness.

As Rick set off for the pub, Jon called across the empty office. 'If you change your mind about the front-line stuff, I'd be happy to work with you again.'

Epilogue

Jon knelt on the nursery floor, spreading the same paint-spattered sheets of newspaper out. He put the tin of red paint on them, then tried to prise off the lid with his left hand. The fingers of his right were no longer bandaged, but gripping anything was still painful.

Reaching for the spoon, he lifted it with a quiet crack from the crusty blob of paint it lay in. The viscous puddle on the floor of Dr O'Connor's cellar appeared in his head. The file notes for Carol Miller, Angela Rowlands and Tyler Young had been found hidden in his surgery. All died trying to achieve some superficial ideal of beauty. Images flashed through his head. Melvyn's salon. Jakes' tattoo parlour. The Paragon Group. TV shows, magazine articles, newspaper reports. All about one thing: trying to look more attractive.

Jon put the paint-covered spoon aside and, still kneeling, rested his elbows on the windowsill. He stared through the glass, unable to stop dwelling on why Dr O'Connor had started to kill his customers. The explanation, if there ever could be one for things like that, had gone with him to the grave. What a world this is, he thought, letting out a little snort of breath.

Alice's voice came from the doorway behind him. 'A penny for your thoughts.'

He looked round, and without getting up held his arms out. 'Come here.'

Slowly she crossed the room, her stomach looking like it was about to burst. She stepped carefully onto the sheets of paper, one foot covering the small ad for the Beauty Centre. It sat discreetly next to the columns of classified entries in the 'Health and Beauty' section. The opposite page was covered in boxed ads for Manchester's assortment of massage parlours and escort agencies, Cheshire Consorts' one of those at the top.

Still kneeling, Jon pressed his cheek against Alice's belly and reached his arms round her until he could grasp his own wrist. It was a gesture that sought to protect them from everything he knew existed outside the window and an attempt to bind all three of them closer together. But it didn't seem enough. A desire for something more tangible engulfed him and he found himself saying, 'Alice, do you fancy getting married?'

Acknowledgements

Once again a rough manuscript was transformed by the expert touch of Gregory and Company and Orion – special thanks to Emma Dunford and Jane Wood for all your time.

Keeping names anonymous for professional reputations, a big thank you to:
   The Turnip – how you sat all those exams, I'll never know
   Ian – for the medical advice and the tour of your cellar
   Nessy – top marks on the police knowledge as usual
   Jo – for showing me round your salon

If you have enjoyed

Shifting Skin

Don't miss

SAVAGE MOON

Chris Simms' latest novel

Available now in Orion hardback

Price £18.99
ISBN 978-0-7528-8929-0

Prologue

The quad bike bounced across the moors, headlight catching coarse blades of grass before rearing up into the infinity of the night sky. Like a rider struggling with an unbroken horse, the woman fought to control the vehicle. But rather than slow down, she kept the revs high, her knees flexed in readiness for the next jarring bump.

Way off to her right the undulating red light that topped the radio mast disappeared behind a rise in the land. Finally she dropped her speed, and the engine's angry growl subsided to reveal the same sound that had sparked her reckless dash in the first place: the terror-stricken bleating of a sheep.

'Not another,' she murmured, eyes turning to the shallow ravine that dropped away to her right. She yanked the handlebars round but the headlight's angle was too high. A turn of the key and the engine shuddered into silence. Suffocating darkness engulfed her. She groped for the heavy-duty spotlight behind the saddle and, as she set off down the slope, began playing the yellow beam before her.

Maybe thirty metres away was a cluster of large boulders. A haze-winged moth homed in on the torch like a heat-seeking missile. It landed on her cuff and she felt the frantic blur of wings against the back of her hand. Ignoring the insect, she trudged onwards, eyes fixed on a blood-stained clump of white fleece. The moth launched itself on a sharp curve, flashed across the trembling shaft and plummeted into the turf. She reached the head-high rocks, stepped round the outermost one and shone the light into the semi-circular grouping.

The sheep was lying on its stomach, its head hanging over front legs that were tucked under its chest. The rear legs were tangled up in entrails that glistened like freshly caught eels. An acrid smell stung her nostrils as she stepped closer, then crouched down. Oh no. The animal was still alive. She swung the torch towards the base of the nearest boulder. Something to put it out of its misery. A rock. Anything. The light picked out a trail of blood dripping down the steep grit surface – the implications were just sinking in when the low snarl sounded from above. As she began to swivel the torch upwards a heavy black form landed on top of her.

One

The house was pitch black as Jon Spicer shuffled, sleepy and naked, towards the mewling little cries. He stepped into the nursery where the soft glow of a nightlight barely revealed the tiny form in the cot.

She was on her back, head twitching from side to side, limbs jerking in mounting frustration. He stared down, mind slowly firing up as he assessed the situation, trying to work out what the problem was. Cold? Hot? Wet? Surely not hungry again, he thought, knowing that would involve a trip downstairs to warm a bottle of milk in the microwave.

He heard a faint plastic click as she flung a miniature fist out to the side. The dummy. Her dummy's fallen out. His movements were slow and clumsy as he patted the soft cotton sheet around her head and, at that moment, finding an object worth less than two pounds became the most important thing in the world.

A fingertip caught on the rubber teat. He picked the dummy up and held it to his daughter's lips. They immediately latched on to it and she began a greedy sucking.

He stood motionless with his eyes half shut, trying to maintain his semi-awake state, desperate to return to his own bed and fall back into the heavy folds of sleep. But the sucking noises continued with the same urgency and a tiny puff of exasperation escaped round the object in her mouth.

Shit, he thought. A dummy isn't going to be enough. She's hungry. Accepting that a feed was necessary, more parts of his brain started clicking into gear. He stepped back into the darkness and towards the stairs.

Movement from the main bedroom as his wife shifted in their bed. 'Jon?'

'It's all right,' he whispered, knowing that however tired he felt his wife was a step closer to total exhaustion. 'Holly's hungry. I'll sort it.'

The bed creaked as she fell back against the mattress. He padded quickly down the stairs.

Punch stirred in his basket as he entered the kitchen. 'Hi there, stupid,' he murmured, opening the fridge. A pool of feeble light spilled out across the floor, casting a ghostly glow across the room. He took a squat plastic bottle three quarters full of the formula they used when Alice was too tired to breast-feed. Leaving the fridge door open, he placed the bottle in the microwave. Holly's whimpers were increasing in strength upstairs. Looking out the window, all he could see was the faint reflection of his head and torso floating in the expanse of black glass before him. He felt a fleeting sense of vulnerability. Anything could be lurking beyond the thinness of the window, watching him from the darkness.

Uneasily, he glanced up at the clock on the wall. Four thirty-seven in the morning. The hours before dawn and the perfect time for raiding a suspect's house. The time when people were in their deepest sleep, disoriented and slow when wrenched from unconsciousness by their front door bursting off its hinges. Or a baby bursting into cries, he thought with a dry smile.

As the microwave whirred he heard Punch's claws ticking on the lino. He looked down and saw his Boxer bathed in the glow from the fridge, the stump of his tail wagging uncertainly. 'Still getting used to these commotions, aren't you, boy?' he said quietly, running a hand over the animal's head. 'Me too, me too.' The machine pinged and he took the bottle out, cupping the base of it in his hand to test the warmth of the liquid inside. 'See you in the morning.'

He pushed the fridge door shut and the darkness instantly surged back, jealously reclaiming the room.

Jon climbed the stairs two at a time, making it back into the nursery just as the dummy tumbled from his daughter's mouth. The whine of frustration was rapidly turning into a toy-like cry.

'Hey there,' he whispered, hooking his index fingers under her arms and lifting her clear of the cot, always amazed at how light she was. He sat down on the padded chair and positioned her in the crook of his arm as her tiny legs kicked about.

'Here you go, greedy young madam.' He offered her the teat and she immediately took it. The squeaks were replaced by bubbling noises and she pressed her fists against the sides of the bottle.

Thank God, he thought, settling into the seat, feeling the cool material against his back. He stared down at the little thing in his arms, sifting through his feelings, searching as usual for the unbreakable bond of emotion that ought to be there.

But he couldn't find it. Of course he loved the baby and knew instinctively that he would lay down his life for her, but the tangible feeling of love that he felt every time he looked at Alice, or Punch for that matter, just wasn't there. Like an oak tree in the dark, he could sense its looming presence but, for now, he couldn't locate it.

Holly was born just over three months ago and he was only now beginning to comprehend how their lives had changed forever. At first, it had felt like she was a temporary break in their routine. The first night feeds were easy – after all, anyone can handle a few interruptions to their sleep. They'd even laughed, feeling relief at how it wasn't that hard having a baby after all.

But then the days stretched into weeks and the weeks into months and slowly it was starting to dawn on him that they were in this for the long run. Things weren't about to settle back to how they'd once been. Not ever.

He closed his eyes and leaned his head back. Almost five o'clock. An hour and a half more sleep if he was lucky, then Monday morning and back to work. Bollocks, he thought, letting out a sigh. The case he was working on seemed to be a total dead-ender. A few elderly homosexuals had been assaulted at night in car parks dotted around Manchester. No one wanted to talk about it, especially not the victims once the ambulance drivers had patched up the minor cuts and bruises to their heads. Normally the Major Incident Team wouldn't be dragged into a case of this nature, but the latest attack had moved the case up several notches in the serious crime scorecard.

The recording of the emergency call was clear in his head. A man's voice, panic making it waver and dip.

'Police? That's the police? You need to get out here, someone's being killed!'

The operator's voice, calm and steady. 'Where are you, Sir?'

'What? It's the car park. The one by the recreation ground. Silburn Grove, Middleton.'

'The public car park on Silburn Grove. Thank you, Sir. Who is being attacked?'

'Listen, I don't know! This lad jumped out on us by the shed. He's got an iron bar. Oh Jesus, I can hear screaming.'

The recording had captured it too, muffled and faint in the background. Someone in terror for their life.

'Good God, hurry. He's killing him.'

'Please stay calm, Sir. Who is being attacked?'

'Oh! I can see him now, he's come back round. He's going towards his car.'

'Who, Sir? The attacker?'

'There's so much blood!'

'Can you see the make or registration?'

'MA03 H something. It's a big estate. Jesus, I don't know where the other guy is.' Movement against the earpiece as the man must have looked desperately around. Just before he rang off an engine surged as the accelerator was pressed down.

By the time the patrol car arrived the car park was deserted. As one of Manchester's more popular sites for gay rendezvous, that was very unusual – especially since it was late evening. The attending officers had swept the area around the shed with their torches and soon found blood spatters arcing in dotted lines up a side wall. Someone had taken a serious beating.

Clusters of drops had then led them across the asphalt towards an area of undergrowth that screened a shallow, dirty stream. The water was clogged with old tyres, bags of dumped rubbish and the odd shopping trolley. No corpse was in the vicinity.

The decision was made to refer the assault on to MIT and Jon arrived at the crime scene two hours later. The powers that be saw it as an escalation of violence that could – if it hadn't already – lead to murder.

The problem was the lack of witnesses. Jon was familiar with cases where victim and witnesses were unwilling to come forward. He was left trying to investigate a case that was doomed to failure. Only when an actual body showed up would the resources needed for a breakthrough be released. Still, at least he was getting home on time each night.

Gurgling noises returned him to the present. He looked down as Holly pushed the teat from her mouth. Her arms slowly lowered then fell slackly to her sides. He held the bottle to the nightlight and saw it was almost empty. Jesus, she could bolt milk like there was no tomorrow. His mum had seen this and, unable to resist a bit of misty-eyed reminiscing, proudly told Alice that, as a baby, Jon could sink nine ounces in a few minutes. But, Jon thought, he'd weighed almost eleven pounds when he was born. The little thing in his lap had been almost half that. Obviously making up for it.

He lifted her to a sitting position, formed a V shape with the thumb and fingers of his spare hand and then gently wedged her chin into it. Her arms hung down and he began rubbing her back, feeling the minute bumps of her spine against the palm of his hand. So tiny. So fragile. Eventually a couple of surprisingly large burps escaped her. 'Good ones, my piglet,' he whispered, planting a kiss on her soft cheek. He lifted her up and gently placed her back in the cot. He was just straightening up when a noise outside caused him to freeze.

The sound, at first low and guttural, suddenly erupted into a hideous yowl. Something deep in Jon reacted to its animal ferocity and his heart started to beat more quickly. The noise came again, dying away into a fearsome hiss.

He stepped over to the window, lifted the blind and peered out into the blackness. A crack had opened in the unseen cloud layer above and moonlight shone down. Balanced on their rear wall was a large tabby cat, back arched upward, fur jutting out in a series of spikes. Its attention was riveted on something on the other side of the wall.

Jon felt like a wildlife photographer observing the secret interplays that take place between the creatures of the night. Sightings of foxes were becoming more and more common in the neighbourhood and he felt a slight thrill that a wild animal could be just metres away, roaming the streets and alleys, using the darkness to claim an urban territory as its own.

Suddenly a tingle worked its way down his spine as he thought about what had taken place up on Saddleworth Moor not three weeks ago. A farmer's wife had been savaged to death by some creature and a frenzy of 'mystery beast' fever had gripped the nation ever since.

Jon knew from recent newspaper articles that the loss of sheep was a fairly commonplace occurrence for many farms in and around Britain's national parks. The problem had got so bad around Bodmin during the mid-nineties that the Ministry for Agriculture, Fisheries and Food had commissioned a scientific investigation to determine once and for all if a wild panther was stalking the bleak expanses of Dartmoor. The study was inconclusive and the issue had lapsed back to occasional sightings of large black cats. But ripped open and disembowelled carcasses of sheep continued to be found in the more remote parts of the countryside.

The Suttons' farm on Saddleworth was suffering particularly badly and the wife, a few years younger than her more elderly husband, had taken to going out at night and patrolling the perimeters of their land on a quad bike. On the fateful night, the husband had been away from home, staying overnight at a big sheep market in Keswick up in the Lake District. According to numerous witnesses, he'd got mightily drunk before staggering off to his hotel room at gone two in the morning. When he returned home the next day his wife was nowhere to be found. Eventually he'd gone out on to the moor, spotted the abandoned quad bike and then discovered her corpse alongside the remains of a partially eaten ewe in a nearby ravine. Both of their throats had been torn out and short strands of wiry black hair were found under the wife's nails. Laboratory analysis revealed that the hair belonged to a panther.

The cat on their yard wall was now backing away, a horrible low noise emerging from deep within its throat. Deciding there was enough distance between it and the unseen adversary below, it turned and leaped onto the adjoining wall before disappearing up and over the neighbour's garage with a frantic scrabble of claws. The gap in the cloud closed up, the scene vanished and silence returned.

From beyond the curve of the earth came a faint glow, just strong enough to separate black horizon from dark sky. Night was coming to an end.

The creature remained motionless, body pressed into the tundra-like grass of the moor. Before it the ground dropped away, clumps of gorse quickly dissolving into the gloom. Further down the slope two sheep sheltered at the base of a particularly dense bush.

The wind shifted and the long hairs that emerged from the tips of the creature's ears bent ever so slightly. This new current of air carried up from the plains of Cheshire stretched out below. Contained in it were some interesting sounds and scents. The noise of engines, the sharpness of exhaust fumes, the presence of Man.

The creature's gaze moved across the uncultivated land, settling on the outermost edge of urban sprawl leading back into the city of Manchester itself. Its eyes narrowed slightly and it examined the lights that twinkled from street lamps and cars and people's homes.

THE ECONOMIC VALUE OF PEACE AND QUIET

The Economic Value of
Peace and Quiet

D. N. M. STARKIE
University of Reading

D. M. JOHNSON
University of Aston

SAXON HOUSE | LEXINGTON BOOKS

Published by
SAXON HOUSE, D. C. Heath Ltd.
Westmead, Farnborough, Hants., England

Jointly with
LEXINGTON BOOKS, D. C. Heath & Co.
Lexington, Mass. U.S.A.

ISBN 0 347 01075 X
Library of Congress Catalog Card Number 74–26358

Printed in England by Eyre & Spottiswoode Limited at Grosvenor Press, Portsmouth

Contents

List of figures

List of tables

Introduction and Acknowledgements

Like long, hot summers, peace and quiet (the corollary of noise) is to many people but a childhood memory. Whether its demise is equally an illusion is an arguable point, but the belief is a political reality. As the effects of advanced technology ripple around the world, issues of peace and quiet disturbed by supersonic aircraft, by new airports, express highways and railways and by motor-traffic in general, preoccupy politicians and are of major concern to governments, both national and international.

Apart from the view, strongly held by some, that noise is increasingly pervasive in modern society (that the supply curve of quiet has shifted leftwards), at least two other possibly interrelated factors combine to imbue peace and quiet with political import. Increased spending on the luxury of less noise as a consequence of rising disposable incomes is one factor. A second is that social values are changing; good environments are moving upwards in the list of social priorities (*Royal Commission on Environmental Pollution, 1971*) and 'people increasingly resent being subjected to noise, particularly in their homes' (*Department of the Environment, 1973*).

The political response to this threat posed to 'civilised' living has taken a number of forms: frequent legislation prescribing standards of sound emission; expenditure of more resources on relocating noisy activities – airports for instance; and, more simplictically, outright abolition of peace-disturbing activities.

But, it must be remembered too that forbidden or curtailed activities have a value, a value which is reduced or eliminated thereby. And the more we spend on noise abatement, the fewer resources there are available for spending on other things, such as housing, health and education or private consumption and investment. The simple fact is that noise exists because some people directly or indirectly benefit by it. Thus, the real problem to be faced is not how to stop noise altogether, but how far it should be reduced (if, indeed, in some cases it should be reduced at all). The need is to strike a balance between gains and losses; the sensible approach is to reduce noise pollution to the point where the costs of doing so are covered by the benefits from increased peace and quiet (*Royal Commission on Environmental Pollution, 1971*).[1]

A necessary, although not sufficient, requirement for the successful application of this approach is some knowledge of the monetary value of the benefit. This book shows that one can derive such values. We firmly believe that with application and focus it should prove possible to indicate the value that society places upon various environmental 'intangibles'. Of course, whether all such values are appropriate for decision-making and whether the game is worth the candle is quite another matter. To many people, it is not worth it; some, for example, would find repugnant ideas that peace and quiet should be subjected to monetary valuation. Although we do not share this view, we can understand it. Noise is an emotional issue and many people are seriously disturbed by it. But because of this it is easy to forget that there are many other people who appear quite unperturbed by very high levels of sound. Around London (Heathrow), Europe's busiest airport, for example, surveys have suggested that about one-third of the adult population are unconcerned by noise, whatever its level (*Committee on the Problem of Noise, 1963*). Such people are either by nature insensitive or have become con- ditioned – they have, to quote Thurber: 'excluded noise by sound-proofing the mind'. Their preference would be for cheaper airline seats rather than for quieter planes. And here lies the crux of the matter.

The book divides into two distinct parts. The first (Chapters 1–7) develops what we believe to be a new and promising approach to what many people think of as an intractable problem, valuing peace and quiet. This new approach, which we call the exclusion facilities approach, is based on the notion that an implicit market for environmental attributes exists. Although the focus of this study is upon aircraft noise, the method is equally applicable to other noises external to the home. Indeed, the basic philosophy is applicable to the valuation of a much wider range of environmental attributes – wherever and whenever money is spent on the creation of artificial environments, one also will find the basis for an exclusion facilities approach.

We hope this text will be read by acousticians and planners, with a pro- fessional interest in the noise problem, as well as by economists. Because of this, Chapter 3 sets out the basic elements of welfare theory pertinent to the valuation of pollution externalities. Conversely, for the benefit of non- acousticians, Chapter 1 describes in some detail the measures of sound, noise and aircraft noise exposure.

The second part of the book (Chapters 8–13) is a case study of the exclusion facilities approach applied around London (Heathrow) Airport. No attempt is made to reappraise past decisions or cost benefit studies in the light of the values for peace and quiet that emerge. Fundamentally, this is because it was not our objective to do so. Our aim is to provide the raw material to carry out such studies. Moreover, we see our study as exploratory. We do not claim to have discovered the ultimate truth, but we do think the values revealed provide a rough guide for those with decisions to make.

The book evolved from research commissioned by the Department of the

Environment in 1971. The results of that industry are to be found in these pages. However, in spite of this pedigree, none of the material contained here should be construed as reflecting the opinions or views of the Department of the Environment. Whatever that corporate view might be, we did nevertheless benefit greatly from the comments of Peter Vass, John Hargreaves (now with Deloitte, Robson, Morrow & Co.) and Alan Lassiere. Our special thanks are to Alan, whose own peace of mind undoubtedly suffered from the burden of in-house responsibility for the research.[2]

We would also like to take this opportunity of thanking many others who freely provided advice, data and material for the original study. In particular, we would like to thank David Foot and Roger Samons of the Department of Geography, University of Reading, who advised on computation and related matters; Dr Andrew Grigg and his colleagues at the Transport & Road Research Laboratory for advice on logit analysis; Miss Livingstone of the British Airports Authority for providing aircraft flight data; David Frost, Planning Department, London Borough of Hounslow; Paul Cheshire, Department of Economics, University of Reading; Dr Gerry Webber of the Building Research Station, Department of the Environment, whose initial index of double glazing households proved invaluable; Mr Kelman of Aero-slim Double Glazing; Sheila Dance and Steven Hale for so expertly transforming rough sketches; and Thelma Warden for editorial work.

We are also very grateful for the kindness of Peter Hall in tolerating the intrusion of such awkward research in the Department of Geography, Reading University. As the writing of the book was the responsibility of David Starkie, all errors and omissions should therefore be attributed to him alone. His individual thanks go to David Pearce and Michael Tyler for commenting on an earlier draft.

Note

1   The formal conditions for Paretian optimality in the context of noise pollution externalities can be found in A. Lassiere and P. Bowers (1972) and D. Pearce (1974).

2   D. N. M. Starkie, *Valuation of Disamenity in Transport Planning*, a report to the Secretary of State for the Environment in fulfilment of contract No CAA9/5/041.

1 Measures of Sound, Noise and Aircraft-noise Exposure

Noise is commonly defined as 'unwanted' sound (*Committee on the Problem of Noise, 1963*). A simple description but one which pinpoints two salient features. First, all noise is sound; second, all noise is subjective, to wit it is a function of an individual's perception and attitudes. It follows that where other things are equal, the greater the generation and propagation of sound the worse a noise problem becomes. Alternatively for a given set of physical characteristics, a noise problem may deteriorate as a result of changes in personal values.

The simple description also highlights the fact that acoustics – the science of sound – is interdisciplinary by nature. At one end of the disciplinary spectrum is a physical science primarily concerned with the measurement of energy transference, whilst at the other extreme lies the relatively unexplored area of human perception and attitude formation which is gradually being delved into by sociologists and psychologists. The interface between these disparate disciplines has met with modest success where 'laboratory' conditions are capable of being established. But the frontier of acoustics, as it pertains to human environments is where measures of annoyance in real life situations are being sought and it is here that research is most lacking and agreement hard to achieve.

Sound is caused by sensations produced in the ear as a result of fluctuations in air pressure. Such fluctuations are normally, though by no means exclusively, the consequence of objects vibrating and creating a series of compression and decompression (or rarefraction) layers in the surrounding atmosphere.

The size and rate of these vibrations determine, respectively, the magnitude and frequency of the pressure fluctuations and it is these two characteristics, magnitude and frequency, that give sound its subjective attributes of 'loudness' and/or 'noisiness'.

1.1 Sound magnitude

Sound magnitude can be described in several different ways. These include the description of sound as a flow of energy (sound power), or as an energy flow per unit of area (sound intensity), or as a fluctuation in air pressure (sound pressure). But whichever approach is used the range of fluctuation and thus

1

of measurement, encompassed on these scales by the human ear, is enormous. The faintest audible sounds are measured in fractions of one-millionth of an atmospheric pressure and the range of magnitude between these and the values for painfully loud sound is of the order of one millionfold. Therefore, it is usual to express the magnitude of sounds in terms of *ratios* relative to some reference value. The ratios are not specified in direct numbers which would still remain inconveniently large, but in logarithmic ratios called *bels* (with one bel equal to 10 decibels). As a consequence, the decibel 'ladder' is a *scale of reference* and not a measure of absolute physical quantities. For example, in the case of sound pressure, the transformation to decibels is made using:

$$dB = 10 \log_{10} \frac{P^2}{P_{\text{ref}}} \qquad (1.1)$$

$$= 20 \log_{10} \frac{P}{P_{\text{ref}}}$$

where P is the sound pressure in units of force per square length and P_{ref} is a reference level, usually the level of the quietest audible sound, considered to be $0{\cdot}00002$ Newtons/m².

With sound intensity (measured in watts per sq. metre), intensity increases at twice the rate that pressure does. As a result, the hearing range in terms of basic intensity measurement is even more unmanageable than that for sound pressure. However, the same solution applies, namely conversion into the decibel scale using:

$$dB = 10 \log_{10} \frac{I}{I_{\text{ref}}} \qquad (1.2)$$

where I is the sound intensity and I_{ref} is a reference intensity. The reference intensity, as in the case of sound pressure, relates to the auditory threshold, in this case, 10^{-12} Watts/m².

It follows from equation (1.2) that a tenfold increase in sound intensity is equivalent to an increase of 1 bel or 10 decibels, a convenient result since an increase of 10 dB is generally thought equivalent to a doubling of loudness.

Table 1.1 shows the relationships between the above quantities of sound intensity, sound pressure and the level of sound in decibels. With respect to intermediate points on the scale of Table 1.1 it can be seen that doubling of sound intensity gives an increase of 3 decibels, whereas a doubling of sound pressure gives an increase of 6 decibels.

The logarithmic nature of the scale of reference has implications also for the addition of different sounds. Because decibels are logarithmic they cannot be added in the same way as other measures of physical units, such as volts and ohms. In the rare case of two identical sounds being experienced the solution is simple, 3 decibels are added to the decibel level of either. This will apply at any level of decibels because if any number is doubled its logarithm (to base 10) will increase by $0 \cdot 3010$ and hence $10 \log_{10} \dfrac{I}{I_{ref}}$ will increase by 3.

Table 1.1

Intensities, sound pressures, decibel levels and typical sounds for sound in air at room temperature and sea-level pressure

Intensity Watts/m²	Sound pressure Newtons/m²	Sound level dB	Some typical sounds
100 000 000	200 000	200	
10 000 000		190	Large rocket engine
1 000 000	20 000	180	
100 000		170	
10 000	2 000	160	
1 000		150	
100	200	140	
10		130	75 piece orchestra
1	20	120	
0·1		110	Car on motorways –
0·01	2	100	Ventilation fan
0 001		90	
0 000 1	0·2	80	
0·000 01		70	Conversational
0 000 001	0·02	60	voice
0·000 000 1		50	
0·000 000 01	0·002	40	
0·000 000 001		30	Soft whisper
0·000 000 000 1	0·000 2	20	
0·000 000 000 01		10	
0·000 000 000 001	0·000 02	0	Threshold of hearing

Source: Adapted from R. Taylor (1970)

In practice, of course, sounds are likely to be coming from a number of sources and will not be of equal magnitude. Here, recourse must be made to actual measurement (or the intensity levels in cases of calculation). Quite often one sound predominates and if this domination is to the extent of being +10 *dB* over the next loudest sound the overall sound level is scarcely affected by the lower sounds.

1.2 Sound frequency

Sound frequency is measured in cycles per second, or equivalently in Hertz (abbreviated *Hz*). It is generally of more interest than magnitude to the acoustician since it is the principal determinant of pitch to the listener. However, since this introduces the human element it takes us away from the concept of *physical scales*, (although with origins related to audibility) into the area of *psychophysical scaling*.

The problem of frequency measurement is caused by the nature of the human ear which varies in its capacity to perceive sounds of different frequencies, and also differs (or rather causes the brain to differ) in its reaction towards them. We therefore have two related problems: first to define the range of audible sound frequencies and second to determine the variance of sensitivity within this range.

With respect to the former it is difficult to delimit a precise range of audibility, partly because of individual variance and partly because other parts of the nervous system may come into operation at extreme frequencies. Moreover, many people for much of the time have a faint 'singing' in their ears at very high frequency, thus making it virtually impossible to pick out external sounds at the top end of the scale. However, generally speaking the lowest audible frequencies are about 20 *Hz* and the highest about 16,000 *Hz* (16 *KHz*).

The second aspect, determining sensitivity over this range, is even more difficult to determine satisfactorily. Again this is partly due to individual variance, but the essence of the problem – and this can probably be considered the basic problem of acoustics – is to determine degrees of human response as opposed to dichotomous response. For instance, we do not require to know simply whether a 50 decibel sound at one frequency is considered 'louder' than a 50 decibel sound at another frequency, but how much louder.

Figure 1.1 shows one 'solution' that is generally acceptable. This is the concept of equal-loudness contours for pure tones. In this context the two 50 decibel sounds are compared with a standard pure tone. The intensity of the latter is then adjusted until it is judged equally as loud as the sound

4

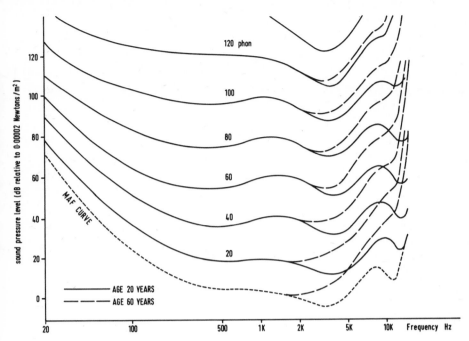

Fig. 1.1 Equal-loudness contours for pure tones

being investigated and the intensity of the pure tone is then measured in terms of the sound pressure level in decibels. The answer is expressed in terms of *phones*. The Minimum Audible Frequency (*MAF*) curve in Figure 1.1, for example, illustrates the basic pattern of sensitivity and it is evident that the ear is most sensitive to sound in the 4 *KHz* region. A 30 *Hz* sound, for instance, would have to have a magnitude of 60 *dB* in order to sound 'as loud' as a 4 *KHz* sound of 0 *dB*.

The dashed lines at curve ends in the figure depict a process that is common to all individuals as they get older and that is a loss of sensitivity towards high frequency sounds, medically termed presbycousis.

It should be apparent from the above that unless a sound is operating on one frequency it is going to be extremely difficult to devise a simple measure of frequency that has any meaning either in physical terms or, more significantly, in human terms. In fact, if the sound is being described for purely physical purposes then it is both unnecessary and misleading not to define the full range and variation of the frequency even if this does involve some degree of generalisation. For instance, the noise from early turbo-jets was described as broad-band noise – indicating that noise was being generated over the whole spectrum, while the term white noise refers to noise of a statistically random nature having equal energy at every frequency over a particular band of spectrum.

Conversely, for purposes of defining human response the full frequency range is clumsy and makes comparison of different situations extremely difficult. On the other hand an 'average' frequency also has little meaning because two identical averages can have different dispersions and hence generate different reactions. The 'obvious' solution is to weight the different frequencies according to some such concept as the equal loudness contours, and thereby produce a single decibel reading.

A number of different weighting scales have been devised, all of which are based upon measurements of sound pressure level within a number of restricted frequency bands (or octaves),[1] covering the whole audible range. These values are weighted in various ways to give a *calculated* single figure. The best known weighting is the *A* scale resulting in the *dBA* measure. A method similar in principle but modified in detail is the *perceived noise level* (*PNdB*). This is especially devised to give most import to those parts of the sound frequency spectra of *aircraft* to which the human ear is most sensitive and to make adjustments according to laboratory based judgements of sounds considered equally 'annoying' rather than equally loud. However, for a wide variety of sounds the *PNdB* tends to bear a constrained relationship to *dBA* and, as a rule of thumb, the *dBA* level is taken to be 13 decibels lower than *PNdB*.

Critics of *PNdB* argue that it adds very little except complexity to *dBA* and Kryter (1970) himself appears to have recognised certain limitations in suggesting (in 1968) a modification called the *Effective Perceived Noise Level* (*EPNL*). The *EPNL* takes more accurate account of discrete frequency components which are typical of the sound from the more recent turbo-fan jets and adds in as well a correction factor for the *duration* of the sound. Nevertheless, the *PNdB* remains as *the* general indicator of aircraft noise.

1.3 Noise exposure

While measurements of single noise events by *dBA*, *PNdB*, etc., are as we shall see later, useful for some purposes, they are often imperfect indicators in themselves of the total exposure in areas continually subjected to noise. In these circumstances what is required is a measure which summarises a *series* of noises.

A recent and sophisticated example of such a measure is the Noise Pollution Index (*LNP*) suggested by Robinson (1971) the basic definition of which is given by:

$$LNP = \text{Leq} + k\delta$$

Where Leq is the continuous 'energy mean' equivalent of the noise levels measured over a specified period, δ is the standard deviation of the instantaneous level considered as a statistical time series over the same period and k is a constant. Leq can use as a basis any of the standard sound or noise measures, *dBA*, *PNdB*, etc. The Index, therefore, introduces the added dimension of fluctuation as well as integrating a series of sounds or noises. It has not been widely adopted as yet and most expressions currently used take a different approach by combining a measure of average loudness or noisiness with an indication of the number of times events are heard.

The majority, as well as the first, of these expressions evolved in the aviation context and the chief ones used internationally are shown in Table 1.2 below.

Table 1.2

Equations for comparison of noise exposure indices

USA:	$CNR = 10 \log_{10} 10^{L_{pn}/10} + 10 \log_{10} N - 12$
	$NEF = 10 \log_{10} 10^{L_{epn}/10} + 10 \log_{10} N - 88$
France:	$N = 10 \log_{10} 10^{L_{pn}/10} + 10 \log_{10} N - 30$
Great Britain:	$NNI = 10 \log_{10} 10^{L_{pn}/10} + 15 \log N - 80$
Germany:	$Q = 13 \cdot 3 \log_{10} 10^{L_{pn}/13 \cdot 3} + 13 \cdot 3 \log_{10} N - 52 \cdot 3$
South Africa:	$NI = 10 \log_{10} 10^{\frac{L_{pn}-13}{10}} + 10 \log_{10} N - 39 \cdot 4$
Netherlands:	$B = 20 \log_{10} 10^{\frac{L_{pn}-13}{15}} + 20 \log_{10} N - C$
ICAO:	$WECPNL = 10 \log_{10} 10^{L_{epn}/10} + 10 \log_{10} N - 39 \cdot 4$

Note: L_{pn} = *PNdB* and L_{epn} = *EPNdB*
N = Number of events heard.

Source: Adapted from W. J. Galloway (1971)

Five of the formulae contain both a $10 \log_{10}$ average of *PNL* or *EPNL* and a $10 \log_{10} N$ expression. The similarity in these cases (North America, France, South Africa and ICAO) arises because all were initially derived by what Galloway terms intuition, or what is more commonly referred to as the deductive process. Implicitly or explicitly, hypotheses are produced regarding the most important parameters of the noise environment and the most logical form in which they should be combined. This logic is firmly based in the physical sciences and is largely concerned with the best way of representing the sum of a series of energy producing events. If each event is termed N_1, N_2, ... N_n and the peak energy produced by each event is termed *PNdB* (or *EPNL*), the addition of these events on an energy basis leads directly to the expression $10 \log_{10} 10^{PNdB/10} + 10 \log_{10} N$.

The British, German and Dutch formulae, on the other hand, stem from the distinctly different inductive approach where relative importance attached to the number of events, vis-à-vis, loudness, emerges directly from the evaluation of an associated human response.

The United Kingdom Noise Number Index illustrates well this process of derivation. In this case the measurement of the response consisted of constructing an 'annoyance' scale and assigning a 'score' to each respondent according to the combined answers to a set of questions related to aircraft noise. The scale used was based on the Guttman technique which tries to ensure that the scale adopted will not be arbitrary and provides for continuous measurement of attitudes. In the UK survey, for example, the questions adopted for the annoyance scale were: (a) Does the noise of aircraft bother you very much, moderately, a little, or not at all? (b) Does aircraft noise, (i) Wake you up (very often, fairly often, occasionally, not at all? (ii) Interfere with listening to the radio or TV? (iii) Make the house vibrate? (iv) Interfere with conversation? (v) Bother you in any other way?

The dichotomous replies to each question enabled a six point scale to be constructed: those who answered the last question in the affirmative had usually given positive replies to the previous five questions (following the very principle of scale analysis).

On the basis of the answers a form of category (or cross-classification) analysis was carried out based on three categories for the average number of aircraft 'heard'[2] on an average summer's day 7 a.m.–7 p.m., and four categories for the average noise level. The resulting 12 category matrix is shown in Table 1.3 with the number of sample respondents falling into each cell and the average score for that cell.

This table was used to construct Figure 1.2 which shows noise plotted against average annoyance for each class of N, with 22·5 and 81 changed to 22 and 88 to obtain N increasing by a constant ratio of 4. It can be seen that for any given level of annoyance a fourfold increase in the number of aircraft is equivalent to an increase in noise of approximately 9 *dB* or nearly a doubling of loudness. Thus N can be transformed into equivalent decibels by using $15 \log N$, since $15 \log (4N) = 15 \log N + 15 \log 4 = 15 \log N + 9$ reflects the result that multiplying N by 4 is equivalent to adding 9*dB* of noise (Hart, 1973). The final element is a scaling factor which is common to all expressions deductive or inductive in origin. This factor is intended to adjust the composite measure so that zero on the scale coincides with an observed absence of annoyance or complaints, etc. In the case of the Noise Number Index, for example, $\overline{PNdB}+15\log N$, was about 80 when annoyance was zero so that a constant term of minus 80 was introduced.

Table 1.3

Number of people and, in parenthesis, their average annoyance classified by noise and number of aircraft, 1961 survey

		PNdB			
		84–90	91–96	97–102	103–108	Total
Av. N per day	5·75	512 (1·1)	158 (1·5)	7 (2)	–	677
	22·5	155 (1·9)	321 (1·9)	82 (2·5)	11 (3·2)	569
	81	38 (2·8)	110 (2·7)	200 (3·1)	137 (3·6)	485
Total		705	589	289	148	1731

Source: Derived from Tables I & II, Appendix XI, *Committee on the Problem of Noise* (*1963*)

In view of the mixed background of the indices shown in Table 1.2 it is perhaps not surprising that no single transformation of one scale to another is available. Figure 1.3, for example, shows for those indices in Table 1.2, the varied effect of increasing the number of identical noise events. Nevertheless, in spite of the variation it appears that all these measures of a noise series are monotonic transformations of each other. Indeed, one can be more precise and conclude that they appear to be *linear* transformations of one another with more or less arbitrary zeros and with equally arbitrary scales of measurement.

Notes

1   The highest frequency in an octave is twice the lowest.
2   'Heard' excludes all aircraft creating noise levels below 80 *PNdB*.

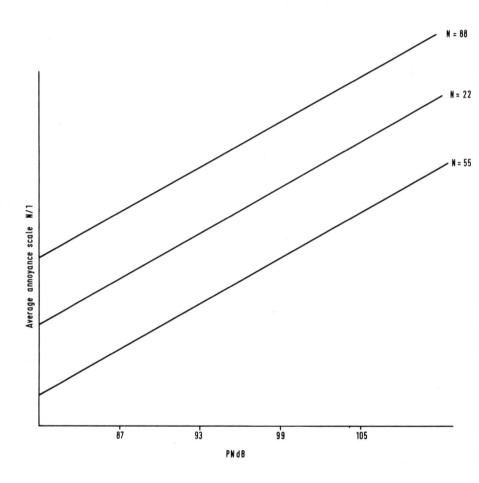

Fig. 1.2 Relationship between average annoyance and average peak perceived noise levels

10

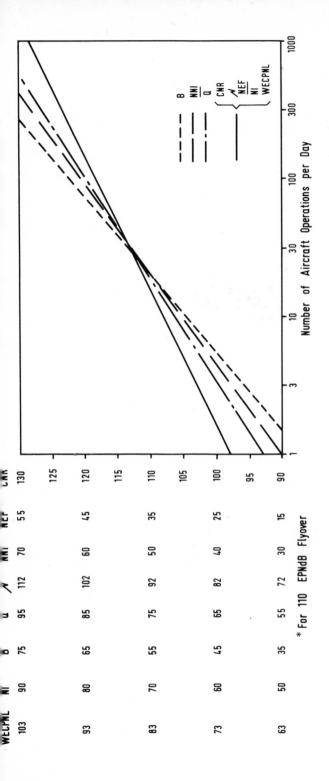

Fig. 1.3 Comparison of various noise exposure indices for a flyover noise level of 110 *PNdB*, effective duration of 10 seconds, for different numbers of operations

11

2 The International Response to The Aircraft Noise Problem

2.1 Noise certification standards

Various measures of sound, noise and aircraft noise exposure form the bases of a multitude of multifarious laws, regulations and incentives aimed at mitigating the aircraft noise problem.[1] The *EPNdB*, for example, forms the basis of one of the few proposals generally agreed to at an international level. This is the International Civil Aviation Organisation's (ICAO) recommended standards for the noise certification of aircraft. These recommendations, ratified in 1971 (as an Annexe to the Chicago Convention) were already embodied, albeit in a slightly more stringent form, in the US Federal regulations, FAR, Part 36 of 1969, and were anticipated in the United Kingdom by the Air Navigation (Noise Certification) Order of 1970.[2]

The specification of the agreement lays down noise levels within which aircraft must be capable of operating. The levels are defined for prescribed points under the take-off and approach paths and to the sides of the runway. They differ according to the maximum all-up weight of the aircraft and at take off, for example, vary from 108 *EPNdB* for an aeroplane of 600,000 lb all-up weight, down to 93 *EPNdB* for an aircraft of 75,000 lb loaded weight. (See Figures 2.1, 2.2 and 2.3.)

The ICAO recommendations relate only to aircraft-engine type designs introduced from 1972 onwards and they specifically exclude supersonic aircraft. Nevertheless the new types of subsonic jets now entering service, such as the DC-10, Lockheed Tristars and the newer versions of the Boeing 747, comfortably meet the requirements; and the US Federal Aviation Administration (FAA) has issued recently (18 April 1974) a notice proposing all subsonic jets weighing more than 75,000 lbs using US airports should meet the requirements of FAA, Part 36 after July 1978. (*Flight International, 1974.*)

Attention has switched, therefore, to the possibility of modifying existing aircraft by the use of so-called hush kits (retrofitting) and a number of feasibility studies have been, or are being, conducted.

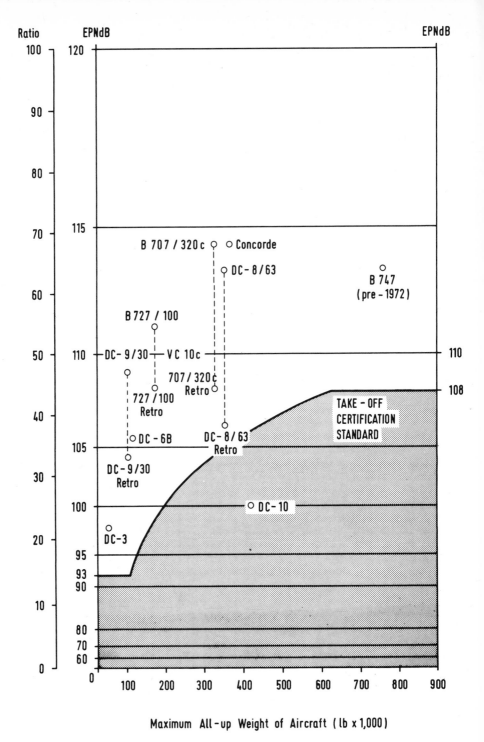

Fig. 2.1 Aircraft certification standards – permitted take-off noise levels
(3·5 n.ml. from start of roll on extended runway centre line)
Source: British Airports Authority (1971)

14

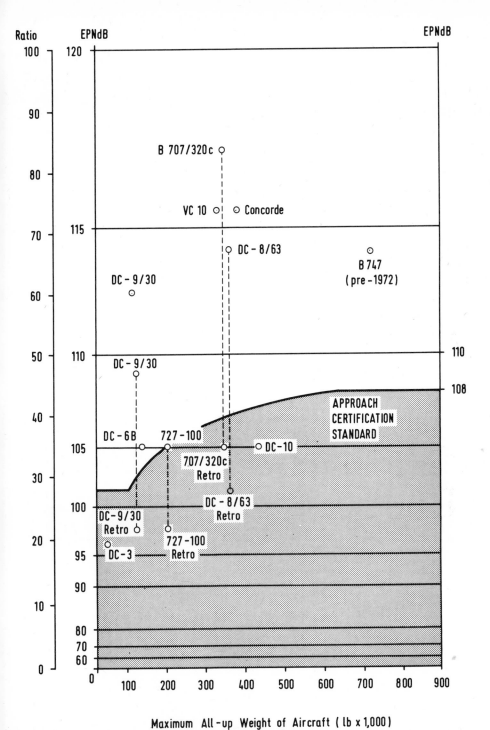

Fig. 2.2 Aircraft certification standards – approach noise levels (1 n.ml. from threshold on the extended runway centre line)
Source: British Airports Authority (1971)

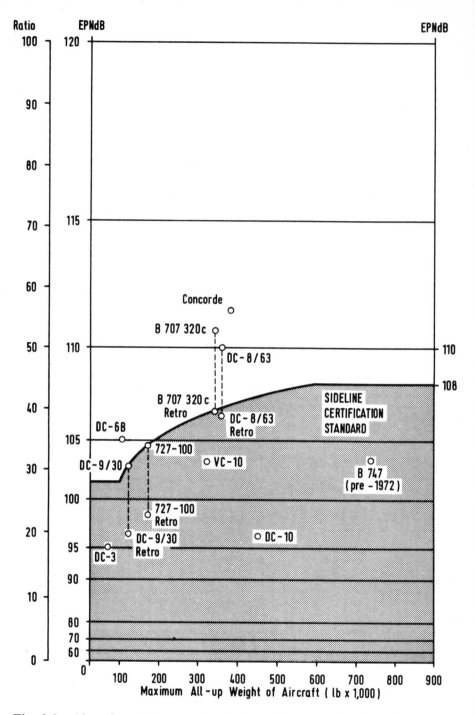

Fig. 2.3 Aircraft certification standards – side-line noise levels (at a point on a line parallel to runway centre line, 3 engines and less, 0·25 n.ml. more than 3 engines, 0·35 n.ml.) *Source:* British Airports Authority (1971)

2.2 Flight procedures for noise abatement

Meanwhile, one of the more commonly used methods for mitigating the effect of the present generation of subsonic aircraft is by means of aircraft operation procedures implemented largely by airport operators.[3]

The United Kingdom 'official policy' (Hart, 1973) of concentrating aircraft flight patterns in what are referred to as 'Minimum Noise Routes' provides not only a specific example of noise reducing operational procedures, but is one of the better examples of regulations based upon measures of *noise exposure*.

The Minimum Noise Routes are narrow air channels into which traffic near airports are concentrated. The location of these channels are chosen with reference to population density, the objective being to confine aircraft noise disturbance to as few people as possible.

The rationale for the argument that it is better for a few people to be overflown many times, rather than many people few times, is found in the *NNI* formula. The formula suggested that annoyance increases with the logarithm of the flight frequency. Thus a point overflown by 100 aircraft, each emitting 100 Perceived Noise decibels will have an *NNI* rating of 50. Each of four points overflown by 25 similarly noisy aircraft will have a rating of 41. Although some of the population will benefit from a reduction from 50 to 41 *NNI*, where population densities are uniform, three times as many will have their annoyance index increased from 0 to 41 (Hart, 1973).

The Minimum Noise Route policy is, comparatively speaking, a sophisticated example of the relationship between policy and measurement. A much more common and down-to-earth approach, again in the context of operational procedures, is the maximum permissible noise level (a maximum which may or may not vary with the time of day). The Port of New York Authority, for example, has established such requirements for airports in New York Metropolitan area:

> ... first of all the plane for which permission to load or take-off is sought must be a type which has demonstrated its capability of operating, on take-off, within a maximum noise limit of 112 *PNdB*, measured in the surrounding communities. Secondly terms and conditions for the operation of jet aircraft are imposed to the effect that take-offs will be permitted only if so planned and conducted that the noise level of 112 *PNdB* is not exceeded (McNairn, 1972).

2.3 Land use controls

Reducing noise at *source* by improved engine technology, by more considerate modes of aircraft operation etc., is one way of trying to reduce the problem of noise from aircraft. A fundamentally different approach is to attempt to ameliorate the impact largely, though not exclusively, by the use of planning controls. Here again the measurement of noise exposure has had an important role to play.

Around the new Charles de Gaulle Airport, Rossy, Paris, three zones which act as *cordon sanitaire* for various land uses have been defined by reference to the *CNR* measure. In the zone of intense noise (more than 115 *CNR*), no dwellings, schools or hospitals can be built; in the other two

A similar policy, also based on the *CNR*, was introduced in relation to proofing, density of housing etc., are in force.

A similar policy, also based on the *CNR*, was introduced in relation to Toronto International Airport in 1969 and has since been extended to other major airports in Ontario Province. In this case implementation is guided by a noise-sensitive zone plan and land use compatibility table based upon *CNR* contours.

The alternative Noise Exposure Forecast (*NEF*) forms the basis of a policy statement by the United States Department of Housing and Urban Development indicating its intention of discouraging (largely by withholding financial support) construction of new dwellings on sites subject to high levels of noise exposure. Noise exposure standards have been promulgated in terms of three basic categories: unacceptable (above forty *NEF*), discretionary (thirty to forty *NEF*), and acceptable (less than thirty *NEF*).

Perhaps better examples of noise exposure measures forming the basis of effective land use policies are provided in the United Kingdom where the authority to regulate development is unambiguously provided by statute and, at least until April 1974 is vested at county level.[4]

Although in the UK it is the *NNI* that is used for this regulatory task, the tendency towards a classification of land use is still apparent.

During the 1960s, the planning authorities whose areas are affected by London (Gatwick) Airport, evolved a basis for the control of development (Sibert, 1969). Having considered this policy, in January 1973 the Secretary of State for the Environment commended the use of the criteria shown in Table 2.1 to all local authorities (Dept of the Environment, 1973).

The use of sound, noise and noise exposure measures as a basis for policies aimed at reducing the aircraft noise problems, may not always have achieved the same degree of refinement as shown in Table 2.1 – the UK *MNR* policy is perhaps a case in point. Nevertheless where and when measures have been used, they have provided at some stage a definite criterion upon which the decision could be based. Yet there are in addition many regulations, restrictions, etc., applied throughout the world which make no reference, overtly or tacitly, to such measurement.

These somewhat more instinctive reactions range from outright bans on

Table 2.1 Recommended criteria for control of development in areas affected by aircraft noise

Level of aircraft noise to which site is, or is expected to be, exposed	60 *NNI* & above	50–59 *NNI*	40–49 *NNI*	35–39 *NNI*
Dwellings	Refuse	No major new developments. Infilling only with appropriate sound-insulation		Permission not to be refused on noise grounds alone
Schools	Refuse	Most undesirable. When, exceptionally, it is necessary to give permission, e.g. for a replacement school, sound insulation should be required to a standard consistent with DES Guidelines.	Undesirable. Sound insulation to be required to a standard consistent with DES Guidelines	Permission not to be refused on noise grounds alone
Hospitals	Refuse	Undesirable. Appropriate sound insulation to be required	Each case to be considered on its merits	Permission not to be refused on noise grounds alone
Offices	Undesirable. Full insulation to be required	Permit. Permit insulation to be required	Permit but advise insulation of conference rooms depending upon position, aspect, etc.	
Factories, warehouses, etc.	It will be for the occupier to take necessary precautions in particular parts of the factory depending on the processes and occupancy expected.			

Source: Department of the Environment (1973)

night flights at such airports as Tokyo, Paris (Orly), Düsseldorf and Oslo (Fornebo); the compulsory dispersal of air traffic between airports (e.g. Stockholm, Sweden) to the imposition of passenger taxes for financing special funds for the purchase of sound proofing for buildings exposed to high levels of noise (Orly).

But the rather coarse nature of these policies merely brings into sharper relief that which is readily apparent even where, first, the problem is subjected to measurement. In either case 'Is it worth it?' is the question begged.

The regulations, restrictions, conformity to set standards etc., all have certain adverse economic consequences to some person(s) or organisation(s). Take for example the apparently simple remedy of closing airports during the night hours:

> Shutting down airports at night . . . entails significant practical and economic disadvantages such as loss of income if air-freight companies prefer to use airports where there are no restrictions on night flights; some aircraft are too long idle on the ground; there are problems of arranging take-off schedules for long distance flights to allow for time differences (flights between Europe and the Middle East or Far East, for example); and so on (OECD, 1973).

In some cases the consequential costs are readily available or are being estimated. For example in the case of flight restrictions at night the British Airports Authority estimated that the Authority alone lost an estimated £1 million in revenue per annum (at 1970 prices) from the limit at London (Heathrow) (*House of Commons, 1971*); and by the end of 1969 the same Authority had paid out sound-proofing subsidies of almost £2½ million (*House of Commons, 1971*).

But even though some cost estimates are available, what is always missing is a calculation of the corresponding benefits of reducing aircraft sounds. The blunt fact is that at the present time we have no conception of the degree to which welfare is improved by a prescribed cut in the level of *NNI*, *CNR*, *PNdB* or *EPNdB*, etc. And until we have such knowledge, there is always the danger that more harm than good will come of well-intentioned measures aiming to reduce the noise problem associated with this form of technological progress.

Notes

1   Comprehensive reviews are to be found in: Informatics Inc (1972); OECD (1973); and C. H. McNairn (1972).

2   Enabled by the Civil Aviation Act of 1968.

3   This is particularly the case in the USA where Supreme Court judgements on litigation for noise damage have placed the onus on the airport proprietor. Indeed, as a consequence, the Federal Aviation Administration (FAA) has, in effect, delegated to local airport authorities the responsibility for monitoring, in day-to-day operations, new aircraft that technically meet the Federal Noise Certification Standards (C. H. McNairn, p. 257).

4   In contrast, many North American and European policy statements are basically guidelines without the force of the law, or where the authority does exist, it is often fragmented, localised and lacking the motivation to restrain development.

B

3 Valuation in Cost Benefit Analysis and its Implications for Noise and Quietude

The conclusion of the last chapter was that if resources are not to be wasted we need urgently to value (in economic terms) the benefits of reducing noise and concomitantly, to value the cost and disbenefits associated with an increase in noise.

So far we have been inclined to use the expressions of noise on the one hand, and peace and quiet on the other, as though there was definitive symmetry between them; an increase in the one matched by a corresponding decrease in the other. Indeed, to many persons this casualness of expression may be perfectly acceptable and without further professional significance. But for the economist concerned with the measurement of value, there is a subtle distinction which *could* be of importance.

Therefore we need first to clarify such matters and to do so we start with the fundamental issue of the theory of valuation in economics. In so far as such a theory exists it exists as part of the wider context of cost benefit analysis (CBA) and the associated postulates of welfare economics. Naturally measurement of costs and benefits, advantages and disadvantages, gains and losses etc., must, for the purposes of CBA be consistent with the underlying theoretical basis of welfare economics and be consistent with the objective function defining social welfare. It is to this aspect that we now turn. As we shall attempt to show, the inconsistencies and controversial issues that surround CBA spill over into the area of valuation.

3.1 The valuation of benefits

A convenient starting point is to consider the valuation of benefits. Layard (1972) writes: ' . . . we must ultimately rely on the individual's own evaluation of his mental state. So that the broad principle is that we measure his change in welfare as he would himself value it; that is we ask what he would be willing to pay'.

It is this concept of the willingness to pay that is fundamental to the treatment of benefits in CBA. It does also, of course, form the basis of the ideas of consumers' surplus developed by Dupuit in the middle of the nineteenth century and later extended into a formal concept by Marshall. The lineage is that we measure benefits in terms of net additions to an individual's consumer surplus; the latter Marshall defined as the excess of a consumer's willingness to pay for a good over and above the price he is actually called on to pay. These ideas can be illustrated by use of the Marshallian triangle. In Figure 3.1, D_1D_1 represents a demand curve for a good x. Quantities are shown on the horizontal axis whilst the vertical axis is calibrated in terms of money of constant utility. This latter assumption (together with the usual *ceteris paribus* assumptions of demand analysis that the individuals' income and the prices of all other goods are fixed) was considered a necessary and sufficient prerequisite for a proper interpretation of consumers' surplus.

If, for example, the individual were at equilibrium at A, then a gift of

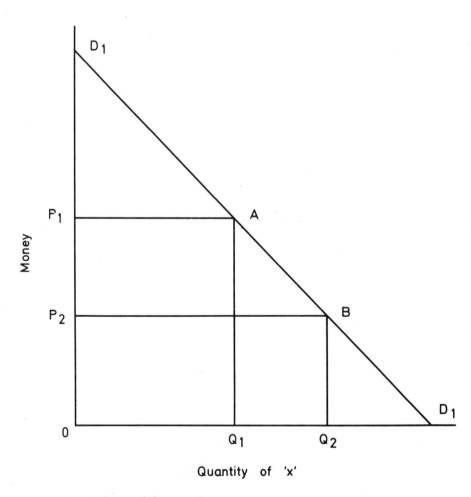

Fig. 3.1 The demand for good x

$0Q_1-0Q_2$ of good x would increase his surplus by ABQ_1Q_2 units. And in circumstances where the consumer receives all as an 'overspill' benefit (consumers' surplus where the price to him is zero) the total area under the curve D_1-D_1 indicates the surplus or benefit received.

This method of expressing consumers' surplus and changes therein, in units of money, is based on the classical notion that utility is capable of cardinal measurement. These premises, of course, were unacceptable to the neo-classical ordinalists and alternatives to Marshall's approach have accordingly been developed by Hicks, Henderson and others. In practice CBA has based itself on cardinal utility. Nevertheless the alternative ordinal measures of Hicks and others have been useful for clarifying the conditions under which the Marshallian measures of benefit are appropriate and valid. Hicks showed, for example, that it was necessary to assume that real income remained constant before a Marshallian measure of consumer surplus change could accurately represent the money value of consumer benefits.[1]

Quite apart from the controversy over ordinal and cardinal utility measures the general approach bases itself on the value judgement that individual preferences (registered as money 'votes' in the cardinalist method) are important and should count. In this sense, as Dasgupta and Pearce (1972) have pointed out, CBA is very 'democratic' – 'it is equivalent to obeying the maxim of consumers' sovereignty'.

In spite of the general acceptance of this philosophy of consumer sovereignty, with its implication that benefits are valued as a consumer would value them in a perfect market, difficulties have arisen. These usually have been in circumstances when the consumer is judged to have, to borrow Pigou's phrase, a defective telescopic faculty.

Issues of myopia have been raised most often in the context of discounting future benefits, although the same arguments have also crept into the discussion about valuing benefits, particularly in regard to the fields of education and safety. Nevertheless, Dasgupta and Pearce (1972) continue: 'Wherever the dividing line between "merit wants" and other wants exists . . . CBA would claim to come down on the side of simple democracy. It aims to record the preferences of the community and recommend on that basis . . . it records preferences in the selfish category.'

3.2 The valuation of costs

On the cost side, the treatment in theory is symmetrical with the valuation of benefits. Cost is measured as an opportunity cost or the benefit of alternatives forgone. The benefit of alternatives forgone is, of course, measured in terms of willingness to pay and in practice is signified by prices paid for factors in a perfect market.[2] Discussion of this issue has centred upon obtaining these correct 'accounting' prices by adjusting actual market prices for aspects such as underemployment of resources, taxes, subsidies, monopoly elements, etc.

Valuing both benefits and costs in this 'democratic' manner is fully consistent with the Paretian value judgement for assessing improvements in social welfare.[3] The Paretian judgement is that if one person is better off and no one worse off, welfare is increased. In these rather restricted circumstances interpersonal comparisons of utility are not required. There are no losers; there is no need to trade gains against 'losses'.

3.3 The valuation of disbenefits

In reality there are losers and indeed our own analysis is based on this essential fact.[4] Consequently, the simple Paretian test of a welfare gain is irrelevant.

The most celebrated attempt to modify the simple Paretian rule to accommodate disbenefits whilst maintaining the basic concept of Paretian optimality is the 'compensation principle' formulated by Hicks and Kaldor. The argument is that if the gainers can overcompensate the losers then an improvement in welfare will accompany change. The Hicks–Kaldor test does not require that actual compensation should take place and it is this aspect of the issue that has been subject to most debate. In the absence of actual compensation paid to the losers by the gainers (in one lump sum so as to leave incentives to work undisturbed) there will be a redistribution of income from losers to gainers. This in turn leads to complications of the Scitovsky paradox quite apart from issues of social justice.

The significance of the compensation rule from our point of view is that it does highlight the distinction between Hick's alternative measures of surplus and the importance of the assumption regarding the constant marginal utility of money.[5] The basic measures are the equivalent and compensating variations. The potential losers' equivalent variation is the maximum sum which, if paid by the loser would reduce his welfare by as much as if the detrimental change in question did, instead, take place (see Appendix 1). The losers' compensating variation is the sum of money that would, if paid, just compensate him for the change by returning his welfare to the previous level of satisfaction (see Appendix 1). For the imposition of a nuisance and therefore for a reduction in welfare, the equivalent variation (EV) corresponds to the willingness to pay approach and the compensating variation (CV) to a measure of hypothetical compensation.

The importance of the marginal utility of money is that

(i) $CV = EV$ if the marginal utility of money is constant
(ii) $CV < EV$ „   „   is increasing
(iii) $CV > EV$ „   „   is decreasing
where the CV is defined with respect to the new set of prices and the EV with respect to the old.[6]

Thus in the case often assumed where the income, or as Mishan (1971) prefers to call it, the welfare effect, is negative (i.e. case (iii) above) disbenefits measured in terms of willingness to pay for their avoidance will be smaller than disbenefits measured in terms of hypothetical compensation. Although, as McKean (1968) has pointed out, there is nothing sacrosanct about Pareto optimality, in these circumstances the general opinion of the theorists would appear to be that hypothetical compensation is the appropriate measure of disbenefits.

3.4   Interpretation of policy

This is perhaps a convenient point to consider whether, in practice, government policy appears to have drawn a distinction between valuation of losses and gains. If it has, then it would appear that the Hicks–Kaldor welfare function is considered relevant and that a constant marginal utility of income does not apply. If it has failed to draw a distinction then it is presumably operating on the supposition that either constant marginal utility of money is appropriate or that Pareto optimality as a criterion of improved welfare is inappropriate.

This general subject has been discussed in two recent quasi-official studies of planning issues. These were the *Commission on the Third London Airport* and the *Urban Motorway Case Studies* carried out for the Department of the Environment by R. Travers Morgan and Partners.

The *Roskill Commission* failed to make their standpoint entirely clear on the matter. Some of their statements were, in fact, contradictory, but in practice they appeared to accept the criteria of willingness to pay for benefits and the minimum sum of money that would return the sufferers to their previous level of welfare in the case of disbenefits.[7]

The R. Travers Morgan *Study* was more definitive in its views, noting that: '. . . when environmental nuisance reduces peoples' welfare, then the cost of that nuisance is the sum which will just bring the sufferer back to his previous level of satisfaction' (Department of the Environment, 1974);
and 'Conversely, for environmental benefits . . . we consider that "willingness to pay" is the appropriate criterion.'

Nevertheless, the opinions of these studies do not necessarily correspond with government policy. For a better indication of this policy we need to refer to statements of policy on the theory and practice of cost benefit analysis or to details in 'official' cost benefit studies. Most of these studies and statements have related to the transport field where non-marketed commodities such as travel time and safety constitute a large proportion of the total benefits and disbenefits. For example, on the issue of the value of time savings, the ex-Ministry of Transport's Economic Planning Directorate (EPD) set out this matter clearly and succinctly:

> In the field of transport, the major effect of a large proportion of expenditure is to *save* the time of those travelling or of those, such as drivers, responsible for conveyance of goods or passengers. The value, therefore, of these *savings* is central to any judgement as to whether or not these expenditures are worthwhile: it is of particular importance in the case of roads since, on current valuations, time *savings* represent a very high proportion of total benefits. Any value used to convert time savings into monetary terms should, therefore, be reliable and defensible. (our italics)

The EPD's technical note then went on to state what values were currently in use within the Ministry of Transport and the principles on which these values were based. The values were divided into values for working time and values for non-working time. In the case of the former, working time, its value is based upon employers' willingness to pay for labour productivity as reflected in the average gross wage (including overtime) plus certain associated costs. The non-working time values were based on a number of studies which attempted to infer values from choices people actually make – 'The value is therefore market based in that it purports to represent what people would be prepared to pay to *save* time. . . .' (our italics) (Harrison, 1969).

Although the pure market approach was subsequently modified,[8] in the context of the time savings the basis of valuation is perfectly defensible in terms of the Pareto criteria of welfare gain or of Hicks and Kaldor's subsequent adaptations of it.

With respect to the valuation of the losses, however, there are no similar statements of principle. Here we have to turn to applications and practice to determine what the situation is.

Presumably the absence of statements of principle follows from the usual application of CBA in the investment appraisal context where, naturally, the focus is upon benefits. But even investments with wide popular support often entail disbenefits for someone and this is equally true in the travel time context. Most studies calculate the change in economic surplus on the basis of 'net' changes in travel time; it is these net changes which form the output of traffic and transport models. The travel time losses suffered by some travellers due to the redistribution and generation effects of new infrastructure are not calculated as a separate item in the balance sheet of gains and losses, and

28

therefore the indications are that policy concurs with an approach that values losses and gains on the same basis.

There are two facets of transport planning where the focus is unequivocally upon time losses and where a separate calculation and valuation of these losses has been made. Both concern 'adjustments' to existing transport capacity. One is concerned with the optimal use of existing highway capacity and the calculation of the social costs (or more accurately, the disbenefits) imposed on other road users by the marginal vehicle. Here, extra journey time imposed accounts for the majority of these losses. The other aspect is the curtailment and reduction of public transport services and it is perhaps of greater significance in the present context because substantive studies have been carried out comparatively recently, and these studies have had a greater bearing on policy formulation and decision making.

The two studies of particular interest in this context are those carried out by the National Board for Prices and Incomes (PIB) as part of their *Report* (No. 159) on London Transport Fares, and *The Cambrian Coastline*, a 1969 study by the Ministry of Transport of the costs and benefits of retaining railway services between Machynlleth and Pwllheli in Wales.

The aim of the PIB study was to estimate the gross 'loss' to passengers from the suspension of service on the peripheral section of a London Transport route: 'This loss exceeds the corresponding revenue by the amount of the consumers' surplus. It [the loss] is defined, in other words, not as what the passengers are actually paying for the service but as the maximum amount that they would pay rather than cease to use it.' (p. 28).

In making the representative calculations the values used for time losses were those values for saved time listed in the EPD's Technical Note 3.

The bases of the Cambrian Coastline Study's calculations were similar: 'We have used the valuation of non-working time of 3s. per hour adopted at the time of the study by the Ministry of Transport for *investment appraisal*. This value was then used to arrive at the cost of *additional* travel time if the railway service were closed.' (p. 10) (our italics).

This evidence can hardly be considered substantial nor does it categorically prove a point about government policy. The National Board for Prices and Incomes was a non-government body while the content or conclusions of the MOT study did not form the basis of any ministerial 'letter of intent'. Nevertheless it does suggest that those advising the Ministers of State endorsed by their advice a willingness to pay a measure for the valuation of both benefits and disbenefits. Therefore the indications are that policy is implemented on the basis that either there is constancy in the marginal utility of money, or that a welfare criterion other than a Pareto one is appropriate. If the latter applies then whatever this criterion is, it does appear to value both disbenefits and benefits on a willingness to pay principle.

Such a conclusion is pregnant with implication for the valuation of intangibles. In our own particular circumstances of noise and peace and quiet, it implies that a single valuation based upon the willingness to pay principle will suffice for both losses and gains. The two aspects are symmetrical; a move from point *A* to point *B* on a scale of noise is of equivalent value to a move from point *B* to point *A*. On the one hand this value is positive (an improvement) and on the other hand, negative.

In practical terms such a view means that a valuation based upon a person's willingness to pay is of relevance not only for examining expenditures and policies designed to reduce noise – noise screens, noise baffles, retrofitting aircraft engines, etc. – but is also of relevance where expenditure and policies involve new losses from a noise viewpoint – airport location, concentration or dispersal of flight paths, etc.

Notes

1   Marshall argued the necessity for a constant marginal utility of money. This constancy would need to hold over all the relevant paths in the range of output/price changes under consideration for the income effect to be zero (see Appendix 1 and D. Winch (1971)).

2   See J. Buchanan (1969) for a dissenting view of opportunity cost orthodoxy.

3   Although consistent, Paretian optimality is not strictly dependent upon cardinal measures of utility.

4   Professor Beesley (1972) has suggested that the Secretary of State was perhaps minimising costs and disbenefits imposed (rather than maximising net benefits) in choosing the Third London Airport site. If policy does operate in this manner then it places particular importance on correctly measuring disbenefits.

5   We will assume for convenience that this constancy does hold over all the relevant points in the applicable range of output/price changes.

6   For an increase in utility the above inequalities are reversed. The *EV* measure now becomes a measure of the *CV* and vice versa and the willingness to pay approach corresponds to a compensating variation measure.

7   Contrast, for example, paragraphs 2 and 87 in *Commission on the Third London Airport* (1970): paragraph 2 states' the cost attaching to some non-material factor, such as the imposition of noise in a previously quiet area, may be assumed to be equivalent to the sum of money which might be subscribed to preserve the initial state of affairs. In other words, things are worth at least what people are prepared to pay for their retention.' Paragraph 87 reads 'the principle underlying the methodology proposed is to assess what

sum of money would be sufficient to leave the sufferer in not worse a situation than he was before.'

8   By rejecting evidence of a relationship between income and preparedness to pay and by using values averaged over the whole population, no matter what the composition of the group of travellers, or transport mode concerned.

4 Previous Attempts to Evaluate Noise

Consistent with the theory discussed in the last chapter previous attempts to place a value upon noise annoyance have concentrated their attention upon preferences revealed by changes or differences in land and property values; they have concentrated especially upon the private housing sector. The majority of these analyses were solely empirical and the interpretation of their findings is open to some speculation. Such studies tried to show that a differential will exist between the market price of properties with low-noise environments and those with high-noise environments.

The underlying concept of the price differential is that if an environmental nuisance such as noise is newly introduced to an area then some of the more sensitive households, generally those who value their properties at or a little above their market price, will leave that area. With a distribution of sensitive people which is random in the initial case, more people will leave the areas of higher nuisance than areas less affected. Incomers to the area with their assumed perfect perception will correctly assess the effect of the noise environment on housing utility and thus expect to be compensated by a lower purchase price. Therefore, proceeds the argument, a house price differential will develop and continue to develop until the differential accurately reflects the perceived variation of the nuisance.

4.1 The house price differential

In actual fact, in spite of the attention it has received from environmental economists, the notion of a house price differential receives little support from the traditional theories of residential location and urban rents. Moreover, these theories suggest reasons why the house price differential might not be at all readily apparent.

The traditional theory of residential location set out in the early 1960s by William Alonso and others is a theory focusing upon a trade-off between rents and transport costs. Households substitute transport costs for rent costs with the rate of substitution governed by the household's preference for high or low density housing (Richardson, 1971). The former costs – transport costs – are regarded as a steadily increasing function of distance from centrally located jobs whilst the latter – rents – are considered to decrease in a similar manner with distance from city centres. Indeed, the reason why rents decrease with distance is that they are supposed to represent a payment for the advantages of proximity. The rent gradient, therefore, is a mirror-image of the transport cost gradient.[1].

Equilibrium conditions in the traditional theory prescribe that, *ceteris paribus*, the combined total of a household's expenditure on housing (rents) and transport will be the same at any location. In this context transport costs are seen as the major determinant of the rent gradient, and thus of any differential between the market price of homes. Environmental preferences on the other hand are given short shrift.

Recently, however, perhaps encouraged by the idea that with increasing affluence environmental quality is gaining added significance in householders' preference functions, environmental considerations have received more attention in general models of residential location.

Richardson's (1971) revision is a case in point and one that inclines towards the opposite extreme of giving pre-eminence to environmental factors. Housing preferences are considered a function of size of house/plot requirements and environmental tastes, and preferences are maximised within an ability to pay constraint. Transport costs are relevant only in so far as they have a bearing on the ability to pay; in this theory travel costs are a secondary determinant. The implication of these 'elements of a new model' is that they prescribe a land value/residential rent surface which is conditioned and moulded by environmental quality.[2]

These nonconforming ideas of Richardson have been rejected by Evans in his restatement of the traditional theory (Evans, 1973). In Evans' model 'the environment as such, is scarcely mentioned and the quality of the environment is never explicitly assumed to be a variable which is taken into account by consumers in deciding their optimal location' which, once again, is seen to be determined largely by the costs of travel, although now broadened to incorporate travel time as well as cash costs.

Where the balance lies between these polemic views of Richardson and Evans is, obviously, not without significance for those who search for a house price differential determined by pollution. But quite apart from such obvious implications there is also a more subtle point at issue here. Centres of employment (factories, offices, shopping centres) which condition the accessibility surface are often, in addition, sources of major pollution (Starkie, 1975). For example, in the case of atmospheric pollution, the *National Survey of Air Pollution* found that broadly speaking there was a marked tendency for pollution to vary directly with distance from city centres and inversely with density (Warren Springs Laboratory, 1972). We might expect a similar relationship to apply in the case of noise pollution because of the systematic variation in traffic densities with distance from the centre of cities. Consequently, the picture that emerges is one where the *dis*benefits of pollution tend to be highly and positively correlated with the benefits of increased accessibility to jobs, with the one factor partially or completely offsetting the other in their respective effect on the structuring of urban rents.

To take a specific example and one particularly pertinent to this study, at London (Heathrow) Airport, the work-force had reached 40,000 by 1967 (excluding some 1,100 employed by airport contractors and the 500 at the London Air Traffic Control Centre) (Sealy, 1969). Indirect employment in associated activities was much smaller – between 3,500 and 5,000, in 1968 (Hall, 1969). Between 73 per cent and 83 per cent of these employees lived within 10 miles of the Heathrow site, with women, the young and the old, the lower paid, the more menial workers all commuting shorter distances. As a consequence in areas adjacent to Heathrow, at least 10 per cent of the resident working men and 5 per cent of the resident working women were airport employees (Smith, 1967). One can only conclude from such figures that the impact on the immediate housing market must have been, and presumably still is, significant with the degree of this significance declining with both distance from the airport site and, generally speaking, with the level of noise pollution also.

Of course it would be argued that it is a sweeping generalisation to say that pollution levels are highly correlated with proximity to employment focii, and that useful exceptions to such a relationship can be found. For example, atmospheric pollution is influenced by prevailing winds while, to take another example, airport noise pollution tends to adopt the shape of a 'footprint' rather than to encircle the airport site. On the other hand, the crucial factor – accessibility, does not necessarily correlate perfectly with linear distance either. Thus while relationship between distance and pollution may be weak, the corresponding correlate between accessibility and pollution can be quite strong. Indeed this tends to be the case at Heathrow. Here the basic east-west axis of the noise 'footprint' appears to correspond to the employment catchment area which is affected by the major east-west transport arteries; the A30, the M4/A4 and, to a lesser extent, the Piccadilly line. At Gatwick, the same coincidence does not arise. On the contrary, the north-south 'grain' of the major transport and communication networks is at variance with the east-west orientation of Gatwick's noise footprint.[3]

Yet a distinction such as this emphasises greatly the need to explicitly incorporate accessibility into analyses which aim to show the effect of pollution on property values. Even more they stress the general complications involved in isolating a pollution-dependent house price differential.[4] It is perhaps not surprising therefore that, in the United Kingdom at least, attempts to *observe* and *measure* a noise determined house price differential have proved thus far singularly unsuccessful. For these data decision-making studies generally have fallen back upon the 'expert' opinion of estate agents and valuers.[5] The argument has been that:

> The professional valuer is constantly in touch with the prices at which houses change hands and with valuations made for other purposes (e.g. estate duty). His professional skill lies largely in making suitable allowance for the multitude of factors entering into the valuation of any particular house, i.e. that part of the problem which causes difficulty for the statistician. (*Commission – Third London Airport*, 1970.)

An example of such professional skill is shown in Table 4.1.

Table 4.1

Variations in judgement regarding house price depreciation (%) around London (Gatwick) airport

	35–45 *NNI*			45 + *NNI*		
	Low price house (< £4000)	Med. price house (£4000– £8000)	High price house (> £8000)	Low price house	Med. price house	High price house
Highest estimate	10	15	25	15	25	50
Average estimate	5	9	16	10	17	29
Lowest estimate	0	3	5	5	10	$12\frac{1}{2}$

Source: CTLA, Research Team (1970)

Quite apart from the practical problems of measurement there are, in addition, theoretical objections to the use of house price differentials, or at least to their use alone, as a means of environmental evaluation. The value of a particular property to the owner is equal to its market price, plus a surplus. This surplus is the difference between the market price and what the occupier would be willing to pay to enjoy the property's advantages (Whitebread and Bird, 1973).

With the imposition of an environmental nuisance this willingness to pay will be reassessed and for some will change. Indeed, it is from such changes, particularly for the potential purchaser and 'marginal' occupier, that the house price differential is derived. Therefore, changes of surplus besides changes in the market price are involved and have to be allowed for.

4.2 The development of the noise cost model

This situation has been recognised and rationalised in the noise cost model, the structure of which purports to be behavioural. A number of variants of the cost model have been developed in the last few years or so. One, namely that developed by R. Travers Morgan and Partners for their *Urban Motorway Case Studies*, although focused on the noise issue, is concerned with the wider environmental impact of urban highways (Flowerdew and Hammond, 1973). It also embraces a community of interest which includes public as well as private housing. Others have been set in the narrower context of noise annoyance, either from aircraft (*Commission on the Third London Airport*, 1971 and Metra, 1970) or from road traffic (Lassiere, 1970).

These models all have common features. They assume that when a noise nuisance is imposed on an area previously free of such annoyance the residents are faced with the same simple choice which was implicit in studies of the house price differential. Either these persons stay where they are and, because they are less sensitive or because they have strong ties to the house or neighbourhood, they put up with the nuisance. Or they move away to a more congenial neighbourhood (perhaps at substantial cost) and are replaced by families less troubled by noise. What these affected people decide to do depends upon their balance of advantage.

If, for example, they are owner-occupiers and they move, they may get a reduced price for their property; they will lose benefits of their location which are invariably greater than indicated by the market price of their property; and of course, they will suffer the cost and inconveniences of removal. If, on the other hand, they choose to remain in the affected area they will suffer the noise nuisance.

The argument is that if one is able to obtain values for a depreciation in the price of houses (which let us denote by D), for the cost of moving (R), for the location rent (S), and for the person's subjective valuation of the likely nuisance if he remains in the affected locality (N), it should be possible to calculate which of the two options – moving or staying – minimises the owner-occupier's total cost, both real and subjective. The 'rational' decision will be to leave if

$$N > S + D + R$$

and to stay if

$$N < S + D + R$$

The total loss to all householders consequent upon the reduction of residential amenity is the sum of the noise disbenefits to those who stay and the cost and disbenefits to those who moved for reasons of annoyance. In

37

addition it is necessary to take into account the depreciation or lower rate of increase in the market value of houses suffered by those who move for reasons other than the noise.

Generally, the higher the level of nuisance, the greater will be the annoyance suffered and the more likely it is that the cost-minimising option will be that which dictates a move. Therefore it is usual for the model to be structured by prescribed levels of noise nuisance. In addition opinions regarding the value of D suggest that this varies significantly with the price of property so that a further refinement of the model is necessary on this account. The model used by the Research Team to the *Commission on the Third London Airport*, for example, included five different levels of noise and three levels of house price: thus 15 sets of inequalities were calculated for each of the four airport sites shortlisted.[6]

N and S are not treated as fixed values. They are presumed to vary considerably between individual households and are taken into account by setting up a joint distribution of N and S and calculating the expected behaviour for each cell in this distribution.

4.3   The dynamics of adjustment

This, however, is a somewhat brief and rather static portrayal of what is, after all, a continually evolving situation. The noise cost model in its more dynamic context has been neatly summarised diagrammatically by Heggie.[7] His illustration of the processes described above is shown in Figure 4.1.

The illustrated model assumes an existing stock of 'quiet' houses. The aggregate demand for these properties is shown by the curve D_0 and their aggregate supply by the curve S_0. The demand represents a stream of potential house buyers continually entering the market and at a given average price level, a number of them will be prepared to make offers: this number will increase the lower the average price. The supply schedule is a description of the number of houses offered for sale during a discrete period of time. This number too, of course, will be a function of price. The demand and supply schedules shown in Figure 4.1 therefore relate to a given time period and the intersection point between them shows the equilibrium price determining the turnover during the period to which they relate.

The S_0 curve shows the implied surplus derived by the present property owners and clearly varies from year to year as the annual turnover alters their characteristics. With the coming of the noise nuisance the amenity value of these properties is reduced and this is represented by a new supply curve S_1.

The demand for properties will probably fall too, from D_0 to D_1, which

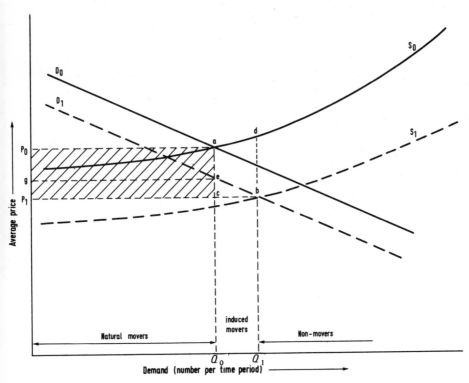

Fig. 4.1   The incidence of noise disbenefits to property owners suffering a noise nuisance

Source: see text

results in a new equilibrium price P_1 and a new turnover per time period of Q_1. As the induced movers leave the area, however, the curve S_1 will rise gradually until the annual turnover again represents 'natural movers' only.

The various 'losses' are as follows:

1   The 'original' owners who move for 'natural' reasons, Q_0, suffer a loss in price equal to $(P_0 - P_1)$ and a loss of surplus shown by the shaded area $P_0 a c P_1$.

2   The induced movers, $Q_1 - Q_0$, also sell at price P_1 but they previously enjoyed a surplus from these properties represented by the arc *ad* on the curve S_0. Their loss of surplus is represented by area *adbc*.

3   The non-movers suffer a loss of surplus equal to the area bounded by the curves S_0 and S_1 and the vertical *db*.

Contrary to the assumption made by the research team to the *Commission on the Third London Airport*, the figure illustrates that there is a further change in surplus attributed to inmovers. The original purchases of good-environment properties derived a surplus equal to $D_0 a P_0$ from them. The new purchasers, represented by the demand curve D_1, derive a different level of surplus $D_1 b P_1$. The difference between these two surpluses represents the net loss (or gain) by the inmovers.

4.4 Conclusion

A great deal of criticism was made of the noise cost model at the time that it was being developed, particularly during the *Roskill Commission's* investigations. But much of the criticism made related not to the cost model concept, but to the specific methods and measures used to derive values for some of the terms used in the model. The absence of incisive criticism of the theory is a tribute to the Roskill team and the undoubted contribution that they have made to this environmental issue.

However, one particular feature of the noise cost model has been the narrow context of its development. In both the Roskill and UMCS instances, the aim was to assist in resolving a particular planning issue. In neither case was it a research exercise aimed at the valuation of an environmental nuisance by examining revealed preferences. That this was not the case is underlined by both the sources of data and by the methods of estimation used. For example, values for D were derived from the *judgement* of estate agents and the values for the distribution S were derived from questionnaire responses to a *hypothetical* situation.

In other words they were a priori models largely uncalibrated to observed behaviour. They were not models designed to derive values per se from the revealed preferences of persons subjected to environmental nuisances. Nevertheless, this does not detract from their usefulness as a starting point for the consideration of such preferences, and it is to this aspect that we now turn.

Notes

1   More precisely the rate of change in total rents with respect to distance is just equal to (the negative of) the rate of change of total travel costs with respect to distance, see A. W. Evans (1973).

2   Unfortunately, Richardson's subsequent discussion on land values appears to neglect his own revision to residential location theory and tends to overconcentrate on accessibility to urban activities at the expense of accessibility to amenity.

3 P. S. Smith (1967). It is interesting that in the opinion of local estate agents the HPD is greater around Gatwick airport than around Heathrow. (*Commission of the Third London Airport* (1970).) Various reasons for this were suggested by the Research Team to the *Roskill Commission*, but these did not include the employment and accessibility issue here discussed.

4 Ridker's seminal study of property values and air pollution in St Louis incorporated along with sulfation rates various accessibility measures into the equations estimating property values. He found some to be significant and their inclusion necessary for the proper estimation of the pollution coefficient, see R. Ridker (1967), p. 136.

5 A celebrated example of a lack of success is a study commissioned from the University of Keele by the UK Ministry of Transport. This careful study of suburban housing, homogeneous except for distance from a major road, produced perverse results insofar as those properties adjacent to the road sold at a higher price than the quieter sheltered properties; see J. Diffey (1971).

6 The Roskill model is summarised by A. D. J. Flowerdew (1972).

7 I. Heggie (1972). The following largely paraphrases Heggie's description of his own figure although there are one or two adaptations.

5 The Exclusion Facilities Approach

5.1 Exclusion facilities

The stay/leaving model is naturally a simplified abstraction from reality. It simplifies to avoid complexity but it is hoped, not too much at the expense of accuracy. It assumes householders are mobile, unconstrained optimisers. In its simple form it also chooses to ignore other options open to pollution-affected householders.

First, it ignores ways in which the activities and thus the behaviour of the household might adapt to the new circumstances while the household remains in situ. Many of these behavioural adaptations can in fact be interpreted as introducing a third option of leaving temporarily. For example, the household might spend its Sunday afternoons in the country or at the seaside instead of spending them in a now noisy garden. More frequent visits to the cinema or theatre might substitute for watching a flickering television screen. In other words, in contrast to the simplifying postulates of the basic model the household could move some of its disturbed activities outside the noise affected area.

The traditional binary form of model also ignores the possibility of households buying, to coin Millward's (1971) phrase, 'exclusion facilities'. These aim to eliminate or mitigate the external effect. Visual intrusion, for example, could be off-set by the household buying shrubs, trees, fencing and other screening devices, or by trying to create visually attractive areas by way of compensation. Expenditure on decorating the exterior or interior of the home could arise in this way. Similarly a household living in an area of air pollution could nullify the adverse effects by installing air conditioning, and noise pollution could be offset by installing sound insulation.

The latter form of expenditure is now a very realistic option consequent upon recent legislation in the United Kingdom, which has reduced the expense of sound proofing and focused attention upon it. The 1965 Airports Authority Act provided airport and local authorities with the rights to subsidise the sound proofing of homes around airports. A number of authorities have taken powers by Statutory Instrument under the 1965 Act to introduce grant-aided schemes. These include Manchester and Luton Corporations and the British Airports Authority: the latter having introduced schemes for Heathrow airport in 1966 and for Gatwick airport early in 1973.

The relevant section of the 1965 Act has now been incorporated in the 1973 Land Compensation Act which greatly extends the scope for grant-aided expenditure on sound-proofing facilities. The 1973 Act has given the Secretary of State for the Environment wide-ranging powers to require authorities to give grants in respect of the cost of sound insulation when households are disturbed by noise from new public works including highways.

5.2 An extended model incorporating exclusion facilities

There does appear to be an argument therefore, for extending the go/stay form of noise cost model to include the possibility that households living in a noisy area may sound insulate their homes. In these circumstances there are two decisions to be analysed. Householders now have to decide whether to live elsewhere or to stay in their present residence. If they choose the latter they have the further option of installing exclusion facilities.

If the cost of these facilities is G and, once having installed them, there will remain an element of annoyance (the subjective capitalised value of which let us call N') then the optimising household will choose to purchase facilities if

$$N > G + N'$$

Thus, sound insulation will be installed if the cost of sound insulation and the subjective cost of the residual disturbance is less than the cost of the full disturbance. In other words, the household will buy exclusion facilities when the benefits of noise reduction $(N - N')$ exceeds the cost of buying the reduction, G, i.e. when $G < (N - N')$. In these circumstances the household will gain a consumer's surplus on its purchase G.

The purchase of exclusion facilities provides, of course, only a partial remedy. Residual annoyance is likely to remain substantial. Sound-insulation glazing, for example, does nothing to remedy the outdoor situation and furthermore, aircraft may cause annoyance by association. Even if aircraft were noiseless some elements of the associated annoyances (e.g. bad TV reception and vibration of the house) would still remain. Thus, for some, leaving the noise affected area *may* still remain the optimal course of action. We need therefore, to redefine our inequalities. Pursuing the cost minimisation hypotheses, for those who decide to stay and *not* to introduce exclusion facilities, the total expression can be rewritten as follows:

$$S + D + R > N < G + N'$$

Conversely, for those who stay and do buy facilities the following relationship will hold:

$$N > G + N' < S + D + R$$

In practice the decision to go and the decision to stay and buy exclusion facilities is likely to interact. Because some householders, given the option, will consider staying with exclusion facilities installed to be a better course of action than leaving, the initial disequilibrium turnover in the housing market and probably the house price differential will be reduced in comparison with a situation where exclusion facilities are not taken into account. A secondary effect is that the more the house price differential is reduced the lower becomes the cost of going and therefore the more attractive this alternative, thus having the opposite effect of increasing disequilibrium turnover and the price differential. Eventually an overall equilibrium would be established taking into account all the choices open to the householder.

Extending the noise cost models to incorporate the possibility that affected households might choose to stay and ameliorate nuisances by the purchase of exclusion facilities, highlights the possibility of inferring a behavioural value from this choice situation. The simple logic is that expenditure on exclusion facilities represents a minimum valuation of the good 'peace and quiet'. If it were possible also to observe the response to a change (or variation) in the price of exclusion facilities then a 'best estimate' valuation could be thus obtained. This best estimate would represent the area under the exclusion facilities demand curve and therefore a Marshallian measure of surplus or value. But if the extended cost model suggests this simple approach to the valuation of environmental goods it indicates also the difficulties of such an approach.

One problem of inferring a value from analysis of exclusion facility costs is the possibility of a direct relationship between exclusion facilities and the house price. The indirect relationship – the possible reduction in disequilibrium turnover (and therefore a smaller change in house prices) consequent upon the introduction of exclusion facilities – has already been mentioned. A more direct interaction may arise from a possible addition to the capitalised value of the house brought about by double glazing. Indeed, in so far as an HPD does exist in a local housing market this should logically follow. Houses with sound insulation will be quieter than those without and will therefore command a premium in this respect. The consequence of this may be a motivation on the part of the double glazing owner-occupier which is a complex combination of both consumption and investment motives. In this respect the terms in the extended model are clearly interdependent.

Moreover any interpretation of the valuation of noise by studying the

$G + N'$ term alone is conditioned also by the cost and benefits of moving. In other words, an analysis of behaviour with respect to the installation of exclusion facilities in a noise polluted area is limited to that proportion of the affected (optimising) population for which staying and installing exclusion facilities (and, by inference, staying and not glazing) is the least cost solution. As estimates of noise cost for the whole of the affected population such values would appear biased and very much dependent upon the vicissitudes of the HPD.

5.3 Constraints on optimising behaviour

On the other hand, such estimates would be biased only to the extent that there are movers for noise reasons and that a realistic choice situation in this respect does exist. The fewer such movers there are the smaller the bias is likely to be. Certainly if an HPD does exist – and of course, in practice the reality of an HPD has been hard to discover – it does not provide a priori evidence that people are moving from an area because they are disturbed. An HPD could easily develop from a sorting-out, by perceptive buyers, of quiet and noisy properties vacated by those moving for reasons other than noise.

Moreover, Paul (1971), Pearce (1972), Jansen and Opschoor (1973) have all argued with conviction that the noise cost models, in the form that they have been applied, overestimate the number of actual movers. They hold this view because amongst other things they claim that the applied models ignore the financial aspects constraining the move.[1] This constraint is perhaps becoming of greater significance with the cost of housing rising considerably in real terms. Many of the transaction costs (agents' fees, stamp duty, conveyancing charges, bridging loans) are related to the house price and therefore have appreciated significantly in recent years. Whereas in basic model D and R are cash flow elements (both the former appearing on the same side of the inequality signs), N and S are monetary equivalents of utility losses usually based upon measures of hypothetical compensation. Moving as a consequence will always result in a financial loss and a liquidity constraint may lead to a decision that the householder will remain in situ in spite of the fact that leaving the noisy area might, nevertheless, lead to a situation of improved welfare.

That fewer people move than postulated by the noise cost models that are usually applied, is also supported by the threshold theory of consumer behaviour touched upon by Wicksteed, Pareto, Robbins and others, and recently discussed at more length by Devletoglou (1971). The theory is in contrast to the normal neo-classical notions of *homo oeconomicus* displaying perfect rationality and a highly tuned instinct of optimisation. This, in a sense, is the notion assumed to apply in the noise cost model regardless of whether it is viewed in its simple binary form or in the extended version suggested here. The argument advanced by Devletoglou is that instead, consumer behaviour is characterised by threshold sensitive response and that the consumer displays indifference until the threshold is reached. Within the threshold range the difference between the alternatives do not amount to a sufficient stimulus to evoke a rational response in favour of one or the other. With this *minimum sensible* hypothesis the costs of rationality are included in the process of choice. With the noise cost model the costs of rationality are obviously high. The information required to optimise upon, for example, a movement of house to a location outside the affected area, is quite considerable. If the threshold theory does operate within the context of the noise cost model then it clearly operates in favour of the status quo: it operates, that is, against moving and in favour of staying.

Quite apart from these considerations, there is another and very substantial proportion of the population for whom the constraints on moving are perhaps even more binding than suggested above. This is the tenant including those households in public housing. With this substantial housing group the basic expression of the noise cost model does not apply without some modification. For the private tenant the concept of a house price differential (D) is replaced by the analogous capitalised rent differential (CR). The rent of less noisy tenancies may rise and that of those tenancies newly affected by a nuisance may fall. For the regulated tenant who enjoys security of tenure (which in the United Kingdom under present law is dwelling specific[2]) this differential may be very substantial indeed. Thus for this group:

$$N \gtrless G + N' \gtrless CR + R + S$$

The case of the council tenant is markedly different. (D) disappears and with it considerations of investment motives in the purchase of double glazing. The normal market mechanisms are replaced by other forms of rationing and trading takes place through a system of barter. Though the clearing house for exchange is sometimes efficiently operated nevertheless the limitations on moving are many. It could be argued that the mechanisms of trading involved in this instance actually add to the degree of uncertainty attached to a move.[3]

In the tenant sector in general, the lower incomes and comparative lack of wealth will reduce access to credit and increase the liquidity constraint. Yet a move might result, for example, in longer journeys to and from work and longer shopping trips which need to be paid for. Although those trans-

47

action costs associated with the ownership of property do not apply in this case, the direct costs of a move are considerable if one takes into account the lower levels of income involved.[4] Indeed as far as tenants are concerned it might be argued that moving solely for reasons of noise and other environmental nuisances is a minimal feature of this sector of the housing market.

5.4 Lack of evidence of noise-induced mobility

For empirical evidence to support the proposition of low or nonexistent noise-induced movement by householders, one is drawn to the singular lack of success by studies, at least in the United Kingdom, in revealing a difference between the price of properties with 'good' and 'bad' environments. However, we also argued earlier in the chapter that an HPD, if it did exist, would not of itself constitute a priori evidence that people were moving from a polluted area becasue they were disturbed. Similarly, the absence of such a differential would not be conclusive proof that there were no noise induced movers.

The reasons for this possibility were discussed in evidence presented to the *Third London Airport Commission* by Plowden appearing for the British Airports Authority. The essence of this argument is that in theory the HPD is determined at the margin by the turnover of a comparatively small number of the total stock of properties in a particular housing market. Whether in these circumstances the HPD develops depends upon the supply of 'noisy' properties relative to the number of imperturbable households prepared to move into that particular localised market. A large number of competing imperturbable customers and a small number of annoyed and intending movers-out may result in no difference between the exchanged price of quiet and noisy properties.

Unfortunately, therefore, in spite of the lack of empirical evidence that HPDs exist in 'disturbed' markets and, indeed, in spite of much evidence to the contrary, we are unable to recognise this as constituting substantive support for our hypothesis. We must look for more direct evidence on this issue of mobility and annoyance.

Data on this matter is rather sparse. However, there is one piece of information which although by no means conclusive, suggests that the argument we put forward is broadly correct. The *Second Survey of Aircraft Noise* was carried out in September 1967 covering an area up to fifteen miles east and west and ten miles north of London (Heathrow) airport. There were 4,678 persons included in the survey and amongst other things they were asked how long they had lived in the actual building in which they were then residing.

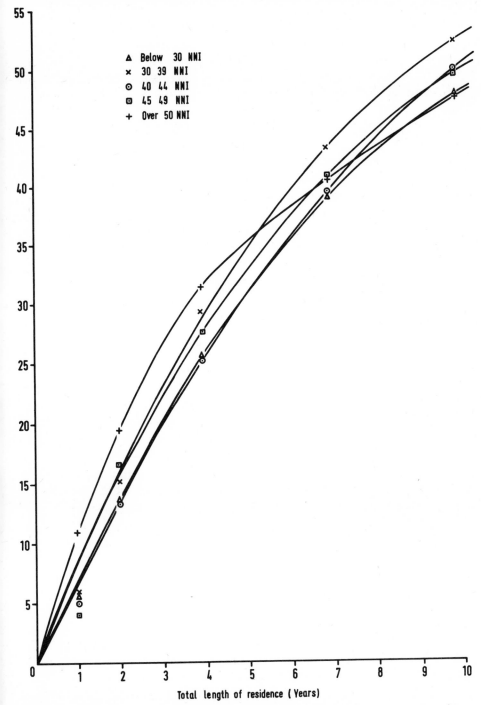

Fig. 5.1 Length of residence by *NNI* band: cumulated percentages for sample population

Source: see text

It might be claimed of course, that such a survey in the area of a long established major airport will only reveal a population that has long since adjusted to the reality of a noisy airport. But this would be to overlook the important point that it was not until the end of the 1950s that the jet aircraft was introduced in significant numbers. Not until the 1960s did the turbo-jet become the predominant mode.

The resulting answers have been analysed by the Building Research Station and the cumulative percentage of informants versus total length of residence in the dwelling for various bands of *NNI* is shown in Figure 5.1. The results are only broadly indicative because the sample sizes in *NNI* bands above 45 were small (30–188) and the *NNI* as an accurate index of annoyance is a matter open to some debate. Nor was the analysis subdivided by tenure group, a drawback incidentally that inhibits the use of published census data for the same purpose. Nevertheless, the analysis suggests that there was not an appreciable difference in the behaviour between the various *NNI* bands.

Confirmation that this finding is broadly correct comes from a less extensive survey relating this time to road construction and traffic annoyance. Surveys were carried out for the *Urban Motorways Committee* in two areas affected by road schemes (Department of the Environment, 1974). A study of household movement from past and present electoral rolls compared the names of voters listed at the same address during successive years. Although certain drawbacks are involved in the use of electoral registers – some households fail to register, others contain wholly persons not eligible to vote, while households which move both in and out between the October qualifying dates are also absent from the roll – the resulting errors are probably quite small. Altogether 730 addresses were studied and the conclusion formed that 'the pattern of household movement from all addresses studied in each area, showed no obvious correlation with the dates of approval, commencement of land clearance, start of construction and completion of the road schemes'. This conclusion, while not confirming our hypothesis conclusively, nevertheless adds further support to our argument.

5.5 A model of constrained behaviour

In these circumstances of powerful sanctions against moving that, in general, householders face, it is most likely that in reality the noise cost type of model simplifies to represent once again a binary decision, but one that differs from that of the traditional model. It now takes the form:

$$N \gtrless G + N'$$

such that the household will purchase sound insulation until:

$$(N - N') = G$$

If variations in the price of exclusion facilities can be observed it should be possible, by observing the quantities of glazing purchased at the various prices, to derive a demand curve for double-glazing. We would expect this curve to move to the right with increasing noise levels and to the left in more peaceful circumstances.

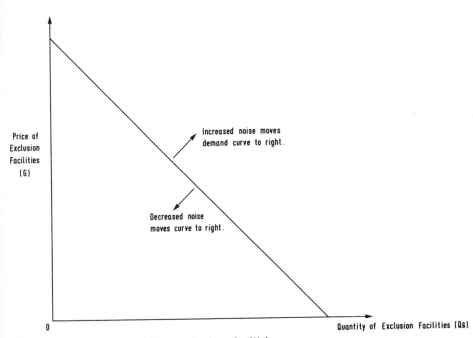

Fig. 5.2   The demand for exclusion facilities

Figure 5.2 shows the essentials of the suggested approach. Consistent with the theory of valuation discussed in Chapter 3, the total area under this curve would indicate the total willingness-to-pay on the part of householders; it would indicate a Marshallian measure of surplus or benefit received.

Opportunities to observe variations in insulation prices may occur for two reasons. First where insulation costs are subsidised by specific grants, changes in the proportionate size of the grant may take place. Second and more especially, variations in insulation charges may arise from the nature of the dwelling. Homes with large picture windows, for example, may be particularly expensive to sound insulate.

Therefore we see the prime focus of the exclusion facilities approach as

51

the discovery of systematic variation in prices and the development of a function, explaining the propensity for householders to purchase insulation, in which both the cost of double glazing and levels of noise are explicit variables. From this function one can derive a value for peace and quiet.

Notes

1 None of the cost models have been calibrated. For a discussion of this issue see A. A. Walters (1972).

2 We are grateful to Aileen Hammond of R. Travers Morgan and Partners for drawing this point to our attention.

3 It is the view of A. W. Evans (1973), p. 21, that the barriers to movement may be greatest for tenants of local authority housing.

4 The cost of the alternative course of action – the installation of exclusion facilities – may be less to tenants than to owner-occupiers because of economies of scale allowed for by certain arrangements between contractors and landlords.

6 The Technical Characteristics of Sound Insulation Glazing

Before passing final judgement on the exclusion facilities approach, we need to examine more closely some of the technical and economic aspects of sound insulation to see if unexpected difficulties are likely to occur from an application of the model. In this chapter we consider some technical aspects.

First there is the issue of how much 'peace and quiet' is purchased when sound insulation glazing is installed in the home. Sound insulation is not an homogeneous product. It is available in many different shapes and sizes and there are a large number of other interacting factors that can affect the precise level of additional sound reduction achieved from extra insulation (Lewis, 1971).

Fortunately too, there are a number of characteristics which simplify the issue from a technical point of view. For example, with secondary window double-glazing – and this is the type normally used to achieve acoustical benefits – the degree of sound reduction achieved is invariant with the pressure, intensity or power of sounds. A double window will, providing the frequency spectra remain reasonably constant, give the same measured reduction in sound whether the external noise level is a bearable 50 *dBs* or an excruciating 120 *dBs*.

Moreover, in many schemes which are grant aided a number of potential sources of variation are eliminated by rigorous standards specified in Statutory Instruments and in other regulations administering the grants. Factors, often of a minor nature such as the fabric of the original window, its condition and the quality of the workmanship involved in fitting secondary windows, are often absent within certain groups or types of housing and can therefore be allowed for in analyses.

But there is one variable – window size – that it seems advisable to consider in more detail. It was suggested in the previous chapter (p. 51) that opportunities to observe adjustments to price variations are most likely to occur as a consequence of sound insulation charges varying with window sizes. If the amount of 'peace and quiet' also varied with window size the simplicity of this approach would be destroyed utterly.

6.1 The effect of window size

Table 6.1 expresses this aspect in terms of the proportional variation in wall

c .

Table 6.1

Average sound reduction (*dB*) from improved window insulation for comparative glazed areas

Percentage of glazed area to wall area	(a) 20 *dB* window	(b) 40 *dB* window	(c) *dB* (*b-a*)
	fitted in a 50 *dB* wall*		
0 (windowless wall)	50	50	0
10	30	47	17
25	26	45	19
33	25	44	19
50	23	43	20
75	21	41	20
100 (fully glazed wall)	20	40	20

Source: Adapted from Table 4 Building Research Station (1972)

* Equivalent of walls weighing about 480 kg/m² for example a 215 mm solid or a 355 mm cavity brick wall.

area glazed. As such it gives a broad indication of how window size might effect the performance of improved insulation. The results suggest that the effect is insignificant over what one may regard as a realistic degree of variation in the proportion. However, the proportion of wall area subjected to glazing is not a variable for which information is readily available. A more apposite form of analysis would be to study the effects of window area per se.

Exhaustive studies of, inter alia, window size and sound insulation efficiency have been carried out by Heriot-Watt University, Scotland, for the United Kingdom Department of the Environment (Heriot-Watt University, 1972).

The specifications of double-glazing systems examined by Heriot-Watt accord reasonably well with those specified in grant-aided sound-proofing schemes. For example, where the existing casement windows were of steel, one of the secondary window systems examined contained glass of 4 mm thickness and was installed with an air gap of 112 mm (minimum) to 130 mm (maximum). This is roughly in accordance with the 6 inch minimum air gap for glass not less than 32 ounces per sq. ft. stipulated in Statutory Instruments for London's airports. The Scottish study also took into account the effect of compressible strips on outer windows (or weather proofing, as they preferred to call it).

The minor disparities of specification were in relation to the lining of the window reveals with sound absorbent material, and fitting of an electric ventilator unit. The former aspect was not examined by Heriot-Watt and the latter was subject to less stringent analysis by them.

The major disparity between the test conditions and those experienced in grant-aided schemes at airport sites arises from the noise frequency spectra examined. The Heriot-Watt tests used white noise as a source of sound. The sound pressure levels were measured in third octave bands in the frequency range 100–3150 *Hz*. This comparatively low frequency range was chosen because the objective of the study was to examine the effectiveness of sound insulation against traffic noise and low frequencies are dominant in the traffic noise spectra.

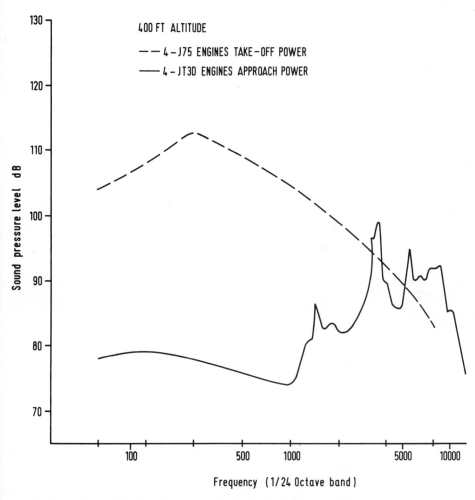

Fig. 6.1   Source spectra of turbo-fan and turbo-jet engines
Source: J. B. Large (1970)

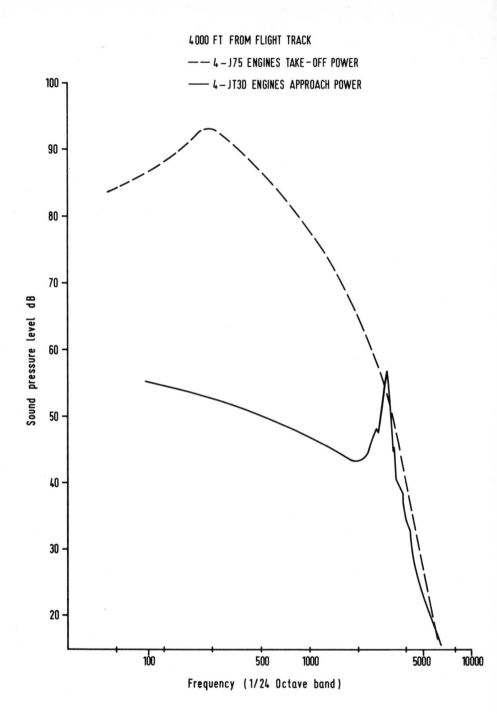

Fig. 6.2   Far-fields spectra of turbo-fan and turbo-jet engines
Source: J. B. Large (1970)

In contrast, aircraft noise is characterised by its broad spectra. This is illustrated in Figures 6.1 and 6.2. The first shows the difference in spectral characteristics between the take-off of a four-engined turbo-jet powered aircraft and that of an aircraft equipped with turbo-fans operating at approach thrust. Both spectra are at the peak noise level reached at a position 400 ft from the source. A similar comparison is made in the second figure but this time the observer is 4,000 ft from the flight track.

These comparisons show that the higher frequencies are associated with the turbo-fan jet. But such jets still account for a very small proportion of

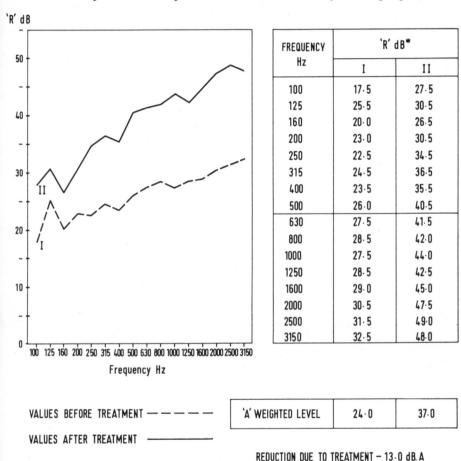

FREQUENCY Hz	'R' dB*	
	I	II
100	17·5	27·5
125	25·5	30·5
160	20·0	26·5
200	23·0	30·5
250	22·5	34·5
315	24·5	36·5
400	23·5	35·5
500	26·0	40·5
630	27·5	41·5
800	28·5	42·0
1000	27·5	44·0
1250	28·5	42·5
1600	29·0	45·0
2000	30·5	47·5
2500	31·5	49·0
3150	32·5	48·0

VALUES BEFORE TREATMENT — — — — —

VALUES AFTER TREATMENT ————————

'A' WEIGHTED LEVEL	24·0	37·0

REDUCTION DUE TO TREATMENT – 13·0 dB. A

Fig. 6.3   Sound attenuation of secondary window glazing on steel casement prime windows measuring 2,515 × 1,520 mm
Source: see text

* The sound reduction index 'R' was calculated, for each frequency in the range, from the formula given in British Standard 2750 (1956).

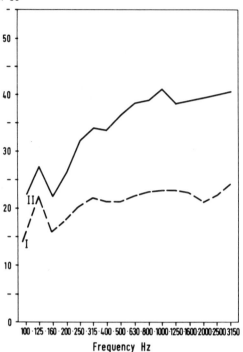

| FREQUENCY | 'R' dB | |
Hz	I	II
100	14·0	21·5
125	21·5	27·0
160	15·5	21·5
200	17·5	26·0
250	20·	31·5
315	21·5	34·0
400	21·0	33·5
500	21·0	36·5
630	22·0	38·5
800	22·5	39·0
1000	23·0	41·0
1250	23·0	38·5
1600	22·5	39·0
2000	21·0	39·5
2500	22·0	40·0
3150	24·0	40·5

Frequency Hz

VALUES BEFORE TREATMENT — — — — —

VALUES AFTER TREATMENT ———————

'A' WEIGHTED LEVEL	18·5	32·5

REDUCTION DUE TO TREATMENT −14·0 dB. A

Fig. 6.4 Sound attenuation of secondary window glazing on ill-fitting steel casement frame windows measuring 2,515 × 1,520 mm
Source: see text

total aircraft movements at UK airports. For the numerically important turbo-jet, the Heriot-Watt experiments, it would seem, are by no means inappropriate.

6.2 The Edinburgh analysis

Careful and detailed analysis by the Edinburgh team appears to suggest that the absolute size of window is of little or no importance as a factor affecting the efficiency of secondary window glazing. For example, when the primary window was well fitted, fully closed, weather stripped and of steel casement

58

construction, dimensions of 2,515 × 1,520 mm produced, compared with single glazing, an additional (arithmetic) mean sound reduction of 13·0 *dBA*. A fractionally higher reduction of 14·0 *dBA* occurred where a simulated twist in the exterior frame allowed an area of opening of 0·002 m² (see Figures 6.3 and 6.4). The corresponding figures for windows of virtually identical circumstances except for a size of 1,215 × 1,113 mm, were 14·0 *dBA* and 15·5 *dBA* (see Figures 6.5 and 6.6). Thus, window size alone appeared to account for a negligible difference of 1·0 *dBA* in the sound reduction qualities of double glazing where the exterior windows were sealed, and a difference of 1·5 *dBA* for casement windows typical of those which would normally be found in a 25-year-old-house. [1]

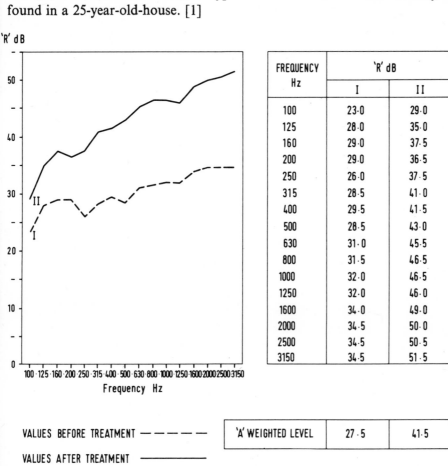

FREQUENCY Hz	'R' dB	
	I	II
100	23·0	29·0
125	28·0	35·0
160	29·0	37·5
200	29·0	36·5
250	26·0	37·5
315	28·5	41·0
400	29·5	41·5
500	28·5	43·0
630	31·0	45·5
800	31·5	46·5
1000	32·0	46·5
1250	32·0	46·0
1600	34·0	49·0
2000	34·5	50·0
2500	34·5	50·5
3150	34·5	51·5

VALUES BEFORE TREATMENT — — — — —

VALUES AFTER TREATMENT ————————

'A' WEIGHTED LEVEL	27·5	41·5

REDUCTION DUE TO TREATMENT − 14·0 dB. A

Fig. 6.5 Sound attenuation of secondary window glazing on steel casement frame windows measuring 1,215 × 1,113 mm
Source: see text

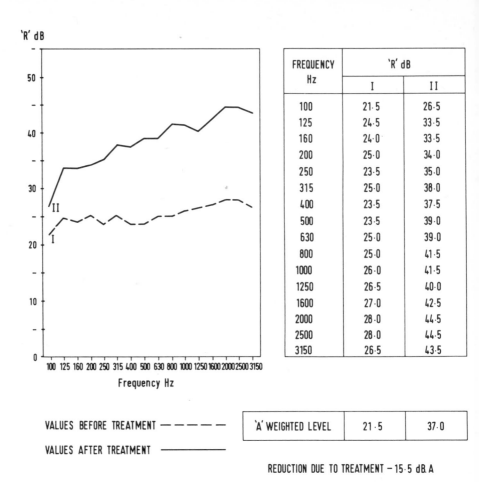

| FREQUENCY | 'R' dB | |
Hz	I	II
100	21·5	26·5
125	24·5	33·5
160	24·0	33·5
200	25·0	34·0
250	23·5	35·0
315	25·0	38·0
400	23·5	37·5
500	23·5	39·0
630	25·0	39·0
800	25·0	41·5
1000	26·0	41·5
1250	26·5	40·0
1600	27·0	42·5
2000	28·0	44·5
2500	28·0	44·5
3150	26·5	43·5

VALUES BEFORE TREATMENT — — — — —

VALUES AFTER TREATMENT —————

'A' WEIGHTED LEVEL	21·5	37·0

REDUCTION DUE TO TREATMENT − 15·5 dB A

Fig. 6.6   Sound attenuation of secondary window glazing on ill-fitting steel casement windows measuring 1,215 × 1,113 mm
Source: see text

We conclude, therefore, that whereas window size may be of considerable importance in relation to the price to be paid for sound-insulation glazing, it is of little consequence in relation to the quality of service to be expected from this 'peace and quiet' good.

Note

1   The transmission loss of single glazed windows does vary a little more with size. This could be of significance; it may have a bearing on the annoyance suffered and therefore the consequent reaction. However, in the

examples considered, the *dBA* difference was $3 \cdot 5$ for the well-fitted windows and $3 \cdot 0$ for the ill-fitted ones. Such differences are barely perceptible.

7 The Characteristics of Sound Insulation Glazing as an Economic Good

7.1 Sound insulation as a 'new' commodity

The general idea of using double glazing to reduce noise is by no means new. As early as 1857 a commission, set up by the government of the day to enquire into the best 'modes of warming and ventilating the apartments of dwelling houses and barracks' advocated double panes of glass in windows, not only for economy in the use of fuel but also for diminishing the effect of outdoor sounds (Attenborough, 1973).

In spite of such Victorian foresight, the commercial development and marketing of double glazing is a comparatively modern affair. Although quickly growing, even today the degree of overall market penetration is exceedingly low. Double glazing therefore, is a 'new commodity' – that is, one with which consumers are not yet familiar (Schumpeter, 1934) – and like other new commodities it fits rather awkwardly within the postulates and conditions of the accepted theory of consumer behaviour. The standard static equilibrium theory of consumer behaviour has been summarised in the following manner:

> This theory is concerned with the situation which an individual faces in making a single act of choice. It is static in the sense that all the variables affecting the single choice are assumed to be constant and also in the sense that the quantities concerned need not be regarded as having a time dimension since there is just a single choice to be made. The theory then uses the comparative static method of comparing two or more isolated acts of choice in which one or more of the variables affecting the pattern of consumption are different, so as to obtain some behavioural relationship between the changes in prices and income and resultant changes in the quantities consumed (Ironmonger, 1972).

Ironmonger proceeded to highlight a number of discordant notes between this standard theory and the characteristics of new commodities. New commodities do not have constant qualities; they are not 'single priced'; they do not directly produce happiness (or utility); they are not always characterised by a continuity of function and they do not necessarily satisfy only one want.

Environmental goods would appear to have many of these characteristics. Quiet housing, housing with a pleasant view, garden screening, garden plants, etc., usually satisfy more than one want. And as a consequence, from the point of view of any such singular environmental want, environmental goods do not have a 'single price'. But of all environmental goods, at a cursory glance, sound insulation glazing would appear to be, in Ironmonger's terms, a new commodity par excellence. It most certainly produces its 'happiness' indirectly and it is a happiness related to several wants – warmth, freedom from draughts as well as quietude. Nor can the consumer, in pursuit of this happiness, consider double glazing one quarter or half a window; the function is indeed lumpy.

Some of these disharmonies produce for the analyst, equipped only with the tools of static equilibrium theory, more problems than others. The satisfaction of multiple wants is obviously a fundamental hurdle but conceptually at least it is easily handled by the methods of multivariate analysis. Similarly, certain methods of multivariate analysis, such as category analysis, can be and have been used to analyse, successfully, lumpy discontinuous functions. But other problems are more difficult from both a theoretical and a practical viewpoint.

7.2 Issues of quality

The issue of constant quality is one that looms large in this context. It is an issue that is by no means exclusive to new commodities as such, but tends to characterise consumer durables as a whole and certain non-marketed commodities of a perishable nature such as travel time. It is also an issue, the difficulties of which are widely appreciated.

A. A. Walters (1968) writes:

> It should be emphasised that quality changes are particularly important and intractable with consumer durables. And most of the characteristics of 'quality' are intangible . . . Many consumer durables are notoriously heterogeneous and it is very difficult to find a scale . . . Various devices are adapted in practice, such as measuring the cubic capacity of refrigerators, the horsepower of cars, and so on. Unsatisfactory as these techniques have been, it is surely better to take some account of quality than to ignore it completely.

The general tendency is to view quality from a cost or producer's point of view. Theil[1] for example, defined quality as 'a perfectly homogeneous good . . . [and] a commodity as a set of qualities'. He then stipulated that a set of qualities is a commodity only if the prices have a certain functional relationship. A similar view was expressed by Houthakkar[1] who defined quality as the price per unit under some basic price system.

But the sound insulation good (or commodity) illustrates a certain absurdity of this approach, at least from the point of view of measuring consumer behaviour. In terms of a price per unit, if we measure this unit as a square foot of glazed area or a window, we have an array of qualities of the sound insulation 'commodity'. And yet over a wide range of window size the crucial factor from the consumer's point of view, namely sound reduction, will remain constant.

Clearly a better approach to this issue is that advocated by Brems[1] who recognised two different meanings of the term quality, 'what the consumer gets from the product . . . [and] what the producer puts into it'. Our concern is with what the consumer gets.

The basic point at issue in the context of double glazing is whether (in spite of the near constant sound reduction that double glazing brings regardless of window size, exterior noise levels, etc.) double glazing of different

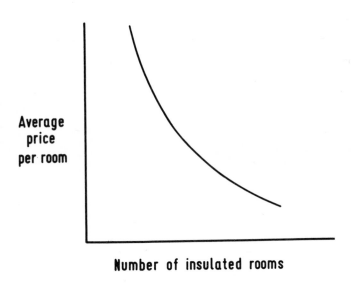

Fig. 7.1 Demand curve for 'peace and quiet' at a given level of noise external to household

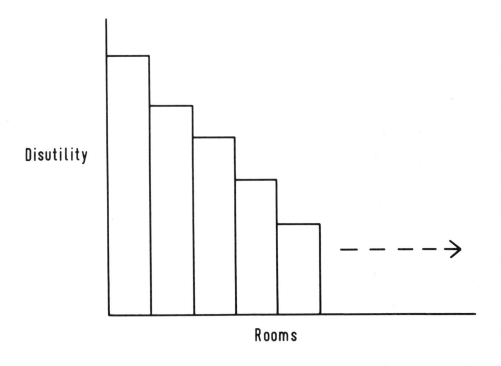

Fig. 7.2 Disutility of noise for different household rooms

household rooms introduces qualitative differences or merely different quantities of the same good, household quiet.

The distinction can be illustrated in the following way.[2] In the one case, households can be envisaged as purchasing various quantities of the same good, i.e., indoor quiet. The quantity of quiet purchased can then be measured by the number of rooms sound insulated per house or group of houses at the average price of insulation per room (see Figure 7.1).

The number of rooms sound insulated per house at a given price will, of course, vary from household to household. For each household the relative disamenity of noise for each room will differ because of different frequencies of use (see Figure 7.2).

These relative distributions will vary also between households as a function of the number of rooms (ability to shift usage) and real differences in disutility for different room usage (i.e., some people cannot sleep with noise, therefore bedroom noise disutility ranks highly relative to others). As a consequence when the new commodity, double glazing, is introduced at

66

price P_1 this will give a unique choice to each household at a given noise exposure level (see Figure 7.3).

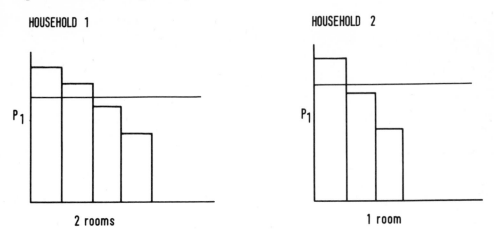

Fig. 7.3   The response of different households to a given price for sound insulation

The alternative argument is that households are buying qualitatively different goods when they have lounges, dining rooms or bedrooms insulated. In this case the demand relationship could be presented as shown in Figure 7.4.

It could be argued that to put the stress on qualitative differences is misconceived in view of the fact that a market demand curve derived from the first approach could be disaggregated to at least resemble the second approach. Although the disaggregation would be in terms of '1st room', '2nd room', etc., and not precisely in terms of 'lounge', 'bedroom', etc., it could be said that such a distinction is of little or no consequence. On the other hand, if households are insulating lounges against daytime and evening noise and bedrooms against night-time noise (which seems a reasonable hypothesis), then it might be considered a debatable point whether household quiet in the two circumstances is of the same, or of a different quality.

We take the pragmatic view that, in the final analysis, whether the distinction is of consequence depends upon the purpose of any valuation. If a valuation is required to illuminate policies with respect to, say, limiting night flights from airports, then the distinction between the demand specifically for bedrooms as opposed to other rooms is of some consequence.

However, this distinction between night and day air operations and therefore between bedrooms and other rooms sound insulated, is probably the only qualitative distinction worth considering.

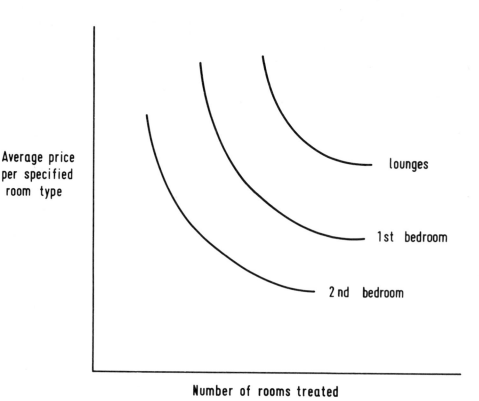

Fig. 7.4 Demand curves for 'peace and quiet' in specified rooms at a given level of noise external to the household

7.3 Market dynamics

Another group of problems arising from the analysis of a new commodity such as sound insulation glazing, involves the dynamics of the market. The dynamic situation stems from a diffusion process as knowledge of the want satisfying power of the commodity spreads through the community. By contrast, the static assumptions of neo-classical theory recognise only that a commodity is made available to the market as a whole at some instant of time.

The diffusion process has been described in the following terms by Ironmonger (1972):

68

The spread of consumption of the new commodity through the population of consumers is due to the successive readjustment, as knowledge is obtained . . . This is to be expected with a new commodity for which virtually the great majority of consumers do not know anything of its want satisfying powers. As some consumers start to consume the new commodity, this consumption is observed by other consumers so that, as time goes on, more and more consumers obtain some knowledge of the want satisfying powers of the new commodity. This process leads to further increases in the number of consumers until stability is reached, if other conditions remain unchanged.

Successful attempts have been made to categorise and subsequently model these dynamic characteristics. It is now recognised that there is, generally speaking, an 'introduction' phase followed by a period of 'take-off' when a surge in consumption occurs. The process slows down and, as a whole, is terminated by the 'saturation' of the market. These stages are well recognised as conforming to a sigmoid-shaped growth curve of which there is a number of variants such as the logistic and Gompertz forms.

Sound insulation is one commodity that lends itself well to a diffusion process. Its precise attributes are by no means obvious and knowledge, spread by word of mouth, can be expected to play an important role.

The fact that sound insulation is likely to diffuse through the market over time would appear to present a particular theoretical problem. The roots of neo-classical demand theory lie in preference ordering. It might be argued, therefore, that because preferences appear to be changing as information on sound insulation diffuses, a neo-classical approach is fundamentally wrong. By way of reply we can invoke the recent theoretical arguments of Lancaster (1966) which are summarised thus by Green (1971):

. . . preferences among bundles of *goods* are not a fundamental determinant of choice, but are derived from preferences among bundles of *characteristics* supplied by these goods . . . Switch of brands is quite consistent with unchanged preferences with regard to characteristics. What has happened is that the information available to the consumer has changed.

This interpretation is, of course, a defence of standard theory for neglecting advertising, etc. Its point is that standard theory on consumer preference ordering is not affected by advertising and flows of information because these aspects (on the basis of the above arguments) cannot change basic preferences or wants.

There is another troublesome aspect of trying to fit the dynamic qualities of the demand for sound insulation within the bounds of static neo-classical theory. Again it is one which is 'disregarded in most theoretical writings'.

This is the possibility that there exists an interdependence between consumption patterns due to what is popularly referred to as the 'bandwagon' or 'snob' effect. Gwilliam and Rees (1973), in reviewing our own research, have referred to the 'imitation' effect.

It is suggested that the take-off phase of growth in the consumption of new commodities receives its stimulus from the revision of the consumer's estimates of the quality of the commodity. In return, it is argued by some 'that the interdependence of consumers' estimates of these qualities is probably of greater importance in effecting these revisions'. If this is so then it runs counter to the normal assumption of neo-classical analysis, that the behaviour of individuals is uninfluenced by the behaviour of others. It is this normal assumption which allows us to derive the aggregate, group or market demand, from the additivity of individual demand curves.

However, true interdependence is not to be confused with the effect of information diffusion. In the latter case, I buy double glazing indirectly because of my neighbour's purchase; in the former, I buy directly because of other's purchases. Moreover, unlike many other consumer durables the pure imitation effect is probably of little significance with sound insulation double glazing. Good double glazing designs stress their inconspicuality while the 'snob' effect relies upon the conspicuous nature of consumption.

7.4 Conclusion

In conclusion, the 'peace and quiet' good, sound insulation glazing, does present certain problems for conventional economic analysis of consumer behaviour. Double glazing exhibits strong characteristics of a 'new commodity' and it is in this context that many of these problems arise. Until recently theory has been inclined to neglect the issues presented by the demand for new commodities with their characteristics of varying quality, multiple want satisfaction, etc. Nevertheless, in the particular circumstances of sound insulation glazing, with certain judicious modification and adaptations of assumptions, neo-classical static equilibrium theory should prove an adequate means of analysis.

Thus, having considered basic technical and economic aspects, we see no insuperable difficulty involved in the exclusion facilities approach. We view this approach as a necessary extension of the more traditional Roskill-type model. Its ability to provide accurate values for peace and quiet, that are representative averages for the community as a whole, is dependent upon an assumption that the number of households moving for noise reasons is relatively insignificant . . . it is this same assumption which undermines the validity of the traditional noise cost model. In view of the constraints operating on household mobility, it is most likely that this assumption is a sound one for tenancies and furthermore, probably one not wholly inappropriate to the private housing sector. If this is so – and the evidence to hand supports the argument – this type of approach to valuing indoor peace and quiet may be of more general application, and we commend further study and use of it in environmental economics.

Notes

1 Quoted by W. Z. Hirsch, in: H. G. Schaller (ed.) (1963), reprinted in F. J. Lyden and E. G. Miller (eds) (1968).
2 We are grateful to Peter Vass for a discussion of this issue.

8 Case Study: The London Airport Noise Insulation Scheme

Heathrow, for some considerable time now, has ranked in passenger terms as the premier international airport of the world. Because of this commanding position the problem of aviation noise, particularly from large aircraft, was apparent at an early date and was exacerbated by the increasing use of jet aircraft during the 1960s. By 1971, when annual air movements comfortably exceeded a quarter of a million, more than two million residents were said to be affected by aircraft sounds in excess of 35 *NNI*, more than tenfold the calculated figure for the Ringway, Manchester area and thirtyfold the figures for Gatwick.

8.1 The origins of the Heathrow scheme

The Heathrow scheme[1] came into operation on 25 April 1966, on the basis that 'dwellings near London Heathrow Airport . . . require further protection from noise and vibration attributable to the use of the aerodrome than can be given by measures already taken . . . ' (*Committee on the Problem of Noise, 1963*). This conclusion was reached following a detailed investigation by that committee, and the view was expressed that:

. . . there are only two practicable ways of improving the present situation at Heathrow or possibly even merely of maintaining it:
(a) to reduce the noise of individual aircraft as new types come into service
and
(b) to provide houses near the boundary of the airport with better insulation against noise (para. 641).

Solution (a) was seen as essentially a long run course of action and it was therefore felt by the committee that sound proofing should be introduced in the meantime. Since the cost of installing suitable sound insulation was 'likely to be greater than the average household could easily bear' the committee recommended that a grant should be paid towards the cost of insulation.

However, the committee had first considered arguments against such a course of action, of which the main two were as follows:

(a) that many people are prepared to live close to the airport as demonstrated by the buoyant price of houses,
and
(b) that it is unprecedented to pay compensation for the loss of an amenity (para. 319).

No significant evidence was produced to support argument (a) and the committee felt that it was outweighed by the evidence suggesting that the noise in the area was the 'worst known' level in the United Kingdom and that the 'people who suffer from it have no right of legal action to secure its abatement'.

Argument (b) was neatly circumvented by the committee's counter point that 'a grant for improving sound insulation is more akin to a house improvement grant than to compensation for being in a noisy area'.

The committee also recommended 'that the grant should never be the whole of the cost', and that the grant should be paid 'on a scale varying from a high proportion of the total cost where the noise exposure is greatest to a small proportion on the boundary of the area within which the grant is payable'.

8.2 Area of eligibility and terms of subsidy

When the scheme was introduced in April 1966 the first of these recommendations was adhered to but the second was rejected. This resulted in one set of subsidy conditions applying to the entire area of eligibility. The latter was defined (largely for reasons of administrative convenience) by the outer boundaries of the ward and parishes intersected by the 1970 (estimated) 55 *NNI* contour (see Figure A2.1 and Appendix 2 for official terms of delimitation). Within this area successful applicants received 50 per cent of the 'reasonably incurred costs'[2] up to a maximum subsidy of £100.

The subsidy conditions for the entire period since April 1966 are detailed in Table 8.1. From the table it will be seen that the grant conditions were improved in December 1968 (up to 60 per cent and a maximum subsidy of £150) but the area of eligibility remained unchanged until September 1972 when a Special Area was created (see Figure A2.1 and Appendix 2 for precise terms of delimitation). Within this Special Area successful applicants receive 100 per cent grants up to a maximum subsidy of £360 whilst in the remainder of the original area – now known as the Standard Area – the corresponding terms are 75 per cent and £206. At the time of writing, the closing date for receipt of applications was 31 December 1974.

Table 8.1

Terms of grant for noise insulation, Heathrow

Dates	Rate of grant (per cent)	Maximum grant payable	Final date for applications	Final date for completion
25 April 1966 1 December 1968	50	£100	31 December 1970	1 January 1972
2 December 1968 13 September 1972	60	£150	31 December 1972	1 January 1974
14 September 1972 (a) Standard Area (b) Special Area	75 100	£206 £360	31 December 1974	1 January 1976

8.3 Conditions of eligibility

Residing or having an interest in property within the area of the scheme is a necessary but not sufficient condition for receipt of a grant. There are further conditions which relate to changes of residence, technical specifications of insulation, and to acceptable levels of cost per unit of work.

Conditions relating to the applicant[3]

Applications may be made by anyone with an interest in the property providing that this interest existed on 1 January 1966. In addition, in the case of tenanted dwellings it is necessary that agreement is reached between tenant and landlord.

The consequence of this ruling for owner-occupiers is that a change of residence after 1 January 1966, even if within the scheme area, annuls one's eligibility. However, in the case of tenanted property eligibility is maintained so long as either the tenant or the landlord has retained an interest in the dwelling since 1 January 1966. Moreover there is no requirement on the part of the landlords themselves to be located within the eligible area.

This distinction between owner-occupied and tenanted property has important implications for the present study. Since all council tenants are eligible for double glazing, even if they moved into their present dwelling after 1 January 1966, a consistent eligibility base is thus provided for analysis. Conversely the exact degree of take-up is extremely difficult to calculate in the case of owner-occupiers since this requires detailed knowledge of property turnover throughout the entire period of the scheme.

Conditions relating to technical specifications[4]

The main specifications refer to the double glazing of windows, ventilation and to the insulation of both chimneys and roofs. In practice less than 1 per cent of householders have opted to insulate chimneys and roofs (Webber, 1972).

An important, indeed fundamental, characteristic of the insulation employed in the scheme is that, unlike the usual form of double glazing (which is generally designed to improve thermal efficiency often to the total exclusion of any noise-reduction benefits), it is designed entirely for the purpose of sound insulation. Inevitably, thermal efficiency is also improved but the technical specifications of the scheme relate solely to sound insulation.

It is generally true that sound insulation improves with an increase in the thickness of glass, with an increase in air space between the glass panes and with a more effective sealing of surfaces; and the specifications discussed these aspects in detail. Because of the compensating trade-off in effectiveness between the first two items, the permitted combination varies between a minimum air-gap of 4 inches where the inner window has a thickness of ¼-inch or greater, to a minimum (inner window) weight of glass of 24 ounces per square foot where the gap is 8 inches or greater.

Surface sealing and insulation is ensured by the requirement for sealing strips on the opening lights of inner windows and for the lining with sound absorbent material of at least two reveals between the outer and inner windows.

Finally there are a large number of requirements relating to the ventilation of each room insulated. An essential feature of the ventilation unit is that it includes a controlled variable-speed fan (which draws air through an airbrick via an external cowl on the house exterior) and an air filter in the fan housing. The unit must be constructed not only to satisfy the conditions for the supply of air, but also must not exceed a sound level of 35 *dBA* in the absence of other sound within the room.

Conditions relating to cost[5]

The cost to the householder of double glazing any given house is a function of the number of rooms double glazed, the size of windows in each of these rooms, the prices charged per square foot of glass and per ventilation unit by the installation firms, and the terms of the grant. In the first three years of the scheme there was a considerable variation in contractor's prices, and the BAA therefore consulted with the local authorities concerned in order to determine the level of costs that might be 'reasonably incurred' for the purposes of obtaining a grant. These levels which still apply, were as follows:

> ... for the essential works (inclusive of necessary repairs to interior decoration) costs of not more than: £1·50 per sq. ft. (£16·15 per sq. metre) of double glazing and associated works
> £40 for the supply and installation of each ventilator unit, with air supply and external cowl.
>
> (British Airports Authority)

Many firms subsequently adopted these costs as the basis for their quotations and a hypothetical example is given in Table 8.2 of the level of gross costs that would be incurred for a common housing type based on these prices.

Table 8.2

Gross insulation cost, inter-war, bay-window, semi-detached house

Room	Window size (sq. ft.)	Window cost (£)	Vent cost (£)	Total cost (£)	Cumulative total cost (£)
Lounge	60	90	40	130	130
Dining room	50	75	40	115	245
Front bedroom	40	60	40	100	345
Back bedroom	20	30	40	70	415
Small bedroom	16	24	40	64	479

In the case of council tenants some authorities have chosen to negotiate special terms with installation firms on behalf of their tenants. Where this is so, the monopsonist power of the authority has often produced installation charges well within the 'reasonable' cost level laid down by the BAA. Moreover, the councils have been free to introduce their own subsidy (or favourable financial terms) over and above those terms laid down by the Statutory Instruments. Hillingdon, for example, have taken this practice to extremes and have decided to sound insulate under the BAA scheme all their eligible council dwellings at no cost to the tenant.

8.4 Administration

The scheme is administered jointly by the five local authorities of Hounslow, Hillingdon, Eton, Staines and Slough and by the head office of BAA at Buckingham Gate. Administration at the local level is usually undertaken by the public health department or, in the case of group applications and special arrangements for council tenants, by the housing department. Initial enquiries are directed to this level of administration. Inspection of work carried out by contractors is usually done under the jurisdiction of the borough surveyor's department. BAA carries responsibility for approval of the application and makes payment of the grant which is either paid directly to the applicant in the case of individual applications, or to the council in the case of special council tenant agreements.

8.5 Publicity and marketing

When the scheme first came into operation in April 1966 it was advertised extensively in the national and local press. In addition BAA circulated all the 60,000-odd eligible dwellings with details of the scheme. Further official publicity was arranged – again mainly in the form of press bulletins – at the time of each change in the terms on which a grant was given.

These forms of publicity aside, extensive advertising was carried out by the installation firms mostly in the form of letterbox leaflet campaigns and press entries. According to the local authority returns there were about fifty such firms involved up to February 1972. Notwithstanding the fact that some of these were undoubtedly subsidiaries of other companies operating in the area, the presence of fifty competitors resulted in a large volume of sales literature being distributed.

As far as council tenants were concerned further official publicity was carried out in those authority areas with special arrangements (Hillingdon, Hounslow, Staines) and it can safely be assumed that council tenant estates in these areas have received 100 per cent information coverage. Council tenants in Slough and Eton have received the same coverage as non-council tenants in those areas.

8.6 Basic response to the scheme: owner-occupiers

In the five local authorities concerned with the scheme it has been estimated, using the 1966 Census 10 per cent sample data, that 34,790 owner-occupiers were initially eligible on 1 January 1966. Of these 3,696 or 10·6 per cent had installed sound insulation by February 1972 when the take-up figures were strongly suggestive of market saturation.[6]

This take-up figure of 10·6 per cent is, of course, not the 'true' take-up since turnover of properties will have reduced the number of eligible properties remaining. But without figures relating to turnover of every single owner-occupied property within the scheme area it is impossible to do more than make an inspired guess at this 'true' figure. If, for example, we assumed that the annual turnover rate from households eligible on 1 January 1966 was 5 per cent, each property standing an equal chance of being involved once per annum, then by February 1972, about 25 per cent of the original properties would have been untreated and ineligible. [7] In this sense the take-up of the eligible properties would be approximately 14 per cent. Table 8.3 shows the distribution of this adjusted owner-occupier response broken down by local authorities.

Table 8.3

Heathrow scheme take-up*

Owner-occupiers April 1966–February 1972

Local Authority	Double-glazed households	Households ('66 census)	% Take-up '66 base	% Take-up estimated '72 base
Hounslow	2216	21270	10·4	13·7
Slough†	494	2540	19·4	25·5
Hillingdon	452	4680	9·9	12·7
Staines	440	4110	10·7	14·1
Eton	94	2190	4·3	5·6
Total	3696	34790	10·6	14·0

Note: * The figures relate to completed work.
    † Precision is difficult in the case of Slough because purchase of properties by council and GLC tenants affect both the figure for double glazers and the 1966 census base.

79

This overall take-up analysis relates only to households which have double glazed irrespective of the number and type of rooms involved. In this additional regard a detailed cross-tabulation was compiled for the 2,100 Hounslow owner-occupiers broken down into the two major categories of downstairs rooms and bedrooms and this is presented in Table 8.4.

Table 8.4

The number of houses with various combinations of upstairs versus downstairs rooms sound insulated:
Hounslow owner-occupiers, April 1966–February 1972

		Downstairs rooms sound insulated		
		0	1	2
Upstairs	0		46 (2·2)	180 (8·6)
rooms	1	20 (1·0)	1118 (53·2)	62 (3·0)
sound	2	400 (19·0)	203 (9·7)	3 (0·1)
insulated	3	64 (3·0)	3 (0·1)	1 (0·05)

Note: No information is available for 116 households.
The figures in parentheses represent the number as a percentage of the total of 2,100 households.

From the table the following points may be drawn: first a very strong preference for double glazing only two rooms (80·8 per cent of the total) and within this modal group, a strong preference for one downstairs and one upstairs room (53·2 per cent of the total). This last point suggests that households are reacting to both daytime/evening and night noise.

8.7 Non-owner occupiers

Of the roughly 60,000 dwellings in the scheme area on 1 January 1966 about 52 per cent were owned by the occupier and 48 per cent were rented properties (approximately twenty-eight thousand dwellings in the latter case). This last total was divided fairly evenly between council property (belonging to both the Greater London Council and other authorities) and private rental, with about one-and-a-half thousand dwellings in the latter category owned by the British Airways Staff Housing Society Ltd (BASHSL).

Take-up differs markedly between these tenure groups. Whereas the private rental sector seems totally unaffected by the scheme (about 0·1 per cent take-up), the council tenant has responded more than any other group of householders with a take-up in the order of 30 per cent, whilst the BASHSL group has an intermediate take-up of 9–10 per cent.

Further analysis of the Hounslow council tenant also shows, on comparison with the owner-occupiers residing in the same area, that it is not only the number of insulated dwellings that is very much higher. In the treated dwellings the average number of rooms insulated is 3·5 compared with 2·14 rooms in the case of the home owner.[8]

In conclusion, perhaps the striking feature of the scheme, looked at overall, is the considerable variation in response from borough to borough and from tenure group to tenure group. Some of this variation will have arisen from variations in the noise environment and from variation in average prices. But there are clearly many other important parameters that are so different in each case – income levels, information flows, motivations, mobility, etc. The picture in the Heathrow area warns against any facile explanation of expenditure on exclusion facilities.

Notes

1 For further details and analysis of the Heathrow scheme, see G. M. Webber (1972).

2 See Conditions of eligibility, p. 75.

3 For full details see Appendix 2.

4 See Appendix 2 for full details and Chapter 6 for a description of the acoustical effects.

5 See Appendix 2.

6 See Figure 9.1.

7 See Appendix 3.

8 These figures relate to the period up to August 1972.

9 Selection of a Population for Analysis

In Chapter 5 we have argued that an exclusion facilities approach would give an accurate portrayal of the benefits of noise reduction irrespective of whether such an approach is applied to owner-occupiers or to tenant households. Both groups of the population we considered to be largely immobile when confronted with environmental nuisances such that reasonably unbiased estimates of the benefits of noise reduction would be obtained from the approach.

In the area of the Heathrow scheme the two housing groups exist in large numbers and, as we have seen, both have installed exclusion facilities on a significant scale. The question arises whether to apply our approach to both groups or if to one . . . which? We need to consider therefore, the practical advantages and disadvantages of each for the application of a cross-sectional demand analysis, in this instance relating to sound insulation glazing.

9.1 Owner-occupiers: diffusion disadvantages

The owner-occupied housing sector on closer examination suffers a long list of disadvantages and few, if any, advantages. New commodities similar to sound insulation glazing are often characterised by long periods of market penetration and it is clear that, in the Heathrow scheme area, sound insulation glazing is no exception, as Figure 9.1 indicates. In the figure, applications for grant-aided double glazing by Hounslow owner-occupiers have been plotted as a frequency cumulative with time. The result is a typical sigmoid-shaped growth curve which a logistic function describes most precisely ($r = \cdot99$). The evidence suggests that the Heathrow market did not approach saturation at the then prevailing terms of grant until 1971–72, six years or more after the launching of the subsidy scheme. Although the grant conditions changed during this period, this did not appear to affect in any marked fashion the rate of diffusion, possibly because the firms offset or partly offset the improved grant with their own price adjustments.

Therefore, the relevant data for analysis is the pattern of demand which had accumulated over the long period from April 1966 to August 1972. This, however, is too long a period to expect the influence of other factors affecting attitudes, such as incomes and noise disturbance, to have remained reasonably

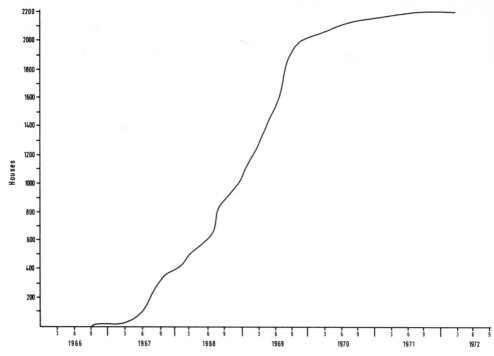

Fig. 9.1   Cumulative up-take of insulation: Hounslow owner-occupiers

stable. Indeed it is obvious that the *ceteris paribus* conditions are by no means complied with. The figures for aircraft movements from Heathrow, for example, illustrate this (see Table 9.1).

Table 9.1

Flight frequencies ('000) – Heathrow 1966–72

Year	Total
1966	223·8
1967	236·5
1968	247·7
1969	258·5
1970	270·3
1971	273·5
1972	279·3

On the basis of these figures, we must conclude that the overall rate of diffusion is too slow to enable the owner-occupied housing sector as a whole to form the basis of analysis. Nevertheless, it is possible that the rate of diffusion may have been much faster in certain spatially defined parts of the owner-occupied sector and that the overall rate of diffusion reflects a spatial dimension which is often associated with the diffusion phenomena. However, regardless of whether this is or is not the case, there are other drawbacks which detract from any analysis of the owner-occupied sector.

9.2   Owner-occupiers: marketing disadvantages

Significant amongst these is the system of marketing whereby at various times about fifty different 'firms' competed for contracts. It is important for our analysis that we are able to assess with accuracy the price quoted for rooms not double glazed in both sound insulating and non-sound insulating residences. In this respect we open Pandora's Box. There was certainly no fixed scale for charges and while in normal circumstances one might expect a variation in costs per square foot of glass of up to $\mp$ 20 per cent (Heriot-Watt, 1972), these were not normal circumstances. In some cases the sales techniques were of dubious nature. Some ventilation units were said to have been bought back by salesmen after the work had been passed by local authority inspectors. In other cases internal doors were removed to avoid the statutory requirements to provide a ventilator unit for each room. Overstating to the administrators of the scheme the real price charged, often with the countenance of householders was also rife – and at one time the police were asked to investigate.

Subsequent tightening up led to the publication of an 'allowable' scale of charges (see Chapter 8). This still left firms free to vary their charges but encouraged by the 'allowable' scale, firms now appeared to adopt a form of average cost pricing. Although stress appeared to be placed upon a 'package' of one downstairs room and two bedrooms, the variance in square footage was much greater than the variance in total (gross) costs, the latter falling at or about the £250 mark (see Figures 9.2 and 9.3). This price is significant because it represents the ceiling charge within which the revised grant of 60 per cent was effective. The consequence was that much of the expected house-to-house variance in price, due solely to variation in window sizes, was thus eliminated.

9.3   Owner-occupiers: eligibility disadvantages

A further, yet equally serious problem to be faced in analysing owner-occupiers' demand for sound insulation lay in the scheme conditions of

85

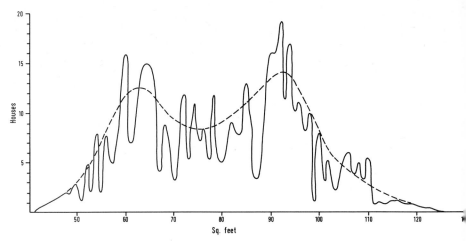

Fig. 9.2 Frequency of square feet of glazing per house: Hounslow owner-occupiers

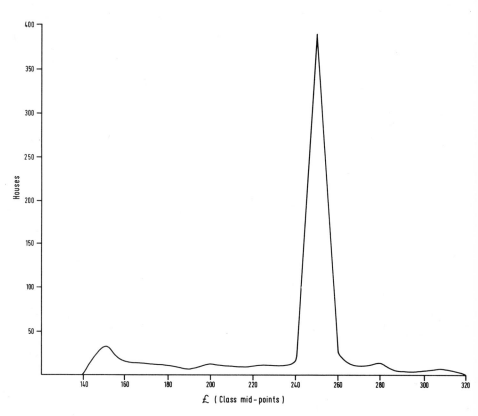

Fig. 9.3 Frequency of total insulation costs per house: Hounslow owner-occupiers

eligibility. These, it will be remembered, require that the house is built before 1 January 1966, and that the applicant has lived in the premises since 31 December 1965. As a consequence new owner-occupiers moving into the area will occupy houses double glazed by the previous occupant or, and this is more likely, houses which are not insulated and for which no grant is available. The analyst therefore is faced with an awkward situation. To make a proper comparison of the effect of different prices, on a like for like basis, requires that the analysis be confined to those householders that have remained in residence since the start of the scheme in 1966. Only in this way can one allow for the distorting effect of turnover on eligibility.

This opens such analysis to the criticism that the resulting price elasticities would relate to the comparatively immobile section of the population and are therefore biased. We do not regard this as a serious criticism because it is our basic contention that people do not move for reasons of environmental annoyance and therefore the immobile do not represent the less noise-sensitive groups of the population.

The real problems are of a more practical nature. It would be necessary, for example, to undertake the tedious and very laborious process of sorting out the long-term stayers by using electoral registers.

9.4   The public housing sector

The alternative housing sector – tenancies – does have a marked advantage with respect to this basic problem of eligibility and turnover. Although the same basic conditions apply, in practice the chief difference from the owner-occupied sector is that either the landlord or the tenant is free to apply for a grant. A change of tenancy does not rule the property ineligible for grant-aided insulation (although the much less common circumstances of a change of landlord would). In this regard the tenant housing sector would appear to be a more fruitful field for analysis.

A further advantage of the public housing market is that it is more likely to be homogeneous with respect to income. Ideally one would prefer, in any behavioural analysis, to introduce explicitly the effect of income. This of course, is not always possible. Such data is not readily available. In its absence the next best approach is to control for such influences, for example, by analysis of a behavioural group with a reasonably homogeneous (and preferably defined) level of income. In this respect too, the analyst of the public housing sector has a comparative advantage.

To these advantages one can mention others which arise not from the way council properties are administered in the Sound Insulation Scheme but from the particular circumstances of public tenancies. One of these, namely the absence in the householders' decision of a complicating investment motive, has already been mentioned in passing in Chapter 5. Although this is a generalisation which does not apply to all public tenants – for example Slough and GLC tenants in the Heathrow area have been able to purchase their houses – Hounslow tenants on the other hand do not enjoy this opportunity.

Within this sector the public landlords – the local authorities – have themselves varied the terms on which the tenant can install insulation within the framework of the Statutory Instruments. Some of these variations unfortunately, do introduce new drawbacks. Hillingdon Council, for example, glazed all properties on the basis of a standard package, in theory at no increase in rents to the tenants. In marked contrast, tenants in Slough, Eton and GLC properties have to fend for themselves on the same terms as faced by the owner-occupier. Although from the point of view of analysis, these council dwellings have the advantage of eligibility regardless of turnover, they continue to maintain most of the other disadvantages that inhibit examination of the private housing sector.

9.5 The Hounslow council tenant

The circumstances in the case of the borough of Hounslow, on the other hand, would suggest that they present a unique opportunity for fruitful analysis. Indeed on closer examination the remarkable feature of the Hounslow tenancies is that they should have so few of the disadvantages that encumber analysis of other housing groups.

The chief reason for this is that the council negotiated, on behalf of the tenants, most favourable terms with one particular double glazing contractor – Aeroslim. The outcome was that insulation charge is a fixed price per square foot of glass and per ventilator unit. Although Aeroslim has not an exclusive contract for council property its competitive pricing and formal links with the council mean that in practice it dominates the market.

The strength of the market penetration by Aeroslim (about 30 per cent by the end of the period of the 60 per cent grant) makes for easier statistical analysis.[1] More important is the comparatively fast rate at which this market penetration took place. The diffusion effect was compressed into a two-year period from June 1970 (soon after the contract was first negotiated) to August 1972.[2]

A number of reasons suggest themselves. There were better channels of both public and private information – to use the diffusion theorists' terminology. In the former case the local authority as well as the BAA dispatched circulars. In the case of the private information channels the higher housing densities and more homogeneous social class will have helped.[3] No doubt too, Aeroslim, who had agreed to the comparatively low price in the anticipation of economies of scale, were systematic, thorough and anxious in their marketing.

The consequence of the short diffusion period is that we can with confidence regard the many other factors influencing the pattern of demand over time as having had little or no effect of changing this pattern during the period. Moreover we can regard the 1971 noise régime as the relevant environment to which tenants were reacting. Although some applications were made in adjacent years, the degree of change in total air movements between 1970 and 1971 (when the bulk of the applications were made), and between 1971 and 1972 was comparatively slight (see Table 9.2).

Table 9.2

Flight frequencies ('000) over Hounslow 1970–72

	Landings	Take off	Total	Per cent of Heathrow's total
1970	94·7	35·2	129·9	48·1
1971	89·1	43·6	132·7	48·5
1972	83·7	48·6	132·3	47·4

However, there is one particular aspect which clouds this otherwise favourable set of circumstances. It is that Aeroslim, with the agreement of Hounslow Council, made a once-and-for-all price increase of 9·7 per cent for glass and 8·9 per cent for ventilation units in 1972.

This aspect apart, however, cross-sectional analysis of the Hounslow council tenant in comparison with the analyses of other tenant or owner-occupier groups, should be relatively free of distortion by time-series influences, by investment motives and by various other complicating factors. The Hounslow council tenant would appear to be the best subject in the Heathrow area for the application of the exclusion facilities approach.

Notes

1   Some eighty-one council tenants applied directly for a grant before the Aeroslim scheme came into operation.

2 Unfortunately the precise dates-of-application are not available in this case.

3 Webber (1972) has placed stress on housing density as an important factor explaining the overall pattern of double-glazing sales.

10 An Initial Search for Significant Factors in the Noise Environment

10.1 The subjective nature of noise

As a precursor to measuring the willingness of households to pay for sound attenuating insulation we have given prior consideration to the further and separate analysis of noise disturbance itself. The reason for this stems from the purely subjective nature of noise annoyance. As a consequence of this we need to know what objective measures of sound are positively correlated with adverse subjective reaction. Put more simply, it is necessary to define, and thus to measure, noise in the way in which it is broadly perceived.[1]

It might be argued that the problem is but a small one and that the solution is to find those measures of sound which best explain persons' behaviour – just as in value of time studies one seeks those mileage costs which most suitably explain modal choice. Basically this is true, but in the present context at least, it is to belittle the practical problems involved in carrying out this suggestion. Sound can be measured objectively in a variety of ways and because of its ephemeral nature, at many different times. Such measurement is laborious, demanding and costly in the extreme.

It can be argued of course, that the necessary knowledge already exists. In Chapter 1 we reviewed a number of aircraft noise exposure measures which purport to correlate well with subjective response. Therefore, an obvious way to proceed is to use one or a number of these indices as the appropriate measure of noise. Thus one could use, for example, the Noise Number Index and seek to show how the propensity to double glaze varies positively with it. As the index increases, either because of an increase in $PNdB$ or N, then other things being equal one might expect a greater proportion of householders to have purchased sound insulation glazing.

10.2 Criticism of the NNI

However, these indices have recently been subject to criticism which has cast doubt on their efficacy as indicators of annoyance and thus on their appropriateness as objective measures of noise. Hart (1973) has put forward a number of such criticisms.

Firstly, he points out that the 'official' *NNI* was based on graphical analysis of survey data (see Chapter 1) and contained no estimates of the dispersion of observation around the averages or information on the goodness of fit.

Secondly, Hart draws attention to the quite different conclusions reached by McKennell (1963) who applied multiple regression analysis to the same social survey data. McKennell's conclusion was that the *NNI* equation could be estimated as:

$$0 \cdot 0418 \, \overline{PNdB} + 24 \log N - 70$$

Thirdly, a repeat of McKennell's formal statistical analysis on data collected by a second social survey (*Office of Population Censuses and Surveys, 1971*), carried out in 1967 on very much the same lines as the 1961 survey, estimated the appropriate equation as:

$$0 \cdot 0747 \, \overline{PNdB} + 12 \log (N + 1) - 87$$

Again, a rather different conclusion from that of the earlier graphical analysis.

Fourthly, the design of the questions and the scale of annoyance (see Chapter 1) did not allow for sensitive differences between respondents. Thus in answer to the question: 'Does the noise of aircraft bother you very much, moderately, a little, or not at all?' a respondent giving a positive answer 'very much', was given the same weight as one answering 'a little'. Similarly, the yes/no answers in the rest of the questionnaire did not allow for the frequency with which conversation was interrupted, TV reception interfered with, etc.

Although these criticisms are specific to the UK *NNI*, Hart goes on to point out that:

> . . . any social survey designed to measure utility (or disutility) using such attitude scales would be subject to the same criticism. For example, the French Indice Isopsophique would be open to exactly the same criticism because it is based on a points score of respondents . . . (p. 143)

He concludes that:

> It is not possible to derive a cardinal measure of utility (determinate up to a linear transformation) from attitude scales which are essentially ordinal. The *NNI* is a glaring example of an attempt to compile a cardinal index from ordinal data on annoyance. While this index could be used to *rank* degrees of annoyance, if it were based on reliable data, it cannot be used to measure the effect of noise or of number of aircraft on annoyance. (p. 143)

Thus, the conclusion drawn from Hart's appraisal is that we should expect the *NNI* to associate little if at all with cardinal measures of disutility expressed in the form of expenditure on sound insulation glazing. Moreover – and this is a point generally overlooked – *NNI* is in any case, basically a measure of daytime noise exposure. Its constituent values for *N* and *PNdB* relate to the 6.00–18.00 GMT period. We are trying to explain annoyance, concern, disturbance, etc., which is partially reflected in the purchase of bedroom insulation; the need therefore, is for measures which incorporate the evening and night-time periods as well. If we are to find a definition of 'noise' appropriate to these particular circumstances then it appears we must start afresh.

10.3   Empirical test of the *NNI*

However, before finally dismissing the *NNI* we decided to examine the situation in the context of our own data. To do this we grouped owner-occupied households in the Borough of Hounslow and analysed the proportional up-take of double glazing for each of these groupings in relation to the appropriate value for *NNI*.

The basis of the grouping was the Census Enumeration District (ED). In the 1966 Census there were 167 EDs in Hounslow, all but 30 of them containing owner-occupiers.[2] The grouped measure of response was expressed either as the proportion of the ED's owner-occupied households that had installed sound-insulation glazing between 1966 and 1972, or as the average number of rooms double-glazed per house double-glazed.

The *NNI* measures used were based on the Board of Trade's analysis of the Heathrow situation during the summer of 1967. For each ED we calculated two measures of *NNI*. One was obtained by fitting *NNI* contours over a map of EDs and then visually interpreting the relevant *NNI* for the ED's centre of (population) gravity. The second measure was based on the *NNI* rating given by the Building Research Station to each household insulation during the 1966–72 period.[3] The appropriate ED rating was taken as the mean of the rating for insulating households in each ED.

The results of the analysis were that neither of the alternative *NNI* measures was, itself, strongly correlated with the up-take of glazing. On the contrary the relationship was decidedly weak. The highest value for *r* the correlation coefficient, was 0.18 (using the BRS's method of assigning index values to the EDs).

The analysis was repeated for 101 EDs in which owner occupation exceeded 50 per cent and 99 in number, thus excluding EDs for which the sample census had estimated a small number of owner-occupied households. Such small numbers were particularly subject to sampling error which could affect, fundamentally, calculations of the proportional up-take of glazing. However, this added refinement did not change the situation to any significant degree. Nor did the use of average number of rooms double-glazed per double-glazing household as an alternative indicator of disturbance.[4]

These, of course, were simple rudimentary tests of *NNI* and as valid tests they can be objected to for a number of reasons. They ignore, for example, the influence of socio-economic factors; the house-to-house variation in the costs of double glazing (crucial to our analysis elsewhere), and they beg the question: 'How appropriate is the 1967 *NNI* as an indicator of the noise environment over a six year period?'

Such objections, however, are perhaps more apparent than real. For example by grouping the households we would expect the influence of cost and socio-economic factors, roughly speaking, to be equal at the different levels of *NNI*.[5] Moreover, the indications are that the *NNI* is reasonably stable with the passage of time (because of the logarithm of *N* term).

Thus, the limited analysis may not constitute a convincing refutation of the Noise Number Index but, taken together with the a priori reasoning of Hart and others, it strongly suggests a need to examine different measures of noise exposure. The fact that other formulae such as *CNR*, *NEF*, etc., appear to be linear transformations of *NNI* (see p. 10) rules them out as alternatives. The answer seemed to lie therefore with what we might term a grass-roots inductive approach of searching for those basic characteristics of sound which correlate, either singularly or in combination with household expenditures on sound insulation.

Such an approach should be doubly beneficial. Not only would it indicate how the valuation of peace and quiet changes with the level of noise, but it should reveal also what it is that persons truly perceive as noise. In the process of deriving noise sensitive values for peace and quiet, one would also be developing a cardinal index of noise.

10.4 The Southampton analysis

As a consequence of this conclusion the Institute of Sound and Vibration Research, University of Southampton, were requested to calculate, by methods of simulation based on flight data, certain environmental variables relating to Hounslow during the summer of 1971. Summer 1971 was chosen because of its relevance to the sound insulation of council properties (see p. 89).

There were two separate commissions. The first one related to the daytime period defined as 6.00–18.00 GMT, a time thus consistent with the time of the day for which the Noise Number Index is calculated. Consistency with the *NNI* was also maintained in other ways. Values for *PNdB* and *N* were calculated in this first commission using the methodology developed in the calculation of the *NNI*. That is, a cut-off of 80 *PNdB* was used to define aircraft 'heard' and calculations were based upon the average mode of operation during the mid-June to mid-September period. The values were calculated for reference position which represented the approximate centroid of Census Enumeration Districts.

Subsequent to this daytime analysis it was decided to broaden the range of environmental variables by including in addition to average peak *PNdB* and the number of heard aircraft, peak *PNdB*. The second commission was prescribed accordingly. This was to provide environmental variables for separate evening and night-time periods. The definition of these periods was assisted by reference to the second survey's (*Office of Population Censuses and Surveys, 1971*) findings on the usual time for going to bed. The 'evening' covered the period from 18.00 hours GMT to 23.00 hours and 'night-time' from the latter hour until 6.00 hours. Further details on the precise methods of calculation used are included in Appendix 4 which summarises the Institute's two reports.

Notes

1   This will be a familiar argument to those conversant with valuation of another non-marketed commodity – travel time. The situation faced in our study is analogous with the problems of measuring perceived motoring costs in value of travel-time studies.

2   The 1966 Census data has the disadvantages of a sample but certain advantages. The survey date is close to the beginnings of the Heathrow Scheme so that the number of owner-occupied households eligible for a grant would be almost the same as the number of households recorded in the Census.

3   The appropriate *NNI* measure for each household was calculated by the BRS from observing which *NNI* band (in intervals of five) the house was in and taking the lower level of that band as the relevant *NNI* measure. The *r* value for the correlation between the two measures of an ED's Noise Number Index was $0 \cdot 85$.

4   There is a certain irony in this situation. The boundary of the Heathrow Insulation Scheme was determined by reference to the *NNI*.

5   Ridker in his study of house prices and air pollution also used 'neighbourhood' observations. (Neighbourhoods were defined census tracts.) H. Nouse (1973) commenting on Ridker's study, pointed out that since census tracts tend to be homogeneous with respect to income and other socio-economic variables, idiosyncrasies of household structure would tend to be 'washed out' in neighbourhood data (p. 70).

11 Modes of Behaviour and Methods of Analysis

11.1 Binary choice

In the demand context that we are considering, the affected population can be thought of as facing a number of alternative, or perhaps complementary binary choices. Either that choice is 'whether or not to double glaze', or 'whether or not to double glaze a specified number of rooms', or 'whether or not to sound insulate a specific room', etc.

These various choice situations could be interpreted as placing, to a degree, a different interpretation on behaviour. Thus the choice 'whether or not to insulate a specific room' might imply that the householder treats the insulation of each room as a separate event to be considered according to its own peculiar circumstances of usage, price of insulation, etc. On the other hand, the choice 'whether or not to insulate a specified number of rooms' implies a view of the household's activity space as an integrated or partially integrated system. As a further comment on the quality issue discussed in Chapter 6, it would suggest that the whole is considered greater than the sum of the parts. Alternatively, the behavioural emphasis may be upon a series of binary choices – first the household decides in principle whether or not to double glaze at all. Then having made a positive decision it decides – perhaps now attaching importance to different factors – upon the treatment of particular rooms, etc.

11.2 Binary regression

However, in each case we are faced with a particular example of a problem of analysis commonly encountered in many fields of investigation in which a response is expressed as a dichotomous variable for individual observations (e.g. Yes/No, Died/Did not Die) but in which the researcher wishes to relate the dependence of the event occurring on certain determining factors.

The problem is well treated in the literature (Cox, 1970) and is often overcome by the adaptation of the linear additive model in which the parameters are defined by least-squares regression:

$$E(y_i) = \alpha + \sum_{j=1}^{K} \beta_j x_{ij} \tag{1}$$

where x_{ij}'s are known values of k independent variables $x_{i1} \ldots x_{ik}$, and α, and $\beta 1 \ldots \beta k$ are unknown parameters.

The adaptation is to retain the fundamentals of (1) but to consider the model

$$\theta = 0 \leqslant \theta \leqslant 1 = E(y_i) = \alpha + \sum_{j=1}^{K} \beta_j x_{ij} \tag{2}$$

in which the method of least squares is directly applied to the binary observations, i.e., we treat the observations 0 and 1 just as if they were quantitative observations. In fact, in the case of double glazing, this is exactly what 0 and 1 do represent and, since the method is computationally simple, the assumption that the effect of the independent variables is both linear and additive would seem a suitable one to examine.

11.3   Conditional probabilities

Because the expected value of y_i, $E(y_i)$, estimated from a set of exogenous regressor values, will as a rule be contained within the limits of 0 and 1, the consequence has been to interpret the outcome of applying this approach as a 'conditional probability'. This interpretation is set out for example, by Goldfeld and Quandt (1972) in the following manner:

> Given estimates of the regression coefficient, the predicted values of Y will not, in general, equal 0 or 1. This suggests that it would be more useful to interpret the conditional expectation of y given x as the conditional probability that the event will occur given x. Put another way a predicted value between 0 and 1 may be interpreted as the fraction of individuals (in the appropriate range of the exogenous variables) that may be expected to have the quality in Question.

The latter rather than the former perspective in the quotation is perhaps a more useful view in the present demand context because it permits for easier interpretation of the resulting outcome as a measure of quantity demanded.

Thus $\theta = f(p)$

and $\theta \cdot n = q$

where θ is the proportion of the population making a specified choice.

   p, is price

   n, is the size of the relevant population

and q, is the number making a specified choice.

On the other hand the notion of the individual at price x having a 'probability' of buying good y, results in a somewhat strained interpretation of the normal demand function. Indeed we would prefer in the present context the terminology 'conditional proportions' to the phrase conditional probability.

Nevertheless, the general approach is a most flexible one and can be usefully extended to examine the consequence of a series of interrelated demands. Extended in this way the model resembles the 'twin linear probabilities model' used for example, by Fisher (1962) as a solution to the bounded regression case. The twin linear probability model involves as a first step, fitting a linear function but treating the regressand in dichotomous form. Then restricting the sample to those with an estimated $y = 1$, a normal linear regression is applied with the regressand now taking discrete or continuous values. The first function estimates if $y > 0$; the second estimates the expected value of y given that $y > 0$.

Our modification to this approach is that the second function also treats the regressand as a binary variable. Thus the first function estimates whether $y > 0$, for example, what proportion of households do install double glazing. The second function estimates for that group of houses with glazing installed what proportion purchase a specified package or insulate a particular room, etc., with the individual household observations taking the discrete values 0 or 1.

11.4   Problems of homoskedasticity and bogus proportions

However, it would be naïve to pretend that this statistical method of using dichotomous regressands in least-squares regression is not without its own peculiar problems. There are, in fact, two of significance.

The first is that the basic requirement of homoskedasticity is untenable. Goldfeld and Quandt (1972) illustrate the point in the following manner:

Denoting by Y the vector of observations on the y and by X the matrix of observations on the x's

$$Y = X\beta + U \tag{3}$$

where $E(u) = 0$

Since the elements of Y can only take on the values 0 and 1, we can deduce certain properties of the disturbance term in (3). In particular, letting X_i denote the ith row of the matrix X, we observe that the ith disturbance, u_i can have one or two possible values:

$$u_i = 1 - x_i\beta \quad \text{if} \quad y_i = 1 \tag{4}$$
$$u_i = 1 - x_i\beta \quad \text{if} \quad y_i = 0$$

Since these are the only two possible values of u_i, they must occur with probabilities p and $1 - p$ respectively. Moreover, the requirement $E(u) = 0$ implies:

$$p(1 - x_i\beta) + (1 - p)(-x_i\beta) = 0 \tag{5}$$

and thus:

$$p = x_i\beta$$
$$1 - p = 1 - x_i\beta$$

The error variance is therefore:

$$E(u_i^2) = p(1 - x_i\beta)^2 + (1 - p)(-x_i\beta)^2 \tag{6}$$

$$= x_i\beta(1 - x_i\beta)^2 + (1 - x_i\beta)(-x_i\beta)^2$$

$$= x_i\beta(1 - x_i\beta)$$

which is not a constant but depends on the values of the regressors.

Although this is a problem of some significance, on the other hand it does not appear to be too serious. Quarmby (1967), for example, was of the view that 'while the literature maintains that these conditions should be met, there is nothing to indicate how accurate or inaccurate are the results obtained under heteroskedastic conditions'.

Faced with the same difficulty, Bayliss and Edwards (1970) considered the bias too small to warrant correction by more complicated and, in their case, more expensive procedures. At the time Bayliss and Edwards were writing, D. R. Cox (1970) tendered his opinion on the matter that Quarmby had found neglected. Cox wrote 'quite appreciable changes in variance y, induce only modest loss of efficiency. Further, at least in the range say $0 \cdot 2 \leqslant \theta_i \leqslant 0 \cdot 8$, the function $\theta_i(1 - \theta_i)$ changes relatively little. Therefore, within this range there is unlikely to be a serious loss of efficiency arising from changes in variance (y_i).'

The other problem is the possibility that the expected value of y might fall outside the range 0 to 1 for certain values of the regressor variables. When this happens it is, of course, inconsistent with both the interpretation of the expectation as a probability or as a proportional response. This possibility alone has been considered an adequate reason in some cases for preferring alternative approaches to the estimation problem. However, it is preferable to first examine the circumstances in which the condition $0 \leqslant E(y_i) \leqslant 1$ is not fulfilled. Certainly the argument that 'it would be extremely easy to choose

100

values of the independent variables which could lead to such uninterpretable predictions' (Wrigley, 1973) is an inadequate criterion for rejection because as Cox (1970) points out, 'all postulated models have at best limited and approximate validity'.

Indeed, this is not a weakness peculiar to the formulation of the regressand as a dichotomous variable taking the value of 0 or 1. Although this problem of uninterpretable values is inclined to be highlighted in the binary content, it does generally apply to all functions linear in the variables regardless of whether the response is quantal or scalar. Thus, just as it would be easy to choose values of the independent variables which generate 'negative' proportions in the conditional probability context, then equally, values could be chosen for a normal demand function linear in the variables which would lead to negative quantities demanded. Therefore, the validity of the approach must be judged on the basis of criteria other than the possibility that the expected value of y might fall outside the range 0 to 1 for certain values of the regressor variables.

11.5 A linear logit model

It is common to find the use of transformations referred to as a solution to this problem of uninterpretable predictions. The procedure is to consider the initial value of the expectation of y as an index which itself is a linear function of the regressor values. To this initial value can then be applied a monotonic transformation constraining the final expectation of y to the 0,1 range. The eventual outcome can then be treated as a stochastic function of the original values of the regressor variables.

There is a close analogy here with the binary modal split models of Quarmby and others. In their case a measure of attractiveness (or unattractiveness) – which Quarmby for example referred to as a Z score – of one mode compared with another, is derived from linear multi-variate analysis applied to binary choice. This measure is then transformed into a probability (Quarmby, 1967).

But such suggested solutions need to be placed in perspective. As one authority, Finney (1964) makes clear, the 'transformation is only a convenient trick for representing the sigmoid by a straight line . . .'. Therefore, the crucial point at issue is whether or not the critical responses are proportional to the logarithm of the stimulus and thus conform to a sigmoid curve. Certainly the use of transformations would be consistent with the nineteenth-century Weber-Fechner psychological law that people do react to stimuli in this way. Hart has pointed out that the use of log N and a threshold value for aircraft 'heard' in the NNI formula is also consistent with this law (Hart, 1973).

So too is the relationship between log N and the Noise Pollution Index (LNP) the latter deduced by Robinson (1971) from the basic nature of sound and from broad observations of human response.

Of the monotonic transformations available there are two that are commonly used, the probit and the logit. We have chosen to use the latter for no other reason than technical convenience. A multiple logit program written by the Transport and Road Research Laboratory was easily adaptable to the computing facilities available to us (Grigg, 1973).

Normally, the linear logit model is derived by regressing

$$\log_e \frac{p_i(y_i)}{1 - p_i(y_i)} \quad \text{on} \quad \alpha + \sum_{j=1}^{K} \beta_j x_{ij} \tag{7}$$

where $p_i(y_i)$ is the probability that y_i takes the value 1 and α, β_j and x_{ij} are as for equation (1).

However, in this case the observed values for y are not group values within the range 0,1 but the values for individual observations which are scored either 0 or 1 only. Consequently, with logarithms involved, the approach has to be modified such that the probability that Y_i takes the value 1 is a logistic function of a linear function of the independent variables.

Thus,

$$pE(y_i) = \frac{e^{E(y_i)}}{1 + e^{E(y_i)}} \tag{8}$$

where pE is the probability that $E(y_i)$ takes the value 1, and $E(y_i)$ is the initial expected value of y derived from equation (2).

This is the basic structure of the TRRL's multiple logit analysis although in the program the estimation of the parameter values in equation (2) is done by the method of maximum likelihood rather than least-squares.

11.6   A model with interaction terms

In both the conditional probability model and the multiple logit analysis the reaction to various stimuli is treated as a simple additive one. For example, referring back to the two-way cross classification from which the Noise Number Index was derived (see Table 1.3, p. 10), both models would assume that there was an effect due to $PNdB$ and an effect due to N and that the combined effect is additive:

Thus,

$$E(y_{ij}) = \alpha + \beta_i + \lambda_j \qquad \begin{matrix} i = 4 \\ j = 3 \end{matrix} \tag{5}$$

where β_i is the effect of the ith level of *PNdB*

λ_j is the effect of the jth level of *N*

and $E(y_{ij})$ is the expected score of annoyance.

Transformation of the variables and the fitting of non-linear response surfaces does not alter this basic additive structure.

However, it is possible that in some circumstances the two factors, *PNdB* and *N* may interact with each other so that the level of *PNdB* may have a different effect on households suffering high levels of *N* from those experiencing low values of *N*. That is to say that the lines in Figure 1.2 may cross. Thus, to allow for this situation, further parameters need to be added so that the basic structure of the model becomes:

$$E(y_{ij}) = \alpha + \beta_i + \lambda_j + \beta\lambda_{ij} \tag{6}$$

where β_{ij} is the interaction term.

These additional parameters are known as interaction terms and one method of introducing them is to use product terms within the approach of normal least-squares regression analysis. An alternative, and more satisfactory solution where, as in these circumstances, the nature of the response surface is not at all clear, is to apply a model based upon dummy independent variables (Orcutt et al., 1961, Starkie 1971).

Written in matrix form the structure is cumbersome although, as can be seen, it is basically simple. For example, where $i = 2$ and $j = 3$ then:

$$
\begin{Bmatrix}
E(y_{11}) \\
E(y_{12}) \\
E(y_{13}) \\
E(y_{21}) \\
E(y_{22}) \\
E(y_{23})
\end{Bmatrix}
\begin{Bmatrix}
1 & 1 & 0 & 1 & 0 & 0 & 1 & 0 & 0 & 0 & 0 & 0 \\
1 & 1 & 0 & 0 & 1 & 0 & 0 & 1 & 0 & 0 & 0 & 0 \\
1 & 1 & 0 & 0 & 0 & 1 & 0 & 0 & 1 & 0 & 0 & 0 \\
1 & 0 & 1 & 1 & 0 & 0 & 0 & 0 & 0 & 1 & 0 & 0 \\
1 & 0 & 1 & 0 & 1 & 0 & 0 & 0 & 0 & 0 & 1 & 0 \\
1 & 0 & 1 & 0 & 0 & 1 & 0 & 0 & 0 & 0 & 0 & 1
\end{Bmatrix}
\begin{Bmatrix}
\alpha \\
\beta_1 \\
\vdots \\
\lambda_3 \\
\vdots \\
\beta\lambda_{11} \\
\vdots \\
\beta\lambda_{23}
\end{Bmatrix}
$$

The model is, of course, over-specified in this form with twelve parameters being used to describe the six possible treatment combinations. Therefore, one dummy from each class $i \ldots j$ and ij, is explicitly not included so that a computer routine, employing a matrix inversion procedure to obtain estimates of the coefficients, can be used (Silk, 1972). That is to say, referring to the above matrix, the 2nd, 4th and 7th vectors are removed. Their relevance to the overall situation re-emerges through the intercept term α Thus, if a similar procedure of removing redundant vectors was carried out in relation to a matrix derived from the two-way cross-classification of Table 1.3 then the value for α would be the estimated annoyance score for the top left-hand cell, i.e., an average N of $5 \cdot 75$ and a level of $PNdB$ between 84 and 90. This cell would be the pivotal cell and the coefficients would represent the differences from it. If interaction is present then the relevant coefficients will be significant.

Although this may appear a complex procedure, it is basically both simple and flexible. For example, the method can be adapted easily to include continuous variables (with specified response surfaces) alongside classes of discrete variables. But of greater import in the present context is the procedures' capability for testing whether interaction between variables suggestive of aircraft noise, has a significant effect on householders' willingness to pay for sound-attenuating double glazing.

12 The Demand Function for Sound Insulation Glazing

In Chapter 10 we examined briefly, the up-take of sound insulation glazing by Hounslow owner-occupiers to try to clarify in broad terms, the environmental factors involved. In that analysis we ignored the influence of price and justified its neglect on the supposition that there would be no systematic spatial bias: its influence would thus be incorporated in the error terms. In this chapter we introduce the price of insulation explicitly into the analysis. In so doing our basic objective is to calculate, using the various methods described in Chapter 11, the householders' demand function for the 'peace and quiet' good.

However, the demand analysis required at this stage the collection of more basic data. Official records contained information on insulation costs only for those rooms that households had had insulated with the aid of a grant. There was no readily available information on window sizes, and thus on prospective costs, for those rooms not double glazed, both within sound insulating and non-sound insulating households, or indeed, on the number of such rooms involved. These data we derived from a sample survey of Hounslow's council properties.

12.1 The sample survey

The sample was drawn from a statistical population which included all council dwellings on all council estates within the area eligible for grant under the 1966 Insulation Scheme. Included therefore, were old people's houses, maisonettes as well as standard council houses – a total of 6,247 units. The size of sample was 12½ per cent (one in eight) producing 781 addresses. These 781 dwellings were chosen by using a systematic random method from a sample frame of dwellings listed by address in street and enumeration district orders. Each address was visited once during the 10.00 a.m.–4.00 p.m. period and non-respondents were classed as 'No Admittance' (*NA*) or 'No Response' (*NR*), depending upon whether admittance was refused or whether there was no answer. A second call was subsequently made at the 'No Response' group of dwellings in a period 6.00 p.m.–9.30 p.m. The overall response is shown in Table 12.1.

The number in the 'No Response' group is surprisingly high. One might have expected such a high proportion of dwellings to be unoccupied during the day but not during the evening as well. Because the survey was carried out during July, it is possible that many families were on holiday at this time.

Table 12.1

Overall response to sample survey

518 dwellings		(66·3 per cent) were successfully surveyed
84	,,	(10·8 per cent) were classed as *NA*
172	,,	(20·0 per cent) were classed as *NR*
7	,,	(1 per cent) were only partially or improperly surveyed (e.g. baby asleep in one of the rooms, etc.)

The dwelling units were classified by numbers of rooms eligible for grant-aided insulation and whether they were a house, flat or other type of construction (e.g. prefabricated units). For the purposes of the analysis a subdivision was made only on the basis of the number of rooms and the subtotals were as shown in Table 12.2.

In the subsequent analysis we have concentrated upon the five-roomed group. The reason for this was that, in contrast to three-, two- and one-roomed dwellings, non-trivial proportions of the population made different choices. These differences in preference would, therefore, allow analysis of different modes of behaviour and model forms discussed in Chapter 11 (see particularly p. 99). Thus, of the 165 five-roomed dwellings, just over one-third (35·8 per cent) had installed double glazing and of these 64·2 per cent had double glazed all five rooms. The proportion of the total number of dwellings that had glazed all five rooms was therefore just under one-quarter (23·0 per cent).

Table 12.2

Breakdown of successful responses by
housing type

Five room dwellings	..	..	165
Four room dwellings	..	..	137
Three room dwellings	..	..	172
Two room dwellings	..	..	39
One room dwellings	..	..	5
			518

From the measurement of window sizes in each sampled dwelling, it was possible to calculate for those non-double glazed rooms the cost that would have been incurred in insulating them. For rooms double glazed of course, the actual prices paid were available from the local authority records.

The prices for non-double glazed rooms in non-double glazed dwellings were based upon the contract prices charged by Aeroslim, prevailing after the 9 per cent price increase (see p. 89). When the diffusion effect was complete these were the prevailing prices and, therefore, we would argue the appropriate prices for the analysis of revealed choice. By August 1972 when information on the sound insulation scheme and the attributes of double glazing appeared to have fully diffused all non-insulating households had the option of glazing at these prices, but chose not to do so.

12.2   Independent variables

The survey of window sizes provided the final item of basic data required for the demand analysis. The assembled variables used initially are shown in Table 12.3.

Table 12.3

Basic variables used in the analysis

		Means
1	Distance from Heathrow airport centre (10^4 feet)	1·376
2	Traffic noise dummy variable	55% (= 1)
3	Rail noise dummy variable	11% (= 1)
4	N day	123
5	$\overline{PNdB}$ day	95
6	N evening	28
7	$\overline{PNdB}$ evening	94
8	Peak $PNdB$ evening	102
9	$\triangle PNdB$ evening	8
10	N night	27
11	$PNdB$ night	93
12	Peak $PNdB$ night	103
13	$\triangle PNdB$ night	10
14	Net cost of insulating five rooms	£89·3

Table 12.4

Matrix of correlation coefficients

Double glazed or not	Double glazed 5 rooms	Distance	Av PNdB Even	N. Even	Pk PNdB Even	Pk PNdB Night	Av PNdB Night	N Night	N Day	Av PNdB Day	ΔPNdB Even	ΔPNdB Night	Traffic Noise	Rail Noise	Cost
1	2	3	4	5	6	7	8	9	10	11	12	13	14	15	16
1.0000															
0.7332	1.0000														
-0.0504	-0.1600	1.0000													
-0.1817	-0.1848	-0.0837	1.0000												
-0.0087	-0.0255	0.1083	0.5182	1.0000											
0.0748	0.0323	-0.2291	0.5938	0.6110	1.0000										
0.0416	0.0090	-0.2077	0.4852	0.7430	0.9126	1.0000									
-0.2139	-0.2256	-0.0482	0.9081	0.4341	0.4240	0.3840	1.0000								
-0.0380	-0.0978	0.4580	0.4248	0.8396	0.4121	0.5521	0.3488	1.0000							
0.0105	0.0084	-0.0522	0.4770	0.9782	0.6160	0.7714	0.4082	0.7644	1.0000						
-0.1057	-0.1376	-0.0660	0.8879	0.7045	0.8171	0.7774	0.7328	0.6041	0.6668	1.0000					
-0.2752	-0.2287	0.1815	-0.3386	0.1792	0.5561	0.5660	-0.4422	0.0431	0.2276	0.0383	1.0000				
0.1823	0.1556	0.1869	-0.0785	0.4991	0.6838	-0.8015	-0.2444	0.3539	0.5458	0.3418	0.8808	1.0000			
-0.1078	-0.1316	-0.1000	0.2366	0.1641	0.1074	-0.0051	0.3731	0.2032	0.1581	0.1617	-0.3700	-0.2471	1.0000		
0.1318	0.1040	0.0802	-0.0507	-0.0851	0.0607	-0.0571	-0.2979	0.0123	-0.1401	0.0222	0.1234	0.1330	-0.3833	1.0000	
-0.3625	-0.3713	-0.1361	-0.2179	0.0409	0.1653	0.1395	0.1320	-0.0284	0.0451	0.2191	-0.0318	0.0610	-0.0301	0.0979	1.0000

With the exception of the dummy variables for traffic and rail noise, and the price variable, the values for the independent variables for each of the 165 sampled dwellings with five main rooms was based upon the values for the ED in which the sampled dwelling was located. Therefore, with few exceptions, the overall means shown in Table 12.3 are in fact (weighted) means of the values for EDs containing the sample.

The derivation and interpretation of most of these variables have been described already. Of the exceptions the distance from the airport centre is self-explanatory.

The dummy variable for traffic noise depended upon whether or not the household was subjected to a Noise Pollution Level (*LNP*) greater than 64. The background data on this aspect is contained in evidence prepared for the Inquiry into the Greater London Development Plan. (Atkins, 1971).

The dummy variable for rail noise depended upon whether or not the sampled household was adjacent to a railway line and therefore likely to experience high, but probably very intermittent, levels of rail noise.

Variables referred to as $\triangle PNdB$ are, in fact, differences between peak *PNdB* and average peak *PNdB*. As such they give a broad picture of the range of, or degree of, fluctuation in aircraft sounds.

The zero order correlation matrix for these independent variables, based on the values for the 165 households included in the analysis is shown in Table 12.4. An unfortunate set of circumstances is apparent from this matrix. It turns out that the variables suggestive of aircraft noise are highly correlated for the three separate periods of 24 hours. Thus daytime, evening and night-time *N* are highly correlated ($r = 0 \cdot 76$–$0 \cdot 98$) as indeed are the corresponding values for $\overline{PNdB}$. Similarly, evening and night-time peak *PNdB* values exhibit the same tendency. The implication of this situation is that the inclusion of the corresponding variables for the different time periods in the same regression analysis would lead to problems of multicollinearity. This was disappointing. It was hoped that the analysis could have been used to illustrate the respective importance of these three periods in the decision to insulate the house as a whole. In the event whether or not five rooms had been double glazed would have to be related separately to the daytime, evening and night-time variables.

12.3 Analysis: model 1

The first model examines what might be termed the package hypothesis. Attention is focused upon the insulation of all the households' main activity space. The dependent variable takes the value 0 or 1 depending upon whether or not the household has insulated a 'package' of five rooms – two livingrooms and three bedrooms – and it is treated as a linear additive function of the independent variables. The price variable is the cost, net of subsidy, of buying the package.

The best result of a stepwise regression procedure,[1] with the Epsilon level (ε) set at $0 \cdot 01$ is shown in Table 12.5.

Table 12.5

Stepwise regression: five rooms insulated

	β	St Error	t values
3 Rail noise	$0 \cdot 186$	$0 \cdot 095$	$1 \cdot 948$
9 $\triangle PNdB$ even	$0 \cdot 028$	$0 \cdot 008$	$3 \cdot 510$
14 Net total cost	$-0 \cdot 023$	$0 \cdot 004$	$5 \cdot 256$

The β coefficient shows the increase in the proportion of households glazing five rooms for a unit increase in the specified independent variables. For example, an increase of one unit of $\triangle PNdB$ suggests that nearly 3 per cent more households install throughout the house, insulation glazing.

With 165 observations there is an infinite number of degrees of freedom and t values of $1 \cdot 282$ and $1 \cdot 645$ are required for an $0 \cdot 1$ and an $0 \cdot 05$ level of significance, respectively, in the case of the one-tail test.

Model 2

The second model examines decision-making on the part of the household as a series of responses to binary events (see p. 99). To be specific the propensity to purchase any sound insulation is examined first. Therefore, the dependent variable takes the value 0/1 depending upon whether sound insulation glazing has been installed in any part of the house. The price variable is entered as the average net cost of double glazing a room in the house. The second stage of this two-tier, or hierarchical model considers, for insulating households only, their propensity to insulate the house as a whole. By combining both analyses thus:

$$E(Yi) = \text{Proportion} \{y^a > 0\} \text{ prop'n} \{y^b > 0/y^a > 0\}$$

it is possible to derive the overall propensity to insulate all five rooms.

The advantage of this two-tier model is that it does allow for the possibility that different factors play a part at each stage of the analysis or that the same factors are of varying importance.

The results of the first stage of this approach are shown in Table 12.6 and the second stage in Table 12.7.

Table 12.6

Stepwise regression: insulation of one or more rooms

		β	St error	t values
1	Distance from Heathrow	−0·168	0·061	3·751
3	Rail noise	0·214	0·109	1·976
9	△PNdB evening	0·021	0·009	2·284
14	Net cost	−0·029	0·005	5·770

In the second stage variable 6 is insignificant. Therefore the same basic picture emerges at both stages although rail noise does not appear to be as important in the latter of the two.

Table 12.7

Stepwise regression: insulation of five rooms in households insulating at least one room

		β	St error	t values
1	Distance from Heathrow	−0·322	0·174	1·853
6	N evening	−0·006	0·005	1·206
9	△PNdB evening	0·034	0·184	1·870
14	Net total cost	−0·015	0·008	1·871

In comparing model 2 with model 1 there appears in this case also to be a basic similarity in the results. Nevertheless, taking into account the error terms at each stage of the two-tier model, its overall efficiency, compared with model 1, appears in this instance to be less.

Models 3 and 4

In the foregoing analysis the environmental variables for the evening period appear more important than the corresponding ones for the daytime or for the night-time. However, because of the high degree of correlation between the environmental variables for the three periods, such a conclusion must be treated with a degree of caution. It seemed advisable therefore to proceed by analysing the up-take of bedroom insulation separately from that of living rooms. This would allow the propensity to double glaze bedrooms to be related specifically and more meaningfully to night-time noise. Similarly analysis of livingroom insulation could concentrate on the use of the day-time and evening variables.

Models 3 and 4 therefore repeat the previous single-stage conditional probability analysis of model 1 but, separately, for downstairs and upstairs rooms. (See Tables 12.8 and 12.9.) That is to say the dependent variable takes the value 0 or 1 depending upon whether in the one case the householder has insulated both livingrooms, and in the others, whether he has treated all three bedrooms.

Table 12.8

Stepwise regression: insulation of two livingrooms

	β	St error	t values
Distance from Heathrow	−0·174	0·063	2·773
Downstairs cost	−0·029	0·007	4·240
Traffic noise	−0·113	0·074	1·526*
Rail noise	0·176	0·119	1·480*

*Not significant at the 0·1 level in a two-tailed test.

Table 12.9

Stepwise regression: insulation of three bedrooms

		β	St error	t values
11	$\triangle PNdB$ night	0·024	0·006	4·058
	Upstairs cost	−0·045	0·008	5·515

Models 5 and 6

Models 5 and 6 are based upon the linear logit analysis (see p. 102). The desirable approach at this stage would have been to reanalyse all variables in a logit context using a process equivalent to the stepwise regression procedure for selecting the most appropriate of the variables. Unfortunately, such a facility was not available in the program available to us which, in addition, limited to five the number of independent variables that could be included in any one analysis. It was decided therefore, to develop the logit based solely on the variables that emerged as significant in the linear analysis.

In practice it is usually the case that there is little difference between linear and sigmoid functions over a considerable range of values. Only at the extreme ranges does the sigmoid differ through its very definition. The linear estimates of proportions or probabilities for most observations generally fall within the middle range. As a consequence it is unlikely that variables that are insignificant in the linear form will prove markedly otherwise when the fitted surface is S shaped.

Table 12.10 contains the basic parameters of the logit function resulting from an application of the multiple linear logit program to the variables of Table 12.8. Table 12.11 shows the corresponding results for Table 12.9.

The multiple logit program prints out a dispersion matrix. By taking the square root of the diagonals, levels of significance for each variable approximately equivalent to the t values of the linear analysis, have been calculated. These are shown in the last column of Tables 12.10 and 12.11.

Table 12.10

Linear logit analysis: insulation of two livingrooms

	β	Significance
Distance from Heathrow	$-0 \cdot 477$	$2 \cdot 59$
Downstairs costs	$-0 \cdot 083$	$3 \cdot 78$

Table 12.11

Linear logit analysis: insulation of three bedrooms

	β	Significance
$\triangle PNdB$ night	$0 \cdot 072$	$3 \cdot 61$
Upstairs costs	$-0 \cdot 155$	$4 \cdot 68$

Model 7

Model 7 introduces the interaction concept. Unfortunately it was not possible to test the interaction hypothesis within a category analysis framework to the extent that was hoped initially.

The first step was to write a complete set of interaction terms based upon (using the night-time model by way of example) three categories of N, three categories of average peak and peak night-time $PNdB$, the presence or absence of an adjacent railway line, whether or not road noise exceeded a certain level and whether or not (for each of the 165 observations) the mean distance from the airport was exceeded. Delta $PNdB$ was excluded on the basis that the interaction terms representing the combinations of average peak and peak $PNdB$ levels would act as a proxy for it. Altogether, after removal of redundant combinations, (see p. 103) there were 33 interaction terms, represented by 0, 1 vectors in the binary matrix.

Unfortunately the data proved to be too limited for such a comprehensive and sophisticated treatment. A large number of vectors were linearly dependent. For example with only 11 per cent of sampled households lying adjacent to a railway it was not surprising that all of them tended to fall within a particular discrete range of $PNdB$, etc.

The problem was partially circumvented by the use of 'continuous dummies' (Gujarati, 1970 and Silk, 1972). In this instance the interaction term is formed by multiplying together a dummy variable and a continuous variable. The latter, in this case, was assumed to be of a linear form, an assumption which could have been avoided had it proved possible to totally 'categorise' the situation.

The final set of 14 independent variables selected is shown in Table 12.12.

Table 12.12

Variables used in the examination of the interaction hypothesis

Continuous	Variable form		
	Dummies	Interaction dummies	Continuous dummies
Bedroom cost	B_1 (i.e. $10 \cdot 31 \leqslant N < 40$)	$B_1 \, F_1$	$F_1 \cdot TN$
Peak $PNdB$ night	B_2 (i.e. $N \geqslant 40$)	$B_1 \, F_2$	$F_2 \cdot TN$
Distance	F_1 (i.e. $91 \leqslant \overline{PNdB} < 95$)	$B_2 \, F_1$	
Traffic noise (TN)	F_2 (i.e. $\overline{PNdB} \geqslant 95$)	$B_2 \, F_2$	

$B_0(N < 10 \cdot 31)$ and $F_0(PNdB < 91)$ have been removed as redundant vectors in accordance with the need to invert the matrix (see p. 103).

This strategy specifically examines interaction between average peak $PNdB$ and N (the two variables that constitute the Noise Number Index) and between average peak $PNdB$ and traffic noise. The latter aspect in the earlier analyses had been represented as a dummy variable i.e. whether or not, for the observation, road traffic noise exceeded a Noise Pollution Index value (measured in dBA) of 64. In the interaction model the LNP was introduced as a scalar variable.

However, in spite of the elaboration only cost and $\triangle PNdB$ proved to be significant at the required level. In other words the results of the stepwise procedure were identical to those of Model 4. In view of this it was not considered worthwhile examining, in a similar fashion, the purchase of livingroom insulation.

12.4 Interpretation

One of the more curious findings was the significance (in Models 2 and 3) of the variable 'distance from Heathrow'. We have come across one previous study which corroborates our findings with regard to 'distance'. It is an extensive study carried out between 1967–70 for the United States National Aeronautic and Space Agency (Tracor Lane, 1970). Over 8,000 interviews were carried out under flight paths up to ten to twelve miles from the centre of the largest airports serving the cities of Boston, Chicago, Dallas, Denver, Los Angeles, Miami and New York.

The findings were that 'distance from airport' ranked fourth of seven social variables used to explain annoyance[2] and, as such, was a much better predictor than the various noise exposure measures examined (CNR, NNI, etc.). In a nonlinear model it was found that the coefficients relating annoyance to distance from the centre of the airport, were at a peak five miles from the airport. The reasons for this 'were not fully understood' and no further speculation on the matter, or attempt to interpret the distance variable, was made.

One obvious conclusion is that distance per se is a surrogate for airport noise – noise from engine testing, from aircraft taxiing, waiting for flight clearance, from aircraft accelerating or braking along runways (in the latter case often with the assistance of the efficient but most noisy procedure of reverse thrust).

No previous study to our knowledge had examined or measured airport noise. Therefore, when the findings relating to distance were apparent, we asked W. S. Atkins to undertake a study of the Heathrow situation for us. The *Report* is included as Appendix 5. It suggests that airport noise attenuates linearly with distance, and that up to two to $2\frac{1}{2}$ miles distance, this noise appears to intrude above the background noise level. Although the level of the intruding noise appears to be fairly low, the number of ground noise events heard close to the airport is quite considerable.

Delta *PNdB*, which emerged as significant in all but the livingroom model and very significant in most, was originally introduced to give a broad picture of the range, or degree of fluctuation in aircraft sound. That it should have proved to be one of the most positive of the noise indicators is interesting for the support it lends to Robinson's (1971) hypothesis that 'other things being equal, the less steady the noise the greater its distracting and hence annoying quality'.

Robinson incorporated this argument in the derivation of his Noise Pollution Index (see p. 6). This index also seems of relevance for a further reason. The first term, *Leq.*, is a measure of 'the total amount of (frequency weighted) sound reaching the auditor [and] is largely governed by the intensity of the loudest intruding noises unless these are brief or so infrequent that the background noise constitutes the major part of the total noise emission' (Robinson, 1971). In other words the nature of the sound source is of less consequence than the intensity of sound emanating from it. Thus, the eclectic nature of the noise pollution measure would seem to make it most suitable for incorporating and integrating noises such as rail noise (and possibly in some cases, airport noise), which appear, on the basis of their significantly positive relationship with the purchase of sound insulation (see Models 1, 2 and 3), to be loud and intruding.

Also of considerable importance in the Noise Pollution Index is background noise. A hint of its relevance also emerged from these findings in the form of a negative sign on a decidedly weakly significant road traffic noise variable (Model 3). The indication therefore being that loud traffic sounds have the effect of masking aircraft sounds.

Apart from these broad indications it is perhaps inappropriate to read too much into these results. Recently, attention has been drawn to the importance of wind drift and straying in the measurement of aircraft noise. The basic data derived from the noise simulation model did not allow for these factors, which may have had the effect of spreading sound outside the relatively narrow flight channels assumed. If this was so, then in practice there was probably less variance in aircraft noise levels in West Hounslow than assumed in the analysis. This alone could have been the cause of the apparent lack of response by West Hounslow tenants to the *estimated* variation in aircraft noise levels.

These considerations apart however, basically the success of the demand analysis must be judged by reference to the significance of the price variable in the functions. In this context, the results are most favourable. The price variable was associated with the negative sign one would expect a priori. And in all but the second stage of the two tier model (Model 2 (i)), price was highly significant. Thus, we have a well-defined demand function for sound insulation glazing by West Hounslow tenants which we can use as a basis for estimating their willingness to pay for comparative peace and quiet.

Notes

1   At each stage the variable is found which, when omitted from the

current regression equation, reduces the fitted sum of squares (*SS*) least. If the decrease in fitted *SS* < ε (total *SS*), then this variable is omitted from the equation. Otherwise, the variable is found which, when introduced into the current regression equation, maximises the increase in the fitted sum of squares. If the increase in fitted *SS* > ε (total *SS*), then this variable is introduced into the equation. The process is terminated when the increase in fitted *SS* < ε (total *SS*).

2   Using Phase 1 survey data and annoyance variable *V*, distance had a value for Eata ('directly analogous to the product moment coefficient') of ·43 and a value for beta ('directly analogous to the product moment partial coefficient') of ·25. The corresponding beta value for *NNI'* ('an updated version of the Old English *NNI'*) was ·13. All seven social variables together produced an *R* of ·67 in a linear model and ·78 in a nonlinear model. The correlation coefficient for the most appropriate measure of noise exposure, *CNR*, when used alone to explain annoyance, was 0·37.

13 Willingness to Pay for a Reduction of Indoor Noise

A number of models were developed in the previous chapter. Some were based upon different basic assumptions regarding behaviour while in other cases the differences stem from more practical considerations.

An example of the latter was the need to distinguish between the insulation of upstairs and downstairs rooms in view of the collinearity problems associated with the basic environmental data. On the other hand, this separate consideration of the upstairs and downstairs activity space is a very useful distinction to make from the point of view of policy, and comment to this effect was made in Chapter 7. Therefore there seems little point in basing the willingness to pay estimates upon Models 1 or 2, both of which focused upon the insulation of the chief household rooms treated as a whole.

This still leaves a choice to be made between two basic functional forms, the linear-logit and the simple linear function. A direct comparison of the relative efficacy of the two is rather difficult because the methods used to calculate the significance of the explanatory variables are not directly comparable. Nevertheless the difference between the levels of significance is reasonably large and favours the simple linear function. Therefore we have used Models 3 and 4 as a basis.

Integrating the functions with respect to the price of insulation between the limiting values of y i.e., $0 \leqslant y < 1$ (holding other variables constant at their means) gives, for the average householder, a total *willingness to pay for the insulation of all bedrooms of £45 and £33 for the sound insulation of living-rooms.*

It has not been possible to introduce household income explicitly into the analysis. We have pointed out that by selecting and analysing the Hounslow public housing group we were examining the behaviour of a group reasonably homogeneous in its social class and income characteristics. Naturally though, we can expect the willingness to pay for sound insulation to vary with household income and therefore it would be especially valuable to estimate the income of our (homogeneous) group.

We have been able to do this by using special tabulations from the 1966 Census prepared for us by the Greater London Council. These special tabulations cross-classify car ownership by tenure group for wards in the Borough of Hounslow. These data enable the estimation of, for example, the number of households with no cars.

The *Selnec Transportation Study* (1972) has calculated conditional probability distributions of the form $E(n/x)$ which relate the expected probability of a household with an income x belonging to car owning category n. These functions are empirical and vary between different residential density types.

It was therefore possible, using the estimated car ownership per household (derived from the 1966 Census) and data on residential densities, to estimate the 1966 average household income for the group in question. The calculated figure was £1,800. Thus, the average willingness to pay for downstairs and upstairs insulation works out at 1·8 per cent and 2·6 per cent respectively, of the average 1966 household income.

At this stage, it is necessary to bear in mind an important characteristic of sound insulation elaborated in Chapter 7. Like so many new commodities, sound insulation glazing tends to satisfy more than one basic want. Apart from the sound insulation aspect, it can reduce the risk of burglary, decrease condensation problems, reduce draughts and increase thermal insulation. Some of these advantages are, one can argue, trivial and unperceived by the majority of householders. The thermal benefit is probably the only one of consequence apart from the sound reduction. Even so, the joint-good characteristics of sound insulation glazing does imply that the measure of willingness to pay should be treated as an estimate of the maximum capitalised value placed upon the extra peace and quiet associated with the insulation glazing.[1]

The extra peace and quiet associated with the installation of sound insulation glazing of the standard specification used at Heathrow is 14 *dBA* or thereabouts (see Chapter 6). As noted in Chapter 6, the use of a standard specification by the authorities was a simplifying feature for the analysis, but it does imply that we have no precise information about the marginal value of peace and quiet. Instead the valuation relates to a reduction within the home of 14 *dBA*, that is, a little more than a halving of sound levels.

On the other hand, a 10 to 15 decibel reduction is a typical reduction in the level of sound associated with many forms of regulation and remedial action which can and do form the basis of various policies. For example the new generation high-ratio by-pass engined jets, such as the DC10 and Tristar, are 10 to 15 *EPNdB* quieter than the existing turbo jet aircraft (OECD, 1973). Similar reductions in sound levels are associated with the hush kits. Research so far carried out shows that retrofitting would reduce noise particularly on landing by about 10 to 15 *EPNdB* (OECD, 1973).

To take some specific examples, for the Boeing 707-320B fitted with a 'Quiet Nacelle', the Boeing Company estimate an 11 *EPNdB* reduction at reduced climb thrust and $14\frac{1}{2}$ *EPNdB* reduction for approach. The addition of a new front fan to the 727–200 series aircraft is expected to reduce take-off noise by almost 11 *EPNdB* and that of the approach by 12 *EPNdB* (Achitoff, 1973).

There are also modifications which can be applied to flight procedures to achieve sound reductions of the same order of magnitude. Apparently the most promising seems to be the two-sequant approach. The first would take place at an altitude of 1,000 metres (at present carried out at 450 metres); then, at some 9 km from the airport, a 6° descent would begin, levelling out at 3° when the aircraft is some 2 km from the edge of the runway. Tests with Boeing 727s and 737s show that noise can thus be reduced by 15 *PNdB*, 8 km away from the airport, by 12 *PNdB* at 5 km and 10 *PNdB* at 3 km (after which distance the reduction is promptly lost) (Bolt, Beranek and Newman, 1972).

Aviation policies such as these – which reduce noise levels by roughly the 10–15 *dBs* valued in this study – should not be thought of as resulting in trivial expenditures which need no justification by conscious, formal analysis. On the contrary, the sums involved are considerable.

To enable the two-sequant approach to be carried out at 58 US airports would require $5 million of airport instrument handling equipment. Assuming all 1,800 jet airliners operating in the US in early 1974 were equipped with required flight deck equipment there would be a further $66·6 millions involved, a figure which could double if general aviation was included (*Flight International, 1974*).

Retrofitting costs are much higher still. The 707/DC8 installed cost of the 'Quiet Nacelle' is almost $800,000 per aeroplane and that of the 727, $175,000 – while the estimated cost of a total retrofit programme for the US falls in the $400 million to $1,500 million range (Achitoff, 1973). A more detailed UK Government study of a UK retrofit programme estimated costs at £34·9 million (Board of Trade, 1970).

Finally, we return to the fundamental theoretical issue of interpreting our own valuations, an issue first raised in Chapter 3. We have studied the preferences of householders as revealed in the market for sound-attenuating double glazing. We have based our approach upon the willingness to pay principle. We can expect to have, therefore, subject to the accuracy of our measurements, a measure of the benefits of 'peace and quiet' consistent with the Marshallian concept of consumers' surplus. Whether we have also an appropriate measure of noise disbenefits is a debatable point depending upon one's attitude to the argument that the marginal utility of income is constant. If one accepts the argument – and public policy, in so far as it is based upon a Paretian welfare function, appears to concur – then we have both a measure of the benefits of additional peace and quiet and a measure of the disbenefits of increased noise.

Note

1   There is an analogy here with the problems encountered in value of time studies. In these studies it is difficult to disentangle the pure value of time from mode, or route, specific disutilities.

Appendix 1

MEASURES OF COMPENSATING AND EQUIVALENT VARIATION
AND THE VALUATION OF NOISE AND QUIETUDE

The distinction between the compensating variation (CV) measure of consumers' surplus and the corresponding equivalent variation (EV) measure can be illustrated for increasingly peaceful and increasingly noisy situations by supposing that a new good which reduces noise is introduced onto the market.

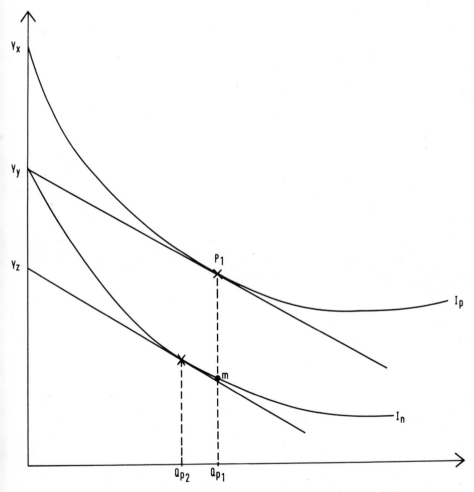

Fig. A1.1   A consumer's indifference map for 'peace and quiet'

In Figure A1.1 units of noise reduction are shown on the horizontal axis. Thus, moving from left to right indicates increasing purchases of peace and quiet (or a less noisy environment). Represented on the vertical axis we have money income intersected at Y_y by the indifference curve I_n. The latter is the indifference curve of the consumer in the absence of the new peace and quiet 'good'.

Now suppose that the peace and quiet good is introduced. We move to a new and higher indifference curve I_p where Q_{p1} of peace and quiet is purchased. The change in real income or welfare brought about by Q_{p1} is indicated by the vertical difference between the straight lines. The upper line is the budget line when the peace and quiet good is introduced at a fixed price and is therefore tangential to the point on indifference curve I_p, vertically above Q_{p1} on the horizontal axis. The other is drawn parallel, and tangential to a point on I_n. This point is vertically above point Q_{p2}. Q_{p2} would therefore represent the quantity of peace and quiet purchased by the consumer if a sum of money was abstracted from him so as to leave him no better off than he had been prior to the introduction of the peace good: this abstraction would return him to his original indifference curve (and thus to his initial level of welfare) vertically above Q_{p2}. Thus, the difference, $Y_y - Y_z$, between the intersection of the parallel lines on the income axis is a measure of the compensating variation of the consumer for the good 'peace and quiet'.

For the corresponding measure of the equivalent variation we need the equivalent change in real income which, in the absence of the peace and quiet good, would compensate the consumer for the good's absence. This measure is indicated by the vertical distance $Y_x - Y_y$ on the income axis. This sum of money, $Y_x - Y_y$, would place the consumer on the indifference curve I_p and therefore at a level of welfare equivalent to that enjoyed by purchase of the peace and quiet good.

If peace and quiet is a good with a positive (or normal) income effect then $Y_x - Y_y$ will exceed $Y_y - Y_z$ to the extent of this income effect. The compensating variation and equivalent variation measures will therefore differ.

The Marshallian approximation of the true consumers' surplus change differs because of the constraint on the quantity of goods purchased. Marshall's definition of consumer surplus was the sum of money that a consumer would pay for a good over and above the sum he actually pays. In this way the quantity purchased is determined and, because of this, the consumer surplus measure will be less than a compensating variation which measures the consumer's willingness to pay with no constraint on the amount purchased. The point can be illustrated again by reference to the figure. In terms of abstracting a sum of money from our 'Marshall' man so as to leave him with the same level of welfare as before 'peace and quiet' was introduced, we return to the indifference curve I_n but because of the quantity constraints, this time at point M. But $P_1 - M$ is smaller than $Y_y - Y_z$. Therefore the Marshallian measure underestimates the compensating variation measure.

There is one set of circumstances however, when the Marshallian measure of surplus and the CV and EV measure are equivalent. This is when the good 'peace and quiet' exhibits zero income effects. With positive income effects the EV will exceed the CV and the CV will exceed the Marshallian measure. With negative income effects (an inferior good) CV will exceed both the EV measure and the Marshallian measure.

In terms of the introduction of a 'bad', noise (or less peace and quiet), the analysis can be treated as symmetrical with that for the good peace and quiet.

However, in this instance the sum of money previously representing the CV now represents the sufferers EV and vice versa. The sufferer, of course, does not buy a 'bad' . . . therefore, we ask – in the absence of the 'bad' what sum of money taken from the potential sufferer would lead to an equivalent reduction in welfare? That is to say – what sum of money would transfer him from I_p to I_n indifference curve? This measure of equivalent variation is given by $Y_y - Y_z$ for, on the I_n indifference curve, the potential sufferer is still free to purchase the good 'peace and quiet' and would in fact purchase Q_{p2}.

With the imposition of the 'bad' (the removal of peace and quiet) the sum of money given to him that would return him to his previous level of welfare (i.e. fully compensate him) is represented by $Y_x - Y_y$. This sum of money will return him from I_n to I_p so that the previous EV now becomes the CV.

Appendix 2

ADMINISTRATIVE AND TECHNICAL SPECIFICATIONS OF THE
HEATHROW INSULATION SCHEME
(Abstracts from Statutory Instruments and Explanatory Documents)

Specification of total eligible area[1]

SCHEDULE 1
Articles 3, 4, 6 and 7
PART I

Local authority	Local Government areas
Council of the London Borough of Hillingdon	In the London Borough of Hillingdon: South ward, and so much of Hayes ward as lies south of the Reading–London railway line.
Council of the London Borough of Hounslow	In the London Borough of Hounslow: East Bedfont, Feltham North, Hounslow West, Hounslow Central, Hounslow South, Hounslow Heath, Cranford, Heston West, Heston East, Spring Grove and Isleworth South wards.
Eton Rural District Council	In Eton Rural District: Parishes of Horton, Datchet and Wraysbury and so much of the parish of Iver as lies south of the Reading–London railway line.
Staines Urban District Council	In Staines Urban District: Staines and Stanwell wards.
Council of the Borough of Slough	In the Borough of Slough: Langley ward.

Specification of special area[1]

PART II

1 In this part of this Schedule a reference to any highway or watercourse
shall be deemed to be a reference to the centre line of that highway or watercourse (as the case may be).

2 The area within a line drawn as follows:

Starting at the point where the boundary between the London Borough of Hillingdon and Eton Rural District crosses the A4 trunk road, following the A4 trunk road (easterly) until it meets the A312 trunk road; following the A312 trunk road (southerly) until it crosses the River Crane; following the River Crane (southerly) until it meets Duke of Northumberland's River; following Duke of Northumberland's River (westerly) until it crosses Beacon Road; following Beacon Road (southerly) until it meets Bedfont Road; following Bedfont Road (westerly) until it meets High Street, Stanwell; following High Street, Stanwell (westerly) until it meets Park Road; following Park Road (westerly) until it meets Stanwell Moor Road; from the junction of Park Road and Stanwell Moor Road going due west (true) to Moor Lane; following Moor Lane (northerly) until it meets Horton Road; following Horton Road (westerly) until it crosses the boundary between Eton Rural District and Staines Urban District; following that boundary (northerly) until it meets the boundary between Staines Urban District and the London Borough of Hillingdon and the boundary between the London Borough of Hillingdon and Eton Rural District; following the boundary between the London Borough of Hillingdon and Eton Rural District (northerly) until it crosses the A4 trunk road.

Conditions pertaining to the applicant[2]

Persons to whom grants are to be paid by the British Airports Authority

Subject to the provisions of this Scheme, the BAA shall make a grant to any person who has applied for the grant at a time when:

(a) he is the occupier of the dwelling, or

(b) if the dwelling is unoccupied at that time, he is entitled to be the occupier, or

(c) if there is a tenancy or licence of the dwelling, he is the immediate landlord or licensor of the occupier or, if the dwelling is unoccupied, of the person entitled to be the occupier,

and the amount of the grant shall be recoverable by that person from the BAA as a debt due to him:

Provided that—

(i) if two or more persons have applied for a grant in respect of the insulation of the same room, otherwise than as joint applicants, the grant shall be paid only to the applicant otherwise entitled to it whose application was first received by the local authority unless such application shall be withdrawn;

(ii) a grant shall not be paid to any person, if he claims the grant by reason of being the landlord or the licensor of the dwelling, unless he was entitled to an interest in that dwelling on 1 January 1966, whether as holder of the fee simple or otherwise; or in any other case unless on that date he resided or was entitled to reside in that dwelling, disregarding any tenancy or licence held by any other person;

(iii) a grant shall not be paid if the dwelling is, at the time when the application is lodged, the subject of a tenancy or licence unless the applicant, being the tenant or licensee, certifies that he has obtained any requisite consent of the landlord or licensor, or being the landlord or licensor, certifies that he has obtained any requisite consent of the tenant or licensee.

Technical specifications[3]

SCHEDULE 2
Articles 6 (1)(c)(vi), 6(1)(e) and 7
Standards for Insulation Works
PART I

Items required to be included in insulation works

1   Subject to the provisions of this paragraph, the insulation works done under this Scheme shall include all the following items:

(1)   the replacement by or conversion to double windows of all existing windows in each room (in which there are to be insulation works under this Scheme) in accordance with the specification in paragraph 3 in Part 2 of this Schedule;

(2)   the provision and installation in each room (in which there are to be insulation works under this Scheme) of one ventilator unit of a type conforming to the standards of ventilation and acoustic performance specified in paragraphs 4 and 5 of Part 2 of this Schedule including connecting the fan unit by wiring of not less than 5 amps capacity to the nearest convenient point in the existing electric supply circuit, or to the electric mains switchboard;

(3)   the adaptation of an existing airbrick in the external wall of each room (in which there are to be insulation works under this Scheme) for supplying fresh air for the ventilator unit, or the provision of a new air supply duct to the unit from outside and the blocking up of the existing airbrick;

(4)   the provision of a new external cowl to shield the supply duct or airbrick through which fresh air for the ventilator unit is supplied:

129

Provided that:
- (*a*) the works may consist of, or include, items different from those specified in this paragraph if the sound reduction and ventilation provided by such items is not less than that which would have been provided by items specified in this paragraph;
- (*b*) where any items or part of an item is provided otherwise than under this Scheme, and complies with the relevant specifications in this Schedule, it shall not be required to be duplicated as a condition for payment of a grant under this Scheme.

Items permitted to be included in insulation works

2   In addition to the items referred to in paragraph 1 of this Schedule the insulation works done under this Scheme may include only the following items:
- (1) making good the existing fabric and decorations (not including curtains) after the installation of new windows and ventilator units, including the adaptation of any existing pelmet;
- (2) improving the sound reduction of the roof structure by the method specified in paragraph 6 of Part 2 of this Schedule;
- (3) blocking by means of board of a minimum weight of 2 lb per square foot adequately sealed around the edges, of chimneys into rooms which have been treated in accordance with paragraph 1 of this Schedule.

PART II
WINDOWS AND VENTILATOR UNITS

Specification for Windows

3   The existing window shall either be retained and converted to a double window by the installation of a new inner window, or replaced by a new double window, and the following conditions shall be complied with:
- (1) any gaps in the outer window shall be effectively sealed by compressible strip;
- (2) the inner window may be framed in wood, metal or plastics, shall be well fitted into the existing window reveal or planted on the wall face round the reveal, with the junction between the wall and window frame fully sealed by means of mastic packing, cover strips or other equally effective means, and shall be glazed with glass having a weight of not less than 24 ounces per square foot;
- (3) both the outer and inner windows shall be adequately openable for direct ventilation when required and for cleaning purposes and for means of escape in case of fire, but with the opening lights of the inner window well sealed round their edges either by compressible resilient strip or by magnetic sealing strip;

(4) if the window is a bay window or bow window the inner window shall either follow the shape of the outer window, or shall be taken straight across the bay or bow, and any projecting surround or window board required to close the gap shall have a weight of not less than 2 lb per square foot;

(5) at least two reveals of the window opening between the outer and inner window shall be lined with sound absorbent material;

(6) the shortest horizontal distance, or, in the case of a bay window or bow window where the inner window is taken straight across the bay or bow, the mean horizontal distance, between the glass of the outer window and the glass of the inner window shall not be less than the distance specified in the second column of the following table in relation to the weight or thickness of glass specified in the first column of that Table:

Less than 32 ounces and not less than 24 ounces per square foot ..	8 inches
Less than one quarter of an inch and not less than 32 ounces per square foot	6 inches
One quarter of an inch or more	4 inches

Ventilation and acoustic performance of ventilator units

4   The ventilator unit shall be fitted with an easily removable and washable air filter and with a controlled variable-speed fan, and shall be capable of supplying fresh air to a room from outside. The unit complete with sound attenuating duct and cover shall be capable of giving variable ventilation rates ranging from:

(i) an upper rate of not less than 65 cubic feet per minute against a back pressure of 0·04 inches water gauge, to

(ii) a lower rate of not more than 35 cubic feet per minute against zero back pressure.

The effective area of the air path through the unit, with the fan switched off, shall not be less than three square inches.

5   The unit shall be so constructed that:

(1) when it is in operation in any room at the maximum ventilation rate the sound level in the room due to the operating of the unit, normalised by the subtraction of $10 \log 10\left(\frac{10}{A}\right)$ (where A is the measured sound absorption in the room in square metre units at each $\frac{1}{3}$-octave frequency) does not exceed 35 decibels on the A scales; and

(2) the sound pressure level difference measured in the laboratory between two rooms separated by a 9-inch brick wall incorporating an agreed sample of the ventilator unit, normalised by the addition of

$10 \log 10 \left(\dfrac{10}{A}\right)$ (where A is the measured sound absorption in the receiving room in square metre units at each $\frac{1}{3}$-octave frequency) is not less than the figure shown in the following Table except for total adverse deviations (at all $\frac{1}{3}$-octave frequencies) not exceeding 32 decibels and an adverse deviation at any one $\frac{1}{3}$-octave frequency not exceeding 8 decibels.

$\frac{1}{3}$-octave frequency band centre cycles per sound	Sound pressure level difference decibels
100	30
125	33
160	36
200	39
250	42
315	45
400	48
500	49
630	50
800	51
1000	52
1250	53
1600	53
2000	53
2500	53
3150	53

Sound reduction of roofs

6 The space between ceiling joists in the roof shall be filled with loose, pelletted, dense mineral wool to a depth that will result in a weight of 2 lb per square foot.

Conditions pertaining to cost

The grant is calculated on the costs actually incurred in undertaking the statutory soundproofing works, after taking into account the full value of all incentives and discounts, etc. provided by builders, contractors or suppliers. For the purposes of grant, the scheme requires that the costs must be 'reasonably incurred'; and this has been interpreted by the British Airports Authority,[4] on the advice of the local authorities, as meaning:

132

for the essential work (inclusive of necessary repairs to interior decoration) costs of not more than:

(a) £1·50 per sq ft = (£16·15 per sq metre) of double glazing and associated works,

(b) £40 for the supply and installation of each ventilator unit, with air supply and external cowl.

for the optional additional items eligible for grant, costs of not more than:

(a) 12p per sq ft. (= £1·30 per sq metre) for the improvement of insulation in the roof structure.

(b) £5 for blocking up each open chimney in the insulated room(s).

Reasonable costs include the cost of builder's labour. If the applicant does the work himself, the reasonable costs would include necessary materials etc. and may include a small allowance towards the cost of any tools the applicant has had to purchase in order to undertake the work, but he may not claim a grant towards the cost of his own labour.

Notes

1 *Source:* Statutory Instruments 1972, no. 1291, Schedule 1, Parts 1 and 2.
2 *Source:* Statutory Instruments 1972, no. 1291, p. 3, para. 5.
3 *Source:* Statutory Instruments 1972, no. 1291, pp. 6–9.
4 *Source:* BAA Noise Insulation Grants Scheme (undated), para. 16.

F

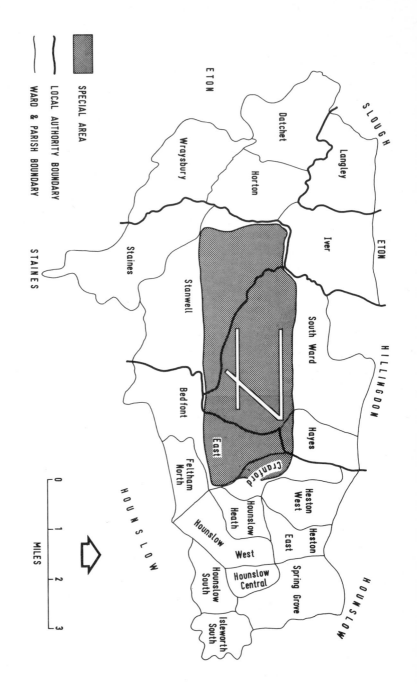

Fig. A2.1 Heathrow double glazing scheme: eligible wards and parishes

Appendix 3

ESTIMATION OF 1972 OWNER-OCCUPIED POPULATION ELIGIBLE FOR GRANTS

If X_0 = eligible houses on 1 January 1966
X_1 = eligible houses on 1 January 1967
t = turnover rate

$$X_1 = X_0 - tX_0$$
$$= X_1 (1-t)$$

Similarly $X_2 = X_1 (1-t)$
$$= X_0 (1-t)^2$$
and $X_6 = X_0 (1-t)^6$

If $t = 0 \cdot 05$
$(1-t)^6 = 0 \cdot 735$

Thus the approximate percentage of houses which have changed ownership since 1 January 1966 is 26·5 per cent and such properties are no longer eligible. However an unknown proportion of these will have been double glazed before being sold. Thus the actual percentage of houses which have not been double glazed but have lost eligibility will probably be less than 26·5 per cent but not less than (26·5 per cent – (10·6 per cent of 26·5 per cent) = 23·65 per cent. A figure of 25 per cent for houses which have not been double glazed but have experienced change of ownership seems, therefore, to be a reasonable estimate of the position on 1 January 1972.

Appendix 4

NOISE EXPOSURE DATA FOR WEST HOUNSLOW, 1971

A4.1 Summer daytime noise exposure data

The Wolfson Unit of the Institute of Sound and Vibration Research at the University of Southampton were requested to estimate, using the methodology set up by the Board of Trade and Industry in preparing their 1967 *NNI* map, the daytime average peak perceived noise levels and the number of flights 'heard' during the mid-June to mid-September period 1971 at 169 positions referenced on an Ordnance Survey Map. These positions related to census enumeration districts in the area of West Hounslow.

The preparation of the data required a knowledge of the aircraft route structure, the area under investigation and the average number of aircraft of each category using these routes between 0700 hours and 1900 hours during the summer months.

The Hounslow area is crossed by ten departure routes and eight incoming routes which, for computation purposes, were numbered respectively 1 to 10 and 28, 29, 30, 32, 33, 34, 35 and 37. Routes 3 and 4 were not used during 1971.

From information given by the Department of Trade and Industry it was found that routes 1 to 10 were used for 31 per cent of departures, the left runway (10L) taking 2·5 per cent of these flights, and the right runway (10R) taking the remaining 97·5 per cent.

Routes 1 and 2 connect via Kilburn with Airways Amber 1 North and Red 1 East which serve 60 per cent of all North Atlantic traffic and 29 per cent of all European. Routes 5 and 6 connect via Detling with Airway Green 1 East which serves 23 per cent of all European traffic. Routes 7 and 8 connect via Wisley with Airways Red 1 South and Amber 1 South, which serve 48 per cent of all European traffic, all the Channel Islands traffic and all long haul traffic except those on the North Atlantic route. Routes 9 and 10 connect via Woodley with Airway Green 1 West which takes 40 per cent of all North Atlantic traffic and the Irish traffic.

The approach routes 28, 29, 30, 32, 33, 34, 35 and 37 took 46 per cent of these, and 33 to 37 for the remaining 54 per cent. The traversing runway (23L) took 4 per cent of the landings. It was assumed that the four stacking areas – Bovingdon, Ongar, Biggin and Epsom were shared equally.

Table A4.1 gives a breakdown of the flight densities into aircraft categories.

136

Table A4.1

Heathrow East air traffic density, 1971

	Average day departures by aircraft category				
Route	Turbo prop	Medium jet	Large jet light	Large jet heavy	747
1	0·2	0·6	0	0·1	0
2	6·0	23·0	0·6	3·3	2·0
5	0	0·2	0	0	0
6	0·2	9·7	0·5	0	0
7	0	0·5	0·2	0·1	0
8	2·6	21·6	6·8	3·8	1·2
9	0	0·1	0	0·1	0
10	0	5·3	0	2·1	1·3

	Average day arrivals by aircraft category				
28 29 30 32	8·5	57·8	16·7	0	4·3
33 34 35 37	10·1	68·0	19·7	0	5·0
Runway 23L	1·2	7·8	2·3	0	0·6

The data was computed by taking a reference noise level in *PNdB* for each aircraft category at 500 ft distance (see Table A4.2) and extrapolating the noise level at National Grid positions by assuming an attenuation of 8 *PNdB* per doubling of distance, except when the angle of elevation of aircraft from the observer is less than 15°, when 10 *PNdB* per doubling of distance is taken. The flight profiles (noise abatement take-offs at 3° glide slope landings) used are those established by the Board of Trade in 1967 (for Heathrow) and used in the 1970 public enquiry into runway extensions at Gatwick.

Table A4.2

Reference noise levels at 500 ft

Aircraft category	Full power climb	Peak perceived noise level			
		Noise abatement climb	Cruise climb	Level flight	Landing
Turbo prop	114	110	—	104	103
Medium jet	121	115	118	111	110
Large jet (light)	128	118	123	115	112
Large jet (heavy)	128	121	124	118	112
B747	121	118	120	115	109

Average peak perceived noise levels and average number of aircraft heard per day above 80 *PNdB* were computed at a scale of six inches to the mile, for 169 reference positions. The results are shown in Table A4.3.

A4.2 Evening and night-time noise exposure

The data was built up from published monthly figures of total movements per runway per day and night given to Southampton by the BAA. A sample of 10 flight logs and 'Min Fly' documents were used to allocate flight densities on each flight route over the periods 1900–2300 hours and 2300–0700 hours local time. The flight profiles used were again those produced by the Board of Trade after their 1967 survey. A cut-off at 80 *PNdB* has been included.

The results are presented in Table A4.4. For ease of tabulation, all incoming routes to 28L are numbered as 28, all incoming routes to 28R are numbered 33. With a cut-off at 80 *PNdB* the approach routes to 23L have no effect on the noise environment at the locations specified.

Table A4.3

Estimated daytime noise exposure at Heathrow East, 1971

Position	Total traffic per day	Average pk. PNdB	Position	Total traffic per day	Average pk. PNdB
218	15·50	85·8	203	170·31	111·4
229	34·50	85·7	202	184·27	104·7
227	40·50	89·6	222	181·47	107·6
228	40·00	89·1	201	232·69	98·0
231	39·80	89·7	204	170·31	97·5
232	56·27	89·7	220	167·51	98·9
234	113·17	89·1	273	232·49	96·8
207	164·11	94·9	216	232·69	97·3
209	116·47	91·6	271	232·49	97·9
210	116·47	87·0	272	191·19	96·0
221	130·91	91·2	243	171·77	105·0
230	122·47	88·4	242	181·47	104·0
223	157·81	98·6	240	157·81	102·0
226	113·37	86·8	276	219·99	99·3
233	113·37	87·7	244	144·87	103·5
236	121·81	92·7	241	157·81	105·2
225	129·21	90·6			
269	174·25	106·8	275	239·39	95·9
213	174·25	107·8	215	231·35	99·5
			211	174·45	106·7
266	230·95	95·1	214	231·35	100·1
250	227·75	94·9	212	231·15	100·8
265	230·55	101·8	417	174·45	110·8
263	173·65	106·2	270	157·98	100·8
264	173·65	104·9	268	231·15	99·7
259	157·18	100·1	277	231·15	100·3
237	128·61	95·3	217	231·15	104·0
239	130·91	96·4	324	134·77	100·7
238	130·91	98·0	332	134·77	100·4
235	113·37	93·3	333	190·79	100·9
246	128·61	98·7	323	183·19	97·3
316	117·61	95·5	334	190·19	97·3

Position	Total traffic per day	Average pk. PNdB	Position	Total traffic per day	Average pk. PNdB
267	231·15	96·2	326	121·61	100·9
258	157·98	99·4	245	143·57	103·2
325	121·41	99·1	335	191·39	97·0
317	117·61	94·4	247	219·99	96·2
331	117·01	97·2	337	199·59	92·3
208	170·31	105·4	219	161·51	93·5
205	170·31	112·7	336	198·49	93·4
224	157·81	100·6	318	179·39	97·9
322	190·29	93·0	420	101·66	95·9
319	179·39	96·5	255	151·18	94·0
341	198·49	91·6	260	157·18	95·4
321	190·29	91·8	349	151·18	92·6
340	198·99	90·9	256	157·18	96·8
329	190·19	91·0	254	157·18	95·9
410	157·98	109·8	350	151·18	91·0
320	130·97	100·4	356	150·88	94·1
328	190·19	91·9	416	209·09	116·8
330	183·75	96·7	262	157·18	105·1
361	184·19	92·0	261	230·35	98·3
374	146·75	95·9	338	187·79	92·6
362	180·39	93·4	251	230·35	99·3
371	170·25	96·3	248	227·75	92·2
327	182·55	94·5	252	173·45	101·6
372	147·25	96·8	339	179·35	93·4
363	175·75	95·2	346	173·45	100·6
370	103·85	96·2	249	227·75	94·2
253	173·65	100·9	257	173·65	102·1
345	227·75	98·3	428	87·70	93·6
347	159·98	102·1	425	71·30	92·8
			432	87·50	90·6
360	155·05	99·6	419	81·70	94·8
357	155·05	99·6	418	101·66	95·0
274	229·69	97·8	424	81·70	93·5
358	147·68	95·5	351	151·08	93·4

Position	Total traffic per day	Average pk. PNdB	Position	Total traffic per day	Average pk. PNdB
359	184·45	97·4	354	124·68	93·1
369	86·78	96·1	352	128·08	91·4
375	79·68	95·2	355	125·28	92·1
368	82·98	94·3	353	123·28	88·9
411	91·86	103·1	364	94·18	93·8
412	101·06	99·4	373	82·98	89·6
408	85·10	94·9	365	86·78	92·5
407	101·66	96·7	367	79·68	92·1
409	157·78	105·6	366	83·48	90·4
422	150·08	97·1	401	78·30	88·6
423	150·08	94·5	405	87·10	96·2
426	101·66	94·8	402	88·30	94·3
421	150·08	97·2	404	87·10	93·6
348	151·18	94·5	403	87·10	91·2
			342	198·99	92·5
406	87·10	96·2	343	217·45	94·8
429	87·70	95·8	344	170·75	100·2
430	86·90	95·6			
413	87·70	93·8			
414	87·10	92·3			
431	87·10	90·6			
415	78·30	88·1			
427	112·06	95·3			
206	239·79	91·4			

Table A4.4

Estimated evening and night-time noise exposure at Heathrow East, 1971

Ref. Pos.	Evening (E) or Night (N)	Peak PNdB	Route causing peak	Number of peak movements	Average peak PNdB	Total number heard above 80 PNdB	Routes heard
201	E	104·2	8	0·19	97·1	54·61	1, 2, 5, 6, 7, 8, 9, 10, 28, 33
	N	104·2	10	0·09	94·2	53·2	1, 2, 5, 6, 7, 8, 9, 10, 28, 33
202	E	109·8	33	8·69	104·8	46·48	1, 2, 5, 6, 7, 8, 9, 10, 28, 33
	N	109·8	33	3·57	102·1	36·66	1, 2, 5, 6, 7, 8, 9, 10, 28, 33
206	E	106·3	7	0·03	99·2	34·06	1, 2, 5, 6, 7, 8, 9, 10, 33
	N	106·3	7	0·01	91·5	16·48	1, 2, 5, 6, 7, 8, 9, 10, 33
142	E	109·7	8	0·19	94·7	54·47	1, 2, 5, 6, 7, 8, 9, 10, 28, 33
	N	115·9	2	0·13	95·0	61·1	1, 2, 5, 6, 7, 8, 9, 10, 28, 33
215	E	107·6	8	0·19	93·8	54·47	1, 2, 5, 6, 7, 8, 9, 10, 28, 33
	N	115·7	2	0·13	94·1	61·1	1, 2, 5, 6, 7, 8, 9, 10, 28, 33
220	E	103·3	33	8·69	99·4	36·18	1, 2, 5, 6, 7, 8, 9, 10, 33
	N	103·3	2	0·13	98·9	17·45	1, 2, 5, 6, 7, 8, 9, 10, 33
221	E	100·8	1	0·02	89·8	30·73	1, 2, 5, 6, 7, 8, 9, 33
	N	100·8	1	0·04	90·3	13·90	1, 2, 5, 6, 7, 8, 9, 10, 33
224	E	105·0	33	8·69	101·3	34·69	1, 2, 5, 6, 7, 8, 9, 10, 33
	N	105·0	33	3·57	100·7	16·66	1, 2, 5, 6, 7, 8, 10, 33
225	E	95·3	1	0·07	89·4	29·61	1, 2, 5, 7, 8, 9, 33
	N	97·1	1	0·04	90·6	13·63	1, 2, 5, 7, 8, 9, 10, 33
227	E	100·2	1	0·02	87·8	6·81	1, 2, 5, 6, 7, 8
	N	100·2	1	0·04	89·3	4·32	1, 2, 6, 7, 10
228	E	100·3	1	0·02	87·4	6·26	1, 2, 7, 8
	N	100·3	1	0·04	88·9	4·20	1, 2, 7, 10

Estimated evening and night-time noise exposure at Heathrow East, 1971

Ref. Pos.	Evening (E) or Night (N)	Peak PNdB	Route causing peak	Number of peak movements	Average peak PNdB	Total number heard above 80 PNdB	Routes heard
230	E	100·5	1	0·02	87·6	25·64	1, 2, 5, 6, 7, 8, 9, 33
	N	100·5	1	0·04	88·7	11·78	1, 2, 5, 6, 7, 8, 9, 10, 33
231	E	100·0	1	0·02	88·1	6·23	1, 2, 8
	N	100·0	1	0·04	89·5	4·19	1, 2, 10
239	E	99·3	33	8·69	96·5	30·53	1, 2, 5, 6, 7, 8, 33
	N	100·5	2	0·13	96·5	13·86	1, 2, 5, 6, 7, 8, 9, 10, 33
247	E	100·9	33	8·69	96·1	51·17	1, 2, 5, 6, 7, 8, 9, 10, 28, 33
	N	104·2	2	0·13	93·2	50·28	1, 2, 5, 6, 7, 8, 9, 10, 28, 33
251	E	106·0	28	8·44	100·5	52·41	1, 2, 5, 6, 7, 8, 9, 10, 28, 33
	N	106·0	28	17·15	102·9	59·64	1, 2, 5, 6, 7, 8, 10, 28, 33
255	E	101·2	8	0·19	93·7	35·15	2, 5, 6, 7, 8, 9, 10, 28
	N	101·2	10	0·09	93·8	53·00	2, 5, 6, 7, 8, 9, 10, 28
258	E	103·9	28	8·44	100·0	37·41	1, 2, 5, 6, 7, 8, 10, 28
	N	103·9	28	17·15	101·2	54·08	1, 2, 5, 6, 7, 8, 9, 10, 28
260	E	104·3	8	0·19	94·6	37·27	2, 5, 6, 7, 8, 9, 10, 28
	N	104·3	10	0·09	94·2	53·97	8, 10, 28
262	E	114·6	8	0·19	104·8	37·29	1, 2, 5, 6, 7, 8, 9, 10, 28
	N	114·6	10	0·09	105·9	54·01	1, 2, 5, 6, 7, 8, 9, 10, 28
263	E	109·7	8	0·19	106·4	45·98	1, 2, 5, 6, 7, 8, 9, 10, 28, 33
	N	109·7	10	0·09	108·4	57·58	1, 2, 5, 6, 7, 8, 9, 10, 28, 33
264	E	110·5	28	8·44	105·4	45·98	1, 2, 5, 6, 7, 8, 9, 10, 28, 33
	N	110·5	28	17·15	107·5	57·58	1, 2, 5, 6, 7, 8, 9, 10, 28, 33
265	E	108·6	28	8·44	102·9	52·61	1, 2, 5, 6, 7, 8, 9, 10, 28, 33
	N	108·6	28	17·15	105·3	60·31	1, 2, 5, 6, 7, 8, 9, 10, 28, 33

Estimated evening and night-time noise exposure at Heathrow East, 1971

Ref. Pos.	Evening (E) or Night (N)	Peak PNdB	Route causing peak	Number of peak move-ments	Average peak PNdB	Total number heard above 80 PNdB	Routes heard
266	E	100·9	2	0·2	95·1	54·22	1, 2, 5, 6, 7, 8, 9, 10, 28, 33
	N	103·2	2	0·13	97·0	60·40	1, 2, 5, 6, 7, 8, 9, 10, 28, 33
267	E	105·0	8	0·19	95·2	54·4	1, 2, 5, 6, 7, 8, 9, 10, 28, 33
	N	105·7	2	0·13	96·7	61·07	1, 2, 5, 6, 7, 8, 9, 10, 28, 33
271	E	104·1	8	0·19	94·9	54·41	1, 2, 5, 6, 7, 8, 9, 10, 28, 33
	N	112·7	2	0·13	93·5	52·53	1, 2, 5, 6, 7, 8, 9, 10, 28, 33
274	E	107·1	2	0·2	97·1	52·7	1, 2, 5, 6, 7, 8, 9, 10, 28, 33
	N	108·1	2	0·13	94·5	51·09	1, 2, 5, 6, 7, 8, 9, 10, 28, 33
275	E	106·9	2	0·2	93·5	59·27	1, 2, 5, 6, 7, 8, 9, 10, 28, 33
	N	108·0	2	0·13	92·1	62·48	1, 2, 6, 7, 8, 9, 10, 28, 33
276	E	106·8	2	0·20	99·0	51·17	1, 2, 5, 6, 7, 8, 9, 10, 28, 33
	N	107·8	2	0·13	96·0	50·28	2, 5, 6, 7, 8, 9, 10, 28, 33
319	E	101·4	33	8·69	96·7	44·58	2, 28, 33
	N	101·4	33	3·57	93·4	46·78	2, 28, 33
321	E	95.7	33	8·69	91·9	49·69	2, 5, 8, 28, 33
	N	95.7	33	3·57	90·7	56·85	2, 10, 28, 33
326	E	103·8	33	8·69	101·1	28·33	1, 2, 5, 7, 8, 33
	N	103·9	2	0·13	100·9	13·27	1, 2, 7, 10, 33
339	E	95·5	28	1·69	93·9	45·35	1, 2, 5, 6, 7, 9, 28, 33
	N	98·5	28	17·15	95·8	54·95	1, 2, 5, 6, 7, 9, 28, 33
340	E	94·6	28	8·44	90·9	51·77	2, 5, 6, 7, 8, 28, 33
	N	95·8	2	0·13	92·1	57·34	2, 5, 6, 7, 8, 10, 28, 33
343	E	101·3	28	8·44	95·9	50·84	2, 5, 6, 7, 8, 10, 28, 33
	N	101·3	28	17·15	98·3	58·02	2, 5, 6, 7, 8, 10, 28, 33

Estimated evening and night-time noise exposure at Heathrow East, 1971

Ref. Pos.	Evening (E) or Night (N)	Peak PNdB	Route causing peak	Number of peak movements	Average peak PNdB	Total number heard above 80 PNdB	Routes heard
346	E	106·3	28	8·44	101·2	45·72	2, 5, 6, 7, 8, 9, 10, 28, 33
	N	106·3	28	17·15	103·3	56·83	2, 5, 6, 7, 8, 10, 28, 33
347	E	101·9	28	8·44	98·1	34·95	2, 5, 6, 7, 8, 9, 10, 28
	N	101·9	28	17·15	99·3	52·33	2, 5, 6, 7, 8, 9, 10, 28
348	E	98·7	28	8·44	95·2	35·15	2, 5, 6, 7, 8, 9, 10, 28
	N	98·7	28	17·15	96·1	53·00	2, 5, 6, 7, 8, 9, 10, 28
354	E	97·2	28	8·44	94·0	30·24	2, 5, 6, 7, 10, 28, 8
	N	97·2	28	17·15	94·9	49·51	2, 5, 6, 7, 8, 10, 28
355	E	95·9	28	8·44	92·8	30·35	2, 5, 6, 7, 8, 9, 10, 28
	N	95·9	28	17·15	93·6	49·59	2, 5, 6, 7, 8, 9, 10, 28
360	E	104·9	28	8·44	100·3	40·54	2, 5, 6, 7, 8, 9, 10, 28, 33
	N	104·9	28	17·15	102·1	53·7	2, 5, 6, 7, 8, 9, 10, 28, 33
361	E	96·9	28	8·44	92·6	47·57	2, 5, 8, 28, 33
	N	96·9	28	17·15	94·2	55·8	2, 10, 28, 33
362	E	98·8	28	8·44	94·0	47·38	2, 5, 28, 33
	N	98·8	28	17·15	96·0	55·79	2, 28, 33
363	E	100·7	28	8·44	96·2	42·56	2, 5, 8, 28, 33
	N	100·7	28	17·15	98·0	53·82	2, 5, 10, 28, 33
364	E	94·9	28	6·44	94·3	25·71	2, 5, 6, 8, 28
	N	96·9	28	17·15	94·8	46·5	2, 5, 6, 8, 28
365	E	95·2	28	8·44	92·9	23·91	5, 6, 8, 28
	N	95·2	28	17·15	93·2	44·8	2, 5, 6, 10, 28
366	E	93·0	28	8·44	90·7	23·91	5, 6, 8, 28
	N	93·0	28	17·15	91·0	44·67	5, 6, 10, 28
370	E	100·1	28	8·44	96·4	33·12	2, 5, 6, 8, 28, 33
	N	100·1	28	17·15	97·7	49·82	2, 5, 6, 10, 28, 33
371	E	101·9	28	8·44	97·2	42·66	2, 6, 28, 33
	N	101·9	28	17·15	99·1	53·7	2, 6, 28, 33
372	E	101·9	28	8·44	97·6	38·03	2, 5, 6, 28, 33
	N	101·9	28	17·15	99·3	51·67	2, 6, 28, 33

Estimated evening and night-time noise exposure at Heathrow East, 1971

Ref. Pos.	Evening (E) or Night (N)	Peak PNdB	Route causing peak	Number of peak move- ments	Average peak PNdB	Total number heard above 80 PNdB	Routes heard
401	E	93·8	2	0·68	89·4	11·64	1, 2, 5, 6, 7, 8, 10
			6	0·54			
			8	1·12			
	N	93·8	2	1·45	89·9	7·15	1, 2, 6, 7, 8, 10
			6	0·12			
			8	0·25			
402	E	99·8	2	0·68	94·4	15·84	1, 2, 5, 6, 7, 8, 9, 10
			6	0·54			
			8	1·12			
	N	99·8	2	1·45	94·5	10·32	1, 2, 6, 7, 8, 9, 10
			6	0·12			
			8	0·25			
403	E	96·7	2	0·68	91·1	15·62	1, 2, 5, 6, 7, 8, 10
			6	0·54			
			8	1·12			
	N	96·7	2	1·45	91·4	10·18	1, 2, 6, 7, 8, 10
			6	0·12			
			8	0.25			
404	E	99·1	2	0·68	93·5	15·63	1, 2, 5, 6, 7, 8, 10
			6	0·54			
			8	1·12			
	N	99·1	2	1·45	93·8	10·18	2, 6, 8, 10
			6	0·12			
			8	0·25			
405	E	104·4	2	0·68	97·1	15·63	1, 2, 5, 6, 7, 8, 10
			6	0·54			
			8	1·12			
	N	104·4	2	1·45	97·7	10·18	1, 2, 6, 7, 8, 10
			6	0·12			
			8	0·25			
406	E	104·3	2	0·68	97·1	15·63	1, 2, 5, 6, 7, 8, 10
			6	0·54			
			8	1·12			
	N	104·3	2	1·45	97·7	10·18	1, 2, 6, 7, 8, 10
			6	0·12			
			8	0·25			
407	E	105·2	2	0·68	96·2	24·21	1, 2, 5, 6, 7, 8, 9, 10, 28
			6	0·54			
			8	1·12			
	N	105·2	2	1·45	94·5	27·43	1, 2, 5, 6, 7, 8, 9, 10, 28
			6	0·12			
			8	0·25			

Estimated evening and night-time noise exposure at Heathrow East, 1971

Ref. Pos.	Evening (E) or Night (N)	Peak PNdB	Route causing peak	Number of peak move-ments	Average peak PNdB	Total number heard above 80 PNdB	Routes heard
408	E	106·8	6	0·54	97·4	14·11	1, 2, 5, 6, 7, 8, 9, 10
	N	106·8	6	0·12	99·5	8·89	1, 2, 5, 6, 7, 8, 9, 10
409	E	117·6	8	0·19	103·0	37·36	1, 2, 5, 6, 7, 9
	N	117·6	10	0·09	102·9	54·05	1, 2, 5, 6, 7, 8, 9, 10, 28
410	E	120·9	8	0·19	106·9	37·41	1, 2, 5, 6, 7, 8, 9, 10, 28
	N	121·0	2	0·13	105·7	54·08	1, 2, 5, 6, 7, 8, 9, 10, 28
411	E	111·0	2	0·68	101·7	21·89	1, 2, 5, 7, 8, 9, 10, 28
			8	1·12			
	N	111·0	2	1·45	100·3	25·91	1, 2, 5, 7, 8, 10, 28
			8	0·25			
412	E	107·8	2	0·68	98·8	24·11	1, 2, 5, 6, 7, 8, 10, 28
			6	0·54			
			8	1·12			
	N	107·8	2	1·45	97·1	27·35	1, 2, 5, 6, 7, 8, 10, 28
			6	0·12			
			8	0·25			
413	E	102·2	2	0·68	94·5	15·77	1, 2, 5, 6, 7, 8, 9, 10
			6	0·54			
			8	1·12			
	N	102·2	2	1·45	95·2	10·3	1, 2, 6, 7, 8, 9, 10
			6	0·12			
			8	0·25			
414	E	101·2	2	0·68	93·5	15·62	1, 2, 5, 6, 7, 8, 10
			6	0·54			
			8	1·12			
	N	101·2	2	1·45	94·2	10·18	1, 2, 6, 8, 10
			6	0·12			
			8	0·25			
415	E	95·1	2	0·68	89·2	11·64	1, 2, 5, 6, 7, 8, 10
			6	0·54			
			8	1·12			
	N	95·1	2	1·45	90·0	7·15	1, 2, 6, 7, 8, 10
			6	0·12			
			8	0·25			
418	E	103·4	6	0·16	93·3	24·25	1, 2, 5, 6, 7, 8, 9, 10, 28
	N	102·2	10	0·09	90·3	27·49	1, 2, 5, 6, 7, 8, 9, 10, 28

Estimated evening and night-time noise exposure at Heathrow East, 1972

Ref. Pos.	Evening (E) or Night (N)	Peak PNdB	Route causing peak	Number of peak move-ments	Average peak PNdB	Total number heard above 80 PNdB	Routes heard
419	E	104·7	8	0·19	93·3	13·69	1, 2, 5, 6, 7, 8, 9, 10
	N	104·7	10	0·09	92·3	9·37	1, 2, 5, 6, 7, 8, 9, 10
420	E	107·0	8	0·19	92·8	24·25	1, 2, 5, 6, 7, 8, 9, 10, 28
	N	107·0	10	0·09	90·0	27·49	1, 2, 5, 6, 7, 8, 9, 10, 28
421	E	109·7	8	0·19	94·1	32·33	1, 2, 5, 6, 7, 8, 9, 10, 28
	N	109·7	10	0·09	91·0	44·03	1, 2, 5, 6, 7, 8, 9, 10, 28
422	E	108·5	8	0·19	94·9	32·38	1, 2, 5, 6, 7, 8, 9, 10, 28
	N	108·5	10	0·09	94·1	44·03	1, 2, 5, 6, 7, 8, 9, 10, 28
423	E	106·9	8	0·19	91·8	32·38	1, 2, 5, 6, 7, 8, 9, 10, 28
	N	106·9	10	0·09	88·7	44·03	1, 2, 5, 6, 7, 8, 9, 10, 28
425	E	102·5	8	0·19	92·1	11·3	1, 2, 5, 6, 7, 8, 9, 10
	N	102·5	10	0·09	94·5	7·81	1, 2, 5, 7, 8, 10
426	E	105·4	8	0·19	92·8	24·25	1, 2, 5, 6, 7, 8, 9, 10, 28
	N	105·4	10	0·09	92·6	27·49	1, 2, 5, 6, 7, 8, 9, 10, 28
427	E	103·8	8	1·12	94·2	26·6	1, 2, 5, 6, 7, 8, 9, 10, 28
	N	103·8	8	0·25	92·8	28·99	1, 2, 5, 6, 7, 8, 9, 10, 28
428	E	102·2	8	1·12	93·7	15·77	1, 2, 5, 6, 7, 8, 9, 10
	N	102·2	8	0·25	94·5	10·28	1, 2, 5, 6, 7, 8, 9, 10
429	E	104·0	6	0·54	96·5	15·77	1, 2, 5, 6, 7, 8, 9, 10
	N	104·0	6	0·12	97·1	10·28	1, 2, 5, 6, 7, 8, 9, 10
431	E	99·7	6	0·54	91·8	15·63	1, 2, 5, 6, 7, 8, 10
	N	99·7	6	0·12	92·5	10·18	1, 2, 6, 7, 8, 10

Appendix 5

AIRPORT NOISE
by A. L. Beaman of Atkins Research and Development (*Edited*)

A5.1 Introduction

Atkins Research and Development were requested to carry out a noise survey in the area around Heathrow Airport to establish:
(a) the existing levels of airport ground operation noise in selected residential areas (ground operation noise includes noise from static aircraft being tested in maintenance areas, pre-take-off run up engine testing and aircraft moving along the runways both under taxiing and reverse thrust braking conditions),
(b) the rate of decay of this noise with distance from the airport in an easterly and southerly direction.

A5.2 Measurement positions and procedure

The noise survey was carried out between 30 July 1973 and 6 August 1973 at the locations indicated in Table A5.1. These positions were chosen because the background noise level was low and the sites were open and aligned along the axis of the airport. By selecting the positions along two perpendicular lines it was thought possible to interpolate the noise levels in the contained area.

Positions 1 to 5 were selected as being representative of housing areas to the east and to the south of the airport; at these positions the existing levels of airport ground operation noise were established.

Positions 10 to 19 were selected along the same axis of the airport at various intermediate distances. Measurements were necessary at these positions in order to establish the attenuation curves.

Because the ground operation noise emanates from the whole airport, the cargo terminal buildings were not expected to screen noise significantly from points 5, 14 and 19.

At positions 1 to 5 the noise level was recorded for five minutes every hour, 24 hours a day over a seven day week. At positions 10 to 19, samples of the noise levels were recorded for five minutes in the hour over three days between the hours of 10.00 and 18.00 – it was arranged that the measurements at these positions were carried out simultaneously with the measurements at positions 1 to 5 in turn.

Table A5.1

Location of noise measuring positions

Measuring position	Approx. distance (miles) south of reference position	Measuring position	Approx. distance (miles) east of reference position
14*	0	1*	0
4, 15	0·125	10	0·23
16	0·3	2	0·5
17	0·57	11	0·76
18	1·0	12	1·13
5	1·43	3	1·33
19	1·8	13	1·7

* Reference positions closest to airport from which distance of other positions measured.

Actual measurements were carried out by observers who tape-recorded the noise level at a height of two metres using calibrated Bruel and Kjaer precision sound level meters and Nagra tape recorders. During the noise recordings they also kept a log of any noise events which they heard (i.e. a clearly identifiable noise heard above the background noise). These included ground operation noise, flyover noise, traffic noise, train noise and local noises such as lawn-mowers, dogs and children, etc. Each event was listed with the time of occurrence.

During the times when the noise level at positions 10 to 19 was being recorded for the noise attenuation assessment, observers were also stationed at the airport and made notes of the various operations there. Aircraft movement schedules for the whole week of measurement were obtained and a record of weather conditions for that week was supplied by the Meteorological Office (see Table A5.2).

A5.3 Results

The number of ground noise events heard and identified at positions 1 to 5 are shown in Table A5.3. On Monday, Tuesday and Wednesday, these data are divided according to the operational use of runways 10 and 28. During Thursday, Friday, Saturday and Sunday, only runways 28 were in operation.

150

Table A5.2

Heathrow weather conditions, 30 July 1973 – 6 August 1973

Date	Time	Wind direction (°mag)	Wind speed (knots)	Temperature (°C)	Cloud over	Weather and comments
30–7–73	13.00	100	7	19	$\frac{6}{8}$ @ 1500 ft	Cloudy, calm, warm.
	16.00	variable	0–6	22		Sunny, slight breeze; slight cloud.
31–7–73	09.00	110	5	16	$\frac{1}{8}$ @ 1500 ft	Bright, warm, little cloud; slight breeze.
	16.00	220	5	23	$\frac{1}{8}$ @ 4500 ft	Sunny, slight breeze.
	24.00	130	4	15	0	Cold, calm.
1–8–73	09.00	060	4	17	$\frac{2}{8}$ @ 5000 ft	Clear, hazy sunshine; cool, slight breeze.
	16.00	220	5	27	$\frac{2}{8}$ @ 4000 ft	Overcast, breeze; thunder later, rain later.
	24.00	–	Calm	19	$\frac{2}{8}$ @ 5000 ft	Cloudy, cool, calm.
2–8–73	09.00	300	3	17	0	Hazy sunshine, warm, calm, wind increasing later.
	16.00	250	9	26	$\frac{1}{8}$ @ 4500 ft	Sunny, hot, breezy becoming cloudy later.
	24.00	230	7	19	$\frac{2}{8}$ @ 3000 ft	Cloudy, cool, breezy.
					$\frac{7}{8}$ @ 6000 ft	Slight rain.
3–8–73	09.00	225	5–8	16	$\frac{6}{8}$ – full over @ 4000 ft	Cloudy, cool, strong breeze. Cloud building up later; heavy rain.
	16.00	230	11	21	$\frac{3}{8}$ @ 3200 ft	Low cloud, warm.
					$\frac{5}{8}$ @ 6000 ft	Strong breeze, cooling later; heavy rain later.
	24.00	260	8	15	$\frac{6}{8}$ full	Overcast, windy.
4–8–73	09.00	320	6	16	$\frac{1}{8}$ @ 1800 ft	Sky clearing, sunny.
					$\frac{1}{8}$ @ 4000 ft	Warm, fresh breeze.
	16.00	260	9	19	$\frac{1}{8}$ @ 4000 ft	Cloudy, cool, breezy.
					full @ 14000 ft	Light rain becoming heavy.
	24.00	200	14	15	$\frac{3}{8}$ @ 900 ft full @ 1200 ft	Heavy rain, windy.
5–8–73	09.00	250	9	17	$\frac{2}{8}$ @ 1400 ft	Cloudy, cool, slight rain.
					full @ 400 ft	Steady rain, increasing.
	16.00	220	12	18	$\frac{1}{8}$ @ 600 ft $\frac{6}{8}$ @ 800 ft full @ 4000 ft	Heavy rain.
	24.00	200	15	18	full @ 2000 ft	Cloudy, cool; strong, gusty wind, slight rain later.
6–8–73	12.00	200	10	18	full	Heavy rain.

Table A5.3
Number of ground noise events heard by time and position

	Monday		Tuesday		Wednesday		Thursday		Friday		Saturday		Sunday		Whole week		
	10	*28*	*10*	*28*	*10*	*28*	*10*	*28*	*10*	*28*	*10*	*28*	*10*	*28*	*10*	*28*	*Both*
Position 1																	
Runways																	
Day	7	9	15	1	3	5	0	14	0	23	0	18	0	10	25	71	96
Evening	1	9	2	4	3	1	0	9	0	12	0	8	0	5	6	18	54
Night	0	5	0	0	0	7	0	9	0	9	0	1	0	4	0	35	35
Total	8	14	17	5	6	13	0	32	0	44	0	27	0	19	31	124	185
Position 2																	
Day	5	0	10	0	1	0	0	15	0	14	0	16	0	7	16	52	68
Evening	3	7	0	0	1	2	0	6	0	9	0	10	0	7	4	41	45
Night	0	6	0	1	0	7	0	5	0	8	0	2	0	4	0	33	33
Total	8	13	10	1	2	9	0	26	0	31	0	28	0	18	20	126	146
Position 3																	
Day	5	0	7	0	0	0	0	6	0	8	0	4	0	4	12	22	34
Evening	1	3	0	0	2	2	0	4	0	2	0	3	0	6	3	20	23
Night	0	3	0	0	0	1	0	0	0	6	0	0	0	0	0	10	10
Total	6	6	7	0	2	3	0	10	0	16	0	7	0	10	15	52	67
Position 4																	
Day	15	0	14	0	13	14	0	37	0	19	0	25	0	6	42	101	143
Evening	3	0	3	2	4	3	0	12	0	5	0	0	0	2	10	24	34
Night	0	8	0	13	0	18	0	6	0	10	0	6	0	2	0	63	63
Total	18	8	17	15	17	35	0	55	0	34	0	31	0	10	52	188	240
Position 5																	
Day	4	0	8	0	6	1	0	13	0	2	0	10	0	3	18	29	47
Evening	1	6	0	0	3	2	0	6	0	2	0	0	0	1	4	17	21
Night	0	2	0	9	0	20	0	2	0	4	0	0	0	0	0	37	37
Total	5	8	8	9	9	23	0	21	0	8	0	10	0	4	22	83	105

Generally speaking, the total number of ground noise events heard is proportional to the distance from the airport (see Figure A5.1), although on a few occasions more ground noise events were heard further from the airport than closer to it. Some ground noise events were lost in local background noise, i.e. passing cars, children, dogs, pedestrians and lawn-mowers, etc.

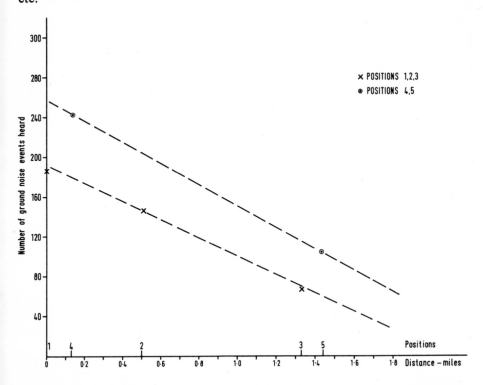

Fig. A5.1 Number of ground noise events heard at varying distances from Heathrow Airport

The difference in $dB(A)$ between the identified ground noise events, as measured simultaneously at positions along the same axis of the airport, was used to establish the two ground noise attenuation curves shown in Figure A5.2 (best fit by eye).

As an indication of ground operation noise levels adjacent to the airport, Table A5.2 shows the arithmetic average noise levels at the reference positions 1 and 4 for day, evening and night-time periods and for each mode of runway operation over the whole week. Although the arithmetic average peak ground noise level is higher at position 1 than at position 4, on the other hand there were less ground noise events heard (see Table A5.2). Position 1

153

lies between the flight paths and closer to the source of flyover noise with the consequence that more ground noise events are masked at position 1 by flyover noise than at position 4.

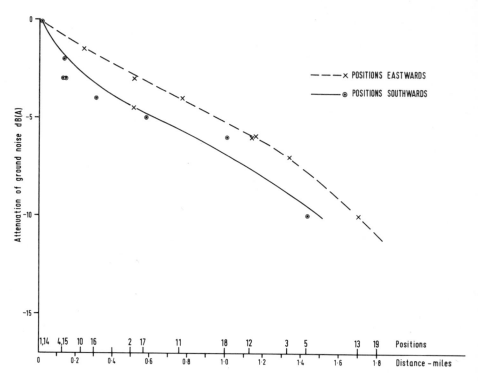

Fig. A5.2 Attenuation of ground noise from Heathrow Airport

Table A5.4

Average peak ground noise levels in
dB(A)

Position	Daytime 700–1900 hours		Evening 1900–2300 hours		Nighttime 2300–700 hours	Whole day 24 hours
	Runway 10	Runway 28	Runway 10	Runway 28	Runway 28	
1	58	65	62	65	60	62
4	55	55	56	56	50	54

154

References

Achitoff, L., 'Aircraft Noise – a threat to aviation', *The Journal of Water, Air and Soil Pollution 2.* 3, pp. 357–63 (1973).

Atkins, W. S., 'Greater London Development Plan, Public Inquiry', *London Borough of Hounslow Support Document S27/210 to Inquiry Proof E27/33* (1971).

Attenborough, K., et al., *The Built Environment*, Open University Press (1973).

Bayliss, B. and Edwards, S. L., *Industrial Demand for Freight Transport*, HMSO, London (1970).

Beesley, M. E., 'Project Selection and Social Welfare' in Worswick, G. D. N. (ed.) *Use of Economics*, Blackwell, Oxford (1972).

Bolt, Beranek and Newman, 'Noise Measurements During Two-Sequant Approaches at Los Angeles International Airport', *Report 2208*, Los Angeles, figs. 5, 6 & 7 (1972). (Quoted in OECD, 1973.)

British Airports Authority, *Annual Report and Accounts for the Year Ending 1971*, HMSO, London (1971).

British Standard *2750*, Recommendations for field and laboratory measurement of airborne and impact sound transmission in buildings, HMSO, London (1956).

Building Research Station, *Digest no. 140*, Table 4 (1972).

Commission on the Third London Airport, Research Team, 'Noise Cost Sensitivity Analysis – Variation in Values of House Price Depreciations caused by Noise', Document presented to CTLA Stage V, *Proceedings* (1970).

Commission on the Third London Airport, *Papers and Proceedings*, vol. VII, pp. 371, and 375 (1970).

Commission on the Third London Airport, *Report*, HMSO, London (1971).

Committee on the Problem of Noise, *Noise: Final Report*, Cmnd 2056, HMSO, London (1963).

Cox, D. R., *Analysis of Binary Data*, Methuen, London (1970), p. 16.

Dasgupta, A. K. and Pearce, D. W., *Cost Benefit Analysis: Theory and Practice*, Macmillan, London (1972).

Department of the Environment, 'Planning and Noise', *Circular 10/73*, HMSO, London (1973).

Department of the Environment, 'Environmental Evaluation: the Cost Benefit Approach' (by R. Travers Morgan & Partners), *Urban Motorways Project Team Report, Technical Paper No. 1* (1974).

155

Deuletoglou, N. E., *Consumer Behaviour: an experiment in analytical economics*, Harper and Row, London (1971).

Diffey, J., 'An investigation into the effect of high traffic noise on house prices in a homogeneous sub-market', *Proceedings*, seminar on house prices and the micro-economics of housing, Centre for Environmental Studies, London (1971).

Evans, A. W., *The Economics of Residential Location*, Macmillan, London (1973), p. 21.

Finney, D. J., *Probit Analysis: A statistical treatment of the sigmoid response curve*, Cambridge University Press, 2nd ed. (1964), p. 253.

Fisher, J. A., 'An analysis of consumer durable goods expenditure in 1957', *Review of Economics and Statistics*, *44*. 2 (1962), pp. 64–71.

Flight International, 18 April 1974, p. 472.

Flowerdew, A. D. J., 'Choosing a Site for the Third London Airport', The Roskill Commission's Approach, in R. Layard (ed.) *Cost Benefit Analysis*, Penguin Books, Harmondsworth (1972).

Flowerdew, A. D. J. and Hammond, A., 'City Roads and the Environment', *Regional Studies*, *7*. 2 (1973).

Galloway, W. J., 'Noise Exposure Forecasts as Indicators of Community Response', Part One, *Proceedings*, Conference on Aircraft and the Environment, Society of Automative Engineers Inc., New York (1971), pp. 56–63.

Goldfeld, S. M. and Quandt, R. E., *Non-Linear Methods in Econometrics*, North Holland, Amsterdam (1972).

Green, H. A. J., *Consumer Theory*, Penguin Modern Economics, Penguin Books, Harmondsworth (1971).

Grigg, A. O., 'A program for logit analysis', *TRRL Supplementary Report SR 16UC*, Transport and Road Research Laboratory, Crowthorne (1973).

Gujarati, D., 'Use of dummy variables in testing for equality between sets of coefficients in linear regressions: a generalisation', *Am. Stat.* (1970), pp. 18–22.

Gwilliam, K. M. and Rees, F. J., 'Urban Transport and Road Design – Classification of Environmental Problems', *Working Paper 5*, Leeds University, Institute for Transport Studies (1973).

Hall, P. G., 'Regional Planning and Airport Location', *Conference on World Airports – The Way Ahead*, Institute of Civil Engineers, London (1969).

Harrison, A. J., 'The value of non-working time: a note on some welfare problems', *Time Research Note 4*, Highways Economic Unit, Ministry of Transport (1969).

Hart, P. E., 'Population Densities and Optimal Aircraft Flight Paths', *Regional Studies*, *7*. 2 (1973), pp. 137–51, and p. 139.

Heggie, I., *Transport Engineering Economics*, McGraw Hill, London (1972).

Heriot-Watt University, 'The Cost Effectiveness of Double Glazing against Traffic Noise', *Report* to the Secretary of State for the Environment (1972).

House of Commons, Select Committee on Nationalised Industries, British Airports Authority, Session 1970–71, *Minutes of Evidence*, Q (a) 462, and Appendix 34, HMSO, London (1971).

Informatics Inc., *An Assessment of Noise Concern in Other Nations*, vol. 1, (prepared for the US Environmental Protection Agency), US Government Printing Office, Washington (1972).

Ironmonger, D. S., *New Commodities and Consumer Behaviour*, Cambridge University Press (1972).

Jansen, H. and Opschoor, H., 'Social and Economic Impact of Aircraft Noise', *Working Document*, OECD, Paris (1973).

Kryter, K. D., 'Annoyance', in Chalupnik, J. D. (ed.), *Transportation Noises*, University of Washington Press (1970), pp. 69–84.

Lancaster, K. J., 'A new approach to consumer theory', *Journal of Political Economy 74*. 2 (1966), pp. 132–57.

Large, J. B., 'Aircraft Noise and Sonic Boom' in Chalupnik, J. D. (ed.), *Transportation Noises*, University of Washington Press (1970).

Lassiere, A., 'The Economic Effects of the Disamenity due to Urban Road Noise in Residential Areas', *Mimeo*, UK Ministry of Transport, London (1970).

Lassiere, A. and Bowers, P., *Studies on the social costs of urban road transport (noise and pollution)*, European Conference of Ministers of Transport (1972).

Layard, R. (ed.), *Cost-Benefit Analysis: Selected Readings*, Penguin Books, Harmondsworth (1972).

Lewis, P. T., 'Real Windows' in Smith, T. et al., *Building Acoustics*, Oriel Press, Newcastle (1971), pp. 116–54.

Lyden, F. J. and Miller, E. G. (eds), *Planning and Programming Budgeting: A Systems Approach to Management*, Markham, Chicago (1968).

McKean, R. N., 'The Uses of Shadow Prices', in Chase, S. B. (ed.) *Problems in Public Expenditure Analysis*, Brookings Institute (1968).

McKennell, A. C., *Aircraft Noise Annoyance Around London Airport*, ss. 337, Central Office of Information, London (1963).

McNairn, C. H., 'Airport Noise Pollution: the Problem and Regulatory Response', *The Canadian Bar Review, L.* 2, (1972), pp. 248–94.

Metra, *The Cost of Noise*, The Metra Consulting Group, London (1970).

Millward, R., *Public Expenditure Economics*, McGraw Hill, London (1971).

Ministry of Transport, *The Cambrian Coastline* (1969), p. 10.

Mishan, E. J., *Cost Benefit Analysis: An Informal Introduction*, Allen & Unwin, London (1971).

Nouse, H., *The Effect of Public Policy on Housing Markets*, D. C. Heath, Lexington, Mass. (1973).

OECD, 'How to reduce aircraft noise', *Working Document*, Environmental Directorate, OECD, Paris (1973), pp. 3 and 6.

Office of Population Census and Surveys, *Second Survey of Aircraft Noise around London (Heathrow) Airport*, HMSO, London (1971), p. 43.

Orcutt, G. H. et al., *Microanalysis of socio-economic systems: a simulation study*, Harper and Row, New York (1962).

Paul, M. E., 'Can aircraft noise nuisance be measured in money?', *Oxford Economic Papers*, 23. 3 (1971), pp. 297–322.

Pearce, D. W., 'The economic evaluation of noise-generating and noise abatement projects', in *Problems of Environmental Economics*, OECD, Paris (1972).

Pearce, D. W., 'Monetary noise damage functions: a technical survey and evaluation of research on the monetary value of noise nuisance', *Report* to OECD, Paris (1974).

Prices and Incomes, National Board of, *Report No. 159* on London Transport Fares, Cmnd. 4540, HMSO, London (1970), p. 28.

Quarmby, D., 'Choice of travel mode for the journey to work', *Journal of Transport Economics and Policy*, 1. 3 (1967), pp. 273–314.

Richardson, H. W., *Urban Economics*, Penguin Books, Harmondsworth (1971).

Ridker, R., *The Economic Costs of Air Pollution*, F. A. Praeger, New York (1967), p. 136.

Robinson, D. W., 'Towards a unified system of noise assessment', *Journal of Sound Vibration*, 14. 3 (1971), pp. 278–98.

Royal Commission on Environmental Pollution, *First Report*, Cmnd. 4585, HMSO, London (1971).

Schaller, H. G. (ed.), *Public Expenditure Decisions in the Community*, Resources for the Future, Washington, DC (1963).

Schumpeter, J. A., *The Theory of Economic Development*, Harvard, Cambridge, Mass. (1934), p. 66.

Sealy, K. R., 'Air transport facilities and regional planning', *The Aeronautical Journal*, 74. 703 (1969), pp. 581–90.

Selnec Transportation Study, 'Calibration of the mathematical model', *Technical Working Paper No. 7*, Manchester (1972).

Sibert, E., 'Aircraft noise and development control – the policy for Gatwick Airport', *Journal of the Town Planning Institute*, 55. 4 (1969), pp. 149–52.

Silk, J., 'Application of dummy variables analysis', in Adams, W. P. and Helleiner, F. M. (eds), *International Geography 1972*, University of Toronto Press (1972), pp. 933–5.

Smith, P. S., 'A study of the economic and social effects of a major airport, with special reference to Heathrow Airport', University of London, M.Phil. thesis (unpublished) (1967).

Starkie, D. N. M., 'The treatment of curvi-linearities in trip end models', in *Urban Traffic Model Research*, PTRC, London (1971).

Starkie, D. N. M., 'The spatial dimensions of pollution policy', in Coppock, T. J. and Sewell, W. R. D. (eds), *Spatial Dimensions of Public Policy*, Methuen (1975).

Taylor, R., *Noise*, Penguin Books, Harmondsworth (1970).

Thurber, J., *The Years with Ross*, Hamish Hamilton (1959).

Tracor Lane, *Community Reaction to Airport Noise, Final Report* (2 volumes) to Bio Technology and Human Research Division, NASA (1970).

Trade, Board of, *The Costs and Benefits of Making Aircraft Less Noisy*, Interdepartmental Working Group on Aircraft Noise (1970).

Walters, A. A., Mrs Paul, 'Aircraft Noise – a correction', *Oxford Economic Papers*, *24.* 2 (1972), pp. 287–8.

Walters, A. A., *An Introduction to Econometrics*, Macmillan (1968).

Warren Springs Laboratory, *National Survey of Air Pollution, 1961–71*, HMSO, London (1972).

Webber, G. M., The Heathrow Airport Noise Insulation Grants Scheme – work done and up-take of grants, *Internal Note 56/72*, Building Research Station (1972).

Whitebread, M. and Bird, H., 'Rent, surplus and the evaluation of residential environments', *Regional Studies*, *7.* 2 (1973), pp. 193–223.

Winch, D. M., *Analytical Welfare Economics*, Penguin Modern Economics, Penguin Books, Harmondsworth (1971).

Wrigley, N., 'The use of percentages in geographical research', *Area 5.* 3, Institute of British Geographers (1973), pp. 183–6.

Index